7.99

Vessel

by

Andrew J. Morgan

Please note: *Vessel* was written and edited in the UK where some of the spellings and word usage vary slightly from US English.

Prologue

First, there was nothing.

Then, a single stellar body flickered in the night sky, and the nothingness ceased to be nothing.

It had arrived, silent and undetected.

It would change everything.

Section 1 — We Have a Visitor
Chapter 1

'Hello TsUP, this is RS0ISS. Reporting unidentified vessel in our region, holding orbit approximately two hundred metres aft of our location. Please confirm.'

The heavy Russian accent, laden with radio static, fell silent. Sitting at his desk — row three of five in the cavernous cylindrical room — Mission Control Capsule Communicator Aleksandar Dezhurov touched his lips against the stiff microphone of his headset and considered his response.

'Moscow TsUP, hello. Negative copy on your last transmission, please repeat.'

He gazed through the three gigantic screens at the front of the room, scratching his head through his greying hair as he waited for the reply. A slow stream of letters and numbers rolled down a smaller screen at his desk, disappearing at the bottom as if being swept along by a digital tide.

The static hissed in his ear.

'TsUP, there is an unidentified vessel approximately two hundred metres aft of our orbit. It is maintaining distance. There are no obvious markings and the shape is unfamiliar to me. Can you verify?'

Aleks frowned. He was not aware of any other operations in the local vicinity of the International Space Station, national or otherwise, and the large screens confirmed this. He adjusted the headset as he always did when he became re-aware of its presence, picked up his pen and jotted a note down on his desk pad as he spoke.

'Copy RS0ISS. Will confirm and verify unidentified vessel.' His emotionless tone broke as worry panged in his throat. 'Let me know if the situation changes, even slightly, okay, Mikhail?'

The nib of the pen paused while his eyes searched their sockets, waiting for the cosmonaut's response.

'Copy, Aleks. Don't you worry about us, we can handle ourselves. Out.'

Aleks nodded, as if to reassure himself. He'd hoped it was going to be a quiet morning. Apparently not.

* * *

Within a few hours, the NASA operatives working in tandem with the Russian Federal Space Agency had confirmed that they were unaware of any American orbital vehicles operating in close proximity to the International Space Station. After half a day, NASA's Washington headquarters clarified this statement, adding that there had been no request for permission to use that orbit by any private aerospace or military programs. They further added that there had been no reported incidents occurring between any of the thousands of satellites they currently monitored orbiting the Earth. The following day, the European Space Agency, Japanese Aerospace Exploration Agency and Chinese National Space Administration denied involvement. As the days trailed on, the Indian Space Research Organisation and a number of other smaller agencies also denied knowledge of the unidentified vessel. It was a mystery to them all.

* * *

The cylindrical room, operated by a small crew a week ago, was now murmuring with the presence of over forty staff in its dimly-lit, theatre-like space, filling every desk with at least one — but in most cases two — people. The NASA presence had become twofold, and the hot twang of American accents punctured the languid hum emitted by its Russian hosts. The air conditioning worked hard, soaking away the heat from the additional bodies — and the screens they watched so intently — yet despite the startling increase in both active personnel and technology in the room, not a single screen, print-out or reading displayed any trace of the as-yet unidentified craft.

'RS0ISS, hello RS0ISS, TsUP,' Aleks called, adjusting his radio headset.

'Hello Moscow, how are you doing?' came Mikhail's cheerful, slightly distorted reply. Mikhail's words were also being emitted through a speaker on Aleks' desk for the benefit of the Flight Director and NASA's representative Flight Coordinator, who both sat in silence next to him with their brows furrowed in concentration.

The unexpected arrival of the vessel had done nothing to dampen the moods of the two cosmonauts and their astronaut guest for whom the ISS was currently home. Even without the Surgeon's report — compiled from the constant stream of health data being broadcast from the station by each of its inhabitants — it was easy to tell that the crew were in good spirits. They were professionals, the best of the best, and they were behaving like it.

'We're good, thank you,' said Aleks, smiling, and he glanced across his shoulder to the Flight Director, who nodded to him. 'Down to business,' he continued. 'We have a no go on ground visibility of the unidentified vessel, require uplink to PC One for visual. Can you get a camera pointed at that thing for us?'

A few seconds passed while the signal shot at the speed of light some two hundred and forty miles upwards to the waiting crew of the ISS. Normally the wait barely registered in Aleks' mind, but recently it seemed like minutes.

'Standby TsUP. Preparing uplink to PC One, copy. No visuals from the ground? Interference?'

'Something like that. Our telescopes won't produce an image at the azimuth of the unidentified vessel, only static. We're trying to figure it out.'

The faint hiss from the earpiece and speaker changed so imperceptibly that the Flight Director and his NASA minder didn't seem to notice. Aleks' ears pricked up, however, and he looked to his screen in anticipation. It blinked and flickered, and the list of numbers vanished. A saturated glow appeared and settled into a view of a white panel criss-crossed with cables and set with rows of buttons. The clean white lab-like scene drifted by, rolling away and down across the monitor in a lazy arc.

'Can we get this on the big screen?' asked the NASA operative in a gruff, business-like voice, and Aleks prodded a button on his desk, which did exactly that. Others in the room looked up from their screens for a moment, before looking back and resuming their work.

The view on screen swayed, guided from behind by an unseen force that steered it away from the wall and pointed it down a long, white tunnel that was punctuated by the occasional narrowing along its length. The camera re-focused and the detail became sharp.

'TsUP, I'm moving through the Lab to the aft of the ISS,' came Mikhail's disembodied voice, distant and hollow, as his hand reached forward into view and gripped a rail with the tips of his fingers. Giving himself a gentle tug, he projected weightlessly forward along the module, gliding past the racks of scientific equipment in the walls and ceiling.

Rolling the camera to the right as he reached for another handrail, Mikhail's broadcast glimpsed the rigid humanoid stature of the experimental R2 GM robotic astronaut, capturing for a second the svelte bronze head mounted to the folded white legless body.

'Passing through into Node One.'

The tension in Mission Control was building. The cursory glances at the big screen from the other operators became hard, unblinking stares, all waiting for their first visual of the mysterious object.

As Mikhail dived through the square hatch that separated the US LAB from the Node One module, the light dimmed up ahead, and he pushed upwards to squeeze into the mouth of the Pressure Mating Adaptor between the US modules and the Russian ones. PMA One was unlit, and its narrowing walls — which formed a cone towards the tight exit at the end of its short length — were completely ringed with soft white cargo transfer bags, held down with stretched bungee cords. A black-and-yellow sign above the entrance jokingly warned of a 17,500mph speed limit.

'FGB,' he said, naming the Russian module as he floated through it. The space inside was a lot narrower than the Lab, and instead of the mess of wires and cables and equipment, the FGB was bare, save for the evenly spaced handrails and the neatly stacked supply containers and water drums that part-filled the cavity from the floor upwards. A pair of running shoes, attached with Velcro to the wall between two handrails, trailed a lace out in front of him, only moving as he brushed by it and through to the last module.

Ahead a stocky, balding man was pedalling on a compact exercise bike. Padded bungees held him down onto the saddle, and he pedalled with his eyes shut, gripping the handlebars tight and puffing his cheeks in and out. The sides of his navy blue polo shirt were dark with sweat, even seeping into the sleeves, framing the stitched American flag with a dark border.

Before entering the Service Module, the camera took a sudden and disorientating dive downwards, pirouetting round into the Multipurpose Laboratory Module.

'I'm just dropping into the MLM,' Mikhail informed them, 'there's a better view from the docking port down here.'

Deftly he sailed down through the module, passing more cables and equipment until he negotiated his way into the ball-like docking station. He spun as he entered, sticking his socked feet into view and slowing himself down with a controlled flex of his knees. Flipping the camera round, he pointed the lens at himself, and a dark-haired man with skin wrinkled beyond his years stared into the lens. His age would be hard for anyone to guess, as his features were still small and well defined like those of someone in their early thirties, but the ravages of long exposure to the sun had hardened and darkened his cheeks and forehead all the way up to his receding hairline. His eyes twinkled with excitement.

'You're in for a treat, Moscow,' he said, a hint of a grin tickling the corners of his mouth, 'it's hard to make out, but it's there.'

He raised his eyebrows before spinning the camera round and offering it up to the small aft window. At first, the camera struggled to adjust to the bright light of the glowing Indian Ocean, but its innards realigned with a whirr and the white flecks of clouds became distinct. The ocean below blossomed into a rich, velvety blue, and grew bigger as the camera motor whirred again and the lens pulled the distance towards it. Then the camera angled upwards and away from Earth, the view tracking along into the black depths of the universe. The darkness only filled the large screen at Mission Control for a brief moment before breaking down into vibrating lines of static.

'What's going on?' the Flight Director demanded, gesturing at the square pool of fuzzy nonsense. Aleks was working on the problem, fingers clacking at his keyboard, an intense concentration dominating his being as he stared unblinking at his secondary desk monitor.

'It's not us, Lev,' he shrugged, turning to the Flight Director, 'we're receiving the signal from the ISS just fine. The problem is occurring at the broadcast end. We're seeing exactly what Mikhail is sending.'

'Tell him,' Lev said, folding his arms. The NASA operative said nothing, but made a note on his touchpad.

Aleks cleared his throat and turned on his mic. 'RS0ISS, TsUP. We have a loss of picture on your downlink, please diagnose and adjust.'

He waited, wondering if the sound on the feed was also down. His finger hovered over the broadcast button as he readied himself to advise an abort on the PC One feed, but the static washed away and a view of the station's interior flooded back in again.

'TsUP, the camera is functional with no obvious faults,' said Mikhail. 'I've adjusted the broadcast channels, please advise.'

An unexpected wave of relief surprised Aleks as it untightened his shoulders, and even Lev breathed an audible sigh. 'RS0ISS, we have AOS. You're looking good.'

As he spoke, he watched the screen as the camera panned back up to that same spot in space and broke down into static again. 'Negative, negative,' Aleks said, his heart sinking, 'loss of signal, loss of signal. Abort PC One and resume Ku Band audio connection.'

With the push of a button, the static disappeared from both his and the main screen. He arched his neck back, shut his eyes and rubbed his face as he waited for Mikhail. He didn't care if Lev or the NASA guy were watching. His palm, or his forehead, or perhaps even both, were hot and clammy with sweat, and his shirt collar was stuck to his neck.

'TsUP, RS0ISS, radio check,' Mikhail said at last.

'RS0ISS, read you loud and clear.'

'Loud and clear, TsUP.'

'RS0ISS, can you give us a verbal on the unidentified vessel,' Aleks asked. He bit at his pen as he waited.

'Copy, TsUP. The vessel is, uh, hard to describe because it's hard to see. It's there all right, but its shape is difficult to determine because I can't see that it has any definite edges. It doesn't seem to reflect the sunlight at all, except to catch it occasionally along its smooth surfaces.'

Mikhail paused, giving Aleks the chance to write down what he was hearing.

'Copy,' Aleks said when he had finished scrawling in an almost hieroglyphic shorthand.

'If I were to say it was any shape,' Mikhail continued, 'I'd say it was trapezoidal, with the top most surface leaning away from centre. You notice it most when it travels past a star, because the star will briefly disappear from view. That's the best I can give you I'm afraid.'

'What colour is it?'

'Uh… it doesn't seem to have one. Sometimes its reflects every colour you can think of, and sometimes it seems blacker than space itself.'

'Copy, Mikhail, thank you. This will do for now.'

'Let me know if you need anything else.'

'Roger. Out.'

Aleks looked down at his notes. Underneath his shorthand glyphs, was a sleek, simple shape scored into the paper with thin blue lines of ball-point ink. As far as he knew, it was the first documented record of extra-terrestrial technology ever made by an official space agency.

'I think we have a visitor,' he said.

Chapter 2

'Give me the full briefing on this one. I want to know every detail,' said the NASA Flight Coordinator, who turned out to be an American man by the name of John Bales. He had summoned Aleks and Lev to his temporary office only ten minutes ago. 'And don't miss a thing,' he added.

Aleks looked to Lev, who gave him a nod. So it would be up to him, then. 'How much do you know about the International Space Station?' he asked.

Bales leaned back in his chair, crossing his legs. 'Assume I know nothing.'

'Er — okay,' Aleks said, looking again at Lev who returned the glance with an *I'm as confused as you are* expression. 'The International Space Station, or ISS as we call it here, was launched in 1998 as a joint effort between us — the Russian Federal Space Agency — yourselves — NASA — and also the European Space Agency, to replace Mir. It's built as a modifiable entity made of self-contained modules, and since its launch has been reconfigured many times, including for the recent addition of the Japanese Aerospace Exploration Agency JEM research laboratory.'

Aleks stopped, feeling a little silly.

'Keep going,' Bales said, smiling in a patronising way.

'Uhhhm … well, the ISS is reaching the end of its serviceable life, and so we have begun the first of many missions to prepare it for its strip-down, deconstruction and eventual decommissioning. It's going to be replaced by OPSEK, a smaller platform that will serve as a stopping point for missions to the Moon, Mars and beyond. There will be an overlapping period between the ISS being decommissioned and OPSEK coming online where the ISS will act as a construction site. Some modules from the ISS will also be used in OPSEK. In the meantime, the ISS will still be used for micro-gravity experimentation.'

Aleks noticed that Bales hadn't made a single note. Did he genuinely want to know, or was this some kind of test? There was something about this man that he found distrustful — he couldn't put his finger on what, but those piercing, grey eyes seemed to hold no empathy whatsoever.

'Can you tell me what the current mission is?' Bales asked. He asked politely, but his tone made it clear that these weren't questions; Bales was *telling* Aleks to answer.

'It's a three-man crew for the Soyuz TMA Ten M mission. They replaced a group of six, who were mainly engineers and scientists doing micro-gravity research. Three is the minimum capacity for the ISS for smooth operation, although it can be run with fewer. Anyway, they're making the most of the opportunity with the free space to undertake some of the modifications required for the start of OPSEK's construction. For the first month of their mission, they're dismantling and removing the equipment from the modules that will form the foundations of OPSEK. At the beginning of their second month, a Progress automated resupply ship will take the old equipment away. Once that's all done, they come back home. Another research team takes over from there.'

'Who are these three crew? Give me a bit of background on them.'

'There's the Commander, Major Mikhail Romanenko —'

'He's a friend of yours, isn't he?'

'Yes. He graduated from the Leningrad Suvorov military school top of his class and went on to operate fast jets. He logged five hundred hours at a record rate, including front-line operations, earning him the Hero of the Russian Federation award. He enrolled at the Gagarin Cosmonaut Training Centre at the age of thirty-one, and after five years served as Flight Engineer on board Soyuz TMA Nine M.

'Major Romanenko's Flight Engineer is another young Russian, Captain Evgeny Novitskiy. He followed the same path as Romanenko through military school and on to the Gagarin Training Centre, although he has shown himself to have an even better aptitude in testing than his Commander. A promising young cosmonaut indeed, although he still respects Romanenko's experience and authority — a trait very favourable among Alpha-males who spend a lot of time together in a close environment.'

'And the third crew member?'

Aleks knew the words he had to say, but didn't want to say them. He looked at the floor, feeling Bales' eyes burrowing into his head. 'The third crew member,' he said, not looking up, 'is an American, NASA's — your — Major Chris Williams. He was born in Ohio, was top of his class in the United States Naval Academy and has since logged over three thousand hours as an experimental test pilot.' He could feel his face flushing hot with annoyance — or was it embarrassment? It was a strange, emasculating feeling he hadn't felt since childhood.

'Very good, Aleks, you certainly know your background. But can you tell me more about Major Chris Williams? What sort of a person is he?'

Aleks shifted his weight from foot to foot. 'He's a short-tempered man, quick to anger.'

'What do you think about that?'

Aleks' face was red hot. 'What do you mean?'

'Is this really necessary?' Lev asked.

'I asked you a question,' Bales said, ignoring Lev.

'I think it's a bad situation to be in,' Aleks said. 'He should have never gone up.' He looked at Bales, who was still — strangely — smiling.

'Thank you Aleks, that's exactly what I wanted to hear. I'm glad you can be honest with me — that's important if we're going to be working together. Is there anything else I need to know? Anything at all?'

'No.'

'Are you sure?'

Aleks didn't know what to say, so he didn't say anything. Nodding to himself, still smiling, Bales stood and held out his hand, an indication for Aleks and Lev to leave. He shook with them both.

'I look forward to working with you,' he said. 'I think we'll make a great team.'

Somehow, Aleks knew that wouldn't be the case.

* * *

'RS0ISS, TsUP, come back.'

Aleks rubbed his eyes as he waited. It seemed like he'd barely left his seat since the vessel had been reported over a week ago. A scratchy sting had formed over his eyeballs, complimented by a dull ache at the small of his back. The scenery around him hadn't changed much either. With not a soul leaving for more than a few hours to catch some rest and have a wash, Mission Control was a constant buzz of conversation. A three-day-old newspaper on his desk read: *METEOR STRIKE ENDANGERS LIVES ON ISS*. A lie, but one plausible and boring enough for the global media to let the story slip off the cover and into the middle pages. The glut of press that swarmed the building a week ago, attracted by the swollen NASA presence, had dwindled to a handful of chancers.

'TsUP, RS0ISS, go ahead,' came Mikhail's voice.

'Good morning, RS0ISS, how are you today?'

Mikhail laughed, making Aleks grin. It always cheered him up to hear his friend's voice.

'Can't complain, TsUP, can't complain.'

'Are you sure? I'm betting Doctor Kotov would love to give you one of his psychoanalytical grillings.'

The man in question, listening to the conversation on his own headset, looked back at Aleks, frowning. Aleks gave him a cheeky nod and a wink.

'No, I don't think that will be necessary,' Mikhail said. 'Spirits are high up here. It's not every day you get to discover something like this.'

'Okay. But in all seriousness, keep us informed down here. Don't bottle up.'

Aleks glanced again at the doctor, who gave a firm nod of approval.

'Although Doctor Kotov is looking very keen —'

'No doctors, no questions, no thank you,' Mikhail interjected.

Aleks laughed. 'I'm sure he'll keep off your back so long as you keep being a smartass,' he said.

'Amen to that.'

'Indeed. Anyway, RS0ISS, we've got a bit of housekeeping to do. Did you attempt a classification of the vessel as requested?'

'We tried,' Mikhail said, sounding uncertain, 'but we can only get a reading on it optically. Anything electrical breaks down into a nonsensical mess.'

'Copy, we've had the same problem our end.'

'X-Ray, ultraviolet, infrared — it all comes back garbled.'

'What did you achieve optically?'

'Not much. The vessel's appearance makes judging size difficult, but we've estimated it at around ten to twenty metres long, five to ten metres tall, and the same for the depth.'

'Big enough to fit people in.'

'Yes, definitely.'

'Has there been any change to the vessel itself?'

'None. We even analysed the static produced by our digital equipment, but it's as random as any other.'

'So the likelihood is that it's dead?'

Mikhail made a humming sound, as if contemplating how he should say what he wanted to say next. 'We don't think so,' he said. 'From what we've been able to measure, the vessel follows us perfectly, with no deviation from our orbit. On top of that, the chances of an object falling into a synchronous orbit instead of bouncing off the atmosphere or falling in and burning up are impossibly small.'

'You think it's here deliberately?'

'Yes.'

Aleks noted down what Mikhail was saying. The conversations were being recorded of course, but it helped Aleks' mind to visualise the situation from his own notes.

'Has EVA approval come through yet?' Mikhail asked.

'Not yet,' Aleks said, finishing his last note. 'Lev keeps pushing for it, but we're being held back on that one, so no spacewalk yet.'

'How about the R2 GM robonaut? Can we get clearance to send that out?'

'We're waiting on that as well.'

'What's the hold up?'

Aleks sighed.

'The usual. Politics, paperwork, red tape — you know how it is.'

'I do, but I wish I didn't.'

'Tell me about it. Alright, next on the list is the METI standard protocol broadcasts.'

Mikhail snorted. 'Really? You want to send some old coded messages to it?'

'Not my decision, so let's run both *Hello from Earth* and *RuBisCo Stars* anyway.'

'Roger. Extra-Terrestrial Intelligence broadcast lined up and ready to go five by five.'

'Copy. Proceed when ready.' Aleks twiddled his pen between his fingers as he waited. Although he was almost certain that the METI broadcasts wouldn't get a response, he couldn't help but wonder what would happen if they did.

'TsUP, METI deployed,' Mikhail confirmed.

Aleks' chest fluttered with nervous excitement that he pushed back down again with reserved reason. 'Roger. Continue with METI broadcasts at one-hour intervals,' he said.

'Copy, one-hour intervals.'

Aleks made a note of the time. 'Stay safe up there,' he said. 'And please, seriously, let us know if there is any change in your situation, any change at all.' He knew Mikhail understood what he meant.

'Don't you worry about us,' Mikhail said.

'Okay. TsUP out.'

'RS0ISS out.'

Aleks took off his headset, and despite the ongoing chatter in the room, he felt a strange sense of isolation. As well as a gurgling unease in his gut about his friend's wellbeing, he didn't know what to make of the knowledge that whatever was up there with them wasn't there by accident. 'And now we wait,' he said to himself.

An hour later, he finished his shift and handed over so he could go and get some rest. He needed it, but despite his exhaustion, he tossed in his bunk for what seemed like the millionth time since he had clambered in. Although his eyes stung and his body ached, sleep seemed to evade him. The air-conditioned room, one of many provided by the RFSA, was cool, but his body burned with a feverish heat that seemed to tie the sheets around his body in a sweaty, sticky jumble of limbs and cotton.

Frustrated, he kicked the sheets off and clicked the lamp on. Its glow painted the darkness away from the mix of browns, beiges and washed-out purples that made up the temporary accommodation. He sat up and yawned, the heavy weight of fatigue hanging from his eyelids, and let the soles of his feet rest on the scratchy carpet. He shuffled into the adjoining bathroom, yesterday's crumpled heap of clothing still on the floor. Yesterday felt like days ago. He looked at his watch, a cheap digital thing his ex-wife had got him, and swore to himself under his breath.

Shit, he thought, *only one o'clock?*

He had been in bed longer than he'd realised, but for less time than he'd hoped. He would need to be up, washed, dressed and back smiling at his station in less than five hours, and the very thought made him want to curl up and die. For a moment he longed for his own bed back home, but he remembered it was just as empty and lonely as the one here. The overnight room was pretty convenient come to think about it. He shuffled back to bed, accepting that he would have to lie there and wait for the sound of the alarm.

But that sound didn't come — it didn't have a chance to. Shuddering awake, his eyes searched the darkness, hunting for the dream that roused him. The screaming silence mellowed, and he eased himself back onto his pillow, taking deep breaths of the cool, dry air to ease his skipping heart.

Thump, thump, thump.

There it was again, the noise from his dream. His semi-conscious brain fumbled for an answer, but the wires weren't connecting. Then, a muffled voice called through the door: 'Mr Dezhurov, sir? Are you there?'

The dream was gone for good as conscious and subconscious snapped back to together in an instant. 'I'm coming,' he croaked. He got up, grabbed a dressing gown from the otherwise empty closet, threaded his arms through the sleeves and wrapped it around himself, yawning as he slouched to the door. He looked at his watch. It read: *3:49am*. Opening the door a crack, he squinted at the silhouette of a man standing outside. As his eyes adjusted, he saw the man was practically a boy, a young soldier wearing the uniform of the centre's security.

'What?' Aleks said.

'Sorry to disturb you, sir. You're needed in Mission Control.'

The soldier looked awkward during the silence that followed. Aleks considered him for a moment, then nodded. 'Alright,' he said. 'Let me get washed and dressed and I'll be right there.'

'Thank you, sir,' the soldier said, looking relieved.

Aleks sighed, and shut the door.

Lev greeted Aleks as he entered Mission Control through the makeshift security point that had popped up overnight. He had concern on his face, even if he was trying his best to mask it. For the first time in a while, Bales was not at his side.

'I'm so sorry to wake you up at this time in the morning,' he said, handing Aleks a polystyrene cup filled with hot coffee. 'But we have a small situation that we thought would be best for you to be in on.'

They walked around the circumference of the room before slotting in at the appropriate row. A relieved-looking junior communications officer stood up as they approached, the suddenly taut cable almost ripping the headset from his ears. Lev had barely dismissed him before he darted away, and Aleks watched him leave, apprehension stirring in his chest.

'What's his problem?' he asked, still watching the man as he left the room.

'He's out of his depth, I suppose,' Lev said, inviting Aleks to sit down, before doing so himself.

'Where's your NASA friend?' Aleks said, nodding towards the empty third seat at his station. He took a sip of his coffee, allowing the lingering heat to flow to his extremities.

'We, er … haven't alerted him. It's only a minor thing. Nothing worth disturbing him about,' Lev said, looking guilty.

'Not minor enough to let me catch up on my rest though,' Aleks said. 'You know I don't sleep well, you know I've been up doing long shifts —'

'As have we all,' Lev interjected, 'and I'm sorry, but we have some very powerful eyes watching over us, so we need to make every decision perfectly. We can only do that with the best personnel on the job.'

Aleks felt numb, cranky and exhausted. He had probably overreacted. Lev was just doing his job after all. He took another sip of coffee, placed the cup down on his desk and started again.

'So what's the deal with Bales? Why is he here?'

Lev pulled a face, one of frustration. 'NASA pretty much funds this entire operation. With money comes control. They may let us think we're running the show, but if they want something, they get it.'

Aleks snorted with disbelief. 'And we let them?'

'We don't have a choice. If we say no, they could pull the plug. As long as they stay happy, and we preen and smile for their puppet, Bales, we'll be okay.'

There was a visible annoyance forming in the creases of Lev's brow at the mention of Bales, so Aleks decided to drop the topic altogether.

'What's going on here, then?'

'Well, you know that solar flare that was predicted for the next month?'

'Yeah. I saw the NASA STEREO report a few weeks back.'

'Well, it's come early. Only a small one at the moment — M Two class I think — but the reports suggest this is the first of many, and they're going to get larger.'

'Do we still have contact with the ISS?' Aleks asked.

'Not at the moment,' Lev said. 'The radiation storm from the first flare is still passing. We estimate another half-hour before comms are restored. I wanted you here ready for the link up.'

Aleks nodded, turning to look back at the double doors. He could hear raised voices, and as a member of security exited, a fragment of the shouting slipped in through the swinging door.

'Excuse me one moment,' Lev said, heading for the door himself. It had barely swung shut behind him when Aleks heard Lev's deep, authoritative bark adding to the muffled cacophony. The voices died down after a minute, and Lev returned looking furious. Bales followed him, his tanned face expressionless and cold below his colourless crew-cut hair. They marched over, and Aleks shot a puzzled expression at Lev when Bales wasn't looking, but Lev either ignored it or didn't see it. He sat down beside Aleks, but Bales continued to stand, looking around the room. Clearing his throat, he addressed everyone in a near-perfect Russian dialect, albeit one tainted with a slightly robotic accent:

'Ladies and gentlemen, can I have your attention for a moment, please?'

He already had it.

'My name is John Bales, and I have been sent by NASA to work closely with you all following the recent discovery of the unidentified vessel that we have code-named *UV One*. It has been decided in a joint negotiation between our two states that should the situation escalate to a point that our astronauts are in a state of immediate danger, our expertise and authority — NASA's expertise and authority — will take command. That time —'

Hushed whispers rippled around the room.

'That time,' Bales repeated, raising his voice a fraction, 'has come, and so I will duly take command of this operation.'

The flutter of whispers became open discontentment, some operators shaking their heads in disbelief.

'It is for the safety of us, our astronauts and for the people of Earth,' Bales said, scanning the room, 'and I expect you all to continue doing your very best. That is all.'

He stood watching as everyone turned back to their stations. Aleks could tell by the look on his face that he was glad — no, worse than that, *delighted* — to be taking control of the mission.

Chapter 3

'Still nothing,' Aleks said, after failing to reach the ISS yet again.

Bales chewed the stylus of his touch pad, thinking. 'Okay,' he said. 'Keep trying, ten-minute intervals.'

Aleks made a note of the time for his next broadcast. Lev, who was sat alongside Bales, was staring into the distance.

'If you'll excuse me,' Bales said, standing up, 'I need to make a few phone calls.'

Without waiting for a response, he strode off, flicking through his touch pad as he walked. Just before he left the room altogether, he turned around and called: 'Please be sure to inform me of any changes to the situation, okay?'

And then he was gone. Aleks, who watched him leave, turned to Lev as soon as the door swung shut.

'Are you going to let him carry on like this?' he said.

Lev, a faint veil of dejectedness hanging over him, shrugged. The expression aged him considerably, and the usual sharpness in his keen eyes seemed to have fizzled out.

'What can I do?' he said. 'It's not my call if the RFSA decides that this is the best course of action. Maybe it is for the best. Maybe the Americans are better trained at this than we are.'

Aleks snorted. '*No-one* is trained for this and you know it.'

Lev looked blank for a moment, and before he could speak, a wiry-looking man with a floppy haircut appeared with a ream of printouts.

'I've got some more readings on the radiation storm,' the wiry man said, flicking his drooping side-parting with a twitch of his head, 'and it looks like we should get an opportunity for communication with the ISS in the next few minutes. But,' he continued, letting the ream spill onto the desk so he could point to a line that slashed up and down in quick succession, 'it'll only be for a minute or two at the most. After that, the next window could be hours, days — even weeks away.'

'Thank you Pyotr,' Lev said, acknowledging the man with a half-hearted smile. Pyotr dithered, looking unsure, then gathered up his printouts and returned to his station. Before Lev could even open his mouth, Aleks was already broadcasting, nudging his headset down to a more comfortable position on his head as he spoke.

'RS0ISS, TsUP, please come back.'

He paused and waited for a few seconds before trying again.

'RS0ISS, RS0ISS, how do you read?'

A loud burst of garbled static gave his heart a jolt, and he instinctively snatched at the gain controls to manage the harsh levels.

'RS0ISS,' Aleks repeated, desperate to hear a voice through the digital mess, 'can you hear me? I repeat, *can you hear me?*'

He held his breath as he waited, searching the soundscape for signs of life. There were nigh on a hundred people in the room, but at that moment it felt like it was him on his own, his world shrinking around him as he focussed his attention on his hearing. The radio hissed and crackled again, this time more quietly, and Aleks' trained ear heard a voice hidden somewhere in the confused mass of sound.

'I think I've got them,' he said, hands darting from one control to the next to isolate the signal. 'Negative copy RS0ISS,' he said, his calm voice hiding the racing energy in his chest. 'Please modulate your downlink on the DSKY using manual. I'm trying a connection through an alternate satellite.'

The static came through again; this time the voice was definite, but still not understandable.

'I've almost got you, RS0ISS. Try again.'

The crackle died and Aleks waited, his thumb and index finger poised on the gain control.

'TsUP, TsUP — RS0ISS, please confirm — signal,' came Mikhail's voice, laden with static and broken up into chunks, but clear enough to understand. Relief flooded through Aleks. He nodded to Lev and switched the main loudspeaker on.

'RS0ISS, readability two, strength four — we're reading you with some noise, but we can hear you clearly enough. Can you confirm your current situation?'

The intermittent replay came intertwined with the hiss of millions of radioactive particles as the solar storm thundered through the ISS at the speed of light:

'The situation — okay — reading — levels of radiation.'

'Copy, RS0ISS, remain inside your radiation protection compartments where possible and limit your exposure time. Anything to report on UV One?'

'Negative — no change to — continue to maintain — aft.'

'Okay, RS0ISS. Please cease all activity and remain inside your radiation protection compartments until further notice.'

'—opy, TsUP.'

Then there was silence, and Aleks waited to see if Mikhail had anything more to add. He did.

'TsUP, how long — we transfer — to Earth?'

Aleks was taken aback by this unexpected question. Looking to Lev, whose corrugated brow mirrored his own concern, he pushed the broadcast button.

'You've got just over a week until Progress arrives with the resupply for the refit and return, and then another four weeks until the next team goes up on Soyuz TMA Eleven M and you come back.'

He released the button, frowned, and then pressed it again. 'Is everything okay up there?'

The response came a little later than felt normal.

'Yeah, yeah — think so. Just getting a little — up here. It feels close.'

There was a pause. Aleks thought Mikhail sounded anxious. Mikhail never sounded anxious.

'Aleks,' Mikhail said, 'I'm getting — that normal?'

'Negative copy, negative copy,' Aleks responded. He could feel his chest becoming tight and constricted.

'I'm — hallucinations — I don't — if — awake …'

'Mikhail, I'm losing signal, negative copy, please repeat, please repeat,' Aleks said, his fingers jumping from dial to dial, adjusting settings as they went. All that came back was static, and then nothing. He called out to the ISS a couple more times, and when not even a distorted signal was being received back, he pulled off his headset and tossed it onto the desk with a clatter.

'Shit!' he growled.

Mikhail's voice still rang discordant in his mind even hours later as he sat in one of the centre's many boardrooms, waiting for Bales. On the opposite side of the long table sat Lev, whose usual aura of capability and authority had all but vanished. A clock ticked, each *tick-tick-tick* long, loud and clear. The atmosphere was thick, but the ticking clock cut right through it with utmost clarity.

When the door opened and Bales entered, striding through in his quiet way, Aleks realised that he'd slipped into a doze. He'd been mesmerised by the clock, the humidity and not least by his exhaustion. An invisible weight pressed down onto his weary shoulders, so he didn't get up to pull his chair in as Bales squeezed past.

'Gentlemen,' Bales said, sitting at the head of the table and placing upon it a thin blue folder, 'I've called this meeting because I need to know what happened in the brief conversation that took place between Mr Dezhurov and Major Romanenko at around zero five hundred hours this morning.'

Lev's face contorted with frustration and annoyance. 'We didn't have enough time to —'

'As you are aware,' Bales interrupted, not looking up as he drew a pile of paper from the folder and sifted through it, 'I specifically requested that any change in the situation be reported to me, particularly any conversation that you may have had with the crew of the ISS.'

He turned to Lev, his narrow eyes unblinking beneath his stark white eyebrows. He was obviously allowing Lev to speak, and Lev seized the opportunity, regardless of why Bales had let him take it.

'The window was small and there wasn't enough time to call you down to Mission Control. Hell, I didn't even know where you'd gone.'

Bales still didn't blink, but he broke eye contact with Lev for a moment as he placed the pile of paper on the table, pinching the corners together so they lay perfectly square.

'Mr Ryumin,' Bales said in a slow, deliberate way, 'there was plenty of time between then and now for you to inform me.'

'But you weren't anywhere to be seen,' protested Lev, who held his hands up in exasperation. 'You would have been informed as soon as you'd returned from whatever it was you were doing.'

If Bales was as frustrated with Lev as Lev was with Bales, he didn't show it.

'Had there been another window for us to resume contact with the ISS,' he continued in his deliberate way, 'I would not have known all the facts and I would not have been able to instruct the crew in the best possible manner. It is imperative,' he prodded the pile of paper, 'that this kind of information be reported to me *as soon as possible*.'

He emphasised the last few words, looking hard at Lev, who glared at the opposite wall above Aleks' head. Bales pulled his chair closer to the table, licked his index finger and flicked through the sheets of paper.

'Before we continue,' he said, as though the previous conversation hadn't even taken place, 'I want to clarify a few details from the conversation with the ISS this morning. I have read through the transcript and listened to the playback, so it would be good to utilise your professional opinions to find the distinction between what we *think* we heard and what was actually said.'

Bales had divided his pile of paper into three smaller piles of equal thickness, and he handed one to Lev and one to Aleks. It was the transcript from the conversation, documented like a script, with initials for the speakers and occasional commentary that allowed for context.

'If you could look at page three,' Bales asked. They all turned to page three. 'You can see that Major Romanenko questions the duration of the mission. What would you say had happened here? Is the Major asking a legitimate and understandable question, or would you say he had forgotten what the date was?'

Aleks could see Bales looking at him from the corner of his eye.

'Mr Dezhurov, would you say that Major Romanenko had forgotten what the date was? It's a simple question.'

'Well,' Aleks said, looking to Lev for help, but not getting it, 'I can't say for sure. Keeping track of time can be difficu—'

'That's not what I asked,' Bales said, clasping his hands together in front of him. 'I just want to know if Major Romanenko was having trouble with his temporal orientation.'

Aleks sighed. He couldn't dance around the question forever. 'It seems that way, yes,' he said reluctantly.

'Good. Thank you,' Bales said as he turned to the next page. 'Could you continue to page four, please.'

He looked on until the other two had turned to page four, then his eyes returned to his own transcript.

'Here, on the eighth line down, Major Romanenko makes a statement that is broken up by interference. I need a best estimate as to the subject and context of his statement, and an assumption as to what he means by it. He says, *just getting a little,* then there's a section missing, before we hear him say, *up here.*'

Bales read the text aloud without any shred of emotion. It sounded so strange read like that. The desperate words, haunting and unnatural, made his skin crawl.

'It feels close,' Bales said. 'What do you make of that, Mr Dezhurov?'

'I don't know,' said Aleks. He could feel his words being led someplace he didn't want them to go. 'I wouldn't want to assume what Mikhail meant.'

'But you must be able to make an educated guess, surely?'

Bales wasn't going to let Aleks get away with not answering this — or any other — question, that much was clear.

'It seems,' Aleks said, 'at a purely hypothetical guess, that Mikhail is experiencing the symptoms of claustrophobia, an expected side effect of the —'

'Thank you, Mr Dezhurov.'

'— of the stresses of being in space during a period of loss of communication and confinement to the radiation protection compartment,' Aleks finished through gritted teeth.

'Thank you, Mr Dezhurov,' Bales repeated, his voice firm, but still calm. 'Lastly,' he continued, 'at the bottom of page five.'

Aleks already knew which bit he meant.

'Hallucinations...'

'We don't know the intensity, the duration or the frequency of his hallucinations,' Aleks said, his face flushing with angry heat. 'He could be seeing stars for all we know, a normal reaction to the increased radiation levels of the solar storm.'

'Would Major Romanenko know that seeing stars was a normal reaction to the increased levels of radiation?' Bales asked.

'Well yes, but —'

'So he wouldn't feel it necessary to waste precious radio time telling you about it, then?'

Aleks had no answer, and that frustrated him even more. Bales gathered his papers together and slotted them back into the folder.

'I think it likely,' he said as he placed the folder on the table, 'that what we heard this morning was nothing more than the symptoms of an anxiety disorder, perhaps induced by impaired cognitive reasoning though long-term and short-term stress. I believe we can expect more behaviour like this, perhaps to an even greater degree than we saw today, with the distinct possibility that Major Romanenko's psychoses may even pose a threat to the safety of himself and the other two crewmen.'

'But that's ridiculous!' Lev shouted, snapping from his distant state. 'He's the best cosmonaut we have, a veteran of many successful missions on Earth *and* in space!'

'I've also seen in his file that he has a history of depression.'

'When he was a teenager for goodness' sake!'

'Depressive behaviour is not something that can be ignored, and as this case shows, cannot be indefinitely cured. Major Romanenko's mental instability should have had him filtered out during the selection process and he should have never been allowed to wear a space suit. He is a discredit to the RFSA, a discredit to the partners of the ISS and a discredit to space exploration.'

Bales shot a look at Aleks. 'I'm disappointed you couldn't tell me about this. I wanted you to be honest with me, even gave you the opportunity to speak your mind, and you held information back — important information. In light of this situation, my conclusion — and the conclusion I shall be reporting to my superiors — is that Major Romanenko is a threat to our mission, the crew, and potentially to the future of mankind. We will retrieve your crew as soon as possible and replace them with our own so we can be certain that the future of this mission is not jeopardised any more than it already has been.'

'This is insane …' Lev said, shaking his head in disbelief.

'Furthermore, Mr Ryumin,' Bales said, standing up and pushing his chair under the table, 'you have been granted three month's leave so you can take some time to rest and recover from this ordeal. It hasn't been easy for you, I'm sure.'

'But — but I'm fine,' Lev said, getting to his feet so fast that his chair snapped back against the wall.

'It wasn't a suggestion.'

The door swung open and a young man rushed in. He was red faced and panting.

'Sorry to disturb you,' he said between gasps, 'but you're needed in Mission Control right away.'

Bales squeezed past and set off down the corridor at a run, and Aleks, with Lev in tow, scrambled out after him. Foregoing the elevator, they clattered down a flight of stairs, crashing one by one through the swinging double doors and into the corridor. When they got to Mission Control, security swept them in, and Aleks entered, hands on hips, chest rising and falling.

'What's the situation?' asked Bales, his apparent fitness allowing him to speak in his usual composed way. The junior flight controller led them to the comms desk as he spoke.

'We had another window — a brief one — and we had enough time to catch a message from the ISS.'

He nodded to the operator sat at Aleks' desk, who, waiting for the command, thumbed the playback button on the recorder.

'It isn't much,' the junior flight controller said, the whites of his eyes bold and bright, 'but I think you need to hear it.'

The speakers erupted with a distorted chatter, swelling and throbbing with guttural hisses and stabs of noise that sounded like tearing paper. An underlying current of speech also seemed to be threading its way through the static, but it sounded distant and muffled, and not quite defined enough to form any recognisable words. The operator turned the gain up, and the hiss rose, becoming almost too loud to bear.

Then, clearly, through the mist of distortion flushing from the speakers, a word — and then another — pressed against the eardrums of everyone in the room, the voice made unrecognisable through the strain of distress:

'Help … me …' it said.

Section 2 — Progress
Chapter 4

An orange flame of dawn light pierced through the small window, straight into Sally Fisher's eyes. She pulled the blind down and repositioned herself so her head was resting up against the small jet's leather-trimmed fuselage.

Sally had received the call from NASA the evening before, around ten thirty at night. A call from NASA wasn't unusual, because they sponsored her SETI work in the search for extra-terrestrial intelligence, but the timing was. Although she had still been working — as she always seemed to be, and that's how she liked it — it was way past what she considered to be an appropriate time for a business call.

Her annoyances were soon forgotten when the voice on the other end of the phone relayed its message. She had been summoned, not to the NASA headquarters in Washington D.C. or to the Kennedy Space Centre like she had been on a few previous occasions, but to Moscow. Her work was her life; there was no spouse, partner, or even cat to consult with, and so her response had been an immediate, resounding, and what she hoped didn't sound too much like an over-excited schoolgirl, *yes*.

Not six hours later, she had met her NASA liaison at the Moffett Federal Airfield, a short drive from the Carl Sagan Centre where she conducted most of her research. She had been ushered onto a small, unexpectedly luxurious private jet. The jet's turbines where already whining at idle as she boarded, and within minutes of buckling up her seatbelt, they were airborne. No one had even asked to see her passport.

The soft, creamy leather should have been comfortable, yet Sally struggled to sit still on its velvety folds. Her brain was a muddle of exhilaration, anticipation, nervousness; a mixed bag of pure ecstasy and unadulterated fear.

They had told her on the phone that she was needed right away in Moscow, but little more than that. The NASA escort at the airport hadn't uttered a word beyond polite pleasantries and the odd instruction. She surmised that whatever it was they wanted from her, it could only be one of two things: firstly, Sally was a communications expert. That didn't mean she was good with radios — although she was — more that her research led the way in the field of deep space transmission. Her first MIT doctorate thesis, completed when she was just twenty-three, helped NASA extend its field of view into the cosmos to make sense of the fine detail received by its space telescopes like Hubble and ROSAT. Her second thesis helped NASA and CalTech push space telescope technology to the next generation, enabling NuSTAR to be launched. Despite her extraordinary technical ability and almost god-like understanding of light in all its wavelengths, Sally had chosen to reject a position at NASA and had joined the SETI Institute instead, driven by an insatiable urge to find life outside the reaches of Earth. This association was the basis of her second assumption for NASA's motives.

Of course, NASA wouldn't let such talent as hers go to waste, and so in exchange for their support of her search for extra-terrestrial intelligence, both through financial investment and access to their facilities, equipment and man-power, Sally would undertake research and assist in the development of technology for NASA and its partners. Her complete lack of ability to put less than her all into what she did meant that she effectively had two full time jobs — one she worked during the day, and the other she worked at night. It would be a strange day — even hour — when Sally Fisher wasn't poring over a computer screen or a printout.

Although it wasn't unusual for NASA to request something vague at short notice, the likelihood of them flying her all the way to Moscow for SETI purposes seemed monumentally slim. She couldn't overlook the obvious fact that her encyclopaedic knowledge of communications could easily be imparted over the phone, by email or through Skype, so to send her to Russia for a mere technical query seemed just as unlikely. Her brain spun, tying itself in tighter and tighter knots as she sat alone in the leather-clad flying cigar tube. She considered turning on the polished wood-framed television, but she knew nothing on that could possibly distract her overactive mind.

The plane, which had been climbing, banked right and levelled out. They were flying East, towards the rising sun and into the new day. With the sun now dead ahead, Sally could slide her blind open again; she watched the criss-crossing grey lines down below give way to open wilderness, and her heart leapt knowing there was so much to explore in the world — and beyond. As she dozed, she hoped she would be getting a chance to discover a whole lot more very soon.

A screech of rubber on tarmac shuddered through the plane, jolting Sally awake. Disorientated, she brushed her hair from her face — peeling away the strands that were sticky with drool — and stretched against the seat as she remembered where she was. She didn't recall falling asleep, let alone travelling nearly six-thousand miles; it only went to show just how sleep-deprived she was, working day and night without even realising it.

The sky was bright but bleak, glowing like a fluorescent tube. As they taxied towards the main terminal building, they turned off the painted yellow line, peeling away from the rows of huge airliners and on to the smaller hangars at the opposite end of the airfield. The nose swivelled as they approached the second to last hangar, and the small plane entered and rolled to a stop. It was dim inside, and Sally struggled to make anything out through her small window. From what she could see, it was empty. The door swung down, and a man in a nondescript dark suit and sunglasses leaned in through the gap.

'If you'd like to come this way, Miss Fisher,' he said, voice as stiff as his suit.

Sally did as she was told. As she descended onto the tarmac, she looked around the hangar; it was indeed empty.

'Please follow me,' the nondescript man said, and she did. He led her to the back of the hangar, opening a door for her. On the other side, out in the open, a black SUV with dark-tinted glass waited for them. As she approached, the back door opened. A man with white crew-cut hair stepped out and offered his hand to her.

'Good afternoon, Miss Fisher,' he said as she took his hand and shook it, 'welcome to Russia. I'm John Bales, and I'd like to thank you for joining us out here on such short notice.'

'That's okay,' Sally said.

The nondescript man entered the front passenger side of the vehicle, and Bales gestured to Sally to climb aboard too. She froze, her nerves taut with a sudden panic, but as quick as the feeling had come, it went, and she stepped into the SUV and slid herself along the rear bench. Her constant struggle with strange people and situations wasn't going to get in her way today.

'I'm sorry for all this secrecy and haste,' Bales said, getting into the car and shutting the door behind him, 'but we want to keep what *we* know and what *they* know entirely separate.'

The car pulled away, accelerating at an uncomfortable pace past the rear of the hangars.

'Who are *they*?' Sally asked.

The car slowed, reaching a chain-link gate that started retracting straight away. Outside, a group of people clutching big cameras with fat lenses and tall flash guns pushed their way in through the growing gap. They crowded the car, thrusting their cameras up against the windows, blasting flash after flash through the glass. Sally recoiled, shielding her eyes from the relentless onslaught.

'Don't worry, they can't see you. You're quite safe in here,' Bales reassured her.

The driver leaned on the horn, edging the car forward through the small crowd. It didn't take long until they were free, and soon they were travelling along a lightly trafficked highway, overtaking everything else on it.

'I take it there's more to this than a simple malfunction on the International Space Station?' Sally said, watching the traffic flying backwards on the dull, grey infrastructure.

'Yes, there is,' Bales said.

'And I don't think you need me just because I'm good with light, either,' Sally continued, eyes jumping from tree to tree as they took over from the bricks-and-mortar landscape. A field rushed by, its crop trimmed to the ground, stumps yellow and withered.

'No,' Bales said.

Sally looked at him; he was studying her. His tanned face was doing well to hide it, but his searching eyes betrayed his curiosity. Sally was used to it. Her reputation often preceded her, and it was one of the reasons she had shied away from the lecture halls and seminars, retiring to the seclusion of SETI research. Ever since she was young, she had been under constant scrutiny.

'What have you found?' Sally asked, breaking eye contact with Bales to hide the excitement crackling inside her belly.

'Well, you could say that *it* found *us*.'

Sally looked back at him, her eyes tracing his features to see if he was mocking her. He wasn't. 'So it's true.'

'What's true?'

'Well, it was just a rumour,' she said, playing with her fingers, 'but word is that the ISS had made contact with an entity … not of this world.'

The rumour wasn't true at all, but Sally thought she might be able to squeeze more truth out of the man if he believed his information had already been compromised. She knew how these things worked: information was dished out on a need-to-know basis, and no one ever needed to know — especially not her. She was a component in a machine, a piece in a puzzle.

They considered each other, and she worried for a fleeting moment that he had seen straight through her ruse. He broke his gaze with her and looked out the window as concrete expanse began to consume nature once again, not saying anything. Sally took this as a cue to drop the conversation — at least for now.

The car slowed as it threaded its way through the tightening asphalt canyons between the tall industrial structures of West Korolyov. It came to a stop outside a dominating yellow brick building whose tall, cuboid structure seemed to have far too few windows for its size, almost like a prison. The barrier opened as they pulled up to it, and closed behind them again right away.

'Please put this on,' the nondescript man said, handing her a lanyard with a plastic card dangling from the end. Although she understood the languages of the cosmos unlike anyone else, she struggled with the languages of other countries, and the Russian text on the card meant nothing to her. She slipped it over her head.

They parked up and climbed out the SUV, and Bales alone led her into the building. They followed corridor after corridor, taking left turn after right turn, burrowing deeper and deeper into the maze until they reached a room whose Russian signage actually meant something to her. Not because she could read it, but because she recognised the pattern of shapes from documentation she had seen before: Mission Control

She showed her pass to the security officer stationed outside and followed Bales in through the double doors. The room inside was dim, which, as her eyes adjusted, disguised its cavernous space. The walls curved around the perimeter, and row upon row of desks filled the width. At the front of the room were three huge screens relaying information about the ISS, and she stopped to take it all in, drinking in the moment. Her involvement in science had never put her on the front line, but here she was and she was overwhelmed with awe.

'It's quite something,' Bales said. 'If you'd like to follow me, we need to get down to business as soon as we can. I'm sorry for the haste, but time is of the essence.'

Sally nodded understanding, and they walked around the room until Bales stopped at a row of desks, guiding her in to an empty seat next to a man who was adjusting his headset.

'If you'd like to take a seat next to our CAPCOM Mr Dezhurov here. He'll be able to fill you in with the details. Mr Dezhurov, Miss Fisher; Miss Fisher, Mr Dezhurov.'

Mr Dezhurov stood and shook her hand. He looked tired — very tired.

'Pleased to meet you,' he said, his English dripping with heavy Russian intonation. 'You can call me Aleks.'

'And I'm Sally.'

They sat down.

'Very briefly,' Aleks began, 'a few weeks ago, the crew of the ISS discovered a unidentified object.'

He continued to describe what had happened, telling Sally about the difficulty in establishing visual contact with the vessel and their failure to communicate with it. He told her about Mikhail's hallucinogenic experiences and, making Sally's skin prickle, the harrowing two-word message that had been their last.

'That transmission was recorded four days ago and was the last time we had contact with anyone on board the ISS,' Aleks concluded.

'Oh my god,' Sally whispered, looking between the solemn faces of Aleks and Bales. 'But I'm afraid even with all my knowledge of long-range communication, we won't be able to penetrate the barrier of radiation from the solar storm to make contact with the crew. It's just not possible …'

Aleks' face fell a little, and he looked at his desk.

'I'm sorry you've brought me all this way to hear that, but there's nothing I can do to help you. You'll have to wait for the storm to die down.'

'That's the problem,' Bales said. Sally looked at him; his narrow eyes were fixed on hers. 'The storm ended more than two days ago. We've had a clear window of communication for over twenty-four hours and there hasn't been a single response to any of our broadcasts.'

Chapter 5

Sally blinked, hearing but not understanding. 'I don't … I don't know what you mean,' she said. 'I mean, I do know what you mean, but I don't know what you need me for?'

That churning, nauseating anxiousness began tumbling inside her again, and she held the desk to steady herself.

'Are you okay?' Aleks asked.

Sally nodded. 'I'll be fine,' she said, not feeling fine at all.

Bales placed his hand on her shoulder.

'We wanted you as an advisor to the ISS crew, to help them figure out how to make contact with UV One, but it's clear that's not going to happen now.' He paused, as if letting his words sink in. 'Sally, we need you to go to the station with one of our astronauts and resume the research yourself.'

'But,' Sally whispered, her throat tightening, 'can't I do that from here?'

'The station is in the best location, has the best equipment and offers you the best chance of making contact with UV One,' Bales said. 'I've been told there isn't anyone better suited to this job than you, and right now we can't do with anything less than that. This is a matter of global security. We can't cut corners.'

He lifted his hand from her shoulder and clasped it together with his other. Aleks' eyes flitted backwards and forwards between them.

'Take some time to think about it,' Bales said, his tanned face breaking into a reassuring smile that his stern eyes did not mirror.

On the plane, Sally had hoped beyond hope that something like this would happen. She had done for a long time before, too. But now it was here, real, it was the last thing she wanted. Sitting in the corner of the canteen, clutching a tepid cup of coffee, she stared through the wall and way into the distance. The people around her came and went, some on their own, some in groups talking among themselves, but they registered only as a blur. She had hoped to find solace on her own in the canteen — it was how she worked best, how she cleared her mind. Solitude was who she was and she sought it out, embraced it even. But this — this was on another level. She felt more than alone: she felt *lonely.* She was already far away from home, from the comfort of familiarity, and they wanted to send her even further away. She didn't cry — she never was one for crying — she just felt lost, confused, and desperate to be back where she belonged.

The sound of chair legs dragging against the floor made her jump, and she looked up. It was Aleks, who placed a steaming cup on the table in front of her.

'I brought you fresh coffee,' he said.

'Did John send you here to try and convince me to go?' Sally asked, staring at the old cup pressed between her palms.

Aleks sat down next to her. 'No, not at all, nothing like that.'

He took a deep breath as though he was going to continue talking, but instead he just sighed a long, loud sigh.

'He's my friend you know,' he said after a while. 'Mikhail, that is. Has been for a very long time.'

'You don't think he's coming back?' Sally asked.

Aleks shrugged. 'I don't know. I haven't known what to think since — since *it* showed up.' He looked around the deserted canteen, his face anxious. 'I just want to know what's going on,' he said. 'I want to get some answers. Find out what happened to Mikhail and the others. For all I know this thing could kill us all tomorrow, and I don't want to go without knowing why.' He took a sip of his coffee. 'That's the reason why we — why *you* — are here isn't it? To ask why?'

Sally gave an inward nod, but outside said and did nothing.

'I don't trust Bales,' Aleks continued, 'and I don't like him either, but for now at least we're on the same team. I *do* trust you, though. I think you could be exactly what we need to sort this whole mess out and find some answers.'

He put his cup down on the table and heaved himself to his feet. 'Do whatever you think's right, okay?'

Sally nodded. 'I will.'

Aleks nodded himself and wandered away, leaving Sally alone with her thoughts.

The next day, with a clear mind, Sally was able to see things afresh, and her decision was made. It came easier than expected, and when she told Bales, she felt a sense of relief. Before she knew it, she was riding in a helicopter bound for Star City. Also known as *Zvyozdny, Shchyolkovo Fourteen* and *Closed Military Townlet Number One,* Star City was home to the secret cosmonaut training centre, *Military Unit 26266,* established during the 1960s space race between Soviet Russia and the US Now called the Gagarin Cosmonaut Training Centre — after the cosmonaut that made Soviet Russia the first power on Earth to put a man in space — and under civil command, it was a thriving town with its own school, shops, post office, cinema, railway station and even museum. Between the old Star City and the new, one thing still remained: its sole reason for existence was to train cosmonauts to cope with the rigours of space. Sally had dreamed of coming to this place since she was a little girl; for her, it was a Mecca of extra-terrestrial exploration and a doorway to the heavens.

The beating blades of the helicopter thumped through her headphones, and Bales gave her a reassuring nod from the opposite seat. She watched through the glass bubble as the patchwork quilt of green fields slid beneath them, her heart pounding with each revolution of the blades. Clinging on to the dangling handhold, she tried to concentrate her mind on the beauty of the view rather than what was waiting for her at the end of it.

'Not long now,' Bales' voice came, muted and muffled, over her headset. He tapped his watch to reiterate what he was saying in case it had been lost over the noise. And he was right: a mere minute or so later and the helicopter was descending down among a network of peeling grey buildings stretched out in uniform rows. The immediate skyline was punctured with other, more unusual buildings; in the fleeting moments of the descent, Sally noticed cylinders and domes dotted around the Eastern Bloc monotony.

The pilot laid the skids on the concrete and gave Bales a thumbs up. Bales slid open the cabin door and jumped down, waving Sally to follow. She clambered out, letting him push her head down as they both ducked underneath the thundering blades. As soon as they cleared the helicopter's footprint, the pilot wound the engine up to full speed, sucking the metal and glass bird into the sky. Bales led the way. They turned onto what seemed to be the main boulevard, a wide strip lined with trees and tall concrete buildings whose patchy surfaces were weatherworn from many decades of harsh winters. The morning cloud had begun to break, letting in a stream of sunlight that glowed on Sally's back. The warmth made her feel at home, like it was an early Spring morning in California, and she shut her eyes for a few seconds to let the soothing reassurance calm her nerves. Just for a moment all was well as she stepped off the mental rollercoaster that had thrown her here and there ever since the call from NASA.

They walked up to what looked like an apartment block, and Bales held the door open for her. Inside it was no different to any of the cheap motels Sally had stayed at during her student days: dirty, flaking paint, cheap fixtures, long corridors and a funny — but not unpleasant — smell.

'Let me show you to your room,' Bales said. He stopped at room twenty-four and opened the door. 'Lunch is at midday in the cafeteria building opposite. Training begins straight after. We've got a window of three weeks before the earliest launch date, and you've got six months of training to get through. It's going to be tough.'

Sally walked into the sparse room and sat on the firm, narrow bed.

'Good luck,' Bales said. 'You'll do just fine.'

And then he was gone. The one window in the room was open, and a gentle breath of air flowed through, carrying with it the mysterious silence of the centre.

* * *

Over two thousand miles due South-East, in a remote patch in the middle of the hot, acrid desert of rural Baikonur, Kazakhstan, a flurry of activity was taking place under the watchful eye of the Cosmodrome Director. Although the parched landscape stretched out for many hundreds of miles in every direction, visible from space as a muted brown wasteland, the few square miles of his jurisdiction was the unlikely home of the space vehicle Soyuz.

Fifty metres tall, ten metres wide and three hundred tonnes, the gargantuan evolution of 1960s rocket design was not where it should have been. The Director's schedule dictated that transport to the pad should have started four hours ago, yet the cylindrical craft remained prone in its folded gantry inside the MIK preparation building. Many anxious-faced engineers and scientists swarmed around it, working at a furious pace.

Watching as the fragile, insect-like cargo was removed from its metal cocoon, it struck the Director — as it did every time he saw it — how incredible it was that such a tiny and delicate object required over one hundred and fifty tonnes of fuel to lift it just two hundred and fifty miles upwards. In the dust-free workshop, its shrink-wrapped foil carcass exposed, it seemed defenceless and frail against an atmosphere it wasn't designed for, a silvery fish rendered useless on dry land. Excess was not a word used in the design of these modules; anything that could be pared back was, leaving only a delicate skeleton behind.

The Director didn't have much time for his muses, though. Following a last minute instruction from NASA via the RFSA, the cargo was to be modified. The Soyuz rocket usually carried one of two capsules: the first, also called Soyuz, was a seven-metre-long transport ship made of three sections. At the front was a pressurized sphere two-and-a-half metres in diameter, used as a docking module and storage space for a small amount of cargo. The middle section, shaped like an egg with a flattened bottom, was home to a maximum of three crew for the short journey to the ISS, and was also capable of withstanding the destructive friction of the atmosphere during re-entry. The rearmost section contained instrumentation and propulsion, including two folding solar panels that stretched out on either side like wings.

The capsule he had been instructed to dismantle was called Progress, an unmanned, automated tug that simply acted as a cargo transport to and from the

ISS. It was not designed to cater for life on its trip; it acted as a hollow space to hold the supplies and equipment needed by the station and its crew, lacking the vital middle section of the Soyuz craft in favour of an additional fuel tank for refuelling the ISS.

As a Soyuz capsule was not ready for immediate replacement, the best possible solution was to reconfigure the Progress craft by replacing the second module. The silver sheath was retracted, and the craft deconstructed, ready for its adaptation. The Director reported that the additional workload would delay the launch by two weeks and four days, pushing it back to three weeks from now. It was going to be tough, but he knew his team could do it.

* * *

'What we intend to do,' the instructor said through a treacle-thick Russian accent, 'is train you in three weeks, what most mission specialists learn in two years.'

'I thought it was normally a six-month course?' Sally asked.

'Six months is the intensive course.'

Sitting at her desk in the musty classroom, Sally said nothing further, waiting for her new mentor to continue. All of a sudden, the weight of her burden seemed a whole lot heavier.

'This, as you may realise, is an impossibility. We can only teach you what is necessary. You must be prepared.'

The first day was easy: she was taken on a tour of an ISS mock-up and shown the basic emergency medical and fire procedures. Then they showed her how the facilities worked, from the bathroom to the galley to the gym. A brief tour of her soon-to-be workplace, the Columbus module, followed. She hoovered up the knowledge and by the time evening rolled in, she was feeling confident about her ability to become space-ready in such a short amount of time.

The next day was physical training, and with it an early start. Still groggy from sleep, she slipped on one of the provided tracksuits, then left the dormitory. Wandering down the deserted main strip, guided by the first few glimmers of morning, she headed for the gym, building up a quick pace to fight off the chill.

'Have you had breakfast?' That was the first thing her instructor asked her as she entered the gym.

'No …' she said. 'Breakfast doesn't agree with me this early in the morning.'

'You need to eat,' the instructor said, hands on hips. 'You need your strength.'

They warmed up and went for a run around the centre. Within a hundred metres Sally's lungs felt full of molten lead, and after a hundred more her tracksuit was thick with sweat. Fifteen minutes later, they were back at the gym and Sally collapsed onto a bench, gasping for breath. She wasn't given long to recover before weight training began.

'Space may seem serene and pleasant on television,' the instructor told her as she forced out another repetition, 'but it has a terrible effect on your body. Muscles, bones, your internal organs — they all need exercise to stay healthy and strong.'

Sally wasn't sure how she made it back to her dormitory by the time the day was done, late into the night. Between setting her alarm for the next day — an hour earlier this time, she was starving — and waking up again, it seemed like a mere blink. A week and a half more of strength and fitness training followed, and at the end she almost whooped with joy when she saw that the first activity on the next day was not until noon. There was a note alongside the entry that told her to have breakfast, but to avoid lunch. She was so tired she didn't give it a second thought.

Chapter 6

It was a warm day, the warmest yet, and the sun beamed down from high in the sky as Sally trudged along to the great domed building at the far end of the centre. Close up, it was bigger than she expected, and its sheer scale took the warmth straight from her body as she was sucked into its encompassing shadow. Her instructor's gym kit had been exchanged for a long, white lab coat. He was joined by two others as she met him in the foyer.

'Follow me please,' he said, and they walked in silence up two flights of stairs into what looked like a small air traffic control room, its desk space dominated by dials and lights and switches that were original from the Cold War era. More frightening was the view outside the letterbox window above the desk: a room, as high as the top of the dome itself and almost as wide. Mounted on a central axle and spanning the radius of the room was a thick blue tube that ended in a sphere. It looked big enough to hold a person. Sally could feel her legs going weak as primal terror rushed into her and a screaming voice bellowed *Run away! Run away!* But all she could do was stand rigid, feeling the blood run from her head to her accelerating heart.

'Don't worry,' said one of the lab-coated people, a smart, square-jawed woman. 'You are fine. We watch; we keep safe.'

She squeezed Sally's arm, and Sally did her best to smile back without vomiting. They led her to a door at the end of the desk, and she followed, semi-dazed and unresisting. Although fear was consuming her every step, a small amount of pride and stubbornness — the same stubbornness she had exhibited since she was a child — carried her forwards, determined not to let her fail.

Behind the door, a skinny gantry cantilevered out to the sphere, which hung open and waiting, ready to devour its human prey. She stepped into the cramped sphere and sat in the deep, curved seat. It hugged and pinched her body from head to toe, although it was quite comfortable once she was in. The lady buckled her up, pulling the nest of harnesses tight across her body, pinning her torso flat against the seat with not a millimetre of give.

'Hold this,' she said, taking Sally's hand and placing it on what felt like an upright tube. 'You press button.'

Sally, feeling for a button, found it and pressed it.

'For if you fall asleep,' the lady said, not being as reassuring as she seemed to think she was. 'Oh, and keep mouth tight closed.'

She left, closing the sphere after her, leaving Sally in near-darkness. Only a small, dim light glowed above her, casting a dribble of yellow on the cramped space. The seat didn't seem quite as comfortable any more, and the tight harness restricted her breathing. She could feel a clammy sweat forming on her palms, sliding her grip from the tube and forcing her to squeeze even tighter. A thought came to her as sudden and confusing as her arrival in Russia: was this what being in the womb was like?

'Please nod your head if you are ready to go,' a loud voice asked her through a speaker above her head. Her eyes hunted through the gloom for a camera lens, which she found just above her. Without knowing why, she nodded. A muted whirr and a rumble shuddered through the sphere, and she felt it droop as she listened to what sounded like the gantry being retracted. When the sound finished — culminating in a solid clunk — the echo left behind seemed to carry through the vast room for an eternity. Then, another deeper more electrical whirr began, building to an unsettling whine.

'Beginning acceleration to one G,' the speaker said, and the whine grew louder, more intense, carrying the sphere forwards with it. The acceleration was gentle, but the disorientation of the darkness made Sally's head light. The button's spring felt stronger under her thumb, but she clung onto it, keeping it pinched down. As she spun faster and faster, an invisible pressure grew, building with the volume of the whine and flattening her into the seat. It was like she was turning into a corner that became tighter and faster with each passing moment. It was uncomfortable, but not unbearable.

'One G,' the speaker informed her.

It struck her then that she did not know when the test would end. Would it stop at a certain number, or would it keep going until she gave in? She grimaced under the weight of her own body as it increased with each revolution of the circular room.

'Two G.'

Her breathing became short and fast, partly because she could feel the clutch of panic constricting her throat, and partly because her lungs struggled to inflate against twice the force of gravity. It surprised her that, although she was not entirely calm, she felt better than she thought she would.

'Three G.'

The light in the cabin seemed to be dimming, but at the same time her eyes felt strange — as though she was falling asleep without being tired. She blinked to try and regain her vision, which worked for a few seconds before it sank back into a dull, misty version of what was in front of her. The weight on her body was worrying; a sickening thought that this was like being buried alive slipped into her head, the crushing weight rising and rising with each spadeful of dirt added to the growing mound. She could feel her soft tissue, both inside and out, trying to find the path of least resistance around her inflexible skeleton. Her face was heavy and numb, doped up with the anaesthesia of the relentless sphere.

'Four G.'

This must be it, she thought, *surely this must be it?*

Her vision had almost faded to nothing. She was at the mercy of the overwhelming forces that ground her into the seat — all except for her hand, which gripped so hard to the button that her fingers stung. Her eyes watered as the crushing power became unbearable, but even her tears couldn't fight the god-like control of the sphere over her body as it thundered round and round.

'Five G.'

A small moan escaped her lips, but the scream of the motor as it slung her into the ever-tightening corner sucked it away, a tiny drop in the sea of rushing wind and roaring electricity. Where she was calm before, almost enjoying the multi-million dollar merry-go round at the expense of the Russian government, she now felt a horrible shroud of mortality smothering her tight and still, suffocating the life from her, straining her blood away from the organs that needed it most. True, real and terrifying death hung over her eyes, blinding her from the only connection she had to the real world: the dim yellow light above her head. Backwards she fell, falling deeper into a bottomless pit that had no rushing wind to whistle through her hair, the yellow light growing smaller and smaller until it was a tiny pinprick that twinkled for the last time.

A hiss of hydraulics and a pool of stinging whiteness cascaded into Sally's body as consciousness hit her with a sudden jolt. She blinked, clarity washing away the dirty smear that streaked her vision.

'How are you feeling?' the lady in the lab coat asked as she stepped into the sphere to help her. 'You did very good.'

Sally tried to get up, but the harness pushed back hard. She exhaled, exhaustion pummelling every muscle in her body, and let the lady unbuckle her.

* * *

Floodlights clicked on one by one as the purple night took over from the last dying rays of the desert sun, and an exhausted Director congratulated himself on a job well done. His team had excelled themselves in the conversion of the Progress resupply craft and had completed the task one day ahead of schedule; all there was to do now was complete the residual checks and begin launch preparations. Progress M Eighteen M, modified for a human payload, was go.

* * *

The last week of training had become just a few short days, and the expedition to the International Space Station — to actual *space* — was hanging over Sally as an ominous shadow. Her stomach lurched every time it crossed her mind, but her stubborn refusal to give up and run away — a trait that seemed as much a burden as it was a benefit sometimes — kept her pinned to Russian soil. Even sitting cold and naked on an uncomfortable bed in the mission doctor's room could not deter her. Velcro ripped as the doctor finished reading her blood pressure and removed the inflatable armband.

'That all looks good …' the doctor muttered to herself, noting the results on her computer. Turning back to Sally, she looked atop her thin-rimmed glasses, her deep-set eyes hard, but friendly.

'Are you on any medication?' she asked, to which Sally shook her head.

'Do you have any history in your family of mental illness?'

Again, Sally shook her head.

'Do you have any history in your family of strokes?'

A shake of the head.

'Diabetes?'

'No,' Sally said.

'Heart disease?'

'I don't think so.'

The doctor stared back at her.

'Are you sure?'

'Actually, I think my great-uncle might have died of heart disease,' Sally said. 'But I can't really remember.'

'I'm sorry to hear that.'

'Does this mean I can't go?'

The hardness faded a fraction. 'No, that's all fine. You can go.'

* * *

Word that SETI expert Sally Fisher had joined the team in Korolyov had seeped through to the global media, and the dissipated interest reignited into a roaring flame of excitement that caught the ear of journalist Sean Jacob. Although he did not know that Fisher was to join the crew of the ISS, or that communication with the ISS had ceased, he had noticed the tell-tale marker of a re-scheduled mission when the plumes of hot smoke had failed to leave Kazakhstan two-and-a-half weeks before. Despite NASA sticking to a shortly-worded press release about the recent solar storms, his speculation ran wild, and the more NASA dug in its heels, the more he suspected something was up.

'I'm telling you, that rocket's taking a crew up with it,' Sean Jacob said, satellite phone pressed to his ear. He waited for a response over the rising desert wind, binoculars trained onto the uppermost module of the Soyuz craft standing tall in the open landscape.

'How can you be sure?' the reply came.

Sean lowered his binoculars and retreated back into his camouflaged tent, where the wind noise died down.

'The Progress module is now a Soyuz module. It's obvious.'

'How obvious?'

'Bloody obvious. One has a stonking great launch escape system sprouting out the top of it and the other doesn't.'

'Alright, alright — I get your point. So they're sending a crew. Why do I care?'

'This is supposed to be a resupply mission.'

'So?'

'So they don't spend millions sending a crew up without reason, do they?'

'Get to the point, Sean.'

Sean sighed, not quite sure if he was battling disinterest or ineptitude.

'It's simple — NASA have flown a UFO expert to the other side of the planet and now they're sending up a crew. She's going with them. There's something up there.'

'That's a bit of an assumption.'

'Then why didn't they just phone her?'

The tent flapped as a strong gust blew through. Sean checked the phone to make sure the signal was still strong.

'I suppose you're right,' the response came. 'Note down your findings and get them sent over to me right away. And keep digging — when we find out what's going on here, this story will go straight to press, front page.'

'Will do.'

* * *

'I want you to meet Robert Gardner,' Bales said, introducing a smart, keen-eyed gentleman to a nervous Sally Fisher.

'Hi ma'am,' Gardner said in a strong, Virginian accent, holding out a hand. Sally hesitated, took it, and they shook.

'Robert here will be piloting you to the International Space Station. He's a superb astronaut, and we're very lucky to have him.'

Gardner grinned, straight white teeth beaming underneath tanned cheeks. 'You're too kind, John. I'm just thankful you brought me along for the ride.'

Bales ushered the pair into the corridor and they wandered along, Bales taking the lead.

'What do you think of Kazakhstan?' Bales asked Sally.

'It's okay,' Sally said. When they'd arrived at the Baikonur Cosmodrome, it was deserted; now it was full of staff busying themselves in preparation for tomorrow's launch.

Bales led them into a large room at the end of the corridor, a space similar to the Mission Control room in Korolyov — except instead of three large screens, there was a single window. A *huge* window. Outside, a wide expanse of dusty-grey desert filled the view, impossibly blue skies resting atop a horizon that seemed to stretch to infinity. In the middle of the window, at the end of a narrow road, a tube, flared at the bottom, pinched at the top, stood tall.

'It's a beauty, isn't it?' Gardner grinned, hands on hips, taught arms flexing under his navy blue polo shirt. Sally nodded, not wanting to be rude. To her, the rocket seemed spindly and delicate, an ugly thing.

'Please, take a seat,' Bales offered, gesturing to an empty row of chairs. They sat, and Bales took out his touch pad.

'Gardner has been fully briefed in his role to transport you to the ISS. He will also serve to assist you in your duties and protect you if —'

'Wait,' Sally said, sitting up in her chair, '*protect* me?'

Bales looked to Gardner and back to Sally. 'We haven't had any kind of communication with the crew of the ISS for weeks now. Chances are the solar storm disabled the antennae array and that everything else is fine, but we need to be certain that you remain unharmed. The ISS can be a lonely, claustrophobic place, and it may have had an adverse effect on some of the crew. It's just a precaution — there's no need to worry.'

Sally relaxed a fraction, but nevertheless she found it hard to continue concentrating on what Bales was saying, her mind conjuring up all sorts of dire scenarios that involved her inevitable death.

'The current crew are a good crew, but they are not the right crew for this mission. You, Sally, are the right crew for this mission. The ISS is endowed with some of the world's best research facilities, and your primary focus — your *only* focus — is to make contact with UV One.'

Sally felt a million miles out of her depth, an imposter in a world that did not belong to her, or her to it. She swallowed the lump back down her throat and nodded.

'I know this seems complicated, but you'll do just great. There's no need to rush into anything — in fact we want you to take your time, plan your methodology and do things slowly. You'll be returning to us in seven weeks. That'll give you plenty of time, and it'll probably be over before you know it.' He slapped his knees and stood. 'Well,' he said, his tune cheerful, 'I suggest you get plenty of rest this evening. I'll send someone to fetch you at zero eight hundred hours tomorrow morning.' He gave a nod and left the room.

Sally looked at Gardner, who was staring out the window at Soyuz.

'Have you been to space before?' she asked him. He looked back at her, all teeth.

'Yes ma'am, I have.'

'Please, call me Sally. How many times?'

'Twice: TMA Four and TMA Eight.'

'What's it like?'

'Space? It's incredible, like nothing you've ever seen before. When you're out there, you feel like you could reach out and touch the hand of god.'

Sally raised her eyebrows.

'You believe in god?'

'Yes ma— yes, Sally, yes I do.'

'Why?'

'When you've seen space with your own eyes — then you'll know why.'

Chapter 7

The fug of cigarette smoke hanging in the air made the dimly lit bar seem even darker. Aleks regarded his companion through stinging eyes, his untouched drink still sitting where the barmaid left it.

'What are we doing here, Lev? My shift starts in four hours and I've not had any sleep from my last double. I've got a launch to do.'

'I'm sorry to bring you out here at this time of night, but I needed to talk to you away from the ears of Star City.'

'Is this about Bales?'

Lev, his face old and tired under the lank shadows, gave the empty bar a cautious glance. He leaned in a little closer to Aleks, handing him a business card, which Aleks took and slipped into his pocket. Lev spoke in an urgent whisper: 'A journalist, Sean Jacob, called me and asked for some information.'

Aleks frowned. This didn't sound good. 'Information? On what?'

'On everything. On Bales, on Sally, on … the mission.' He cast another anxious glance over his shoulder. 'He was particularly interested in Gardner.'

'Gardner?' Aleks said. 'The American astronaut?'

'Yeah.'

'Why?'

'He didn't say. But he was very keen to iterate that any information I get on Gardner would be of great value to him.'

Aleks felt uncomfortable, both physically and morally. He knew the walls had ears even a hundred miles out from Star City. 'You're not going to do it, are you?

Lev looked distant for a second, before a sudden flash of mischief danced across his shadowy eyes.

'I've got to do something. I can't let Bales get away with what he's doing to us.'

'To *you*, Lev,' Aleks said, 'what he's doing to *you*. And what you intend on doing back is tantamount to treason.'

'Treason? *Treason?*' Lev hissed, his voice raising a register as temper fought control. 'Getting that interfering American off Russian soil is the complete opposite of treason!'

The flash flickered and died, and he leaned back in his chair, covering his face with his gnarled, working man's hands. When they retreated back to his lap, the expression they left was one of dismay.

'I'm sorry,' he said. 'You're a good friend to me, as good as any I've had, and I know that you're saying what you're saying because you want to protect me.'

But … Aleks thought.

'But this is something I've got to do, Aleks. There's something not right with this picture, I can feel it' — he thumped his chest with a balled fist — ' in here. Jacob knows it too. I need you to help me.'

Aleks sighed. He knew in his heart and in his mind that his friend had beaten his sensibilities. They may have been craggy, emotionless relics on the outside, but deep within both of them beat an unbreakable friendship. It was a friendship that would get the better of him.

'Alright,' he said.

Colour washed into Lev's face as though Aleks had released a vital artery with that one word.

'Thank you,' he said. 'Thank you.'

Aleks said nothing, taking a sip of his drink instead.

Chapter 8

Getting the suit on felt like a lifetime ago.

'T minus sixty seconds and counting,' Aleks' voice came over Sally's radio headset. 'How are you both feeling?'

'Good. I'm good,' Gardner said. Pinned down by the harnesses and with the added restriction of her suit, Sally couldn't turn to see him even though he was sat right next to her.

'Fisher?'

'I'm fine,' she said, her own voice sounding distant and thin.

'Good. Launch sequencing start.'

Gardner: 'Timeline is good.'

'We have internal separation of the first tower.'

A shudder breached the tiny cylinder; Sally drew a sharp intake of breath. They were blind to the outside world, suspended fifty metres in the air and about to be forced into orbit at over ten thousand miles per hour.

'Umbilical tower separation in progress.'

'Copy that. T minus twenty seconds and counting.'

A tremendous roar flooded the capsule, so loud it shook Sally in her seat. From the corner of her eye, Sally could see Gardner pressing buttons using a slender metal rod from his own restricted position. It didn't fill her with confidence to observe such a primitive tool being used on board such an expensive piece of equipment.

'Ignition,' Aleks confirmed, and if the roar had been loud before, it was deafening now. The shaking was so violent that it made Sally's vision blur.

'Second tower separated. Reaching maximum thrust. Lift off, we have lift off.'

Sally squeezed her eyes tight shut. Through the shaking and noise, a pressure rose into her back, lifting her off the Earth's surface. She pictured the gap between the rocket and the ground — first small, growing larger by the second — then her mind took her to a dark place of veering trajectories and screaming voices. She did her best to push those thoughts away, but they hovered with frightening clarity on the backs of her eyelids.

'Trajectory is nominal, flight speed is nominal, vibration is nominal. Everything's looking good.'

'Telemetry nominal, combustion chamber pressure nominal. Stage one ignition successful. We're one minute into the flight.'

'Pitch is good, roll is nominal.'

The rocket continued accelerating. It was nothing like the centrifuge, nothing like Sally had *ever* expected, and with tremendous effort she opened her eyes. Light rushed in, and the horror of her imagination was washed away. It was *really* happening. She was *really going to space*. As the rocket rolled, her stomach squeezed into a new corner of her insides and was held fast by the gargantuan thrust that drove them on.

'Seventy seconds into the flight. Flight is proceeding nominally.'

'Ninety seconds.'

'Stage one is continuing to operate nominally. Spacecraft is nominal.'

'How are you doing, Fisher?'

It took Sally a moment to realise that she had been spoken to, having lost who was talking to who in among the noise and vibration.

'I'm fine.' She had to force the words out.

'Good. Gardner?'

'I'm feeling great.'

'Excellent. One hundred and ten seconds. Stage one booster separation. Stage two core booster ignition.'

A deep clunk, a groan, and the rocket unleashed a fresh burst of acceleration, pushing Sally even harder into her seat. She was glad Aleks didn't ask her how she was now, because she wouldn't have been able to speak.

'Vehicle stable. Stage two engines are stable.'

The vibration calmed, and with a small jolt the shroud protecting the crew module was jettisoned. For the first time, through a tiny circular porthole, Sally could see the stars, unencumbered by the blanket of atmosphere cradling the planet. Up here they glowed brighter and sharper.

'Launch shroud jettison is confirmed.'

'Copy.'

'One hundred and ninety seconds. One nine zero. Rocket structure parameters are nominal.'

'Everything looks nominal. We're good.'

The shaking had all but gone, but the pressure remained. Despite the excessive forces trying to squash Sally flat, a tiny flutter skipped in her stomach. She couldn't help but grin. She was in space; she was going to the ISS. It was amazing.

'Two hundred and fifty seconds. Roll is nominal. Stage two core booster separation. Third stage ignition.'

'Stage three engines nominal.'

'Copy.'

'Three hundred and twenty seconds. Structural parameters are nominal.'

Gardner continued prodding buttons with his stick. Sally was impressed by how calm he'd been. If he felt nervous, neither his voice nor his actions revealed it.

'Third stage engines are stable.'

'Four hundred seconds, four zero zero. Everything is nominal.'

'Copy, loud and clear.'

'Four hundred and thirty seconds, four three zero.'

'Still with us, Fisher?'

'I sure am. Feeling great!'

She let out a whoop. Probably against protocol, but what did she care?

Gardner laughed. 'That's the spirit.'

'Five hundred seconds. Glad you're having fun, Fisher. Pitch and roll nominal.'

'Separation.'

'Copy, third stage separation.'

Progress, now stripped of the rocket that launched it, had reached a stable velocity of 13,421 miles per hour. The number had seemed meaningless in books and on the internet, but now it made perfect sense. As the ferocious g-forces abated, an invisible hand pushed up through her abdomen, a sensation that reminded her of driving over a humpback bridge too fast.

'We're standing by for docking proximity to the International Space Station,' Aleks said. 'That'll be in about six hours. Congratulations Progress M Eighteen M, and thank you for a great flight.'

'Copy, speak soon, and thank you,' Gardner replied. 'Phew. Quite a flight, huh, Sally?'

'You're telling me,' she said. The repeated realisation of where she was gave her sparks of excitement, making her grin with uncontrollable glee. It gave her a strange feeling of alertness, a new level of being that buzzed through her core. She was glad Gardner couldn't see her face, because she was probably pulling some ridiculous expressions. 'What do we do now?'

'We sit and wait. Progress will automatically deploy all its sensors and antennas, make a few changes to the pitch and roll. All we need to do is kick back for six hours and wait to dock with the ISS.'

'As easy as that? Don't you have to dock us yourself?'

'Nope. Automatic.'

'How much do they pay you?'

Gardner laughed. 'I'm not here for when it goes right.'

Gardner's words hung like a sour mist in the fresh silence. Sally remembered what Bales had said about the crew of the ISS, that she might need protection from them. Unease doused her elation. Gardner must have picked up on her dipping mood, because he fired up a different conversation altogether.

'So, you're a communications expert, right?'

'Yeah.'

'The best?'

'Apparently.'

'Well, for a communications expert you sure are difficult to communicate with...'

Gardner laughed at his own joke; Sally didn't. 'I didn't mean anything by it,' he said. 'Just a bit of humour. That's all.'

Sally gazed out at the moving stars, watching each burn with more brilliance than the last. 'What do you think's waiting for us there?'

'At the ISS? Some folks who'll be pleased for some new company I expect. Being an astronaut is lonely business, even when you're with others. Some spend years at a time up here.'

'Coming back to Earth must be strange after that long.'

'That's what they say.'

'What's the longest you've stayed up here for?'

Gardner thought about it for a moment. 'Six months, I think it was. Yeah, six months.'

'How did you find it when you came back?'

'It was hard to walk what with all the muscular atrophy,' Gardner said, chuckling.

'No, I mean, how did you find it *mentally*? You said you found god up here. Did that change who you were when you came back?'

Gardner stayed silent.

'Is that why you haven't been up here for so long?'

'I don't know what you mean.'

'Come on — TMA Eight was seven years ago. What happened? Why are you up here with me now?'

'What use are all these questions? We're up here now. Nothing's going to change that.'

Realising that six hours was a long time and that it wasn't the best idea to cross the man sent to protect her, Sally stopped asking questions, even as they continued to burn a hole in her mind. Before long, Gardner was back to his usual chirpy self, laughing and joking about any and every subject — except the mission. *He* may have been avoiding the topic, but it was all Sally could think of.

* * *

'Jacob here.'

'Sean! How did the launch go? Got anything for me?'

The muffled voice coming from the satellite phone was difficult to make out, but not impossible.

'She was on board, I know it.'

'So you were right. Well done. What proof do you have?'

'They flew her in yesterday. She's got to be on board.'

'What's NASA saying?'

'Well, NASA's still talking about some kind of space storm. They're denying Sally's involvement completely.'

'And you don't believe them?'

'Hell, no. Why send a communications expert — from SETI no less — to look at some space weather?'

'Why indeed.'

'And not only that, but guess who they've got going up with her?'

'I give up. Who?'

'Robert Gardner.'

'Of TMA Eight?' the satellite phone said, after a pause.

'The very same.'

* * *

Sally attempted to shuffle in her seat, but the harnesses restricted even the slightest movement.

'Are you uncomfortable?' Gardner asked.

'I'm fine. I just need to … go.'

'Then go. You've got your MAG on. They don't call it maximum absorbency for nothing.'

Sally wrinkled her nose at the thought. She may have been wearing a diaper, but she sure as hell wasn't going to use it.

'If it's any help,' Gardner said, 'I've been in mine.'

'That's disgusting. How long until we reach the ISS?'

'About three-quarters of an hour.'

'I'll wait, thanks.'

She curled her toes, trying to think of anything but the need to urinate. The feeling passed, and before she knew it Aleks' voice came crackling over the radio.

'Progress M Eighteen M, TsUP. First stage of docking approach underway, range, three zero zero zero metres. How are you doing?'

'Copy TsUP. We're both doing great,' Gardner responded. 'Switching to docking camera.'

Gardner reached with his metal rod and pushed a button on the instrument panel. A small screen illuminated. In the middle was the ISS, a white smear against the blackness of space.

'Viewfinder looking good. Approach is nominal.'

The white smear grew bigger, consuming the screen a pixel at a time.

'Range, one thousand metres, one zero zero zero. Engaging Kurs automated rendezvous sequence.'

'Copy.'

The smear, which had been drifting down, veered back to centre. As it did, a flash of white enveloped the screen, falling back to nothing but grinding static.

'TsUP, TsUP, loss of visual, repeat, loss of visual.'

A trace of nerves strained Gardner's voice.

'Copy, loss of visual. Standby.'

Sally realised that the pulsing noise coming through the headset wasn't coming through the headset at all; it was coming from her head, as blood flushed through at an ever-rising rate. The seconds ticked by as minutes, each one further from home.

'Progress M Eighteen M, we've lost all visual down here too. Kurs downlink failed. Proceed to manual rendezvous sequence.'

Gardner's response was slow.

'Copy.'

Sally watched from the corner of her eye as Gardner stretched out to reach two small nipple-like joysticks. He craned his head down as far as the harness would let him.

'Visual on the periscope good. Range looks to be about five hundred metres, five zero zero. I — wait …'

He paused, straining hard against the harness to see into the optical viewfinder. 'I can see it …'

His voice had taken a flat tone, emotionless and dry.

'Confirm visual — what can you see, Gardner?'

'I'm not — I don't know. It's hard to describe.'

He shook his head, as if breaking himself from a trance.

'TsUP,' he said, his voice somewhat closer to normal, 'can you give me the docking location of TMA Ten M?'

'Copy. Standby.'

'What is it?' Sally asked, the words coming from her mouth without her realising. When they crackled in her own headset, it startled her.

'I'm not sure.'

'Progress M Eighteen M, TsUP. TMA Ten M is docked at MRM Two. You should have a visual.'

'I — I don't. It's not there.'

'Please repeat.'

'TMA Ten M … it's not there, repeat, not there.'

The urgency in Gardner's voice elicited a pause from Moscow.

'Proceed with rendezvous. Dock with MRM One.'

Gardner took a breath loud enough to be heard on the radio. 'Permission to abort,' he said, his voice wavering.

A new voice came on the radio. Bales'.

'Negative. Permission denied. Proceed with rendezvous.'

'But —'

'Gardner — proceed with rendezvous. That's an order.'

Gardner sunk back into his seat.

'Copy.'

'You'll be fine.'

A crackle, and Aleks returned to the conversation.

'Uh, Progress, please confirm range.'

Gardner stretched out again to get a glimpse at the optical viewfinder.

'Range about two zero zero. Adjusting pitch, one degree.'

With a gentle nudge, he thumbed the left-hand joystick. Sally watched, dumbfounded by fright, afraid even to speak in case it made a bad situation worse.

She wanted to shut her eyes until it was all over, but they stayed wide open, locked in place.

Range one hundred metres, one zero zero. Pitch, one degree.'

'Copy. We're still receiving telemetry. We concur adjustment of pitch, one degree.'

'Range eighty metres. Visual on docking target.'

'Copy.'

'Seventy metres.'

Sally's temperature-controlled suit was feeling stuffy, her breath fogging in fast-shrinking patches on the inside of her bulbous glass visor. She looked at the ambience controls on her side of the console, but she dared not move to adjust them. Her skin itched with trepidation and sweat.

'Fifty metres. Roll, one degree,' Gardner said.

'Negative, negative — do not roll one degree. Telemetry suggests to hold.'

'The telemetry is wrong. Rolling one degree.'

A sideways nudge of the right joystick confirmed Gardner's intentions.

'Forty metres, pitch one degree.'

He gave a joystick a nudge, quite a big one.

'Shit … pitch two degrees.'

'Take your time, Gardner.'

Gardner nudged the stick again, this time without radio confirmation.

'Come on …' he whispered, just loud enough to be picked up by his mic. 'Twenty metres. Docking target off by four degrees. Pitch one degree, roll two degrees. Reverse thrust, one second.'

'Do you have alignment on the docking target?'

Gardner prodded the left joystick again.

'Gardner, do you have alignment?'

'Almost … ten metres … five … *come on* …'

A convulsion of screaming metal jerked Sally's head forward, throwing her into her harness. The capsule lights flickered, dimmed, then reignited, while a brace of flashing red buttons on the console blared for attention. A whoosh of fast-moving air built to a deafening roar of gale-force extremes, billowing up the loose sheets of paper tucked away in the footwell compartment.

'We've got to get out of here!' screamed Gardner, already clawing at his harness. Sally felt for her own, remembering what she'd been told: *twist and pull.* Time seemed to slow and the rushing wind became distant, the lone pulsing of her heart the only thing that stayed clear. With a shaking hand, she managed to grasp the locking mechanism. Her fingers seemed numb through her glove. As she rotated the buckle, she felt a click. She pulled. The straps fell, taken by the rushing air and slapped across her chest.

'Progress M Eighteen M, we're detecting depressurisation. What's going on?' Aleks' said, just audible above the rushing wind.

Neither Sally nor Gardner responded as both fought their way past bulging payload bags to the sealed egress hatch at the front of the tiny module. Gardner got there first. He grabbed the slender locking bars and heaved them anti-clockwise, turning them to their stop and swinging the hatch open. He pushed his way through, gliding along in an awkward ball; Sally followed.

'Gardner, Fisher — do you copy?'

As Sally left the descent module and entered the front most orbital module — the last between them and the ISS — the thunderous wind increased in tenacity, and she could feel the powerful suction pull at her as she negotiated the narrow hatch.

'Seal's blown on the descent module hatch,' she heard Gardner shout as he tumbled into the far side of the spherical orbital module. Unable to stop her own momentum, Sally crashed into Gardner's back, sending him bouncing away. He grappled for a handhold, drawing himself along to the open hatch.

'Come and give me a hand — we need to seal this thing!' he bellowed and Sally did as she was told, pulling herself hand over hand to help Gardner heave the hatch shut.

'Just a bit more!' Gardner shouted. As they strained, the rushing wind quietened as the hatch clunked shut, the last molecules of gas escaping as they slid the locking mechanism home. In the sudden quiet, Sally's heart beat loud as a drum. Gardner's face was greased with sweat.

'The hatch seems to be holding,' he gasped between breaths. 'The breach must be on the other side. Let's get to the station before it fails on this side, too.'

Motivated by his own words, Gardner swum — with more grace than the tumble that brought him into the module — to the hatch that separated them from the ISS. He heaved the lever to the unlocked position and pulled the thick, round door open. Sally looked through the growing gap and was confused by the sight revealed to her. Another hatch, conical in shape and sporting a gleaming scar from the poorly aimed guide probe, stood between them and the safety of the station. Gardner reached out and touched it as if he didn't believe it was real.

'I don't understand,' he said. 'Why haven't they let us in?'

Chapter 9

The last of the trailing smoke dissipated on the desert breeze as staff at the launch site and at Mission Control held their breath in unison. The usual celebration of a flight well done fizzled into nothing as speakers broadcast the on-going disaster in a disjointed, patchwork fashion, rushing wind distorting every shouted word from Progress M Eighteen M into an unrecognisable mush. Aleks had dialled the gain down a tad without even thinking about it, now the shouting had stopped and he was presented instead with empty silence.

'Progress M Eighteen M, please respond,' he said, trying to maintain a steady voice. 'Progress, please respond'.

'TsUP, Progress,' came Gardner's voice, and although it was strained with nerves, a shudder of relief flooded through Aleks. 'We've got a hull breach on the descent module hatch, pressure lost. No access to ISS, repeat, no access to ISS.'

Aleks' brain ticked through an internal checklist practiced for such a situation. The telephone-book-like emergency-procedures manual was on his desk, ready, but he didn't need it.

'Progress M Eighteen M, do not attempt to board the ISS,' Aleks said. 'Isolate the breach and report. Your suits have two hours' life support, so take your time and be thorough. Please confirm.'

'The breach is on the other side of the descent module hatch, so I think we're okay.'

'Progress, please check the hatch for breaks in the seal.'

'Copy, TsUP, I'll go check.' Gardner's voice could have been that of a frightened boy.

As Aleks waited, he adjusted the firm-fitting headset, running over the possible scenarios in his mind. The decisions had been left to him, since Bales had abandoned his role as Flight Director and left Mission Control, mobile phone pressed to his ear. A worried look had been passed around the room, mirrored from face to face as his absence became apparent.

'TsUP, are you still there?' said Gardner. 'I've found a hairline fracture — it's on the inner face of the descent module hatch, about four inches long, forty-five degrees anti-clockwise from the hinge. How long have we got?'

The rigid tension in Aleks' shoulders hardened; this was the response he'd hoped not to hear. The ever-changing odds of survival just went down.

'Copy, Progress. My readings show the pressure in the module at a quarter of an atmosphere. I need you to increase the pressure in the orbital module to point five atmospheres.'

'Copy.'

Aleks waited as Gardner negotiated his way to the module's atmospheric controls to do as he had requested. He looked behind him to the double doors, but there was still no sign of Bales returning.

'TsUP, pressure now at half an atmosphere and holding.'

This was good news: the module could hold pressure, if at least for a while. That bought them time, as the two-hour life-support in the suits could be preserved a little longer.

'Progress, bring pressure up to one atmosphere,' Aleks said. 'Do it slowly.'

'Copy, TsUP.'

From his own readout, Aleks could see the pressure continue to rise. He held his breath as the blinking red pressure warning light extinguished. The needle continued to climb, passing the three-quarter mark and topping out at one atmosphere, a hundred percent.

'TsUP, pressure seems stable,' Gardner said, confirming Aleks' readout.

'Okay, Progress, hang tight. We're looking at getting you inside the ISS as soon as possible.'

'Copy, TsUP. Don't take too long.'

Aleks glanced at the pressure readouts again, which now read at ninety-nine percent. He watched them for a minute, and they dropped yet another percent. A quick sum in his head told him the remaining oxygen in the O2 tanks would last just over an hour and a half before Gardner and Fisher were reliant on their suits again. He moved his finger from the external broadcast button to the internal one.

'All stations, CAPCOM. I need a procedure for external entry through the MRM One hatch, and fast.'

'Copy, CAPCOM.'

'Copy.'

'Copy, CAPCOM.'

The chorus of confirmations filed one by one through Aleks' headset, and although the steadfast allegiance of the mission team ran as a trickle of confidence in his chest, it had become a knot of sickness by the time it reached his stomach. He knew almost for certain that there was no way to open the MRM One hatch from the outside. It could only be opened from within. Russian and American minds fused as they scoured procedural manuals and diagrams, hunting for the elusive answer. The pressure readout slid a few percentage points more.

'TsUP, are you there? We're losing pressure up here,' Gardner said, breaking Aleks from his thoughts. He sounded more than a little worried.

'Were still here, Progress,' Aleks responded, looking up from his desk to see if any of the huddles of bowed heads were looking over for his attention. None were. 'Give us a few more minutes.'

The digital display counting mission time seemed to have wound into overdrive, each second ticking by another step closer to what seemed an inevitability. Aleks swallowed the thought away and pressed the internal broadcast button once again.

'All stations: has anyone got anything? Anyone close?'

The stinging silence in his ears gave him his answer, until a light illuminated on his switchboard.

'CAPCOM, flight dynamics.'

'Go ahead, FIDO.'

'There's no possible way of opening the hatch without compromising the structural and atmospheric integrity of the station' — Aleks' heart sank — 'but we do think there's another way in.'

'Where?' Aleks asked.

'In through Quest.'

An uncomfortable hotness settled over Aleks' brow. There had to be a better way than this. There *had* to be. But he knew there wasn't. He scratched at the grey prickle of stubble forming on his chin, glancing over his shoulder in the hope that Bales would return. He didn't.

'Quest,' he repeated, turning back to his desk.

'Affirmative, CAPCOM. An EVA would be required from Progress to the Quest airlock. The distance is about forty metres.'

'A spacewalk? What are the odds of survival?'

'In those suits, about forty percent.'

That was better than the odds of staying put.

* * *

'Thanks for meeting me,' Sean said, offering a hand as he shouldered his tatty duffel bag. Lev Ryumin grasped it with both of his own and gave it a firm, singular shake.

'Mr Jacob, It's a pleasure to meet you.'

'Please, call me Sean.'

The two men wandered through the long, straight expanse of corridor that overlooked banks of parked aircraft and, beyond that, Sheremetyevo airport's main runway. The tall panes of glass that separated them from the view ticked with falling rain.

'Can we get a coffee?' Sean asked, pointing to a concession that looked to sell it.

'Of course,' Lev said. 'How do you like it?'

'Er — black please. It was a rough flight.'

Lev ordered drinks for the pair of them and they sat down at a bench in a quiet corner, away from the noise of the other airport-goers. Sean emptied two sachets of sugar into his coffee while Lev stirred his own, watching him. Sean could tell Lev was unsure about him.

'I appreciate you taking the time to talk to me,' Sean said, blowing steam from his cup. 'I think you'll be interested in what I've been able to uncover so far.'

'Go on,' Lev said.

'I think there's something up there. Something big. Well, not physically big perhaps, but something amazing. Something … alien.' He took a swig of coffee, watching Lev to see how he reacted. His emotionless expression remained steady.

'That's a bold assumption. Do you have proof?'

Sean shrugged. 'All the pieces fit. Heavy NASA involvement, a sudden mission change, loss of contact —'

'What makes you think there's been a loss of contact?'

'Come on, it's been weeks without a peep from the station.'

'We could be using encrypted channels.'

'And why would they be encrypted?' Sean said, grinning. 'Hiding something … extra-terrestrial?'

Lev folded his arms. He looked impressed. 'You're clever — perhaps too clever. I would be careful who you share this information with. I'm sure there are many who would go a long way in keeping you silent.'

'So why are you here?' Sean said, leaning in close, eyes fixed on Lev's. 'Why are you helping me?'

The questions seemed to catch Lev off guard. 'That's — that's not important,' he said.

Sean's stare remained unbroken. 'I think I can trust you, and you can certainly trust me. We both have our reasons, and as long as those reasons point towards the same end game, we can work together.'

Lev nodded in agreement. Sean had given him no other choice. He leaned back, breaking the intense stare. 'I need to find a hotel. Know any good ones?'

Lev paused for a moment, as if deciding if he liked Sean or not. His hard expression broke into a smile. 'There's the Novotel. It's just across the street.'

It was a short walk to the Novotel through the late afternoon rain. Before long, Sean, key card in hand, opened the door to his modest room. He gestured for Lev to sit down at the table by the floor-to-ceiling window and then jumped on the bed, which sagged and bounced. 'Some habits die hard,' he said, grinning at a bemused Lev.

He leaned over to his duffel bag, retrieving a notepad that was already half-filled with notes from his investigation so far.

'You won't be putting my name down, right?' Lev asked, looking concerned.

'Of course not.'

'Okay. Good.'

Sean shuffled the pillows around, getting himself comfortable. 'We can talk a little more openly now we're out of earshot,' he said. He thumped the pillow behind his back. 'God, why are hotel pillows always so damn thin?'

Lev didn't say anything.

'Right then,' Sean continued. 'I might as well ask the big one: can you confirm the presence of an alien object in orbit around Earth?'

Lev stiffened. 'I can't answer that.'

Of course not. It probably wasn't in his nature to give away state secrets to men he'd just met. 'I thought you wouldn't. Still, no harm in asking.'

Lev appeared to relax. 'If I told you that information,' he said, 'it would be obvious that I was the source. And I don't want that.'

'That's fair enough. What can you tell me about John Bales then?'

'I don't know anything about John Bales.'

Sean didn't believe him. They way he sat so awkwardly made it clear he was lying. Sean made a mental note to press him on it, but not right now. He needed to earn his trust first. 'What about Robert Gardner? He's definitely NASA, trained by NASA, but beyond his last mission into space — TMA Eight — his files are blank. Well, there's some hokum about a deep-space exploration program in Europe that he supposedly consulted on, but I don't see any training records or mission prep logs or anything prior to the launch today. Not even a ticket for the simulator — nothing. Besides, no one goes to space after a break that long, with or without training.'

Lev was nodding as though he knew something. 'TMA Eight.'

'Tell me about TMA Eight,' Sean said, pen poised ready.

'Gardner was the commander. It was a routine mission, nothing exciting. Well, it shouldn't have been.'

'What happened? The files don't show anything out of the ordinary.'

Lev looked as though he was digging up memories he'd rather forget.

'There was a big cover-up. Budgets were being cut hard and the last thing the Russian space program needed was a disaster. I was CAPCOM at the time and I was sworn to secrecy. The whole team was.'

Sean was scrawling at lightening pace. 'Does anyone outside of the TMA Eight mission crew know what happened?'

'No. Just me. Bales too, most likely.'

'So why was there a cover-up?'

'Gardner panicked. Despite a clean psyche evaluation, he lost control of himself on the flight back from the station. He nearly ended three lives on that day, but he was lucky enough to have a crew who reacted in time to save them all. Why he's back in space, I don't know. He was chosen by Bales, not by us.'

'So what exactly did Gardner do wrong?'

Lev folded his arms, shaking his head as he recalled the memory.

'He said he found god.'

* * *

'Why are they taking so long?' Sally said, pressed up tight against the capsule wall. The pressure gauge on the wall was in the orange zone, flitting just outside the red. It was horrible to watch the needle dip in and out like that.

'They're thinking of something, don't worry,' Gardner replied, his own voice small. Between breaths, it was very quiet in there.

'What if there's no way to get in, then what?'

'There's always a way.'

They both waited for the inevitable hiss of the radio, for the delivery of a message that hung in the balance between good and bad, life and death. When it came, it made Sally jump, her hands grasping at her chest.

'Progress M Eighteen M, TsUP. Prepare to receive instructions.'

'TsUP, Progress ready to receive instructions — go,' Gardner replied.

'Progress M Eighteen M, you will not be able to access MRM One, repeat, you will not be able to access MRM One.'

Although Sally didn't know for sure that the thick, curved hatch that stood between them and the station was MRM One, she was pretty certain it was, and a heavy ball of nausea grew in her stomach, micro gravity letting it slop and bounce against her insides. They were so close, yet so far.

'You must leave Progress and negotiate the station externally, re-entering via Quest.'

Sally guessed judging by the ashen colour Gardner's face had taken that this was bad.

'An — an EVA? To Quest?' Gardner stammered, radio protocol forgotten.

'Copy, Progress, we want you to perform an EVA to the Quest module.'

Gardner didn't say anything, just licked his lips. Aleks continued.

'Use the handholds along the station to make your way to Quest. You wont be able to clip on, but with careful negotiation, the risk of detachment should be minimal.'

Gardner tried to scratch his head, his hand banging against his visor. He looked at it, surprised. He seemed to have lapsed into a stupor.

'Gardner, are you there?'

He blinked, freeing himself from his dumbstruck gaze.

'Er, yeah — yeah I'm here … what do we do once we reach Quest?' he said. Sally realised that the pain in her chest was a result of her holding her breath and she puffed out, steaming her visor. The mist vanished in the same way her hope had. She watched Gardner, almost as if waiting for him to announce her death sentence.

'Progress, once you've reached Quest you should be able to open the outer airlock externally. Enter, seal the outer airlock and flood the chamber. Then you will be safely on the station's life support.'

'But — doesn't that assume that the inner airlock is closed? What if it's not closed?'

Aleks' voice seemed absent for a long time, but it could have been dreadful anticipation playing tricks with Sally's mind.

'That's correct,' Aleks said, 'but with the recent solar storm, all the internal hatches will have been closed — including the Quest inner airlock. The station should still be in this state of protection as no orders have been given to stand down.'

'Okay …' was all Gardner seemed able to say.

'Pressure inside the orbital module is at thirteen percent, and the oxygen in your suits is at ninety-four percent, so you have two hours and twelve minutes to make the EVA. Take your time, move slowly and carefully. Once you've left the range of the orbital module broadcast unit we will no longer have radio contact. Good luck.'

'Thanks,' Gardner said. And then Aleks was gone.

'So what do we do now?' Sally asked, although she knew full well what the answer would be. A small part of her still believed she'd misunderstood what was about to happen, and she clung to it even though she knew it was hopeless. Gardner's eyes seemed to look through her rather than at her, as hollow and empty as the orbital module itself.

'We go outside,' he said.

Chapter 10

'*God*? He found *god*?'

Sean felt more than a little perplexed, his pen frozen mid-word on the pad.

'So he says,' Lev said.

'What exactly did he see?'

Lev pulled a face, dismissing himself of the question. 'No one knows but him. I don't think it was necessarily what he saw that made him do what he did, but what he felt. A presence, if you like.'

'Is this the same as the philosophical crap astronauts seem to go through when they see Earth for the first time?'

'I suppose so, yes. I've been led to believe that seeing Earth in that manner is a very profound and humbling experience.'

'But Gardner had already been up once before.'

'He had.'

'So if he was fine the first time, what happened to him the second time?'

Lev shrugged.

Sean could see from a mile off that this was a dead end — at least for now. Time to change the subject. 'Let's talk about Sally Fisher,' he said.

'I don't know anything about Sally Fisher. She was brought in by Bales. I think she's NASA.'

'*I* think she's SETI.'

Lev shifted in his seat.

'If she's SETI,' Sean continued, 'what's she doing on board a hastily-converted Russian resupply mission?'

Lev took a breath. 'She's a communication expert who —'

'I appreciate you need to protect yourself,' Sean said, 'but that doesn't mean you can serve me shit and call it steak. NASA values the work SETI does, and no doubt Sally Fisher is a comms genius, but there's no hope in hell of any SETI bod making it to space — unless there's something up there we didn't invite.' The words were satisfying as they came off his tongue. Then he noticed an odd thing: Lev looked frightened.

'It seems you've got it all figured out,' he said.

Sean shuffled to the edge of the bed, closer to Lev. He spoke in a low voice. 'I know a lot more than you think I do, but I don't know half as much as I want to. *You* know something more. Something important. You're here because that something is driving you off the rails. Never mind that stuff about Gardner — you've got a weight you need off your shoulders. Well, here I am to take that weight. Talk to me.'

Lev looked out of the four-storey window, watching a small passenger jet puncture the low, grey clouds. 'I know who Bales is and what he's doing. But — but telling you is a hell of a risk for me. I'm not sure if I can do it.'

He stood, knocking the table and making it wobble.

'I have to go,' he said, and all at once he was leaving the room. The door clinked shut behind him.

'Godammit,' Sean said.

* * *

The hole was the darkest thing Sally had ever seen. Despite the abundance of shining white prickles, the blackness in between seemed to suck the light away to nothing — and she was about to go out there.

'Keep one hand on a handhold at all times,' Gardner said, 'particularly as you exit the hatch. And stay close. Let me know if I'm moving too fast.'

Although her body trembled with the same nerves as Gardner's voice did, Sally nodded her understanding, trying to keep her focus on the cosmic abyss in front. Gardner reached out and grasped the lip of the hatch.

'I'm going to climb out first. I'll let you know when I'm clear so you can follow.'

He shut his eyes, took a breath, then threaded himself through the hatch, gently spinning and rolling a little here and there to keep on track. Sally watched him, the ball in her stomach fast becoming a writhing jelly. A shock of adrenaline fizzed down to her fingers and toes when Gardner's feet disappeared from view altogether. She waited, alone.

'Sally, you can come out now. Go slowly. Take your time.'

Surprising herself, she kicked off against the module, drawing the gaping hole closer. So far, weightlessness had felt like swimming, but it fast became apparent that once she was in free motion, no amount of waving her arms or kicking her legs would adjust her course. She tumbled as she headed towards the hatch, clawing and grabbing to find purchase and right her course. She hit the far side of the module backwards, and the shock of the unexpected stop sent a blackness to her vision that almost made her pass out.

'Let me know if you need some help, okay?' Gardner said.

Sally had found a handhold that she clung to with a panic-strong grip. She didn't need her thumping chest and burning throat to remind her she'd nearly drifted off into space, to tumble forever with no hope of return.

'I'm fine,' she croaked. 'Just give me a minute.'

Despite her undeniable introversion, Sally had made it her life's work never to be beaten. She had surprised others — and herself — many times before, and she felt a familiar determination feeding strength to her body, pushing her to do what she never thought she could. It was the same feeling she had somehow conjured when she'd won the Barry Goldwater Scholarship at MIT, despite her father dying in a car accident a month before; the same feeling when she had pitted her mind against CalTech's brightest to earn a communications contract despite the intense competition; the same feeling when she — at the age of six — had watched her mother fall asleep for the last time, succumbing to the hold of a tumour-riddled lymphatic system. Her death had been so gentle, so undramatic, and she would never forget just how hollow she had felt. It had seemed like she should cry, but the tears hadn't come. All she'd felt was insignificant, one of the billions of mammals on a rotating ball of earth and rock, playing her part in the cleansing cycle of evolution.

But that insignificance was nothing compared to what she felt now, looking out the hatch into the vastness of the universe. As she drew herself out, she saw something new, below the shimmering folds of the station's photovoltaic arrays, beaming an impossibly bright assortment of browns, blues, greens and greys — Earth.

'Oh my god …' she breathed. Sally was far from religious, but looking at the sight below, the sentiment seemed apt.

'How are you doing?' Gardner asked.

He was down and to the left, clinging to the next module along, looking back up at her.

'I'm okay. Just …' She took a breath. 'Just readying myself.'

'Take your time.'

The orbital module was almost spherical in shape, flattened at the nose where it mated with the station. It was shrouded in a shimmering foil that looked almost the same as the blankets given to runners after a race, and it was completely lacking in anything to hold on to. Gardner must have anticipated this.

'Try to gather some of the material to pull yourself out with. Make sure you've got a firm grip with one hand before you let go with the other.'

Sally could see that the foil had been bunched up and creased in a staggered pattern, and she reached out to grab a handful.

'Be careful when you pull. The material is very delicate and tears easily.'

She hesitated, then grasped a fresh ripple of foil. It thrummed in her hand as it crumpled, and although her logical brain understood why no sound joined it, her instinctive brain itched at its absence. It was now or never. She could pull herself out or she could stay here and suffocate. It sounded so simple in her head.

'Here I go,' she said, easing herself out.

'Good. Take your time, no sudden movements.'

The slight tug against the foil was enough to arc her body out from the hatch, floating around until she was facing down towards the station. But she didn't stop turning, her momentum indefinite and unrestricted.

'Tense your arms, slow yourself down,' Gardner said.

She did so, squeezing her grip tight, trying to keep her breathing slow. The shimmering material flexed, its slippery folds sliding free of her grasp. Her dream of visiting space became a nightmare as the last few millimetres of foil slipped out from between her fingers. She tried to grab something — anything — but every brush of her gloved hand sent her that little bit further away from the module.

'Help me!' she screamed, flailing and kicking as she inched away into infinite space.

A sudden tug at her arm stopped her moving any further, and a strong grip pulled her back to the station.

'I've got you …'

Sally grabbed hold of the first protrusion she could find and pulled herself in close and tight. Inside her helmet, a lone drummer pounded away, her limbs throbbing to its beat.

'You gave me a bit of a fright there,' Gardner said.

'Thank you,' she gasped, 'thank you for saving me.'

'No problem. We'll go when you're ready.'

Once she'd calmed enough to continue — or at least calmed enough to unlock her rigid fingers from the handhold — they moved together in single file, arm over arm along the station's length.

'Keep close, and tell me if I'm going too fast,' Gardner said.

As they pulled themselves along, Sally tried to distract herself from the daunting chasm of space by reciting the modules over in her head as they passed them.

FGB.

Her arms ached already: holding herself flat against the surface of the module was asking a lot of her upper body. The moment she relaxed, even a little, she could feel her feet wanting to try and loop over the top of her. She gripped harder and moved on.

PMA One.

'Are you still okay?' Gardner asked. 'You're being very quiet.'

'I'm fine. Let's keep going.'

Muscles burned. Sally's hands and wrists felt numb from gripping so hard, and she could feel her grasp weakening with each swing.

'Alright, difficult bit coming up. Try not to catch your suit on any of the masts.'

Sally could see what Gardner was talking about. Ahead was the truss that crossed the station, supporting the great solar panels that grew outwards like wings. What was it called? Oh yes. *S One*.

S One had a gathering of tricky protrusions sprouting from it, and Sally relished the chance to let her arms recover as she watched Gardner negotiate them. He moved slowly, checking to his left and to his right, then back again, making sure nothing caught. When he'd cleared the truss, he waved to Sally, and she moved towards it. Manoeuvring her torso across the truss was easy; it was her legs she found hard. Trying not to let herself loop around, she lifted one leg up and hooked it over — clear — and then the other — clear. Gardner turned away to continue on up the station, and Sally went to follow when —

'I'm stuck!'

Sally looked back to see what was stopping her moving forward. A small antennae had caught in her boot, tearing through and out the other side. She wriggled it, but the barbed nodules at the end of the antennae hung on tight. Gardner had paddled back to help, and was trying to look over her shoulder to see what had happened.

'It's okay,' he said. 'It's only gone through your boot. Your suit's still sealed.'

As reassuring as that was, it didn't stop Sally's pulse rising up again. She tugged again at her boot, but it was stuck fast. 'I can't bend round without making it worse,' she said, and Gardner nodded in his helmet.

'I'm going to have to squeeze past,' he said. 'You'll have to move over to let me through.'

The only way that was going to work was if Sally held on with one hand and leaned out to the side. 'Are you sure?'

'I can't see any other way round that won't take longer than we've got.'

That answered the question, but not in the way Sally wanted. She took a breath, preparing herself, then took another one. Then she held it for a bit.

'Sorry to rush you Sally, but we really need to get a move on here.'

Sally breathed out slowly. He was right — she had to do it. With one gentle swing, she pushed away from the station with one hand while holding on as tight as she could with the other. Silver station gave way to black space and she dangled, holding on with one hand and one stuck boot, listening to her blood thumping around her body at a hundred miles an hour.

'I'm squeezing past, so hold on tight.'

She felt Gardner brush against her, and already the strain on her hand, wrist and arm was beginning to show. 'Hurry,' she said.

'I'm going as fast as I can.'

There was a tug against her boot, a gentle one, then another harder one. With each slight movement she could feel the tendons in her forearm scream in unison, each one betraying her grip a fraction at a time.

'Almost there …'

Her little finger began to slip, weakening beyond her ability to control it any longer. She could feel her other fingers going the same way soon after. 'Please hurry …!'

'Almost … there …'

Her ring finger gave, then her middle finger. Her index finger pulsated with agony as she crushed it as hard as she could around the handhold; then it too gave way. She screamed, but before it had fully left her lungs she felt her boot snatch free and Gardner's hand grab her suit. He pulled her back to the station, and she cowered against it, looping her weak arm around a handhold.

'That's twice you owe me now,' Gardner said, his voice brimming with relief.

'Not funny,' Sally wheezed. She couldn't believe how out of breath she was. And how tired she felt. 'Let's get inside the station before anything else bad happens.'

They moved on once again, and Sally noted in her head as they passed Z One and Node One to reach the base of Quest. By then not only was she physically exhausted, she was mentally exhausted, too: the concentration required was taking its toll, and she was starting to feel dizzy.

'Nearly there.' Gardner said. He sounded tired, too. 'We just need to work our way around the underside of Quest.'

Quest, being as it was an entry and exit point for the station, bristled with an array of handrails, much to Sally's relief. Together they monkey-climbed their way around the cylindrical module until they were faced with a flat white hatch. Gardner took hold of the long lever recessed in its surface.

'Come on,' he muttered. 'Please don't be locked …'

The handle moved, unhindered, giving Gardner cause to whoop. Sally couldn't help but grin. Gardner lifted the hatch open, the flimsy disc wafting outwards.

'You first,' he said.

Resisting the urge to throw herself in, Sally moved from bar to bar and into the hole. Once in the airlock, she allowed her body to float to the other end. It was such a relief to be able to relax, to feel safe and not worry about drifting to a long, slow death. Gardner followed, locking the outer door behind him. Seeing him pull the lever home was almost delicious in its satisfaction.

'Phew,' Gardner said. 'We're in.'

He breezed over to her, tapping the walls and floor to guide his movement with expert precision. For some reason, the slippery motion made Sally's grin even wider. Or perhaps it was the elation of being alive? She didn't care which: the last time she had felt this relieved seemed so long ago.

'I didn't see it,' Gardner said. 'UV One, I mean. Did you?'

Sally's grin faded. 'I didn't even think to look.'

* * *

'Wait!' Sean shouted down the corridor after Lev, who turned out of sight. He darted back in for his key card then slammed the door shut and sprinted after him. Dodging an elderly couple, he charged around the corner to see a pair of elevator doors closing and no Lev in sight.

'Damn …'

The elderly couple shuffled past, both muttering something incomprehensible.

'Sorry,' Sean said, embarrassed. The old lady shook her head, and they shuffled on.

Wandering back to his room, Sean pulled out his mobile and dialled. It rang for a while. A voice answered.

'Hello?'

'Hi. Jacob here. I need intel on Bales, and I mean *deep* intel.'

'Hold on a minute there, Sean. I thought that Lev Ryumin has what you need?'

'Yes, he does, but he's just run off.'

'Run off?'

'Yeah — he actually ran out of my room while I was talking to him.'

'Weird.'

'Tell me about it. He's got something on Bales, though, something serious. Serious enough to make him sprint like his trousers were on fire.'

'So he got cold feet, then? Figures. Okay, I'll see what I can do. We've got a few people that owe us some favours at the White House. You think this is worth using up those favours for?'

'Hell yes,' Sean said, stopping outside his door and fumbling in his pocket for the key card. He pulled it out, but before he inserted it into the door he noticed it wasn't his key card at all.

'Hold that thought,' he said, examining it. It was a top level RFSA security pass. 'You sneaky bastard,' he said, grinning. Then he realised he was locked out of his room.

Section 3 — Welcome to the ISS
Chapter 11

An uneasy hush lay heavy in Mission Control. The engineers, scientists, physicians, mathematicians and other experts had prematurely outlived their usefulness, a collective limb severed from a body that wandered on alone. Despite the weight of a twelve-hour shift pressing down on his aging muscles, Aleks couldn't leave. It didn't feel right. No one would say anything if he took a break, caught up on some sleep — in fact they'd probably encourage it. Yet still he sat at his post, watching as other weary staff members dropped one by one from the fold. The clock ticked onwards. Perhaps Gardner and Fisher were working on repairing whatever damage there was to the station's communication systems, readying themselves to broadcast? Aleks could feel the tingle of expectant frustration twitch in his knee as he bobbed it up and down, watching the clock tick … tock … tick … tock. Any minute now the call would come through, any minute now. Unless the comms systems were well and truly dead, of course.

Dead. That was a word he didn't want to think about. Somehow he felt if he exited the room, he would be abandoning Gardner and Fisher to face whatever hellish form of death awaited them. He knew there was nothing he could do for them sat at his desk, but even if he did leave, all he'd do was worry somewhere else.

'Aleks, go get some sleep.'

Aleks looked up to see Bale's stern face staring down at him.

'I —'

'That's an order. You've done a fine job today, but I'm going to need you rested if you're going to do the same again tomorrow.'

Aleks went to protest but thought better of it. He was too tired to argue, particularly with John Bales. Removing his headset and rubbing his eyes, he creaked up out of his chair, shuffled out of Mission Control and headed towards bed. A wall of cold night air hit him as he exited the main building, and stepping up his pace, he cut across the grass to the dormitories. He heard the door clink shut behind him, but almost immediately it opened again. Quick footsteps slapped on the damp grass towards him, and he turned to see who it was.

'Aleks, can I have a quick word?'

It was Bales, his white hair glowing silvery in the moonlight.

'Sure,' Aleks said, rubbing his hands together to stave off the chill.

'I wanted to thank you again for what you did in there,' Bales said, his voice thick with sincerity. 'You stayed calm and performed when it was needed of you the most.'

'Just doing my job.'

'I need to ask you something,' Bales said. 'May I?'

'Sure.'

'You've had an admirable career. You've served your country — and the world for that matter — with utmost loyalty. Can I count on you to keep that up?'

This took Alex aback. Maybe he was reading too much into it, but it seemed to him like Bales was questioning his loyalty, even if it was draped in a thin veil of complementation.

'Yes, of course, but what —'

'Not everyone is like you,' Bales interrupted, 'not everyone can see the bigger picture.' He took a step towards Aleks, his hardened face looming in the night's mist, his hands reaching out and clamping down on Aleks' shoulders. 'I think you know what I mean, Aleks. And I think you know why I'm telling you this. I want to know that we're on the same team, that we're fighting for the same side, because when things come to a head I need to be sure that you'll be there for me, doing as I say.' His grip tightened, fingers digging into Aleks' flesh. 'I need to know what Lev Ryumin has been doing, who he's been talking to.'

'I don't know what —'

'Don't answer me now, Aleks. Take some time to think, to relax. It's been a hard day, and I don't want you to make any rash decisions with a tired mind.'

Aleks blinked, dumbfounded.

'If you make the right decision, I can promise that your career with the RFSA — even with NASA — goes better than you could ever have dreamed. If you don't, well — I can't promise that you'll be spending much longer on this base.' Bales gave Aleks a pat on the shoulder and released him. 'I hope what I've said makes sense to you. Go get some sleep, and we'll talk some more in the morning.'

Without another word, Bales turned back the way he had come. The door into the main building had long shut behind him before Aleks even moved.

* * *

'All we have to do is flood the chamber and we can go in,' Gardner said, prodding at a collection of fat, well-spaced buttons on the wall-mounted control panel.

'And then what?' Sally asked, watching him work, then looking at the circular hatch that stood between them and the rest of the station. 'We just wander in, say hi, kick back and watch some TV?'

Gardner stopped pressing buttons.

'Look, I know as much about this as you do, but we both know we can't stay in here forever.'

He paused, as if thinking, before resuming his button pushing. A quiet hiss that built into a gigantic roar in a matter of milliseconds startled Sally, but its presence seemed to reassure Gardner, who looked pleased. As fast as it started, it quietened again.

'Why didn't they let us in when we were back on board Progress?' Sally said.

'Any number of reasons. They might still be in the radiation protection compartments. They might be asleep. They might not have seen us coming.'

It seemed that Gardner was clutching at straws.

'But it's a good thing they didn't open that hatch,' he continued, 'because it could have ripped Progress apart and dumped all the station's atmosphere outside.'

He ended the sentence in a cheery way that lingered in Sally's mind. The silence in which it lingered wasn't an awkward or uncomfortable one: it was one charged with electricity, a capacitor for whatever uncertainty awaited them. The glowing red light next to the hatch was bright and angry, and Sally willed it to stay red forever. It turned green. Neither of them moved — they both just stared at it.

'I suppose this is it,' Gardner said.

Sally couldn't be sure if she'd said, *I guess so*, or just thought it.

Giving himself a little nudge, Gardner drifted over to the hatch and grasped the lever with both hands. Sally heard the breath he took before guiding it anti-clockwise, taking one of her own and holding it. A gentle nudge was all Gardner needed to push the hatch open.

The white walls of the airlock continued into the Quest module, only the space between them was wider, but not by much. Following Gardner, Sally negotiated the inner airlock hatch into what looked like a space cloakroom. On the walls hung two bulky American EVA suits, much larger and thicker than the Russian ones they had worn for the launch. Their helmets were covered in soft drawstring bags, hiding the shining visors. Motionless and in line, she imagined the bagged spacesuits queuing on some medieval death row, waiting to be decapitated. The feeling of eyes watching her through the soft material gave Sally a prickle that crawled all over her. She shivered.

'We can de-suit here,' Gardner said, 'it'll be easier to move around.'

'I thought you said you'd … *been* in your suit?' Sally said, wrinkling her nose at the thought.

'I was kidding! You don't think I can hold myself for six hours?'

Sally didn't respond, but she gave him a glare anyway.

'I just wanted you to feel comfortable,' Gardner said, holding his hands up, 'that's all.'

A bit at a time, they helped each other take off their suits, unclipping and releasing the helmets, gloves and boots first, then unzipping and peeling off the main carcasses, leaving them in their shorts and vests. The work was hard, particularly in near-zero gravity, and it made Sally hot. She was glad to be free of the suit, and she enjoyed the cool air that flowed across her bare arms and legs. Having secured their suits, Gardner headed for the exit, beckoning Sally to follow.

'Let's go and find the others. Then we can put some more clothes on and get something to eat.'

Sally hesitated, so Gardner slowed himself against the ring of wall that surrounded the open hatch between Quest and the rest of the ISS.

'It'll be fine — I promise,' he said, holding his hand out to her.

Giving herself a mental slap, Sally nudged away from the wall towards him. Without the suit, the weightlessness felt remarkable — fun, even — but right now she had neither the mind nor the stomach to enjoy it. As she approached Gardner, she brushed the ceiling with a casual hand, steering and slowing herself to a stop next to him.

'You're a natural,' Gardner said, smiling.

'Thanks.'

The open hatch led to another small module, connected at each end, at the top and bottom and ahead by more modules. The hatches ahead, above and below led to darkness; to the right stretched out at least thirty or so metres; and to the left was a pink wall with a tight conical tube that bent upwards and out of sight.

'Hello?' Gardner called out in a raised but uneasy voice.

They waited, but all that came back to them was the sound of the slow moving air and the electrical systems that moved it.

'Follow me,' Gardner said, pushing out to the right and down the long, white tunnel. Sally followed, drawing herself along handhold after handhold. Every surface was covered with them, as well as laptops, cables, buttons and all sorts of complex-looking equipment. It was a menagerie of science, with not a single space wasted. She ducked and weaved through cluttered spots, past semi-folded tables and around lumpy pouches held to the wall with Velcro.

'Strange — none of the hatches are closed,' Gardner muttered to himself as they reached the end of the long tunnel. He looked left and right down into the two modules attached either side of them, and Sally did too. Empty. Sally shivered despite the pleasant ambient temperature, leaving her exposed skin prickled with goosebumps.

'Let's check out the Russian side,' Gardner said, kicking off back the way they had come. Sally followed, not wanting to be left alone, and pushed herself off into a spiral, steadying herself as she caught up with him. She had somehow angled herself so that what was the ceiling was the left wall and the floor the right. Everything was familiar: the wires, the laptops, the buttons, the equipment — but it was all rearranged. The disorientation made her head swim, so she looked forward, concentrating on Gardner's socked feet, and pushed on. This was going to take some getting used to.

It was easy to recognise where they had started because of the tightening conical section that blocked their path and the pink wall that surrounded it. Following Gardner, she ducked below a black and yellow speed-limit sticker and into the cone. It was unlit and surrounded with bulging padded bags, which closed in around them as the cone narrowed. Although the exit was tight, they fitted through no problem, emerging into yet another module.

But this module was different. Soft white fabrics and high-tech equipment gave way to olive green metal and rough beige material. The noise was different too: the soft hum of processing air had become a louder, more industrial whine, emanating from the metal pipes that threaded from wall to wall, countless manual valve taps sprouting from them.

'Stay close,' Gardner said.

Sally tried to avoid looking into the yawning mouths of dark modules that passed by on either side. They left the module and entered the next, which was covered in its entirety with beige material. It was also littered with storage cylinders and boxes that were piled up and secured with bungees, filling half the module's height. Sally realised the walls themselves were lined with the softer of the two Velcro weaves, and the objects clinging to it were stuck there with the other. Ahead, Gardner had stopped, so Sally did, too. She tried to look around him, but he had manoeuvred himself upright in the tight space, blocking the view.

'Hello …' Gardner said, keeping himself steady with a handrail.

'Hello,' an unseen voice responded in a thick, Russian accent. 'I wondered when you'd get here.'

* * *

While munching on a piece of lukewarm toast, Sean turned the card Lev had left him over and over between his fingers. The first piece of toast finished, he stretched over to the room-service tray and picked up another, then continued with the newspaper article he was reading. He finished the second piece of toast, brushed the crumbs off the newspaper, put Lev's card away and retrieved his mobile phone. Number dialled, he held the phone to his ear, picking soft, mushy toast from his teeth with his tongue. There was a ringing, and a voice answered.

'Hello?'

'Hi. Sean here.'

'Sean.'

'Did you hear?'

'Hear what?'

'It's in the paper.'

'Sean, it's three in the morning. Enough with the riddles.'

Sean looked at his watch and did the math.

'Sorry — my mistake. But this is important.'

'What is?'

'Lev's dead.'

The phone went silent, except for the hiss of static.

'Lev Ryumin? Are you sure?'

'Positive. It's in the local paper right here in front of me. Page fifteen mind you, but it's here.'

'What happened?'

'Car crash, apparently. Rolled it off an embankment and into a ditch. I'm surprised it killed him.'

'Do the police think it's suspicious?'

'I don't know, but I know I do.'

A crackled sigh.

'Okay, get on it. And see what you can find out with that card. But stay safe — don't do anything unnecessarily risky.'

'Of course,' Sean said, and hung up. He helped himself to another piece of toast.

Not much later Sean was battling commuter traffic as he weaved his way through the Moscow suburbs and South, out to a little town near Podolsk. He felt a relief to leave the concrete-smothered city behind, enjoying the refreshing feeling open expanses of countryside always gave him. After a few hours of driving, he pulled off the main road and crawled down a rutted track towards a dilapidated farm building. He parked up next to a rusted tractor with three wheels and a hole in the roof. This place always creeped him out. Letting himself into the building he called out:

'Hi! David?'

A crash was the response, followed by a short, middle-aged man with a mop of shoulder-length brown hair who popped into the hall from a dingy doorway. His face turned from annoyance to elation the moment he saw Sean.

'Sean! How are you?' he said in a strange blend of Armenian and American accents, rushing out to shake Sean's hand.

'I'm great, thanks — how are you?'

'Good, I'm very good,' David said, pulling Sean by the sleeve back through the doorway he had just sprung from. 'Can I get you anything to eat, to drink?'

'No thank you, I'm fine.'

'Are you sure?' David said, stopping to look at him with a quizzical expression. 'I have plenty!'

'Really, it's fine,' Sean said, wriggling free of David's grasp. As much as David annoyed him, he couldn't help but like the strange man. He was his go-to guy for all things computer technology, and had been since he'd arrived in Moscow many years ago as a keen-eyed and fresh journalist looking for his first big story. David had irritated him as much then as he did now, but the affection that had built in the intervening years kept them firm friends.

David grabbed him again and continued leading him through the horrible and rather unsafe-looking building. They entered a large room, an old barn judging by the smell of manure and mildew. At the back was an array of computer monitors around an old office desk. Next to them was a scattered heap of tin cans, presumably the source of the crashing noise Sean had heard upon his arrival. Once dragged to the computers, David let Sean go and sat down on his moth-eaten desk chair. He looked up at Sean, expectant.

'So, what can I do for you?'

'I called by,' Sean said, 'because I was hoping you would be able to help me get some information.'

David continued to look at him, bright eyed.

'So …' Sean continued, 'I've got this key card' — he pulled it from his pocket and handed it to David — 'and I was hoping to see what we could get from it.'

David took it and looked closely at it, turning it over, inspecting it.

'Russian Federal Space Agency, huh?' David said, looking at Sean with narrow eyes. 'That's serious business.'

'Are you okay doing it?'

'Sure, no problem. I charge more for government hacks, though — you know that, right?'

'Of course.'

David grinned, a keen twinkle in his eye. What he did with all that cash, Sean thought as he looked around the disgusting habitation, was anyone's guess. He probably slept on a big pile of the stuff.

'This isn't any old door-opening hotel key card,' David said, turning his attention back to the thin slip of plastic.

'You're telling me …' Sean muttered.

'What?' David said, looking at Sean with the sort of expression a confused dog might have.

'I — never mind. What can you tell me about the card?'

David resumed his studying. 'It'll be encrypted. Cryptographic hardware, true random number generator, that sort of thing.'

'Can you do anything with it?'

'This isn't the movies! I can't just plug it in and click a few keys!' David screeched, looking both agitated and terrified.

'Sure, of course,' Sean said, stepping back to give the small man some room. 'Whatever you can do and whenever you can do it is fine by me.'

David's cheeks were flushed pink and his fringe hung limp over his face. 'Sorry,' he said. 'Sometimes people expect too much, you know?'

'I know,' Sean said.

'But not you, though.'

'Not me.'

David grinned.

'I'll have a look at it now for you,' he said, swivelling on his chair to rummage through a pile of what Sean had dismissed as broken and discarded electronics. From it he pulled a card reader, which he plugged into his computer. He slotted the card in. Navigating the on-screen menu, he opened a window filled with — to Sean — meaningless code.

'Interesting …' he mused, scrolling through the mess of letters and numbers.

'What is?'

'This isn't an RFSA key card at all. It's printed on one, but the data is from something else. It's a key card alright, for a man called John Bales — Major General John Bales.'

'Bales?' Sean repeated, confused. 'A *Major General*?'

'Yes, US Department of Defense.'

'Are — are you *sure*?'

'Positive.'

'Jesus Christ …' Sean said in a quiet voice, propping himself up against David's desk to support his weakening knees.

Chapter 12

'Are you Major Romanenko?' Gardner asked, guiding his weightless body closer to the man with cautious apprehension. Sally followed him through the narrow hatch between the modules and drew up alongside him to see the source of the Russian accent for herself. A skinny man floated at an unfolded dining table, a vacuum-packed meal pouch held halfway to his mouth. His black, patchy beard didn't quite meet his black, patchy hair, and the void between was filled with pale skin that glowed under the fluorescent tubes.

'No,' he said. He put the tube protruding from the top of the pouch into his mouth and squeezed, eyes narrowing with satisfaction. 'We don't get beans in Russia. We generally don't seem to like them for some reason.' He pointed the pouch at Gardner and Sally. 'The Russians, that is.'

He sucked the pouch clean and deposited it in the waste disposal, then propelled himself towards the two Americans. Sally felt an instinctive urge to pull back, but she followed Gardner's lead and held fast, even though she could feel him stiffen up. The Russian outstretched his hand as he brought himself to a stop in front of them.

'I'm Captain Evgeny Novitskiy,' he said.

Gardner took the hand and shook it. Novitskiy then offered it to Sally; she did the same. Novitskiy beamed. 'You must be hungry.'

At the word, Sally's stomach growled. She hoped no one heard it.

'Let me get you some coveralls and then I'll prepare you some food.'

He squeezed past them and shot off down the station with startling speed and agility. Sally and Gardner shared a look, and Gardner leaned in to whisper something almost imperceptible to her.

'Stay close to me.'

Sally recognised the wariness in his voice: it was the same feeling that troubled her gut as well. They both watched the Russian scoot into a module and out of sight.

'I'll guess your sizes — don't be insulted if I get them wrong!' he shouted to them.

Before long he was back with two pairs of coveralls similar to the ones he was clothed in, which he handed to them with a grin. He was either ignoring the ashen look Gardner was already wearing — Sally assumed she looked about the same — or he just didn't see it. They dressed in silence while Novitskiy helped himself to something more to eat.

'I love the food you Americans have,' he said wiping his mouth on the back of his sleeve. 'Every visit to your food supply is another sweet surprise. Normally everything we eat is monitored, but not any more.'

Sally pulled the zip to the top and fastened the Velcro strip across it, trying not to take her eyes off the small Russian for too long at a time. Gardner was done, and remained where he floated.

'Come and sit down,' Novitskiy said, patting the table. 'I'll get you some food. Do you like sausages? We have some quite delicious *bangers and mash*' — he forced a strange interpretation of an American accent onto the name — ' that I can get for you.' He paused, looking bemused. 'Or is bangers and mash British? I forget.'

Still beaming, he glided to a wall-mounted compartment and retrieved fresh food pouches for his guests. He fed them into another compartment, shut the small door behind them and jabbed a button. 'It won't be long. Please — sit down,' he said.

Sally looked to Gardner, and he nodded, so she followed him to the table where they both waited in silence. A ping, and the food was done. Novitskiy retrieved the pouches and passed them to Sally and Gardner, who took them. Sally tore the nozzle open and, with trepidation, started to eat. The first mouthful was nauseating — because of nerves, not taste — but the second went down with ease. Her stomach rumbled in agreement as she squeezed food into her mouth, and her light-headedness began to fade. Novitskiy watched on, looking pleased. When the food was finished, he took the pouches and disposed of them, and sent two drink cartons tumbling their way.

'Catch,' he said, a playful lilt to his voice.

Sally did, and Gardner too. Having plucked the tumbling pack from the air, she quenched her thirst. The silence as she drank was almost buzzing in her ears, yet Novitskiy did not seem to take offence — if he had even noticed. He continued grinning, watching the pair of them nourish themselves on his provisions. Her body and mind refreshed, Sally was able to think clear thoughts. The thoughts smouldered into questions, which in turn burned upon her tongue. But as much as she wanted to spit them out, she waited, leaving the situation to Gardner's discretion. She gave him a look she thought said all that, and the slight hint of worried resignation on his face seemed to confirm he'd understood. He sealed his water pack, stuck it down onto the table and cleared his throat.

'Where are the others?' he said, the bold, matter-of-fact tone he'd attempted cracking towards the end.

Novitskiy shrugged, his pleasant humour unwavering.

'Williams, the American — he's down in the MLM,' he said, pointing to an open hatch in the floor.

'What's he doing down there?'

'Watching, I suppose. He spends a lot of his time down there now.'

'And Romanenko?'

Novitskiy's pleasantness faded a fraction, if only in his eyes, but it returned before he spoke again.

'He had to leave.'

Sally frowned. *What are you talking about?* she wanted to say, to yell, but she didn't dare.

'Leave?' Gardner asked.

Novitskiy shrugged again, like a schoolboy who didn't want to tattle. 'I don't know. You'd have to ask him.'

'But he's gone, right?'

'Yes.'

Novitskiy's short answer and sliding pleasance indicated the conversation had reached a dead end, and Sally looked from one man to the other as they considered each other. This odd relationship was evolving fast — too fast.

'Can you take me to Williams?' Gardner said.

Novitskiy's beaming expression returned. 'Sure. Follow me.'

He turned, gliding in his organic way, and darted down towards the MLM. Gardner beckoned Sally to follow, and she trailed behind him as they went after Novitskiy. As they plummeted down, the disorientating somersault gripped Sally's full stomach and she slowed, pausing to shut her eyes and take a breath. Her bubbling insides churned, then eased. She released her breath in a gentle blow.

'Good god, Sally, you've got to come see this,' Gardner called out from below.

Dinner under control, Sally opened her eyes and pushed on into the MLM, which opened up into a dim shell with a few soft storage bags and an airlock at the far end. Gardner and Novitskiy had joined a stocky, balding man — Williams, she presumed. All three focussed their attention on a small window. As Sally drew alongside them, a gasp escaped her as she saw what they saw: a shimmering, black object, trapezoidal in shape, tracking their orbit a few hundred metres behind.

* * *

Aleks had been in that cylindrical room more times than he could remember, yet today it felt like the first visit all over again. The usual people were there, using the usual equipment; the usual hum radiated through the air as chatter and air-con sang in harmony. But, as a flagpole claims the land in which it penetrates, Bales stood in the centre of Mission Control, his command absolute. As Aleks approached his station, Bales gravitated towards him, his dominance radiating from him like heat from a fire. Aleks could almost feel it burn.

'Good afternoon, Aleks,' he said, taking a seat next to him. 'Did you have an opportunity to think about our little discussion?'

The mere sound of Bales' voice made Aleks want to throw up.

'I know what you did,' he said, the words tasting bitter in his mouth. 'I know what you did to Lev.'

'An unfortunate accident from what I hear,' Bales said, pulling a sombre face, 'and I am truly saddened to be made aware of it.'

A hot throb swelled in Aleks' temples. The fire was raging, and he needed to get away from it before it consumed him. 'I'm sure you are.'

Bales gave him a thin smile. 'So I trust you'll be dedicating yourself to the program,' he said, 'to the others here, to those on board the ISS whose safety is reliant upon our performance?'

Aleks thought his teeth might crack his jaw was clenched so hard. He could almost *see* the fire twinkling in Bales' eyes. 'Fine,' he said at last. He felt hollow, as though he had just coughed up his soul. But it was necessary, and he had to remind himself of that. *It was necessary.*

Bales nodded. If he was revelling in Aleks' defeat, he didn't show it. 'Thank you, Aleks. You've made a wise decision.' His face wrinkled into a snarl and he leaned in close to whisper, 'But if you do neglect your duty, you will be *finished* …'

He lingered, the fire heating his breath, then stood back and gave Aleks the thin smile again. 'Thank you for your time, and I'm sorry for your loss.'

Bales returned to his post. Aleks couldn't help but stare at the back of his head, revulsion making his hands quiver. Sure, he would do what Bales told him to do. He would sit at his desk like the trained lapdog he was, pressing buttons and flicking switches. But he would be watching. Watching and learning. He reached into his pocket and pulled out a small piece of card, a business card, given to him by his late friend, Lev Ryumin. It read:

Sean Jacob — Journalist

* * *

'It's beautiful …' Sally whispered, nose almost pressed against the window. When at last she broke herself away from the view, she was met by the hollow stares of both Novitskiy and Williams, who had moved in close behind her. She hadn't noticed them, and for a moment she felt locked in, before realising they were staring past her and into space.

'You're Williams, yes?' Sally asked the balding man in as calm a voice as she could muster. Like Novitskiy, his chin too had an unkempt patchwork of beard sprouting from it.

'Uh huh,' he said, his words slow and slurred. He blinked, and a more alert state of consciousness seemed to snap on. 'But you can call me Chris.'

'Okay, Chris,' Sally said, nerves tingling, 'what can you tell me about UV One?'

'UV what?' Chris said, looking confused.

'The vessel,' Sally said, pointing back over her shoulder with her thumb.

Chris shook his head. 'There's nothing to tell. It just floats there, following us — watching us.'

Watching us?

'What do you mean by that?'

Chris raised his eyebrows, as if it were a question he'd never asked himself before. 'I don't really know,' he said. 'I just — feel it.' He looked straight at Sally, his cold blue eyes glinting in the Earthlight. 'You will too. You wait and see.'

A sudden blanket of claustrophobia smothered Sally, shrink-wrapped and close. Her skin itched with sweat.

'Do you know where Major Romanenko is, Chris?' Gardner asked, his voice loud in the silence.

Chris broke his gaze away from Sally and looked at Gardner. 'He's gone.'

'Gone where?'

'I dunno. He took Soyuz.'

'Shit …' Gardner muttered.

So that's were Soyuz had gone. Sally's stomach dropped when she realised they had no way to get home. It was a sickening thought that she tried to ignore, but couldn't. Gardner seemed to be grappling with the same revelation. He chewed his lip, a distant look in his eyes.

'Shall I show you to your quarters? Novitskiy asked, breaking Gardner from his daze.

'Sure. Why not.'

Novitskiy led the way, and he, Gardner and Sally drifted back through the station to the American end. As they neared the rear airlock, Novitskiy stopped himself on a handrail. 'This is the Harmony module,' he told them, 'and these are your quarters.' He pulled open the narrow door on a tent-like unit that wasn't much larger than a cupboard. Inside, a sleeping bag nestled against the wall. 'The other one is on the opposite side,' he said, pointing to an identical unit. 'The toilet, if you need it, is that unit over there.'

Sally looked where he was pointing and remembered she'd needed to go earlier. Her bladder twinged anew.

'If you'll excuse me,' she said. She looked to Gardner who, after realising she was asking permission, nodded.

'Well, I'll leave you both to it,' Novitskiy said, rubbing his hands together. He turned tail and slipped off towards the Russian end.

'I'll be back in a minute,' Sally said, heading to the toilet.

Gardner was investigating his quarters. 'Take all the time you need.'

She guided herself into the tiny cubicle, pulling the doors shut behind her. She had been shown how the system worked in her weeks of training, and so she did what she remembered: remove her coveralls, sit at the lavatory, affix the suction unit. It was an odd fit, but she managed it, and she used the time to shut her eyes and let the unimpeded quiet wash over her. Questions popped off in her head like fireworks, the fiery spray of each one obscuring the next until she didn't know what she was really thinking at all. The faint nick of a headache gnawed at the cavity behind her shut eyes as the thoughts quietened, leaving her head empty but for one: *It floats there, watching us.*

She wondered what had caused Romanenko to take Soyuz, leaving his crewmates and duty behind. It was obvious that the psychological effects of being isolated up here with UV One were enough to make any man nervous, but Romanenko's reaction seemed unbefitting someone of such experience and training. It just didn't make sense. And why hadn't he made it back to Earth? Surely he knew how to pilot Soyuz? Perhaps there was a failure on board. Perhaps he panicked. Perhaps it wasn't as simple as jumping in and setting a course for home.

A tapping noise jolted her from her daydream, and she bumped her head against the plastic roof of the cubicle.

'Are you okay in there?' came Gardner's voice through the door. 'You've been a while.'

Sally righted her mind again and pulled herself back to reality, remembering she was sitting on a toilet.

'Yeah, I'm fine. I'll be out in a sec,' she called back.

She returned the suction unit to its holster, redressed and exited.

'Everything okay?' Gardner asked, concern lacing both his tone and expression.

'Sure. I was just dozing. I'm pretty tired.'

'Yeah, me too.' He looked around as if checking to see if anyone was listening, before turning back to Sally and speaking in a low voice. 'Look, they seem okay. A little traumatised perhaps, but okay. I reckon we're safe to get some sleep now. We can resume our mission with fresh minds tomorrow.'

That made sense to Sally. 'You're probably right,' she said, yawning at the thought of a warm bunk.

They clambered into their respective quarters, and Sally zipped up her door behind her. Wriggling her way into the upright sleeping bag, she clicked the light off and shut her eyes, and within minutes she was asleep. She slept without a single dream and did not stir for almost ten hours.

When she awoke, it took her senses a good long minute to re-acclimatize to where she was. Her quarters were cramped, the air was close, and the folds of her limbs were clammy with night sweat. She peeled herself from the sleeping bag and emerged into the Harmony module, where she stretched her whinging muscles out. Gardner's quarters were already open and empty. The Harmony module was deserted. Yawning, she paddled her way along the station to the galley and, sure enough, Gardner was there, alone.

'Where are the others?' Sally asked, hanging from a rail.

Gardner, who was eating, shrugged. 'Sleeping, I think. I haven't seen them. Here, I prepared you some breakfast.'

Sally joined him, and they ate together. It was a strange experience: the intimate and vulnerable state of the breakfast meal combined with the knowledge of their location, and indeed their mission. It made for an uneasy feeling in her stomach. She picked at the food with none of the appetite of yesterday, while Gardner ate on.

'Why do you think Romanenko left?' she said, playing with a globule of porridge as it tumbled on the spot in front of her.

'Dunno,' Gardner said through a mouthful.

'I wonder if it has anything to do with what Chris said?'

'What did Chris say?'

'You know — about being watched.'

Gardner dismissed her with a look. 'I dunno,' he repeated.

'Don't you want to know?' Sally asked, frustration growing at Gardner's disinterest.

He stopped eating. 'Look,' he said, 'I'm here to get you to the station and keep you safe for the duration of the mission. I don't know or want to know what's going on with' — he waved his hands around — 'all this. I'm not in the habit of poking sleeping bears.'

He resumed eating. Sally scooped the floating porridge into her mouth and swallowed it down.

'Fine,' she said. 'At least I know not to ask.'

Gardner sighed. 'I'm sorry,' he said, 'it's not like that. It's just … it's just that I don't want to get caught up in a wild goose chase and end up like these guys.'

'Wild goose chase?' Sally repeated, incredulous. 'You've seen UV One with your own eyes. You know it's real.'

'I know, but what's happening to our crazy new friends isn't going on out there,' he said, pointing towards the MLM. He then pointed at his own head. 'It's in here.'

A noise from the other end of the module made Sally turn and look. It was Novitskiy. How much had he heard? Not too much, she hoped.

'Morning,' she tried to say in a cheery way, but her voice ended up as an unnatural squeal instead.

'And to you,' Novitskiy replied. His grin was absent. 'Did you sleep well?'

'Yes,' Sally and Gardner said at the same time.

'Good.'

He floated up alongside them. His face seemed to have aged decades without the smile tightening the lines of his cheeks and jaw.

'I want to apologise,' he said, 'for not being forthright with you about Romanenko.' He scratched his beard, eyes unfocussed. 'Let it be said that he was a good man. A great man, in fact. But for some too much is just too much.'

Sally looked at Gardner, whose face was blank, like he didn't know what to think. Novitskiy's smile re-appeared, but it was heavy with sadness. His bushy black eyebrows upturned, making his eyes sparkle with regret.

'He hadn't been able to cope with it, with being here. I should have done more to help him, but I just didn't think to.' He stopped talking, his face flushed. He looked to the floor and sniffed a wet sniff. 'He didn't deserve this — none of us did,' he said, still looking at the floor. He sniffed again, and when he looked up, his eyelids bulged with weightless tears. 'Excuse me, I have to go,' he said, and he turned and left, swimming through the module and out of sight.

Chapter 13

'Hi, David, Sean here. Have you managed to dig up any more information with that card?'

Sean waited, mobile phone pressed against his ear, while David proceeded to knock over a pile of something loud.

'Sean — I've hit a dead-end. This thing is seriously well protected. I can't get anything off it, I can't use it with anything — this is proper homeland security level stuff. To be honest, I'm not comfortable playing with it any more.'

Sean swore to himself and took a second to recompose. 'No worries, thanks for trying. I'll come and get it off you now if that's okay?'

'That's fine. And Sean?'

'What?'

'I'm sorry I couldn't be of any more help. I know how much this means to you.'

David really was a good egg. Sean smiled. 'Don't worry about it.'

'Okay. Bye then.'

'See you soon.'

Sean hung up the call and tossed the phone on the bed. He leaned back in his chair, cradling his head in his hands, cursing the cul-de-sac he seemed to have wandered down. He had tackled some difficult stories before, but this — this took the biscuit.

'What am I going to do now?' he said to himself, watching through his hotel window as yet another aircraft thundered overhead. Easing himself up from the chair, he shuffled to the bathroom, unbuckling his belt on the way. As he sat on the toilet, a familiar digital chiming chirped in through the doorway.

'God damn it …' he muttered through gritted teeth, wrestling his trousers up again and stumbling back into the bedroom. He picked up the phone: unknown number. Frowning, he put it to his ear.

'Hello?' he said, answering in a cautious voice.

'Is that Sean Jacob?' a Russian accent replied.

'Who's asking?'

'My name is Aleksandar Dezhurov. I work — worked, I mean — with Lev Ryumin. He gave me your card. I was hoping that I could talk to you about — well, you know.'

Sean's heart skipped a beat. 'Sure, of course.'

'Where shall we meet?'

'Can you get to the Novotel hotel next to Sheremetyevo airport' — he needed time to get the card back first — 'in, say, four hours?'

'I'll be there.'

* * *

'This has been given a proper going over,' Sally said, looking in disbelief at the brutalised wiring that made up what was left of the communications system. 'Long range comms are shot, short range comms are shot — even the inter-module comms are shot.'

'There's nothing you can do?' Gardner asked.

'Not a thing. There isn't a component here that hasn't been trashed.' She probed inside with an insulated rod, re-examining the extent of the damage, and shook her head. 'I wonder why Romanenko did this?' she muttered.

'I'll be damned if I know,' Novitskiy said. 'Chris and I discovered the damage when we tried to radio him after he'd taken Soyuz. Perhaps he didn't want us to contact him. Is there any way we can use the communications module on board Progress? That should still be working, yes?'

'Progress is decompressed,' Gardner replied. 'Seal failure. We'd need to make some repairs before we could use it again. Chris is an engineer, isn't he? He'd probably know how to repair Progress.'

Novitskiy pulled back as though he'd been shocked by the exposed wiring. 'Ahhh, I don't know …' he said, crinkling up his face. 'He's very delicate at the moment. I don't think that would be a good idea.'

'Do we have any other choice?' Sally asked.

She and Gardner looked at Novitskiy, who opened his mouth, then shut it again. 'I suppose not,' he said.

'Great. I'll go and talk to Chris,' Gardner said. 'You never know, it might be good for him to have something to focus on. Oh, and Sally — do you feel up to starting your research on UV One? That's why we're here, after all.'

'Yeah, I think so. I'll have to make do with the equipment on Columbus what with this lot being out though,' she said, gesturing to the bird's nest of severed cables.

'As long as you're sure. It's fine if you want to take a day out to recover.'

'I'll be okay. Like Chris, I probably need the distraction.'

Silent nods all round confirmed agreement. Gardner and Novitskiy floated away to the MLM to talk to Chris, while Sally headed to the Columbus module to begin her research. On her own, she noticed how quiet the station was. Yes, there was a constant low-level hum from the air extraction vents, but the silence of space seemed to permeate through it, mask it somehow. She was certain it was just her mind playing tricks on her, the very knowledge of being in space making her awareness so acute. That didn't stop it being unnerving, though.

As she perused the equipment on offer — and there was a lot of it, from floor to ceiling and left to right — she could hear voices getting louder. They were talking to each other, varying intonations passing a verbal ball back and forth, muffled by the many twists and turns between them and her. The voices got almost loud enough for her make out the conversation they shared, but before they did, they faded again into a muted burble. Gardner and Novitskiy must have persuaded Chris to come and help them.

Now Sally knew the MLM was empty, she felt an urge to go and look out the rear-facing window again. It was a silly thing to want to do, she knew that — after all, what possible benefit would looking at UV One bring over the quantifiable results of scientific equipment? But still, she wanted — almost *needed* — to go.

Oh, what the heck … she thought, and dusted off into the main shaft of the station. As she slid towards the Russian section, the voices grew louder again, peaking as she flew past the junction with MRM One where Progress was docked. She shot into the FGB module, excitement pounding in her chest, and changed direction with a clumsy roll down into the MLM. It was dark at its end, darker than before, and as she tumbled to a stop she realised the window covering was down. A small crank underneath the window with directional arrows marked in Russian seemed the obvious way to open it again. Sally turned the crank and sure enough the covering retracted. She blinked as the stunning bright glow of Earth's multi-coloured surface shot in through the growing gap, and by the time her eyes had readjusted, the crank had reached its stop.

And there it was, floating in the vacuum of space, its course so resolute that it did not bob or shimmy as it followed them. It was uncanny the way it did that, almost serene, as though its existence could have been explained as a smear on the window. Colours danced and sparkled on its surface, a kaleidoscopic ripple of an alien sea somehow coming from deep within it, like it was a window to a distant planet. Perhaps it was? She could imagine the warmth of a faraway sun as she looked out over the iridescent sea, the dancing glimmer bright but never harsh, the radiant heat even and soothing.

'Sally, are you okay?'

Gardner's voice slashed through her with diamond-sharp clarity, and she jumped.

'Oh,' she said. 'I didn't see you there.'

She looked back out the window. UV One trailed along, lifeless and dull, bar the occasional wink of a star disappearing behind its black hull.

'You weren't in the lab, so I came looking for you. You had me worried.'

Sally snorted, thinking he was joking, but his expression was that of genuine concern. 'I'm fine,' she said, feeling a little foolish. 'Sorry if I scared you. I just came down here to look, that's all.'

'Okay,' Gardner said, 'but I'm not sure I like you spending time down here alone.'

'Why?' Sally said, bemused.

Gardner narrowed his eyes, as if he misunderstood what she'd said, or didn't believe she'd said it. 'Sally, do you know how long you've been down here for?'

'I don't know, ten minutes maybe?'

'Almost two hours.'

* * *

The door knocked and Sean got up to answer it. 'Aleks?' he said to the drenched Russian on the other side.

'Yes. Hello.' They shook hands. 'I got here as fast as I could.'

His soaking coat pattered water onto the floor.

'Come in, please,' Sean said, moving aside to let him by. He bolted the door shut behind him.

'The traffic was a nightmare,' Aleks said. 'It must be the weather.'

Sure enough, the rain that had drenched Aleks was still streaming down from slate-grey clouds. Sean had managed to miss it when he'd returned from David's not half an hour ago. It was clear then, and now the rumbling of jets overhead was almost lost among the steady thrum of droplets hitting the window.

'You can grab a towel from the bathroom and dry off if you like,' Sean said.

Aleks thanked him and went to mop himself up. While Sean was waiting, he hung up Aleks' coat — which dripped onto an expanding patch of dark carpet — and clicked on the coffee machine. 'Just chuck the towel on the floor when you're done,' he called out. When Aleks emerged, looking fuzzy and damp, Sean handed him a cup and they sat down.

'Funny,' Sean said, taking a sip, 'it wasn't long ago that Lev was sat right where you're sitting now.'

Aleks, who was hugging his cup, smiled a forlorn smile. 'I'll miss him,' he said.

'He was quite the character.' *And look where that got him.*

Aleks nodded, looking around the room in a non-committal kind of way. 'Yes, he was.'

Although Aleks seemed to be keeping his feelings as close to his chest as the cup of coffee, Sean could tell he and Lev had been close. Why else would he risk his life coming here?

'When I last saw Lev,' Sean said, 'he left me this key card.' He passed it to Aleks. 'It's registered to Bales, I know that much, but I can't get anything off it and I can't do anything with it. Do you think you might be able to help?'

'I can certainly try,' Aleks said, examining the card. 'It looks like it should work with our card system. Do you have the login details for it?'

'I don't.'

'Hmm. Do you know how Lev got it?'

'I don't know that, either. Can you crack it?'

'I'm not really sure. Lev was the computer expert, not me.'

'That figures.'

'He was always very keen to keep our work secure. If he could break in, it wasn't good enough. Cold War habits die hard.'

'I bet. Do you think he might have left any clues?'

Aleks pondered the question. 'It would make sense.'

'Where would we find them?'

'We could check his blog?'

Sean laughed, but his laugh faded as he realised Aleks wasn't joking. 'That guy — sorry, Lev — *had a blog*?'

'Yes. He enjoyed posting on it.'

'Did you ever read it?'

'No.'

'Do you know how to find it?'

'Yes, of course.'

Sean booted up his laptop and put it on the table where he and Aleks could both see it. He pivoted it towards Aleks. 'Type in the address at the top.'

Aleks typed and hit return. The website loaded.

'That's a pretty straightforward Wordpress template,' Sean said, 'nothing you could really hide anything in. Oh look — his last post was from the night of his death.'

They read the post. Sean shifted in his seat, disappointed. 'It's about his cat.'

'He loved his cat.'

This wasn't going to be easy.

'Maybe if I look in the image metadata …' Sean said, clicking on the image and looking through its properties. Nothing. He scrolled back through previous posts, which were prolific, but nothing jumped out at them. Sean scoured the code, hunting for any clues or hidden messages, but every avenue was a dead-end. 'Well, I'm stumped. Must be nothing here,' he said, returning to the blog's home page where the shot of Lev's cat stared back at them. 'Any other ideas?'

Aleks started to chuckle, a small titter at first, then loud bursts of laughter.

'What?' Sean said. If this was a joke, he really didn't get it.

'That old dog …'

Sean looked at the page again. Still Lev's cat. 'What is it?' he said, frustrated. The cat seemed to be taunting him.

Aleks composed himself, patting his stomach as if to wring out the last few laughs. 'I'm sorry,' he said, his grin wide. 'When we were younger, we used to write secret messages into our dissertations to see who could get the most ridiculous statements published by the university. The best one was Lev's: *I have nothing but contempt for the odious man, Professor Tselner*. Tselner even read the thesis to the class it was so good, but the message always stayed a secret.'

'So there's a message in this post then?'

'Yes — it's right there, clear as day.'

Sean looked again, leaning in close to scour the text. Frustration was becoming desperation, to the point where he was staring through the screen rather than at it. 'Please just tell me,' he said, despondent.

'Write down the last letter of the last word of every sentence and tell me what you read. If the last word is a number, write down that number instead.'

Sean's eyes bobbed up and down as he tried to work it out in his head, but he gave up after a minute and snatched his notepad from the bedside cabinet, almost knocking a stale glass of water over. 'T …' he said as he wrote, '… H …' He continued writing until there were no more words. Then he spaced out the letters, organising them into more a understandable arrangement. He looked at his pad in disbelief.

This key card will give you access to Bales' file. You need to see what's in there. Lives are in danger. Be careful. User JohnRBales Password USDF1T42

'That old dog …' Sean whispered. It was no joke after all.

Chapter 14

While Gardner and Chris worked on Progress, and Novitskiy took care of the station's day-to-day operations, Sally spent her time analysing UV One. Patience was a virtue she was blessed with in abundance, but after four endless days of futile effort, she was beginning to tire. Coupled with the onset of insomnia — weightless sleeping seemed to be evading her, a common problem she'd been told — and life on the station was taking its toll. How she longed for the exhaustion-fuelled sleep she'd had on the first night.

She hadn't been into the MLM to see UV One since her conversation with Gardner, conducting all her experiments from the Columbus module on the opposite side of the station. As she ran a thirty-second pulse of microwaves one more time before wrapping up for the morning, she decided she could no longer ignore the fact that the only response she'd had from the vessel was when she'd looked at it, deep into its formless shape. The thought made her shiver; in retrospect, what she had experienced in the MLM was more akin to a reaction than an action — as though it knew she was watching it and it was watching her back. Alone in the quiet of the American end of the station, she couldn't be sure that it wasn't looking for her still, and the last thing she wanted to do was to expose herself to it again. She knew in her heart that it was the cause of her insomnia as well, that in her sleeping state she would be vulnerable to — to what? She didn't know. But she could feel it.

The morning shift over, she affixed her notepad and pen to the wall, logged off her computer and guided her way to the galley at the Russian end. She was hungry, but like every mealtime she felt a nauseating sense of unease as she floated over the downward hatch to the MLM. It yawned at her, open and dark, threatening to suck her down into its belly. Looking forward, she gave a firm kick to propel herself over it, catching herself on the far side next to the food store.

She was alone: Gardner and Chris were performing an EVA, examining Progress in a survey that seemed to be taking a very long time — 'We need to check absolutely *everything*,' Chris had said — and Novitskiy was — well, she didn't know where Novitskiy was. She only came upon him every now and then, most often crossing paths to and from the galley as he shepherded storage bags along like cuboid sheep, still performing the mission he came here to do in the first place.

The food heater pinged. She retrieved the pouch from its hollow and brought it to the table. Steam wafted from its nozzle in that strange micro gravity way as she tore off the cap, and with it came an aroma she still wasn't used to. She couldn't place her finger on what it was, but it was present no matter the flavour, and it clung to the back of her nostrils like mucus. Wrinkling her nose, she tucked in anyway. She'd almost finished half when she froze, nozzle still in her mouth. Was that a noise she'd heard, or had she imagined it? She listened hard, the loud whooshing and humming of the Russian module masking the last essence of detail. Nothing. She carried on eating. But there it was again. It sounded like — like crying. She affixed her meal to the table and tried to trace the source of the noise, following it as it got louder. It seemed to be coming from the next module along, the FGB. But wait — as she neared the downward tunnel to the MLM, the sound changed direction. It was coming from its dark mouth. Chest tightening, she peered into the gloomy hole.

'Hello?' she called, watching the shadows in its belly flicker.

There was no response, but the weeping had taken on a more three-dimensional quality. It was definitely coming from down there. Taking a deep breath, she fed herself into the hatch, wide eyes searching as her hands nudged her along rail by rail. As she got further in, she could see a person at the bottom, a small, scruffy-looking man who was pressed up against the glass, looking out into space.

'Novitskiy?'

Novitskiy jumped, spinning around so fast he ended up at a lop-sided angle. He looked around until his eyes met Sally's, blinking as they readjusted to the gloom. His chest rose and fell, his expression strained with terror.

'Sally ...' he said, sounding relieved, and he wiped his eyes on the back of his sleeve. 'I didn't hear you come down.'

'Are you okay?' Sally asked, keeping her distance.

Novitskiy sniffed. 'Yes, I'm fine,' he said, looking a little sheepish. 'I'm just feeling a little, ahm, how you might say, "sick for home".'

'Homesick?'

Novitskiy nodded, sniffing again. Over his shoulder, Sally could see the ponderous shape of UV One, following them from a distance.

'Let's get out of here and have some lunch,' she suggested, breaking her eyes from it and back to Novitskiy's own puffy, sodden ones. 'It gives me the creeps down here.'

Novitskiy agreed, and they drifted back up to the galley. Sally prepared some food for him, and they sat at the table and ate together in silence. Sally considered the unkempt man; she couldn't believe this frail thing in front of her was the result of intense selection and training by the RFSA, or any professional organisation for that matter. She considered her words before she offered them to him. 'Do you feel like it's watching you?'

Novitskiy stopped chewing mid-mouthful, swallowed, then took a large gulp of drink. 'I don't know what you mean.'

Despite him trying to avoid her gaze, Sally held it until he put his pouch on the table and stared straight back. He licked his lips, twitched, then spoke. 'It didn't start like this. It gets worse. It gets worse the longer you stay here. I can feel it *in* me, in my head, picking at every detail of my brain. It's searching for something, but it can't find it, and the longer it searches the deeper it searches and the more it makes me want to —'

He cut himself off, looked back at his food and carried on eating. Sally could see that he was quivering, although he was trying to restrain himself. 'You should probably get back to work,' he said.

Sally rose from the table, not breaking her eyes away from him. 'Will you be okay?'

He nodded. 'I just need to be alone. It's easier when I'm alone.'

'Okay,' Sally said, and she deposited her waste and left, gliding over the open mouth of the MLM as fast as she could. As she entered the American section of the station, she was certain she could hear sobbing coming from behind her.

* * *

'Hello?'

Sean swapped the phone from one ear to the other. 'Hi, it's Sean. Just a quick catch-up call.'

'What have you got?'

'Well, I've just had a very interesting meeting with a rather disgruntled friend and employee of the late Lev Ryumin.'

'And?'

'We've cracked the key card.'

'So what can you tell me?'

Sean paused. He had hoped for a bit more praise, but no matter. 'We discovered some coded instructions from Ryumin explaining how to use it.'

'Well, get on with it then.'

Sean held the phone to his chest and rubbed his forehead. Sometimes he wondered if it was all worth the hassle. He brought the phone back to his ear. 'Aleks — Ryumin's friend — he has the card. He's going to log in at an RFSA terminal and relay the information back to me.'

'Can you trust him?'

'I think so.'

'And what about this Gardner character? Any more news on him?'

'Any information there is on him that hasn't been deleted will be in Bales' file.'

'Which you'll access with the key card?'

'Right.'

'Okay, good work. Looks like we're really close on this one.'

A bubble of pride swelled in Sean's chest. Better late than never. 'Thanks.'

'Talk to you later.'

Sean hung up the phone. Rain continued to batter the window, as it had done since he'd last spoken to Aleks those few days ago. He really did hope he could trust him.

* * *

When Sally awoke, she checked the time to see how long she'd slept, something of a habit she'd developed. To her surprise she'd gone through the night without waking once, and she felt refreshed for it. Wiggling free of her canvas cocoon, she dressed herself and exited her quarters. Finally, *finally*, she was getting used to sleeping in space. Since the guys hadn't yet fixed Progress, she wasn't sure how much longer she'd be sleeping there for, but she was glad that it was making sense to her disorientated brain at last. The mission was supposed to be seven weeks, but she felt sure that no-one here wanted to stay as long as that.

Morning exercise, a wash and then breakfast, she decided. Stretching her sleep-tightened muscles off the rails as she pulled herself along, she yawned a long yawn that was a sorely missed by-product of a good, deep sleep. Slipping from one module to the next, she breezed along with minimal effort, touching a surface here, a surface there, to keep her direction true. If there were any freeze-dried bananas left, she decided she would have some of those. They were no banana milkshake, but they would make a welcome change from the gungy porridge that seemed all too commonplace on this tin-pot station. Up through PMA One she went, along the FGB and into the service module, where the exercise bike lived. Popping two panel fasteners, she unfurled the spindly contraption, swung her leg over the saddle, snapped the bungees into place over her shoulders and started pedalling.

As the virtual miles passed, microdots of perspiration became bulging droplets, each forming a glistening, spherical mound over her pores. She checked her watch — seven minutes to go. Lungs burning, she squeezed out the last few revolutions, slowing as she hit her target. Twice a day every day she'd done this, and still it didn't seem to get any easier. Panting, she unstrapped herself from the bike and dismounted, retrieving a towel to dry herself off with. She gripped the towel under one arm while she disassembled the bike, occasional stopping to mop fresh sweat from her brow. Then something caught the corner of her eye, and she looked up. The hatch to the FGB — and the rest of the station — was closed. She hadn't seen or heard it close, yet it was. She attached her towel to the wall and floated over, still not quite believing it. She looked up, and the hatch to MRM Two — the docking port that Romanenko had taken Soyuz from — was also closed. She looked down: the hatch to the MLM was still wide open. The darkness within it seemed to be sucking all the light away, drawing it down into its murky gullet. Bubbling up from its depths like a frothy bile was an energy, fizzing and throbbing, that swelled in time with the heartbeat in Sally's temples. She tried to cover her ears to block the sensation, but it pushed through into her body, into her head, and she squeezed her eyes tight shut. It was a primal fear that gripped her, made her want to shut everything out, but she knew it was no use. She could feel the force guiding her, steering her down, and even with nothing to see but the blackness of her eyelids, she knew where it was taking her. Then the blackness began to glow blood red, a bright light shining through her eyelids and into her very being. She opened her eyes, shielding them from the brightness with her hand, until they adjusted.

And there it was, UV One. But it was unlike anything she'd ever seen before, a display of colours that folded and spun beyond the visible spectrum. But she could see it, its intensity, and what she saw she understood in a whole new way, as though a door had been opened in her mind and the secrets of the universe had been poured in. The colours stretched out beyond the vessel, growing in a sphere that expanded by the second, engulfing the station and her in it. And then it hit her, a feeling of familiarity, of knowing, like she shared a kinship with another mind. The feeling grew, becoming stronger and stronger, until a torrent of agony scored the insides of her eyeballs, and she screamed, tumbling away from the window. A pair of hands grabbed her by the shoulders, stopping her mid-spin. She blinked, and through her burning, streaming eyes, Gardner came into focus.

'Are you okay?' he said.

'I …' she croaked. She could barely get the words out.

'What happened?'

'I … don't …'

Gardner looked over her shoulder, out of the window. He turned back to Sally, his face creased with worry. 'You — you see it too, don't you?'

Sally nodded. She felt drained. Gardner gripped her shoulders harder, and a strange look came about him. 'He's here …' he said.

'Who … who's here?'

Gardner looked around, eyes distant. 'God.'

Cold liquid ran through Sally's veins as, with a sudden clarity, she realised what had happened to him on TMA Eight. 'You mean … you mean you've seen this before?'

Gardner nodded. He was looking out of the window rather than at her. 'He's been here a long time, watching, waiting,' he said. 'I tried to ignore him at first, but I couldn't. He's just so beautiful.' His eyes bulged with tears, the Earthlight catching the shimmer and the puffy red skin around them. He let go of Sally and hugged himself. 'I couldn't bear to go,' he said, wiping his eyes on his sleeves. 'It — it broke my heart to leave him behind.'

Sally felt an odd sympathy for him, seeing this strong, confident man reduced to a fragile child. 'Are you talking about UV One?'

'I want to do what he's asked me to do,' Gardner continued, ignoring Sally. 'But I don't think I can do it. I'm too weak …'

'Hey, are you both okay?' a voice said from above, making Gardner jump. Sally looked up to see Novitskiy hovering overhead, his pasty face reflecting concern back down at them. 'I heard screaming.'

'We're fine,' Sally said, but as she did Gardner pushed passed Novitskiy and out of the MLM.

Novitskiy watched him leave, and when he turned back to Sally his look of concern had grown into one of fear. 'I don't think he's holding up well. He's doing even worse than Chris.'

'I'm not sure any of us are doing particularly well,' Sally said, folding her arms to try and mute a shiver. 'How long until Progress is fixed?' Novitskiy didn't answer. He looked guilty; Sally knew he was hiding something. 'Tell me! *How long?*'

Novitskiy fiddled with a seam on his coveralls. He seemed to be orchestrating an internal debate, determining whether or not he would tell her something. He stopped fiddling. The debate was won. 'We can't fix Progress,' he said, looking down at himself.

'*What?*' Sally breathed, the chill in her veins now ice cold.

'There's too much damage to the airlock seal. There's no way to repair it without replacement parts.'

'Well what about the comms — they still work, right?'

'The batteries have frozen because of the decompression. They're dead.'

'How long have you known this?'

'Two days.'

'So why didn't you tell me then?'

Novitskiy scratched at his stubbly beard. 'We didn't want you to give up hope.'

'*Give up hope?* What do you mean? NASA knows what happened to Progress, surely they'll be sending a rescue mission? *Right?*' Sally realised she was yelling, her chest rising and falling as hot anger boiled within her. 'Sorry …' she said, unballing her fists. 'I didn't mean to shout at you.'

Novitskiy came a little closer, and as he did, Sally could see that it wasn't fear in his eyes after all, but sadness. 'They're not coming.'

What was left of Sally's anger fell away, leaving her hollow. '*What?*'

'There is no rescue vehicle. Progress was our only chance.'

'But — why?'

Novitskiy took a deep breath, as if preparing himself for something. 'Because of Gardner.'

Chapter 15

Aleks felt sick. He had woken up that morning after a few measly hours' sleep with fever, nausea — the full works. But he still turned up for his shift. At his station, he drained his fifth cup of water to dampen his dry throat, but the churning feeling all the way from his oesophagus to his bowels persisted. He wasn't actually sick, however — he knew that for sure. He felt terrible because he knew he was about to risk all he had ever worked for. His job was his life and his family, replacing what life and family he ever had outside of these walls. It was everything to him, and there was a strong chance he was about to throw it all away.

The minutes had stretched to hours, everything and everyone passing by as if in slow motion. He filled his cup again at the water cooler, returned to his desk and waited. The days since his meeting with Sean had gone by as a blur. He had put off what he needed to do until he thought the time was right, and today was that day because Bales was not here. The man himself had told him about a week ago that he would be attending a meeting off site. When he'd first heard the news, Aleks looked forward to Bales' absence for his own reasons, but after his meeting with Sean he realised it was a chance that offered so much more. He downed his cup of water in one go.

'CAPCOM to all stations,' he said into his mic. 'I'm handing over. I'll be back in five.'

'Copy, CAPCOM,' came the plethora of responses. A NASA lad twenty years his junior appeared beside him to cover his post.

'Thanks,' Aleks said to him. 'My bladder's not what it used to be.' He forced a laugh, regretting it as soon as he heard it. His replacement didn't seem to suspect anything, or at least his polite smile didn't suggest so.

'No problem, sir,' he said.

Aleks fought the urge to run as he left Mission Control, and even the breeze as the double doors swung shut behind him seemed to push him onward. He turned a corner, heading in the direction of the toilets, and as he neared them he checked over his shoulder and kept on walking. He exited the corridor into a dank concrete stairwell and started climbing. The stairs were meant for use as a fire escape, so he didn't expect to meet anyone on his way. With each step grinding at his hips, two floors up and one more to go, he wished he *had* stopped off at the toilets after all, his bladder ripe and ready to burst. Too late now — onwards and upwards. A tingle of adrenaline spurred his steps and he skipped the last few a pair at a time, pausing just inside the door to catch his breath. *Nearly there*. Taking a last deep lungful to calm his nerves, he burst through into the empty corridor and resumed marching. Not this door, not this one, a couple more — he stopped outside a door that looked no different to the others, apart from its number. He entered.

Inside was a meeting room, seldom used because of its compact size. Two small desks filled the space, one of which bore an old computer. He sat down, and the dust that puffed from the chair's padding confirmed how long it was since anyone had been here. He clicked the mouse and the computer came to life; a barrage of update warnings lit up the screen which at first he mistook for some kind of alarm. *Don't be ridiculous*, he thought, heart racing. *Bales has no idea what I'm doing.* He inserted Lev's key card into the appropriate slot, opened the RFSA's intranet page and navigated to the secure log in. Two empty boxes appeared, a cursor flashing in the first. His heart skipped again, his confidence in Bales' ignorance wearing paper-thin.

Retrieving Sean's hand-scrawled note from his pocket, he turned it over to read the login details and punched them in key by key. He hit return and waited, the stale air of the room feeling warmer and closer by the second. A loading bar appeared and when it reached completion, the screen went black. Aleks' heart sank. But then it lit up again with an unfamiliar window that was emblazoned with the US Department of Defense logo. The page read: *Bales, Major John R.* Below that, a series of options presented themselves. Aleks clicked *Mailbox* and waited. The screen refreshed and a list of messages appeared. The inbox count was 2,438. Scrolling through, scanning the subject lines, he looked for something useful in among the weekly reports and general communications.

Footsteps and two muted voices plodded past and he stopped scrolling, hovering the cursor over the close button, skin prickling with horrible anticipation. The footsteps receded and he continued to browse. And there it was. Marked as confidential, it was the order for the RFSA to step down and re-assign Bales as Flight Director for the International Space Station. It was sent by Bales himself, and the response was a disgruntled but non-resistant acceptance. Aleks scrolled on. There was another message, confirming Gardner's place on board Progress M Eighteen M. The email chain started seven years earlier with a simple message from Gardner that read: *He's here.*

What the hell? There were more messages, recounting details of Sally's flight to Russia, technical requirements for launch, training schedules and shift patterns at the Baikonur Cosmodrome. It was all very strange Bales getting so involved in the intricacies of the mission, to be engaging on such a front-line level, but yet he had sent confidential emails stipulating all sorts, right down to the specification of the Progress conversion —

Aleks clapped a hand to his mouth. Taking his mobile phone from his pocket, he fumbled out a text message, but before he could finish, the door burst open. As quick as a flash, he clicked off the page and yanked out the key card, then looked to the open doorway to see none other than John Bales himself. His expression was grim. With Bales was the young NASA guy who'd covered his post, his expression also grim.

'What are you doing, Aleks?' Bales said, watching him from the doorway.

'I — nothing,' Aleks said, slipping his phone into his pocket, trying hard to reduce the tremor in his voice.

Bales strode towards him, looking at the blank desktop on the computer screen. 'What are you doing?' he asked again.

Aleks' mind raced, thinking hard for a way out. There was only one thing for it. 'I was … I was looking at pornography. I came here for a bit of a of privacy.'

This off-the-cuff excuse seemed to take Bales by surprise, and he recoiled, as if in embarrassment at disturbing Aleks at such a personal moment. But it didn't last long. Bales leaned across Aleks to take control of the mouse, which he steered towards the RFSA intranet icon. He clicked it. The home page opened and he clicked the button to log in. The screen refreshed and Aleks' heart sunk: in the username box, Bales' details had been remembered, and they burned in bright, digital letters as clear as day. The game was up. Bales stood tall, triumphant, and gestured to the security guards that had also appeared in the doorway.

'Take him,' he said, and left the room.

Just before the guards got to him, Aleks put his hand in his pocket, found his phone and squeezed the button he hoped was *SEND*.

* * *

'Because of Gardner? *Why?*' Sally said, grasping Novitskiy by the lapels.

Novitskiy pulled himself free and moved away from her. 'Maybe you should ask him,' he said. 'It's his fault, not mine.'

A scuffle from the MLM entrance made them both look up to see Chris making his way towards them. He was out of breath. 'Guys, come quick. You need to see this.'

Without another word, he flipped around and shot back out again. Novitskiy followed, and Sally after him. She tried to keep up with them as they darted from module to module, but at this speed she kept crashing into things as she misjudged her trajectory. She kept close enough to see Chris and Novitskiy disappear left into Node Three, where the Cupola was. She had been in there once before: it was a viewing module that bulged downwards and had the best view of Earth on the station. She tumbled in to find all three of the others looking out in the same direction.

'What is it?' she said, scrambling over to look. Through one of the Cupola's many windows, she could see what looked like a metal can with a ball at one end and squared off wings at the other.

'It's TMA Ten M,' Gardner said. 'It's the Soyuz capsule that Romanenko took.'

It drifted on a path that seemed to be taking it close by them.

'Mikhail ...' Novitskiy whispered.

Both hope and horror stirred inside Sally at once. She tried to dismiss the thought that TMA Ten M had become a floating coffin. 'Can we use it for spares?'

'We can do better than that,' Gardner said, staring out at the spacecraft. 'We can use it to go back home straight away.'

'If it's in good condition we just need to fuel up and we're out of here,' Chris said. They all looked at it in dreamy silence.

'So how do we get it?' Sally said, her voice sounding loud after the quiet.

'We'll have to do an EVA,' said Gardner. 'The robotic arm won't reach. Two of us in EMU suits should have enough thrust to dock it. At a rough guess, it looks like it'll pass by in about an hour, so we need to move fast.'

Sally and Novitskiy stayed in the Cupola as Chris and Gardner left to suit up. Soyuz seemed to be moving quicker than Sally had first thought, and she wasn't sure they even had an hour. 'How long does it take to get outside?' she asked.

'About half an hour at a rush. It's very risky doing it so quickly, but they've done it many times. They should be okay with the buddy system checks.'

Now Sally was alone again with Novitskiy, she couldn't help but ask the question burning in her mind. 'Why is it Gardner's fault that NASA aren't coming for us?'

Novitskiy made a noise in his throat. 'NASA don't send astronauts like him. Not unless — well, lets just say his being here is a bad omen.'

'You're talking about TMA Eight, aren't you?'

'Yes.'

'Were you on it?'

'Yes. We were lucky to get out alive.'

'This is a suicide mission, isn't it?'

Novitskiy was staring out at Soyuz, the Earthlight soft on his face. 'It's called *forlorn hope*. When they send someone like Gardner, it's because they don't expect them to come back.'

Sally looked at Soyuz with him. Its foil shell and paper-thin solar wings made it look so delicate she could crush it between her thumb and forefinger. 'Do you think he's still alive in there?'

Novitskiy didn't answer.

Soyuz had drawn level with the station when two white figures came into view. Their gleaming gold visors twinkled as they directed their bulky EMU jetpacks towards the craft. They negotiated a path that intercepted the vehicle, and as it passed by the Cupola, they used their EMUs to steer it towards the MRM Two docking module. Working together, they pivoted the vehicle onto its end, slowing it as it drew level with MRM Two. Watching the slow, graceful manoeuvre was mesmerising, every gentle change of speed and direction fluid and controlled, every metre closer causing Sally's chest to flutter with anticipation. The journey home was within their grasp. 'Come on …' she whispered.

With the nose of Soyuz in line with MRM Two, all they needed for a safe docking was a straight line. Sure enough, the two white-suited men directed Soyuz's guide probe into the mating adaptor, where it locked in and came to a rest.

'Ha haaaa!' Novitskiy cried out, and Sally hugged him, charged with excitement. Novitskiy pushed her away, and she looked at him, hurt, only to see that his face had become pale. Fearing the worst, she looked back out the Cupola window where one of the astronauts was grasping at his helmet, writhing and spinning out of control away from the station. The other, on the opposite side of Soyuz, hadn't seen, and was making his way back to the station in the opposite direction.

'Follow me!' Novitskiy yelled, and Sally sprang after him, paddling as hard as she could to chase him down the station. She reached Harmony where her sleeping quarters were; just beyond, Novitskiy had stopped, pulling at Velcro tabs holding a sheet of wall panel to the module's frame.

'Help me pull this off,' he said, but Sally was already on it, peeling the sheet away to reveal the bronze head and white body of the R Two GM robotic astronaut. 'Grab an arm and lift.' Sally did as she was told. Together they hoisted the strange, legless figure from its cradle. They headed back towards the Cupola with it, turning into the opposite module, Quest, where Sally and Gardner had first entered the station. The room seemed bigger, as the two space suits were missing. Novitskiy opened the inner airlock and they fed the robot in, shutting the door behind it.

'I'll pilot the R Two from Harmony. You go back to the Cupola. Come and tell me if you see anything I need to know about.'

'Okay,' she said, nodding, and they left Quest, Novitskiy turning right into Harmony and Sally heading straight on over to the Cupola. It took her a moment to locate the drifting astronaut: he had travelled a long way already, and when she found him her stomach lurched. He was no longer thrashing — he was still. The other astronaut had seen and was heading straight for him, but Sally could tell that the distance between them was too great to catch up. From the right, the bronze headed R Two robot darted into view, moving with a speed the EMUs couldn't hope to match. It caught up with the drifting body, slowing him down and guiding him back towards the station. The other astronaut met them on the way back, and with a wave of relief washing through her, Sally watched as man and machine towed the limp body to safety. She rushed across to Quest and waited as the warning light for the outer airlock door clicked on and then off again. There was a muted rushing of air, then silence.

'We have to wait a few minutes before they can come in,' Novitskiy said, drifting in behind her. 'But they'll be here soon.'

Sally remembered her own experience of coming in through the airlock, the relief of sharing the station's life support after her journey on the outside. The red inner airlock light glowed deep, and she swapped between staring at it, then the airlock door, then it again every few seconds. It took her brain a moment to catch up when it did switch off, and everything sank back into clarity as Novitskiy rushed to the door to help Chris — helmet already removed — tow Gardner's floating, lifeless body in. His helmet was off too, and Sally let out a tiny gasp as she saw the look on his face. It was part surprise, part — no, that couldn't be right. But the more she stared, the more she realised she *was* right, that the expression frozen on Gardner's face was one of elation.

'His vitals are fine,' Chris said, his own face reflecting the polar opposite, 'but he's completely non-responsive. He's in some sort of coma.'

Chris and Novitskiy steered Gardner's body to the medi-station in the Harmony module, as Sally followed on behind. Other than a brief and foggy stint in her weeks of intense training, Sally had never had any sort of formal first aid education, and so all she could do was look on at her only friend, helpless. As Novitskiy and Chris peeled off Gardner's suit, revealing his soft naked flesh beneath, the feeling became one of claustrophobia, and it engulfed her like a thick skin, numbing her mind. Once what could be done for Gardner was done, they retreated to the galley where she stared at her untouched meal.

'He seems to be stable,' Novitskiy said, the first words spoken in a while. 'I'll keep an eye on him for any changes.'

Somehow, Sally knew — and she felt the others knew too — Gardner wouldn't be coming back.

'We'll investigate the Soyuz capsule tomorrow,' Novitskiy continued. 'We don't know what kind of condition it's in, so we'll need our wits about us. That means a good night's sleep before we attempt to breach it.' He paused, drumming his fingers on the table. 'Or at least as much sleep as we can manage, anyway.'

He took a mouthful from his food pouch, struggling to chew and swallow. He didn't take another, but sat back, scratching at his face. Sally wondered if he wanted to leave the breach until tomorrow because he couldn't face seeing his friend in the inevitable condition they expected to find him in.

'I didn't know he was in trouble …' Chris whispered, jarring Sally from her distant thoughts. 'I just left him out there.'

'It's okay,' Sally said, putting her hand on his. 'I saw the whole thing. You did the best you could have possibly done.'

Chris snatched his hand away, sending his drinks pouch spinning from the table.

'I didn't help him!' he bellowed. 'I didn't help him like I didn't help Mikhail!'

Sally watched in shock as he left the module, loud bangs and thumps reverberating back up the station after him, each one making her flinch.

'He'll be okay,' Novitskiy said. He sounded weary.

'What did he mean?'

Another muffled thump travelled up the station.

'I used to love American food,' Novitskiy said, massaging the paste in the pouch, then holding it up to his face to look at it with big, longing eyes. 'But now I can't stomach it.' He slopped the pouch back on the table.

'Novitskiy!' Sally snapped.

'What?' Novitskiy said, looking up, a child-like surprise replacing his distant expression.

'What did Chris mean when he said he didn't help Mikhail?'

Novitskiy pursed his lips.

'He didn't take it well,' he said. 'Williams — sorry, Chris — had real admiration for Mikhail, despite what everyone says. When Mikhail asked him to help run some pressure tests on the Soyuz airlock, he didn't think for one moment that he would just up and leave in it. He blames himself for that.'

'I'm sorry.'

'Don't be. There's nothing any of us can do to make things different, so it's best not to linger on it. I prefer to think that Mikhail's just — gone out for a bit.' That same awkward smile he'd smiled when Sally had first met him bloomed on his face.

'Is there any chance at all he's still alive?' Sally asked, not really knowing what else to say.

Novitskiy's smile dimmed, and his woeful eyes looked deep into hers. He shook his head. 'Not even a remote one.'

* * *

The waiter refilled Sean's wine glass. Sean brought it to his nose to savour the musty tones of such a fine vintage. It wasn't often he treated himself, but since his investigations had taken such a positive turn, he felt it was a justified luxury. That and the wine was taking the edge off the grinding worry in his stomach as he waited to hear from Aleks. Aleks had messaged him earlier today to let him know he would be trying the key card, but he was yet to follow up with the results. Sean glanced — as he had a thousand times since being seated at the hotel restaurant — at his phone, which remained silent. He drained the glass.

When his dessert arrived, his appetite was somewhat waning, partly due to the big steak he'd just consumed, and partly because it was ten o'clock and he still hadn't heard anything. *When did Aleks' shift start?* He couldn't remember. Aleks had mentioned it in his earlier message, so Sean prodded the menu key on his phone and scrolled through to read it. As he did, the phone vibrated in his hand, the resulting jolt of adrenalin almost causing his steak to make a reappearance. He opened the new message and read it. As he consumed its few words, his mouth went dry, and he re-read them in disbelief. Sure enough, they said the same thing they had read the first time: *Bomb on Progress*

Chapter 16

In that moment everything became very real for Sean Jacob. Too real. He was used to chasing leads and getting into tight corners, but this was another level of government conspiracy he wasn't prepared for. Panicking, he looked about the restaurant, half expecting a squad of Kevlar-clad troopers to crash through the doors. His frenzied stare was met by the sympathetic smile of an old couple sat on the table opposite, while the few other diners hadn't even noticed. His heart seemed loud in this quiet, serene environment, and for a second he felt silly. They wouldn't be coming for *him*, would they? How would they even know of his existence? He looked at the message again, then deleted it. *Shit*, he hadn't meant to do that. Not that it mattered — the words still burned bright in his mind.

Hands trembling, he retrieved his wallet, scooped out of wad of cash and, hoping it was enough, dropped it on the table. Just because they hadn't come for him now didn't mean they wouldn't come for him at all. He didn't want to end up like Lev Ryumin. Negotiating the tables in a daze, Sean exited the restaurant and hurried towards the elevators. He could see the main entrance at the other end of the lobby, and he watched for the inevitable black SUV to pull up outside. The elevator pinged its arrival, taking him by surprise, and the businessman that stepped off smiled at him as they traded places. But *was* he a businessman, or an undercover government agent? Sean watched him with suspicion while tapping the button for his floor.

'Come on …' he said to himself. After what seemed like forever, the doors closed and the elevator ascended. It arrived at his floor and he disembarked, checked the route was clear and headed for his room. At the door, he paused, grasping the handle. Visions of what might lay in wait for him turned his throat dry, but still he took a breath and slotted the key card into place. The green light illuminated and the bolt retracted. Trying not to make a sound as he opened the door, he slid into the room. It was dark, and there didn't seem to be anyone there. He bolted the door and put the chain across, and only then did he switch on the light. Everything was as he left it. Relief swooped over him, and with it, exhaustion. He dropped onto the bed, just for a little while, to let his thoughts catch up with him. But his thoughts weren't the only thing to catch up with him: the red meat and wine intoxicated his body with slumber, and he fell asleep.

The next morning he awoke in a pleasant mood, despite a bit of a throb above his left eye. He lumbered to the bathroom to top up his glass with water, and as the cold liquid filled his stomach, the events of the night before came back to him. How could he have been so stupid as to fall asleep? He dashed to the window, cracked the curtains and looked out at the road below. There were still no black SUVs parked outside, which was a mild reassurance, but he still needed to get out of there fast, and there was only one place he knew to go.

An hours' drive shrank to forty minutes as he urged the taxi driver on. The recent rain storms had left the road damp, but that didn't seem to phase the driver as Sean encouraged him to go faster. With every mile between them and Moscow, Sean relaxed a bit more, and by the time he arrived at David's farm he was feeling a lot more level-headed.

'Sean! What are you doing here?'

David flicked his straggly, shoulder-length hair from across his face, a welcoming smile revealing his dirty teeth.

'I need somewhere to lie low for a bit. I figured you could help.'

The smile waned.

'Er … sure. Come in.'

David backed up to let Sean in, before looking both ways out the door.

'Where's your car?' he asked.

'Left it at the hotel and got a taxi here.' Anticipating David's next question, Sean added: 'I was dropped off up the road and I made sure I wasn't followed.'

That seemed to satisfy David; he shut the door and bolted it twice.

'Everything alright?' Sean asked.

'Yes, I'm fine,' David said, pushing past and wandering through to the back. Sean followed him. 'It's just … I had a couple of police officers here, you know, snooping like they do, asking questions. They didn't have a warrant or anything, but I locked the door after they left just to be safe. Can I interest you in some cake?' He had stopped by a rotten workbench that was almost black with mould. There was a cake atop it.

'No … thanks,' Sean said, eyeing the scene with a grimace. 'But I'd really appreciate it if I could use your internet.'

'Sure,' David said, helping himself to a slice. 'The password's my birth date.'

'Really? Your birth date?' Sean said as he watched David push the cake into his mouth in one go. It occurred to him that this man must have the most resistant immune system in the world to live in these conditions and not get sick.

'I'm just kidding,' David said through the mouthful. 'It's actual a fifty-digit hexadecimal code. But it was my birthday last week, which is why I have cake.'

Sean forced what he hoped was a pleasant smile over his true feeling of revulsion. 'Happy birthday.'

'Thanks,' David said, beaming. 'Give me whatever device it is you want connecting and I'll hook it up for you.'

Sean retrieved his laptop and passed it to David, who took it with sticky hands. At least the cake, being a week old, wasn't too greasy. 'Is the connection secure?'

David snorted.

'Don't be silly,' he said, 'of course it is. It doesn't come any securer … securer …'

'More secure?' Sean suggested.

'Yes, exactly. It doesn't come any more securer than this.' He looked pleased with himself, swelling with pride.

'Very impressive.'

'Isn't it just? You'll need to use a wired connection though, I hope that's alright?'

'That's fine, thank you.'

'Wireless connections just aren't secure enough.'

'I figured.'

David clicked away at Sean's laptop for a few minutes, sucking crumbs off his fingers as he worked. 'All done,' he said, handing the device back. 'Cable's pretty long, so you can take it to the workbench if you want.'

'That's okay,' Sean said. He assumed the workbench was the same rotten one with the cake on it. 'I'll sit here and use it on my lap.'

'Okay, but that's not good for your back.'

'I'll be fine, thank you.'

'Can I get you a drink?'

'No, thank you.'

'How long will you be staying?'

'I'm not sure.'

Sean opened his browser and tapped *Major General John Bales* into the search bar.

'What are you looking for?' David asked.

Sean shut his eyes. He'd forgotten how annoying David could get. 'Actually, I will have that drink, thank you,' he said. That seemed to appease David.

'What would you like?'

'Some water would be great, I've got a bit of a headache.'

'Would you like some aspirin, too?'

'Okay, sure.'

David, grinning, left to get Sean's drink and pills. Sean scrolled through the results, but he couldn't see anything relevant. He scanned page after page, with nothing catching his eye. It wasn't a surprise, but he couldn't help but feel disappointed. He tried a different search: *SETI Sally Fisher*

After he and Aleks had cracked Lev's code, they'd spoken more about UV One and Sally Fisher, and of the whole picture, it was Sally Fisher that bugged him most. She was the anomaly in all this, the sore thumb that stuck out from here to the International Space Station. If Bales wanted to destroy UV One — and it was hard to imagine he wanted to do anything else with the explosive on board Progress — then it didn't make sense to send her. Maybe she was a last resort, a bridge to burn if communications failed. It all seemed very drastic.

He scrolled through the results and found a bio of her on a university page. She was a plain-looking girl, yet Sean found it hard to take his eyes off her. When he finally did, he read through the post, scanning past the details he already knew. He re-read it, and then again. Something twigged in his mind, but he wasn't quite sure what it was. He searched for: *Robert Gardner TMA-08*. Again, it was no surprise that nothing came up, save for a mission report that said everything had gone as expected. The report was accompanied by a photo of the crew: Gardner, some other guy, and someone that for some reason he recognised. He opened a new tab, loaded up the mission page for the current Soyuz TMA Ten M expedition, and the same face was there. Captain Evgeny Novitskiy.

Sean's brain thundered with electricity as he untangled threads at random in the hope that something would come from it. Bales, Novitskiy, Gardner, Fisher, TMA Eight, TMA Ten M — it was all somehow linked, and no matter how close he was to understanding that link, he just couldn't grasp it.

'I've got your water. And your aspirin.' David wandered back in, carrying a glass that was brim-full of cloudy water. He handed it over, looking pleased with himself. 'Didn't spill a drop.'

Sean nodded his thanks and took a sip. It tasted chalky.

'And here's your aspirin.'

He opened a dirty hand to reveal two pills sticking to it. Sean peeled them off, looked at them, figured that he could do worse than to cure his headache, and placed them on his tongue. Taking another long swig of the chalky water, he swallowed them both down. 'Thanks,' he said, his tongue tingling in a most unsavoury way.

'You're welcome. What are you looking at?'

Sean's train of thought was well and truly derailed, so he decided he may as well share it with David. It couldn't hurt. 'I'm trying to find a link between four people. One guy reckons he found god and nearly killed two others doing it; another guy is one of the guys the first guy nearly killed; there's a girl that doesn't seem to fit in at all; and the last guy, he's in charge, and he's about to do something big.' He made an explosion sound, throwing his hands apart to simulate what he meant, but David just looked blank. *Never mind.*

'I don't believe in god,' David said.

Sean smiled. David may be simple, but he wasn't stupid. And he was damn handy with a computer. 'No, me neither. It's too easy to believe in something so conveniently inexplicable.'

'They used to kill people who didn't believe in god. Can you imagine that? It's madness.'

Sean smiled. 'Yes, it is.'

Then it hit him, all at once. Novitskiy was on TMA Eight with Gardner, when Gardner almost killed everyone on board. Novitskiy continued going into space, but Gardner didn't. Why? Because Gardner was a liability. Yet he had been sent up again seven years later on TMA Ten M, with Sally Fisher riding shotgun. It would have been Bales' decision, but why pick Gardner? Why not someone else? Because last time Gardner went into space, he saw something. God. Or at least that's what he thought he saw. And Bales knew as David knew that people who didn't believe in god got killed, so he was getting in early and killing god first. But not before he sent his messenger, Sally Fisher. What was the message? That's where Sean's mind hit yet another dead end.

Something in his pocket vibrated, making him jump.

'Shit!' he yelped, dropping his laptop in shock. It was his phone. He pulled it out of his pocket and looked at the number: Aleks. He answered the call.

'Hello?' he said.

'Hello, Sean.'

'Who's this?'

'You don't know me, but thanks to a mutual friend, I know you. He says you have something of mine, some information. I want it back.'

'I don't know what you're —'

'Listen,' the voice cut in. 'You need to know there is nowhere on this planet I can't find you, nowhere you'll be safe from me. But I'm willing to cut you a deal.'

Sean could feel a cold sweat beading on his forehead. His worst fears had come true: they had found him. 'Go on.'

'Come to the RFSA headquarters tomorrow morning. Bring this phone.'

'And what do I get in return?'

The voice laughed a slow, deep laugh.

'Let's just say you'll have a guilt-free conscience.'

Sean tried to think of a way out, but he knew he didn't have much choice. 'Okay, okay. I'll be there.'

'Good. And one more thing: if I discover the information you have has been leaked, then, well — I'm sure I don't have to explain what would happen.'

The line went dead. Sean lowered the phone from his ear.

'Is everything okay?' David asked.

'No …'

'Can I do anything to help?'

Sean looked at him. Beneath his scruffy hair and permanent layer of dirt, David was a good man. He shouldn't have got him involved in the first place. 'Look, David — no matter what happens, you mustn't tell anyone I was here, or what we've spoken about. Do you understand?'

'Sure,' David said, nodding.

'And keep your door locked.'

David invigorated his nodding.

Picking his bag up off the floor, Sean headed for the exit with David following. Before he left, he turned back to David and held out his hand. David looked at it, then took it. They shook.

'Take care, David.'

'You too.'

Sean marched off down the long drive and didn't look back.

* * *

Sally awoke after six dreamless hours. After trying to get back to sleep, she gave up, got dressed, and worked her way free of her tiny cocoon. Outside, Gardner was still affixed to the wall, clear tubes winding from his arms to the IVGEN unit mounted to one side. His elated expression hadn't changed; it creeped Sally out. He was like a giant toy, a glass-eyed puppet hanging from the wall, pulling a playful gurn at nothing in particular. As Sally propelled herself past him she got a horrible feeling that his eyes were following her. What made her skin crawl wasn't the thought of Gardner himself watching her, but something else watching her *through him.*

She shook the thought from her mind and continued along the station. Novitskiy, if he was up, would be in the Russian section, so she headed over in that direction. He wasn't there, but Chris was.

'I — I'm sorry I shouted at you yesterday,' he mumbled.

'That's okay,' Sally said, giving him a reassuring smile. She helped herself to a yoghurt pouch from the fridge.

'No, I really am. Since I've been here I've realised that I do have a bit of a propensity to, well — snap.'

'Really, don't worry about it,' Sally said, sucking yogurt from the pouch.

'I'm learning more about myself every day. Before, I would stop at nothing to be the best. I would trample on people just to get that bit higher. But now I realise that I can achieve more by using my strengths to help others.'

Sally stopped eating. She was getting a strange feeling that she couldn't pinpoint. 'What made you figure that out?'

Chris shrugged. 'Our situation, I suppose. Being so close to thinking there was no way out, that I was going to die up here.'

Sally resumed eating her yoghurt. She couldn't be sure, but she felt certain that Chris was leaving a particular detail out of his story. 'Do you think it — UV One I mean — has been communicating with us?' she asked.

Chris frowned, as if the thought hadn't already crossed his mind. 'I don't know. I mean, you're the communications expert. What do you think?'

'I think it has. At least I think it's trying. Perhaps it doesn't know how.'

'Perhaps. Maybe that's why Gardner ended up like … you know.'

Sally didn't say anything.

'Look,' Chris said, 'Novitskiy wants me to check Soyuz out and I need someone to give me a hand.'

'I'm not really qualified to do —'

'It'll be fine. Novitskiy's looking after Gardner, so that leaves you free to help me.'

Sally could sense an energy building around Chris, the source of her strange feeling. The way his nostrils flared, the creases forming in his brow — something wasn't right. She backed away under the guise of putting her yogurt pouch in the disposal. 'I'll check with Novitskiy first —'

'No!' Chris yelled, slamming his fist on the table. 'You're going help me so we can get off this god-forsaken hell-hole and go home!' His eyes flashed with anger and his chest swelled.

'Okay,' Sally said, trying to maintain calm. She was backed up flat against the wall. 'I'll help you. Let's just keep it together, shall we?'

Chris watched her, and she watched him as his breathing returned to normal. He blinked his savage expression away. 'Okay,' he said.

They suited up in silence, except for the odd word as they helped each other check zips and seals. Chris had already explained it was just a precaution in case Soyuz hadn't maintained pressure, but still Sally felt sick with nerves. The list of worries was long, topped by a fear of being sucked into empty space, finding Mikhail's corpse — which was a given — or finding something … worse. Worse how? She didn't know, and she didn't want to know, either.

The MRM Two module where Soyuz was docked was right above the dining table, so as another precaution they closed and sealed all the hatches in the service module. It was something of a relief to shut the hatch that led down into the MLM. Module secured, Chris waved Sally after him, and they negotiated the tight funnel to the airlock. With a raised palm he told her to hold position, then unsealed the airlock to Soyuz. Sally held her breath, waiting for a horrible rush of wind to suck her out, but none came. Chris pulled the station's hatch inward, then unlocked Soyuz's hatch and pushed it outward. Sally looked past him into the cramped spacecraft, a feeling of dread creeping up inside her. Soyuz, however, was empty.

Chapter 17

Aleks had never been in so much pain in his life. His eyes, his lips, his ribs — all at once they pulsed with white hot agony in time to his palpitating heart. The taste of blood was strong in his mouth, but his jaw ached too much to spit it out. All he could do was swallow, making his face burn twice as much under the fire of his tenderised skin and his stomach roil with the metallic-tasting fluid.

Through the small window, a bleached light began to glow. The sunrise, after the longest night of his life, brought fresh hope, but that feeling faltered at the sound of a key turning in the door. Tied to a chair, he could only turn his head to see who was coming for him next. Bales walked in.

'I've brought you some breakfast,' he said in a jovial kind of way that made it seem like he hadn't noticed Aleks' bruised and battered state.

Aleks said nothing, watching Bales with a mix of loathing and apprehension as he walked towards him across the small room.

'I got you porridge. I hope you like porridge.' Bales dragged a chair in front of Aleks and sat down, ladling a spoonful and holding it to Aleks' mouth. 'Here. Eat.'

Aleks turned his head away, flinching at the pain triggered by the movement. 'I don't want any,' he mumbled through lips sticky with blood. It wasn't true; he did want it, having not eaten for around twelve hours — or maybe more, he had no way of knowing — but the thought of chewing and swallowing made him nauseated. Also, he didn't know what kind of trickery Bales was trying to pull, and he needed to be on his guard.

'Come now,' Bales said, lowering the spoon. 'You need to eat.' He held the spoon up again, closer to Aleks' mouth.

Again Aleks turned away. 'Why are you doing this? What do you want from me?' he said.

Bales put the spoon and bowl down on the floor. When he sat straight again, his face was grave. 'You've done a bad thing, Aleks. But I understand why you did it. You're a proud man. You're a man who wants to do what he thinks is right. This time, however, you made a mistake.' He leaned towards Aleks, who stiffened. 'But people make mistakes, and I'm willing to overlook this one if you help me set it right again.' He sat back, lips spreading into a broad grin as if they were the best of friends sharing a joke together.

As much as Aleks felt wary of Bales' newfound friendliness, a part of him crying out for relief latched on to this sudden goodwill, believing it without hesitation. It was going to be hard to keep that part of him suppressed for long. 'What do you want me to do?'

Bales chuckled, spreading his affability on thick. 'You gave me Sean,' he said, looking down at Aleks' blood-soaked shirt, 'albeit with a little persuasion, and I'm grateful for that, really I am. But I need you to do one more thing. The trap is set, and now I need you to get him to walk into it.'

Guilt joined the throbbing nausea in Aleks' stomach. He had tried so hard to resist the never-ending torrent of blows, but he was just too old to stand up to that kind of treatment forever. After all, Sean was a journalist, sticking his nose where it didn't belong, so he should expect to get on the wrong side of people — and in this case, the wrong side of the wrong people. He was young and fit; he should be able to fend for himself. That was the thought that helped ease Aleks' conscience as much now as it had done when he'd given up Sean's phone number. That part of him crying out for relief had won over, leaving him powerless to resist it. 'What do you want me to do?' he whispered, swallowing his shame deep down.

Bales' grin spread even wider.

* * *

The taxi, as they all did, smelled funny. It was a strange blend of cinnamon and cigarettes, and Sean did his best not to heave as its driver negotiated the back roads of Korolyov at frightening velocity. His stomach could normally handle the pace, but today his nerves wouldn't allow it.

'Here will do,' he said, clutching his seatbelt, and the driver stopped. He paid the fare and got out, surveying his surroundings as the old Trabant took off, tyres chirping. It was a deserted street, damp with early morning rain, and as he walked along it he stretched out the aches left by a night in his pop tent. As miraculously small as it folded up, the miracle only went so far: it wasn't the most spacious of sleeping environments. Still, it was better than sleeping in a hedge, and he wasn't going to be staying in any hotels for a while.

It was strange being back on the street again, homeless. As a journalist in his field he knew a certain level of dedication was required of him, but it always made him feel like a small country mouse in a very large city when everything he owned was slung over his shoulder, including the place he laid his head at night. The bag he carried — which went with him everywhere — contained the ideal journalist's survival guide inventory — at least it would have done if such a thing as the journalist's survival guide existed. *Perhaps I should write one*, he thought to himself as he trudged on.

In with his tent was a penknife, custom built into the base of a torch to make carrying it through customs easier; his phones; three Kendal mint cakes; a notepad and several pens; a global phrase guide; and a few other knick-knacks. He also had a stun gun — but this was no ordinary stun gun. He'd picked it up in a camping store in east Sormovsky a few years ago; it was disguised as a travel radio that slipped easily into a pocket. It packed a hell of a wallop, depleting its entire battery charge in five blasts. *It may only be five blasts*, the man who sold it to him had said, *but one is enough to get the message across*. The shopkeeper had demonstrated it on a goat tied up behind the counter, which made a noise Sean would never forget. But still he bought the stun gun, which even played FM and AM band radio.

This constant chatter in Sean's head served as it always did to stop him turning on his heel and running away. He found distracting himself before a big interview, a stakeout or potential capture and torture as he might be experiencing today, a necessary device to keep his head in the game. But as he drew closer to the RFSA building, he could distract himself no longer: he needed to be prepared. As he crossed the road he fumbled around in his bag, retrieved the radio-shaped stun gun and pocketed it. He expected to be searched and hoped it would go unnoticed.

A familiar buzzing fizzed through his leg, and he withdrew his phone. It was Aleks' number. 'Hello?'

The voice that answered was not the same as before: it was Aleks himself. 'Hello, Sean, it's Aleks.'

'Aleks! Are you alright? Where are you?'

'I'm fine, I'm fine. Look, I need you to do me a favour.'

'Sure, anything.'

'I —' Aleks sounded nervous. 'I need you to give yourself up. Bales will kill me if you don't.'

Sean slowed, his heart and mind racing. 'Okay …'

'Listen carefully to what I'm about to say and do *exactly* as I tell you,' Aleks said.

Sean wedged the phone between his ear and shoulder and grabbed his pad and pen from his bag.

'Come to the RFSA office,' Aleks said in a slow and deliberate voice. 'Be here in thirty. Bring your phone, too. You'll be met by some guards. Don't try to fight them — it's no use. Bales just wants what belongs to him back. Oh, and meet them at the main entrance.'

Sean scribbled as fast as he could.

'I don't want to end up like Lev's cat …' Aleks said. He stuttered a nervous laugh.

'Okay,' Sean said, reading the transcript over. 'I'll be there soon.'

* * *

'He's not here …' Sally whispered, not believing what she was seeing.

Chris unclipped his helmet, and Sally did the same. Pushing himself into Soyuz, Chris negotiated the cramped vehicle and returned with a confused look on his face. 'The airlock bolt would be open if he'd left Soyuz. He can't close it again from the outside. But it's still completely sealed. He's — vanished.'

A chill prickled Sally's skin. It didn't take much thinking to realise where Romanenko had gone. 'UV One,' she breathed.

'What's that?' Chris said, drifting closer to her, head cocked to one side.

'UV One.'

Chris heard her this time, and recoiled at the words. 'But — why? Why would it take him? And how?' He looked over his shoulder into Soyuz, as if expecting to see something he didn't want to. Pushing Sally away, he heaved the airlock shut again and sealed it.

'Can this take us home?' Sally asked.

'Uh, yeah,' Chris said, pulling the locking lever tight. 'Seems in good condition to me.'

'Do you think the communication system still works? I wonder if Romanenko got to that as well?'

'I don't know,' Chris said, floating by to reopen the module hatches. 'I'll run what we've found by Novitskiy before I do anything else.'

Sally could see it in his face and hear it in his voice: he was scared. Not just scared, terrified. The silent ghost ship had returned, the man he blamed himself for killing, gone. Worst of all, obvious physical evidence that UV One was not just in his mind, or any of their minds, had turned up right at their front door. The cage was open for him to leave, but just outside its safety lurked something he didn't want to see.

'How long do you think it'll take before we can go home?' Sally asked as Chris opened the final hatch, the one down into the MLM.

He stopped, flushed pink, the exertion of opening all the hatches painting a sheen of sweat on his face. 'Couple of days or so at the most. Got to make sure the hull is structurally sound and all the systems are operating as they should.' His eyes were big and white, an expression that looked out of place on a man like him. He gave Sally a curt nod, then retreated from the module, leaving Sally by herself.

A couple of days, she thought. *A couple of days and we can go home.*

Later that day they all reconvened for the evening meal. Eating together was an unspoken tradition that brought Sally comfort, even if the atmosphere at the table was tainted with nerves. They shared a joke or two between them, cursed Novitskiy's cooking and recounted amusing anecdotes about their individual lives back on Earth. It wasn't until they'd finished eating that the subject of the craft docked right above their heads came up, and only because Sally forced it to.

'So I hear it's just a few days until we can pack our things and leave,' she said, broaching the topic like it was no big deal.

Chris looked at Novitskiy. Novitskiy looked at his lap.

'What?' Sally said, picking some food from between her teeth. 'Will it be more?' She looked between Chris and Novitskiy, their silence turning her nonchalance into concern, then worry. 'What's wrong?'

Novitskiy sighed deep and slow. 'I'm sorry, Sally,' he said, not looking up at her. 'I should have mentioned it sooner, but I didn't. I didn't want you to worry.'

Sally's mouth went dry. She tried to speak, but couldn't.

'Soyuz should be fine,' Novitskiy said, 'and it'll only take a few days to check it over. But we have a problem.' He looked up, straight into Sally's eyes, and she could almost feel his weariness weighing her down. 'There are four of us, and only space for three on board Soyuz.'

'There's enough space to squeeze a fourth person in, surely?' Sally said. 'It looked like there was — I checked.'

Novitskiy looked more and more broken up. 'I'm afraid not. The extra mass would likely kill all of us on re-entry.'

The silence after Novitskiy had finished speaking echoed in Sally's ears. 'So who's going to stay?' she whispered.

'I don't know,' Novitskiy said, looking down again.

Chris shuffled on the spot. 'Why don't we leave Gardner?' he said in a low voice, almost as if he didn't want Gardner's frozen body at the other end of the station to hear.

Novitskiy looked at Chris, then at Sally, his face expectant.

'We're not leaving him here,' Sally said. 'I can't believe you'd even think that.' She folded her arms, appalled by the suggestion.

Chris shuffled again. 'But he's in a coma —'

'No!' Sally snapped, and Chris stopped talking. Silence resumed.

'We don't have to leave him like this,' Novitskiy said. 'We can — you know — help him …'

Sally stared at him. 'Are you serious? You want to *kill* Gardner?' She leaned back, shaking her head. 'I can't believe I'm hearing this.'

Novitskiy didn't respond. He just floated at the table, frail and exhausted-looking, his neck so thin his coveralls looked several sizes too big. As her anger washed away, a sympathy grew — for both of them. It was easy to forget how long they'd been up here and what had happened to them, the fragile wrecks they'd become. She suspected that if she met their former selves before they'd left Earth, she wouldn't recognise them. 'Okay then,' she said. 'In that case, I'll stay.'

Novitskiy and Chris exchanged glances, then looked at her, expressions cautious. 'You mean it?' Chris said.

Sally nodded.

'No, Sally,' Novitskiy said. 'I'm not going to let you do this.' His tone was flat, as if he were fighting an urge to stay quiet.

'I want to. You've both been through way more than I have. I can hang on a bit longer.'

'But you don't know how to look after the station —'

'You can show me,' Sally interrupted. 'I've seen you doing it. It doesn't look like too much work.'

Novitskiy's eyes had gone distant and he was shaking his head. 'I won't have it,' he said. 'I'm staying. Me. Not you.'

'You're not staying —' Sally began, but Novitskiy slammed his fist down onto the table, shocking her into silence.

'I outrank you, and I'm telling you that you will be going, on Soyuz, back to Earth. And I won't hear another word of it.'

With that, he left the module, leaving Sally and Chris by themselves. Sally didn't know what to think: on the one hand, she was mortified at the thought of leaving Novitskiy up here on his own with nothing to keep him company but UV One, and on the other, she could already feel an elation fizzing like electricity in her chest at the thought of returning to Earth. She couldn't believe it — she was going home.

* * *

'Someone get Bales, quick — I'm getting a signal.'

Scott Thomas, the NASA scientist appointed as CAPCOM in Aleks' absence, watched as a junior-level staff member scooted from his post and out the door. 'Can you get me noise clean-up, please?' he said. 'And put this on the main speakers.'

His Russian counterpart leaned across the desk and tweaked the controls. Scott listened to his headset again.

'TsUP, do you read?' an American voice said over the speaker. 'Come back, TsUP.'

Scott pressed his broadcast button. 'This is TsUP, reading you five by five. Is this RS0ISS?' He waited for the response, his breath caught in his throat.

'Copy, TsUP, this is RS0ISS.'

A cheer rose up from Mission Control.

'Quiet please, people,' Scott said, and the murmur faded. 'RS0ISS, what is your present situation?'

'We're comin' home!'

A long whoop followed the message, and it was met by another cheer from Mission Control. Behind Scott, the double doors swung open and he turned to see Bales march through.

'What've we got?' he said. He seemed distracted.

'RS0ISS, Flight,' Scott said pulling off his headset. 'They're back online.'

'Sitrep?'

'Uh, I don't know yet, we've just made contact this minute.'

'Get on it.'

Scott nodded, returned the headset to his head and pushed the broadcast button. 'RS0ISS, please confirm your situation.'

They waited for the signal to reach its target and come back.

'Not so good. Romanenko's dead, Gardner's in a coma. But we've recovered TMA Ten M so we should be able to return in a couple of days.' Chris' voice paused. 'Say, where's Aleks?'

Bales beckoned, and Scott handed the headset over to him. He held it to his ear and signalled to Scott to broadcast. 'Williams, Flight Director John Bales speaking.

The severity of the situation has required NASA to take command, so you will be speaking to me from now on. Please repeat last.'

'Okay — we've, uh, lost Mikhail, and Gardner is in a coma.'

'Causes?'

'UV One.'

Bales chewed his lip. Scott thought he seemed nervous.

'There's four of you still alive. Who are you leaving behind?'

'Novitskiy volunteered.'

Bales frowned. This didn't seem to be the answer he wanted to hear. 'Okay, that's not a problem. We can work around this. Good job — you've done well.'

Bales passed the headset back to Scott, who put it on.

'Make sure everything is in place for their return,' Bales said to him. 'I've got something I need to take care of.'

* * *

The RFSA building stood tall and ominous in front of Sean, the small windows peering down at him from on high. He patted the stun gun in his pocket to make sure it was still there. 'Well, here goes nothing,' he said aloud to himself.

* * *

'He's on his way, sir.'

'Thanks,' Bales said, and put the phone back in his pocket, feeling pleased with himself. It was all coming together. He looked at Aleks, whose eyes widened at his stare. 'I'm a man of my word, Aleks. You've given me Sean Jacob, and I will give you your life back in return.'

'Don't hurt him,' Aleks pleaded. His bruises had swollen overnight and he looked a mess. Ignoring him, Bales left the room, and without looking back, said, 'If it helps ease your conscience, he won't feel a thing.'

A guard closed the door behind him, muting Aleks' cries, and he set off down the corridor. He unclipped his chest holster, pulled out his pistol, cocked it, checked the round was seated in the chamber, made sure the silencer was tight, and returned it. At the end of the corridor, another guard waited for him.

'Come with me,' Bales said to him, and they walked on through the building, navigating their way through the long, beige corridors to the entrance lobby. Bales felt his chest holster under his jacket again, double-checking the clip was released and ready for a quick withdrawal. The entrance lobby was deserted, just how he needed it to be.

'Room's clear, sir,' the guard said.

'Good. He should be here soon.'

They waited, watching through the glass frontage for Sean to arrive. They waited ten minutes, then twenty, and by half an hour, Bales checked his watch.

'Where is that son-of-a-bitch?' he murmured to himself. He pulled out his phone, re-dialled the last number and put it to his ear. 'Where is he?'

'We last saw him turning into the entrance about a half hour ago. You haven't got him yet?'

Bales hung up the phone and broke into a run back towards the cell. 'Secure the building!' he yelled to the guard as he ran off. He sprinted back through the corridors, taking a left turn, then a right, not slowing until he reached his destination. But it was too late. Seeing a pair of bodies lying in a heap outside Aleks' temporary cell was enough for him to know what had happened. He stepped over one of the dazed guards and entered the room. Emptiness yawned back.

Chapter 18

Sally slept well that night. The relief of her imminent departure made the station a much more pleasant place to be, and her quarters didn't feel quite as claustrophobic as they had done before. The mood of her companions was the best it had been since she had arrived, the good cheer even rubbing off onto Novitskiy. Although, he was probably just being polite in sharing the good news with them, holding back his real feelings to keep her and Chris in high spirits for the journey home. This thought made her feel sad and, if she was honest with herself, a bit guilty. She wished she could do something to help him, but he wouldn't let her, dismissing her with his new mantra that he delivered with a warm smile: 'I'll be alright.' As for Chris — he was a changed man. After he'd discovered a functional comms system on board Soyuz and made contact with Mission Control, his grin had become permanent.

The next day, while Chris continued his inspection of Soyuz, Sally chatted with Novitskiy as they tended to Gardner. Even Gardner's unnerving stare couldn't sway the cheer.

'I promise you, as soon as we get back to Earth, I won't leave NASA and the RFSA be until they send someone back up to get you,' Sally said, as she watched Novitskiy unclip Gardner's IV bag. 'In fact I'll make it my life's work to bring you home.'

Novitskiy laughed. 'I'm sure you will,' he said. He passed Sally the IV bag, which she set aside. 'And I'm sure I'll be fine up here in the meantime.'

'You're taking this very well.'

Novitskiy's smile stretched from ear to ear, although Sally couldn't be sure it carried any depth.

'I'll be alright.'

The more Sally spoke with Novitskiy, the more she thought he was at peace with staying. A spike of endorphin-fuelled generosity would have worn off by now, but he continued to smile and engage in light conversation without showing any signs of distress. Perhaps there was even some relief in there, but relief at what? She figured it must have been because Chris was leaving. He was a handful, teetering on the brink of an unpredictable breakdown, and being up here without him would be something of a respite. What was it that Bales had said? *The ISS can be a lonely, claustrophobic place, and it may have had an adverse effect on some of the crew.* He'd got that right.

And what of UV One? What if it sent Novitskiy crazy and drove him out the airlock like it had done Romanenko? What if it broke him down into an emotional mess like it had done Chris, or worse, the comatose state of Gardner? The more she contemplated, the more she believed — hoped, even — their minds had been playing tricks on them the whole time. Cabin fever, isolation sickness, whatever they wanted to call it, it must be happening here, and she was almost ashamed to have been caught up in it. The brain was a powerful tool, she knew that much, but she had also discovered just how easily led it was. With any luck, some time alone would give Novitskiy the space to clear his mind and rid himself of the contagious paranoia that had built up between them. But what about the empty Soyuz module, the disappearance of Romanenko? She tried not to think about it as she passed Novitskiy a new IV bag, which he took with a thankful grin. She had no idea if the thoughts she was having were anything like the ones going on in his own head; perhaps he *was* relieved to have some time to himself. Or perhaps he was terrified.

A muffled yelp came from the Russian end of the station, and they both looked up.

'Are you okay?' Novitskiy called out, but got no response. 'I'd better go check that out.' He stuck down the IV bag and pushed off. Sally followed, drifting after him through the station.

'Chris?' Novitskiy called again. Silence.

'I hope he hasn't hurt himself,' Sally said, a horrible feeling of dread swelling in her abdomen.

As they entered the FGB, a small bead darted past.

'What was that?' Sally said, but before Novitskiy could respond, another bead shot towards her. It hit her on the arm, leaving a deep red splat.

'I think it's — blood,' Novitskiy said, his voice weak.

Looking at the stain on her arm and not where she was going, Sally bumped into the back of him. She looked up to see more beads of blood coming towards her, a mass of droplets expanding from a central point. That point was in the middle of the service module: Chris. His hands, soaked in blood, covered his eyes. Thick globules of life-giving liquid seeped out from between his fingers, floating away and smearing anything they touched with a dark red sheen.

'Chris …' Novitskiy said. 'What happened?'

Chris sobbed, drawing his hands away to look up at them. Where his eyes had once been were two gaping holes. 'I just wanted to get it out of my head,' he gurgled, covering his face again. 'I couldn't get it out of my head …'

Novitskiy swore, grabbed a first aid kit from the wall and took it to Chris, who was moaning something incomprehensible under his breath. Sally, frozen, could only watch on in horror as Novitskiy did his best to patch Chris up. Once he was sure Chris was stable, Novitskiy took him to the medical bay, leaving Sally to clean the mess he left behind. Before she knew it, Novitskiy was back, alone.

'I have to go,' Novitskiy said, lifting a shaking hand to run his fingers through his hair. He hadn't yet changed his coveralls, which were streaked with red. His face was too, a stark contrast to the whites of his wide eyes. Sally had managed to mop up most of the floating blood with a couple of towels, but still a dark sheen covered several large patches on the walls, and a metallic smell lingered in the air.

'I have to go,' Novitskiy repeated.

The instant Sally had seen Chris, covered eyes seeping blood, she knew she was staying. She couldn't pilot Soyuz, and she wasn't about to let either Chris or Gardner die up here. 'Will he make it?'

'I've had to sedate him. Hopefully he's not done too much damage, other than — well.' He didn't finish the sentence.

'Are *you* okay?' Sally said, touching his arm. He looked surprised at the question, as if it hadn't occurred to him how he felt.

'I'll be fine,' he said, shaking his head. 'I'll be fine. We'll go tomorrow morning.' He looked like he was about to cry. His emotional barrier had crumbled.

After they had cleaned themselves up, Novitskiy checked Chris over again, while Sally disposed of the bloodied towels. She did it without thinking, her chest hollow and her mind empty. When Novitskiy spoke to her again, she just smiled, reassuring his concerns with her new mantra: 'I'll be alright.'

* * *

Throat burning, Sean hailed the first cab he saw. It pulled over, and before it had even stopped, he bundled Aleks in, jumped in himself and yelled, 'Get us out of here!' The taxi driver was obviously no stranger to a client in need of distance from his current predicament, because he stepped on it. He took them east out of Korolyov, and it was only after the tall, industrial buildings began to thin that he pulled over and asked them where they wanted to go.

'To Podolsk, the main road. I know a place where we can lie low for a while,' Sean said.

They set off for Podolsk, and Sean wound the window down a little, letting the cool air chase the heat away, dabbing his brow with his sleeve.

'How did you find me?' Aleks asked him.

'It's surprising,' Sean said, eyes shut, 'how far you can get with an attitude that says, *I belong here*. That and a stun gun. Service entrance at the rear, a few corridors along to office thirty, and there you were.' He took the device from his pocket and returned it to his holdall. He'd completely discharged it on those two guards. Thank goodness he hadn't run into Bales or he'd have most likely been … well, he didn't want to think about it.

'I think you had a little help from Lev's cat …' Aleks said, a smile coming through the swollen lumps and bruises on his face.

Sean grinned. Then he laughed, an uncontrollable euphoria making him giddy and silly. He was happy to still be alive. 'Aleks, my friend, if it wasn't for you and Lev's damn cat, we'd both be smoking holes in the ground by now.' He took his notepad out from his bag and showed it to Aleks. '*Office thirty. Two guards. Use back entrance.* A genius bit of secret code if ever I saw one.'

'Well, what can I say. You learn fast.'

'To be honest I thought there'd be more security. The only weapons I saw were in the hands of your two guards, thank goodness.'

'It's a place of science, not the gulag …'

The car made a left and they hurtled on down the country roads at the usual taxi-driver breakneck pace. As the adrenaline wore off, the soft fuzz of exhaustion enveloped Sean's senses, and he dozed for a while, only to be woken by Aleks jabbing him in the ribs. 'Huh? What?' he groaned, wiping drool from his chin.

'Look,' Aleks said, pointing out in front of them.

The taxi had stopped. They were in familiar surroundings, and Sean's sleepy brain took a few dopey seconds to realise they had arrived. What confused him was the smell of ash that blew in through the gap in his window. He traced the source of the ash and saw what was left of a dilapidated farm building. It rippled from within towering flames that turned the dreary afternoon orange. All at once he was awake, his throat bone dry and his stomach twisted into a hard knot. Without knowing what he was doing, he jumped out of the car and sprinted down the road, his lungs stinging as he ran, his eyes joining them as smoke engulfed him.

'David!' he yelled as he tore up the driveway, but the deafening roar of the flames drowned out his voice. His streaming eyes blinded him and soon he was lost in among the smoke and ash, the searing heat of the fire sucking the oxygen from him and leaving him breathless. It was clear there was nothing he could do. The fire was so intense that if he went any further in, he knew he would be dead. Stumbling towards cooler air, he retreated, and once he was free of the smoke he toppled to the ground, great hacking coughs overwhelming his body. Thumping footsteps approached him, and in an instant Aleks was on him.

'Are you okay?' he said, helping Sean sit up, brushing the ash from him. 'I thought you were gone for sure ...'

Sean said nothing. His coughing had subsided, and so had the stinging in his eyes, but tears still ran from them. David was innocent. He had never harmed anyone. He was the nicest, most welcoming person Sean had ever met. He was a shining light in a dark world full of bitter, nasty people — and now he was dead. Worst of all, Sean knew it was his own fault he was dead. He thumped the ground, grinding his flesh into the stony dirt, punishing himself with the pain. He had led Bales right to David, given him up on a silver platter. His death was a message, a warning.

'I can't do this anymore,' he said, his voice barely a whimper. He tried to thump the ground again, but his swing was weak and pathetic, just like him. 'I can't do this.'

Aleks sat down next to him and drew him close. The embrace was strange, but somehow comforting. Its warmth was different to the intense heat of the fire that had taken a man's life: it was kind. Sean knew that, without words, Aleks was telling him it was okay, and that to give up now would be a waste of David's life. After he had calmed, Aleks helped him up, and they hobbled together back to the taxi. Aleks said something Sean didn't understand to the taxi driver, who nodded, and they set off back the way they had come.

'I have a brother,' Aleks said. 'He will look after us until we know what to do next.'

'I don't want to bring anyone else into this.'

'Grigory is strong man and can look after himself. It'll be fine.'

Reluctant, Sean nodded. What other choice was there?

The grey clouds turned deep purple as the sun sank below the horizon, and street lamps blinked on as they entered a small, quiet town. The taxi turned off the main road, weaving through a compact estate of rough housing, and pulled up at the kerb. Aleks paid the driver and they disembarked, Sean stretching the ache from his limbs as the taxi pulled away. A sting from his grazed hand made him flinch. He brushed off the dirt to inspect it.

'Is your hand okay?' Aleks asked.

'It's fine, I think,' Sean said, shaking the pain from it. He looked at Aleks, whose bruised face shone under the street light. He couldn't help but laugh at how pathetic his own graze was in comparison. 'More importantly, how are you? You look terrible.'

'I've had worse.'

Once the taxi was out of sight, Aleks led Sean down a side street, and they stopped outside a small, single-storey building with rickety shale walls and a moss-covered roof. They wandered up the path through the front garden, which was littered with old building materials. A bag of cement propped the porch door open, next to a pair of dirty trainers. Aleks knocked, and they waited.

A light clicked on behind the door, which then opened. A wave of hot, nauseating smell flooded out, and following it came a man who was well over six feet tall, had a scratchy beard, deep-set features and a stained vest. In one hand he held a bottle of something that looked home-brewed, and in the other, a pistol. He lowered it as soon as he saw Aleks and a grin broke upon his face.

'Aleks!' he boomed, pulling the man in and thumping his back. He let go, and they exchanged some cheerful chatter, and then Aleks explained their situation. The tone dipped; they both looked at Sean, and then back at each other. Grigory nodded, stepped back, and waved them in.

'Thanks, Grigory, we really appreciate it,' Aleks said. 'Come on in, Sean.'

Sean didn't respond. As he followed Aleks into the house, the hot odour grew stronger. The smell, he decided, was blood.

* * *

When Sally found Novitskiy the next day, he was already working on Soyuz. She could hear him talking to himself long before she saw him, and as she helped herself to her morning meal, he carried on working, unaware of her presence. Her meal was half-finished before he realised she was there.

'Oh, hello,' he said, stopping himself as he flew out of Soyuz at breakneck speed. The wide smile he had been carrying faded almost the instant he saw her. 'How are you today?'

'Fine,' Sally said. In reality she was unsure how she felt; the dread that had overwhelmed her when she'd been alone in her quarters was gone, but it hadn't been pushed aside by fear, or regret, or even resentment. She just felt — numb. Tomorrow was a blank page with no clues on it to guide her, and she was left empty and unsure. She recognised it as a mental defence mechanism, and was grateful for it. 'How are you?'

Novitskiy didn't answer right away. He looked like he wanted to speak, but he didn't, his lips twitching as they formed words, yet held them back. 'Look …' he said at last, but Sally already knew what he was going to say.

'It's fine,' she reassured him. 'It's the only way.'

'It's just that Gardner and Williams are injured, and I'm the only one that can —'

'I know, I know. I've told you, it's fine.' She rubbed his arm, forcing as comforting a smile as she could manage. 'I mean it.'

Novitskiy nodded, and behind his eyes a little glimmer of excitement twinkled. She could hardly blame him for that. 'Thank you,' he said, and left her to carry on with his preparations.

Sally spent the rest of the morning helping Novitskiy ready Soyuz for departure. He also showed her what daily maintenance she needed to do on the station. It was straightforward stuff: pretty much all the systems were self-monitoring, and all she had to do was check readings and levels and tick them off a list, plus give the place the odd clean. It was nice to have something to do to take her mind off things, and the hours rolled by far quicker than she was accustomed. By the time they had buckled up a comatose Gardner and a sedated Chris, she had built up a healthy sweat.

'What else can I do?' she said, moving herself towards an air outlet to let the cool stream wash over her.

'That's it,' Novitskiy said. 'All you need to do now is seal the hatch behind me.'

Sally tried to ignore the horrible flutter in her stomach. 'Well, I guess this is goodbye then.'

'I *will* come back for you,' Novitskiy said, and before Sally could decide whether it was the light, or if his eyes were filling with tears, he had swung his arms around her and squeezed her tight. She reciprocated, although she couldn't match the desperation with which he clung to her, the trembling in his arms that he couldn't hide. He let go, and his eyes were indeed shining with tears.

'I won't ever forget what you've done for me,' he said in a strained voice. He looked at her for a moment, then turned and entered Soyuz. Sally did as she had been instructed and manoeuvred the large hatch shut, watching through the shrinking gap to savour her last few moments of human interaction. Her eyes met Novitskiy's just before the hatch shut completely, and the flutter in her stomach became a nauseating jolt. Hatch met seal, and she pulled the locking lever home. That was it. She was now the loneliest human being to have ever existed.

Chapter 19

Grigory, as it turned out, was a gracious host, and made Sean and Aleks' stay a pleasant one. He was a former special forces operative, and through patchy English, had some fascinating stories to tell. He had been discharged following a leg injury on a tour of duty, and had so far spent his retirement in the countryside. He dabbled in hunting, particularly for musk deer, which were abundant in the area. It also turned out that he was a fantastic cook, and Sean's anxiety had dropped the instant the smell of cooking venison had overpowered the smell of blood. They would need to lay low for a while, stay off the grid, and this place was ideal.

Once Sean had decided it was safe enough to report home on the satellite phone — having ditched his mobile — Grigory drove him twenty miles into the hills for him to make the call. Better to be traced to a knot of trees in the middle of nowhere than back to Grigory's house, Sean figured, and the others agreed.

'Hi, it's Sean. Can you hear me okay?'

'Sean — I've been wondering what happened to you. I was starting to get worried.'

'I'm touched. Look, I've got to make this quick, so here's the gist: the US Department of Defense are planning on detonating a weapon to destroy an unidentified vessel they've codenamed UV One. Not only that, but they have a crew up there and —'

'What are you talking about?'

'What? I'm talking about the unidentified —'

'Have you not heard?'

'Heard what? I don't really get to read the news where I am at the moment.'

'They've come back to Earth. The whole crew. It turned out to be a communications problem after the solar storm knocked out the main array. Nothing sinister at all.'

'What …?' Sean said, the revelation disorientating his mind in one sucker punch.

'They landed a few days ago. There *is* a story worth running though — the International Space Station is now empty. First time it has been since it was launched. NASA and the RFSA are sending another crew as soon as they can.'

'But …' Sean stammered, searching his brain for something that made sense. 'But Aleks said —'

'Aleks? Dezhurov? Jesus, you are out the loop, aren't you? There's a nationwide search going on for him after he was named chief suspect in the murder of Lev Ryumin. The man killed his best friend — can you believe it?'

Sean had nothing to say. All the questions he had prepared in his mind escaped him in an instant.

'Anyway, it looks like this whole thing is a dead duck. I suggest you get yourself back here for debrief and reassignment. There's some crazy stuff about to happen in North Korea, and I want you on it.'

'How many people came back?'

'What?'

'How many people were on the Soyuz craft that returned?'

'The same number of people that were on the station — three.'

'What about Sally? And Gardner?'

'What about them? I know what you're thinking, but they never went up. They were on the ground as consultant experts. And the Progress vehicle that went up had no one on it. We checked into that, and NASA confirmed.'

'And you bought that?' Sean yelled, not believing what he was hearing.

'It's a damn sight easier to swallow than aliens, Sean.'

For the second time in that brief conversation, Sean was knocked speechless, but not by shock this time — by blind fury.

The voice at the other end didn't wait for him to talk. 'Why don't you take a couple of weeks off before you come back. Have some time to get this whole thing out of your system. We've got people here I can put on the empty space station story, so take this opportunity to recharge your batteries. I know what you're like — you work too hard, get too involved, and I don't want you wearing yourself out. You're no good to me like that.'

'This is bullshit.'

'Alright, well I've got a meeting now,' the voice continued, ignoring him, 'so I'll speak to you later.'

The speaker clicked. The voice was gone. Sean continued to hold the phone to his ear, lost in a flood of thoughts and feelings that pinned him to the spot. He stood like that for a long while before he made his way back to the house with Grigory, where he relayed the story to Aleks.

'*What?*' Aleks said, his face looking like he'd just been slapped.

'That's what he said. That you killed Lev.'

'That's … that's …' Aleks spluttered, his cheeks blooming with red anger as he paced around Grigory's living room. He stopped, balled his fists and yelled something incomprehensible. Then he sat down. 'Bales …' he moaned through his hands. 'This is all Bales …'

It made perfect sense. Bales could destroy Aleks without needing to point a weapon, without even needing Aleks at all.

'I'm sorry,' Sean said. 'I'm sorry I got you into this.'

Aleks dismissed him with a wave.

'I'm a grown man. I chose to get involved. This isn't your fault.'

'So what do we do now?'

Aleks sat back in his chair and sighed, his bushy, greying eyebrows forming a frown. 'We nail this son-of-a-bitch.'

Sean tossed and turned that night, the phone conversation going round and round in his head. Was it true? Had he been misled by his trusting nature? That would make him an aide in all of this … He turned over again, the sheets clinging to his skin. No, Lev Ryumin had been killed by Bales. He knew it was true. Or was it? Perhaps Aleks had him roiled up in a big web of lies, all fabricated to protect himself from the long arm of the law. After all, the only person who had mentioned UV One to him *was Aleks*. Lev had only implied its existence. The whole thing seemed to be unravelling in his mind the more he thought about it, and it made his stomach heavy as a rock to realise how deep in he was. But what about the email from Bales, his orders to investigate and destroy UV One? Sean winced when he remembered he hadn't seen the email with his own eyes — everything he knew he'd been told by Aleks. All at once he felt anxious about being in a house in the middle of nowhere with a wanted criminal and his ex-special forces brother, who, he realised, was pretty handy with a butcher's blade.

The next morning, Sean woke to find the house empty. There was no sign of either Aleks, who had been sleeping in the main bedroom, or Grigory, who had taken refuge on the sofa, and the house looked as it had done late the night before.

'Hello?' Sean called, his voice loud in his ears. No answer came. He looked out the front window; Grigory's truck was gone. Trembling panic made his knees weak, and he stumbled to the front door to slide the bolt shut, which slammed home with a dull thud. What was he going to do now? He couldn't run, he was in the middle of nowhere, and … well, he was starting to feel silly. Sitting down, back leaning up against the door, he shut his eyes and took measure of the situation. Aleks couldn't have killed his best friend. Why would he? In the cold light of day, the voices in his head that had wound him into a stupor the night before seemed a lot fainter.

He groaned as the predicament rolled around in the wash of his mind, and in a single frustrated moment, he decided what to do. Hauling himself to his feet, his heart spiked as he realised his stun gun, which he was about to get, was drained flat; he had forgotten to recharge it. *Shit.* Rethinking his plan, he went to the kitchen, listening out for Grigory's truck. He took the biggest knife he could find, the one Grigory was using to carve up musk deer the night they had met. It was weighty, imbalanced by the long, thick blade. Along its cutting edge it shone bright, the metal sharp and gleaming only where it needed to be.

The crunch of tyres on the loose road and the chug of an engine sent Sean running to the window, heart thundering, knife in hand. Peering through the blinds, he saw Grigory's truck pull up to the kerb outside. He and Aleks got out. Sean unlocked the bolt and backed up, grasping the heavy knife in both hands. He held it out in front of him like an axe, ready to drive it home the moment he was provoked. The handle turned and the door opened. Aleks walked in. He was chatting with Grigory, who was following him up the footpath, laughing. When Aleks saw Sean, his face dropped, wide eyes moving from the knife, to Sean, then back again. Grigory pushed past Aleks, and also stopped when he saw Sean. They all stared at each other, locked in an unspoken stalemate, and the silence that held them apart grew longer. It made Sean tired, his heart beating fast and his limbs moaning with a dull ache. He wanted to say something, but he didn't want to be the one to push the first domino.

'What are you doing?' Aleks said, breaking the unsteady truce.

'I'm protecting myself,' Sean tried to say with force, although his voice came out flat and thin.

'From what?'

'From you.'

Aleks' face was one of shock, of confusion, but it wasn't a look his brother shared; Grigory had the same expression he'd worn when Sean had first met him: suspicion.

'I don't understand …' Aleks said, his wide eyes unblinking.

'I'm not sure you've been telling me the truth.'

Something changed on Aleks' face. 'Everything I've told you is the truth,' he said, taking a step towards Sean.

Sean retreated back, thrusting the knife out further in front of him. 'Stay where you are!' he yelled through gritted teeth. 'Don't come any closer!'

Aleks lifted up his hands, palms outward, but the instant Sean glanced at them, Grigory pounced. Sean slashed with the blade, but Grigory countered, knocking back against Sean's arms with his own. Then Sean felt a large, hot hand clasp his wrist, and a sudden agonising pain shot through it. Grigory retreated. Nursing his empty hand, Sean stumbled back, quivering with pain and shock. Grigory passed the knife to Aleks. He then reached into his jacket and retracted a handgun, matt-black and snub-nosed, which he cocked and pointed at Sean. He walked over to Sean, gun levelled at his face, and stopped with the muzzle inches from his forehead. Sean shut his eyes, his tightening throat suffocating him, forcing his breaths to become fast, ragged gasps. All at once he felt numb, distant, as if he were buoyant and weightless. He waited, but the pain never came, nor the flash, nor the thunder.

He opened one eye, and then the other. Grigory was still standing in front of him, still holding the gun inches from his face, but now it was reversed, pointing the other way. Grigory jiggled the weapon, making Sean's insides squirm, but he realised that Grigory had done it in a, *here, take this,* kind of way. Sean lifted his hands, moving them towards the grip until his fingers met cool steel. As he took the gun, Grigory released the muzzle, and backed up next to Aleks. Now Sean was pointing the gun, which was shaking in his hands. He moved it to Aleks, whose eyes looked back deep into his, and then to Grigory. Neither of them spoke. Sean didn't know why he did what he did next, but he did it anyway: he lowered the gun and put it down on the coffee table. Then he fainted. He didn't know how long he was out for, but when he came round, it was because a shadow was hanging over his face.

'Sean, are you okay?'

Pain smouldered in a pocket behind his eyeballs, and as he opened his eyes, it seared with vicious agony. 'Eurghhh …' he gurgled as he sat up, reaching for the source of the pain, the back of his head. When he looked at his hand, there was blood, but not much. 'What happened …' he groaned.

'You fainted,' Aleks said, helping him to stand. 'You knocked your head on the table.'

Bit by bit it all came back to Sean. The knife, the gun … the fainting. *Shit.* But he was still alive.

Aleks helped him to the sofa and lowered him down. 'I'll clean you up and get you some pain killers,' he said. 'It doesn't look too bad. You'll be fine.'

The pain in Sean's head had begun to subside already, but in its place came nausea at the thought of what happened before he fainted. 'I'm sorry. I didn't know what to do.'

'That's fine,' said Aleks, who had returned with a damp cloth. He mopped the back of Sean's head with it. 'I can understand your position. But I hope there will be no more knife waving from now on.'

Sean shook his head, which reinvigorated the pain, and he winced. Not that there was any point in threatening him with a knife — Grigory had plucked it from his hands without so much as a thank you.

The front door opened and Grigory himself walked in, carrying a bag of shopping. 'Food for tonight,' he said. 'You're not going to stab me over it, are you?'

An embarrassing stupidity burned on Sean's cheeks. 'No,' he mumbled. 'I'm sorry.'

'It's fine,' Aleks said, chuckling. 'Here, take these.'

Sean took the pills and water and swallowed them down. He handed the empty glass back and shut his eyes to stop the room from spinning. 'So, what next?'

'I don't know,' Aleks replied from the darkness.

Sean didn't know either. There were a few ideas floating around, but when he tried to think about them, it hurt his head. There would plenty of time to think about them tomorrow — but first, sleep.

* * *

It was strange being alone. Not that Sally was unused to being by herself, but isolation at this magnitude was a whole new experience. It wasn't creepy, but it was … quiet. Even during her most sedentary times as a researcher, she'd still swapped the occasional *hello* with other staff. Here, she had no one. As the days passed, she noticed herself talking out loud, and although it was a concern at first, she began to embrace the sound of a human voice — even if it was her own. At one point, something she'd said aloud triggered a spore of a memory, and she'd realised she sounded just like her own mother. The thought had made her sad.

She busied herself with her research, and even found the time for more: those little experiments she had always wanted to do. Deep space radio waves, big bang evidence — the kind of things she *really* enjoyed. They were the sort of activities that helped keep her mind off the cold fact that she was over two hundred miles away from anyone, floating alone in lifeless space. She had even been down into the MLM on occasion to look at UV One, which still tracked behind the station as it had done since its arrival. Nothing strange happened, even when she stared at it. She began to believe that her previous experiences had been amplified by contagious hysteria. Space wasn't the domain of the action hero — it was the working environment of the mentally accelerated, and that was bound to have consequences.

Shoulder elastics pulling each long stride into the treadmill, Sally wiped a towel across her sweaty face as she finished the last ten minutes of her two-hour fitness regime. As she warmed down, she thought about where she was going to take her experiments next. With no idea how long it would be until the next Soyuz came to collect her — and she presumed it would be soon since the ISS had been left manned by an astronaut with only three weeks' training — she needed to make the most of the time she had.

'I'll probably finish the deep space pulses, then move on to a broad range scan of that neutron star, erm … what was it called?' She snapped her fingers. 'R X J one eight five six point five dash three seven five four. That's it.'

Her memory was something she prided herself on, and she grinned at her achievement. Sometimes, it was the small things that made her happy. She slowed and stopped the treadmill, took a moment to catch her breath, unfastened the straps and dabbed herself with the towel. It had taken her a while, but she was getting used to the fitness routines, and she was even starting to enjoy them. A run and a wash left her feeling fresh and invigorated, ready to study.

* * *

'How is he?'

Evgeny Novitskiy stood over the bed of Chris Williams, who was still sedated and had his entire head bandaged. A clutch of tubes poked out where his mouth should have been.

'He's not doing well I'm afraid,' the nurse tending to him said with a sad smile. 'He's got damage to his trigeminal nerve, so he's in a lot of pain. We can't wake him — the agony would be too unbearable.'

'And Gardner? Any change?'

The nurse shook her head.

'Thank you.'

Novitskiy left Chris and the nurse be, and, walking stick in hand, took a stroll around the corridors. He was at a hospital in Moscow — where exactly he didn't know — along with Chris and Gardner, having been flown in direct from

Kazakhstan. He hadn't seen Gardner since their arrival — he was in a closed room with the curtains drawn. The nurses kept him up-to-date with his progress, which was minimal.

It had taken Novitskiy a few days to gain the strength to walk again after the weightlessness of space, but now he was mobile — if a little unsteady — he had been restricted to his floor. All the other rooms were empty — it was just himself, Chris, Gardner and the staff occupying the whole level. Quarantine, perhaps? They wouldn't tell him. They said it was an order from above, but wouldn't say from who. He'd asked to talk to someone from NASA or the RFSA. The nurses kept telling him *soon*, but soon didn't seem to be coming. He aimed himself for the ward desk and pottered on.

'I hope you're not thinking of escaping?' the nurse at the desk said, giving him a warm smile.

'No, sir.' Novitskiy replied, hobbling over to him. 'You don't know when I'm going to be debriefed, do you? It's really important I speak to someone.'

The nurse sifted through his paperwork, shaking his head. 'I'm sorry — we still haven't heard anything. I'll make sure to let them know you asked.'

'Thanks,' Novitskiy said, and hobbled back down the corridor to his room.

'Hey, Novitskiy?' the nurse called after him.

'Yeah?'

'No running in the halls.'

Novitskiy rolled his eyes, grinning, and carried on walking while the nurse chuckled to himself. The smile faded as the thought of Sally Fisher panged in his chest.

The next day, he awoke early to the warmth of the sun poking in between the blinds. He felt tired, even more so than usual. His dreams had jarred him awake again and again, leaving him before he could remember what they were. He sat up, stretched and yawned, and when he'd finished he saw a nurse wheeling a trolley though the door with his breakfast on it.

'Here you go, Captain,' the nurse said as she lifted the tray onto his lap.

'Thank you, very kind.'

'And this came for you, too.'

The nurse handed him a letter. It had a US Department of Defense logo on it. He took it, but didn't open it. 'Thank you.'

'Enjoy your breakfast.'

The nurse smiled, then left. Novitskiy watched her, and when she was gone, he tore open the letter. It was short.

Dear Captain Novitskiy,
You have been summoned to a meeting with Major General John Bales.

Other than the time and date of the meeting and a note to say a car would come to collect him, that was it. There wasn't even a signature. He looked at the bedside clock — the meeting was tomorrow. He turned the letter over to see if there was anything else written on it: there wasn't. *Major General* John Bales? He'd never even heard of this high-ranking man, let alone met him. This was very strange.

Chapter 20

'Hello — is this the NASA press centre?'

The person on the other end of the line — in her middling forties by the sound of it — confirmed that, yes, it was the NASA press centre. 'And can I ask who you might be?'

'Ah, yes — my name Is Steve Philips. I'm the foreign affairs and technology correspondent for the *New York Times*.'

Steve Philips was indeed the correspondent for foreign affairs and technology at the *New York Times*, but that wasn't making the pretence of being him any easier. Sean transferred the bulky satellite phone from one ear to the other, and gave a thumbs-up to Aleks and Grigory, who were sitting on the back of Grigory's pickup truck, watching. Although Sean had explained his plan to them as they drove out into the wilderness, the expressions on their faces didn't suggest they were convinced by it. *Whatever,* Sean thought. *I think it's a good idea.* The plan was simple: dig up as much information on Sally Fisher and Robert Gardner as possible to try and prove their present whereabouts, thus forcing NASA to make a new statement. And sometimes — just sometimes — the easiest place to get that withheld information was via the very people trying to withhold it, so that's what Sean — now also known as Steve Philips, foreign affairs and technology correspondent for the *New York Times* — was doing. As Professor Klein had often repeated to his class during journalism school: it was all about confidence.

'Mr Philips, thank you for calling. And how might we be able to help you today?'

'I'm doing a piece on the relationship between America and Russia, and the joint program on the International Space Station. You know, astronauts working with cosmonauts, that sort of thing. Quite the teamwork story, don't you think?'

Too much information, Sean, too much information. Keep the lie simple. He could almost hear Professor Klein's voice in his head.

'Yes, that does sound very good.'

Keep it simple.

'I'd like to interview some of the team on the ground. I understand Sally Fisher, the communications expert, and Robert Gardner, former astronaut, were both recruited as consultants on the matter. I'd like to interview them if I can.'

The woman didn't reply. Sean felt hot, his shirt tight and clammy around his chest and neck. Perhaps he had triggered some kind of keyword? Were they trying to track him down, trace the call? They were miles out into the woods, but were they far enough away from civilization? He listened for the thump of helicopter blades over the trees, anxious, but —

'Would you like to do a telephone interview, or interview them in person, Mr Philips?'

The response stunned Sean, and he regrouped his thoughts to speak. 'In person, please.'

'Would you like to interview any of the Russian team, too?'

He hadn't thought of that. 'Er … okay.'

'Who would you like to interview?'

Think, Sean, think.

'The surgeon and CAPCOM, please.'

Shit. CAPCOM was sat opposite him, looking concerned.

'I'm afraid the CAPCOM isn't available for interview at present. I'm sure you understand. You can most certainly interview his cover and the mission surgeon, though. When shall I arrange that for, Mr Philips?'

'Is tomorrow too soon?'

'Not at all. Shall we say ten thirty?'

'Yes please.'

And it was done. He thumbed the call disconnect button, and took a breath. His heart was pounding. Who'd have thought the most intense phone call he'd ever make would be to a middling forties woman?

'Well?' said Aleks, gesturing for Sean to reveal all.

'We're in. I don't believe it, but we're in.'

Aleks hopped down from the truck to give him a slap on the arm, which in his present state of nervous shock nearly toppled him over. He was thankful that Grigory only gave him a smile.

Back at Grigory's house they fired up Grigory's computer and set a search running for the terms *Sally Fisher* and *Robert Gardner*. Sean was convinced there was something more to find online, and while they waited for day to become night to become day again, he wanted to use the time to scour the web for more clues. He routed the searches through proxy servers to prevent them being traced, and left the computer to whizz through billions of fragments of data, sorting, disposing, sorting, disposing, hunting until it found a piece that might be of interest. When it did, it flagged it up. So far all the flagged data had been irrelevant, and Sean had dismissed it, leaving the computer to continue its digital treasure hunt.

'This soup is really delicious,' Sean said after a mouthful. 'How do you get it so thick?' He dunked the spoon in again, waiting for Grigory to finish his own mouthful and reveal the secret.

'Potato,' Grigory said. 'Mashed.'

'Huh. As simple as that?'

'Yes. Always use good potatoes.'

Sean nodded, his mouth full of creamy soup. It struck him that the three of them could have been friends on one of those character-building wilderness trips, were it not for the undercover journalism and criminal fugitive.

'I think the computer's found something,' Aleks said, putting his bowl down to go see.

'Anything useful?' Sean asked.

'I'm not sure. Come and have a look.'

Sean finished his last spoonful and went over. It was obvious why Aleks was uncertain: the computer seemed to have pulled a result from a long-since abandoned conspiracy site.

'This page doesn't exist any more,' Aleks said. 'It found this in the cache of an online search engine. It's six years old.'

Underneath a header consisting of B-movie graphics and some text that read *The Vault of Mystery* in a slimy font, there was an article about extra-terrestrial visits to Earth. It described incidents such as Roswell and the Bermuda triangle, linking them to a theory about unmanned space probes and alien abduction. It all seemed far-fetched and tenuous, but knowing what he knew about UV One, Sean had a hard time laughing it off. There was a time when he would've scorned it as second, even third-rate journalism, but now it was a gold mine of possibilities. He skim-read the rest of the article, which continued to talk about present day sightings and abductions, and featured a few snippets from astronaut Robert Gardner. Seeing that name made Sean's stomach lurch with excited anticipation.

We have been able to track down former NASA astronaut Robert Gardner, it read, *who was unfairly dismissed from NASA in a massive alien cover-up that would have shocked the world. 'It was like there was something in my mind, calling me,' he told us. 'It made me think and feel like I've never done before.' Such was his trauma that he couldn't answer any more of our questions, and he now denies ever meeting with us at all.*

The article went on and was uncredited. Aleks clicked some of the links on the page, but they were all dead.

'I feel like I'm missing something obvious here,' Sean said, so Aleks scrolled back to the top of the page and they read it through again. A paragraph caught Sean's eye and he read it aloud, word for word.

'In 1947, a probe was sent to Earth, where it crashed in Roswell, New Mexico. It is believed that government scientist Dr R. Bales was in charge of the classified research —' he stopped reading, his brain doing a mental loop-the-loop. 'Dr R. Bales — I don't believe it …'

'I'll run a search on Dr Bales,' Aleks said, fingers flying as he spoke. He hit the return key and a new window of results appeared.

'Dr Rupert Bales,' Sean read, 'was born on the sixteenth of July, 1917, to Daniel and Molly Bales in Longview, East Texas. After graduating with honours from Stanford, Dr Bales joined the National Advisory Committee for Aeronautics as a molecular research scientist. His pioneering work at the closed Walker Air Force Base in Roswell, New Mexico, aided the development of early rocket propellants. He is considered one of the leading scientists of our time, advancing rocket propulsion technology by several decades with his work. Dr Bales died of unknown causes in 1954. His only son, John Rupert Bales, was born the following year.'

Sean took a moment to digest the information, which swilled around inside him like tainted bile.

'It can't be — can it?' he said in a thin voice. 'Did John Bales' father die because of something like — like UV One?'

As a key turns in a lock, each thought pushed a mental tumbler into place, unlocking the conscious as a whole. Did Bales know his father had died at the hands of an interstellar traveller — *if* his father had died at the hands of an interstellar traveller — and was this his motivation for sending Gardner up with a payload full of explosives? If it was true, he could imagine the message Bales had given Sally to pass on: *See you in hell.*

Taking the mouse from Aleks, he scrolled to the bottom of the entry. In the list of references there was a link to a page on Rupert's molecular research team, and he clicked it. A brief summary paragraph and a list of names came up. He clicked the first name.

Albert Levard — 1916-1949

He was only thirty-three when he'd died. Coincidence? Sean navigated back a page and clicked the next name.

Joseph Collins — 1923-1955

Sean clicked the next name, a sick feeling rising in his throat at what he knew was coming.

Charles Freeman — 1913-1960

And the next:

Edward Warner — 1905-1955

All nine of the ten names followed the same pattern, all having died soon after the 1947 Roswell incident. Except the last one: Ruth Shaw. Her entry suggested that she was still alive.

'I need to see Ruth Shaw,' Sean said.

'She'd be ninety-three,' Aleks replied. 'Are you sure she's still alive?'

Sean was thinking exactly the same thing.

'I hope so.'

* * *

'Captain Novitskiy, there's a car here for you.'

Novitskiy gave the nurse a nod, and she disappeared back around the door. Looking in the mirror, he straightened his tie, brushed down his dress jacket with the back of his hand, took his walking stick and doddered to the exit. Muscle atrophy always made him feel older than he was, and he thumped the floor with his stick in frustration as he walked. At the end of the corridor, a black-suited man waited for him.

'Good morning, Captain,' he said, holding the door open for him as he approached. 'I hope you're feeling better.'

The words seemed more of a statement than a question, but Novitskiy responded anyway. 'I'm much better, thank you.'

The suited man didn't say anything further, and together they walked down and out to the SUV that was waiting for them. Novitskiy climbed into the back. The suited man closed the door behind him and got in himself. They pulled away.

Out of the hospital, they turned onto the main road. Novitskiy didn't know the area, but he soon saw familiar landmarks and could tell they were heading to the RFSA building. When they arrived, they were ushered straight in, and before he knew it, he found himself outside an office on the second floor.

'The Major General will see you now,' the suited man told him, just as he was about to sit down.

'Can I catch my breath please?' Novitskiy said, holding his weight up as best he could with his walking stick. He had a pain in his chest and his legs were shaking.

'I'm afraid the Major General is a busy man, so you will need to see him now.'

Begrudgingly, Novitskiy went in. A man, the Major General he assumed, was sat at a desk leafing through a wad of files. The office must have been temporary, because the desk was bare beyond a few folders and the decor was sparse. The Major General looked up, saw Novitskiy, stood, and offered his hand. They shook and sat.

'I'm sorry to bring you here on such short notice,' Bales said, neatening his files. 'Our situation calls for a quick reaction.'

'I agree,' Novitskiy began. 'Sally Fisher is still —'

'We will get to the matter of Fisher shortly,' Bales said, 'but not right now. We must start from the beginning.'

'Okay, sir …'

'Captain, I've seen your record, and it is very impressive.'

'Thank you.'

'You have surpassed the expectations of your commanding officers, excelled in your training and in my opinion, bettered your immediate superiors.'

Novitskiy said nothing. He didn't know where the conversation was going, but he didn't like it. He could sense something was up.

'You're a man I believe I can trust,' Bales continued, 'and I need to be able to trust you now more than ever. What's at stake is far beyond what you could ever possibly imagine.' He paused to open the first page of the topmost file. 'We know very little about UV One. The little we do know gives me cause for great concern. What can you tell me about it? About your experiences?'

Novitskiy had spared little thought for his time in the presence of UV One, and back on Earth those experiences seemed distant and muddled. He would have preferred to keep them that way, and even the mention of the vessel caused an immediate surge of panic in his veins. He gripped the arms of his seat, hard.

'Ahm …' he said, his throat drying, 'it's hard to describe. Sometimes you have your good days, and sometimes your bad. On a bad day it's as though your mind is being stretched to breaking point, being forced to experience thoughts and feelings that far surpass its capabilities. Sometimes that translates as an overwhelming euphoria, other times as horror beyond imagination. As time passes, it gets worse, more intense, harder to fight. I believe it was too much for Major Romanenko. Gardner and Williams, too.'

Bales wasn't writing anything down. To Novitskiy's surprise, Bales' hardened expression had melted to one that seemed almost concerned. 'Thank you, Captain. That is helpful, if worrying news. And I hear that Gardner has returned with you?'

'Yes, sir. And Williams.'

Bales seemed distracted, troubled.

'Sir, I have to ask,' Novitskiy said, breaking Bales from a distant thought. 'When is Sally Fisher returning?'

'We're looking into assembling a mission as soon as we can.'

'I want to be on board.'

'I'm afraid that's not possible.'

'But I made a promise —'

'That's not my problem, Captain. This is my mission, my concern. Not yours.'

Novitskiy figured out what didn't feel right. It was Bales that didn't feel right.

'I'm sorry,' Bales said. 'I'm sure you understand.'

'Will that be all?'

'Yes, that will be all.'

Novitskiy stood and left the room.

* * *

'I'm not sure this is a good idea,' Aleks said, touching the almost faded bruises on his face as if the memory of their origin had risen anew.

'It'll be fine,' Sean said.

They rumbled through Moscow, Grigory at the wheel, heading for the last place Sean wanted to be right now: the RFSA building.

'They aren't going to be there, you know,' Aleks said. 'There'll be no interview. It's another set-up.'

'I know, I know. I'm not stupid.'

And he did know. He knew that Sally Fisher and Robert Gardner were still on board the ISS. It was simple math. Three guys had come down; two must still be up there. NASA could try and bluff them with whatever fabrications they liked, but he knew in his gut that the conversion of Progress had been intended for one thing and one thing only: the transportation of humans.

'So what are you going to do?'

That, he didn't know. Maybe he could just wing it, turn up and see what was what. That's pretty much how he plied his trade, and it had got him what he wanted in the past — but in the past the US Department of Defense hadn't been trying to shoot him dead.

'I'll probably go in for a quick recce first, assess the situation.'

'I'll go with you,' Grigory said.

Sean was going to refuse, but then he realised that having an ex-special forces bodyguard wasn't that bad an idea. 'Thanks.'

They pulled up a few streets away and Sean and Grigory got out. Aleks slid over to the driver's side.

'I'll be waiting for you,' he said. 'Don't be long.'

Sean and Grigory set off towards the RFSA building, its tall structure just about visible between a couple of industrial units. Sean walked fast and stuck to the shadows, checking back over his shoulder every few seconds to catch the eyes he felt sure were watching him. They turned the corner at the end of the street and the entrance loomed open.

'Are we going in?' Grigory asked.

Sean looked around. An emergency escape ladder scaled the building next to them, leading up to the roof. 'Let's climb up there,' he said. 'We'll get a better view past the entry barriers and into the lobby. See if there's anyone waiting for us.'

They climbed up to the flat roof and shuffled on their bellies to the edge. They watched a delivery vehicle arrive; it checked in at the gate and went through. People milled in the lobby: one was talking to a receptionist, who pointed down a corridor; another mopped up a pool of something spilled; others stood about, chatting.

'There doesn't seem to be anything out of the ordinary,' Sean said.

Another man entered the lobby. Although he walked with a limp and was supported by a walking stick, he walked fast. Two suited men followed close behind. They were talking to him, but he was ignoring them. Sean watched as the man left the building, forcing his way past a group that had decided the doorway was a good place to stop and chat, and marched on towards the barriers.

'Hey,' Sean said. 'I think that's Captain Evgeny Novitskiy. I wonder what he's doing here?'

He squinted, trying to make out the man's face as he approached. As he reached the barrier, one of the two men following him tried to grab his shoulder. He responded with a quick thwack of his walking stick, sending his aggressor hopping on one leg. He walked around the barrier, nodded to the gatekeeper and continued up the street. The man who had been whacked was helped out by the other, and together they followed after him.

'That's definitely Novitskiy,' Sean said, scrambling back along the roof and down the ladder. Grigory followed.

The two suited men caught up with Novitskiy. Having learned from their mistakes, they snatched his stick away and he fell. Between them they took his arms and legs to carry him away.

'Hey!' Sean yelled, breaking into a run. 'Leave him alone!'

The two men reached into their jackets, but it was too late. Sean thundered into them, crashing head first into one man's chest as he tripped up the kerb. They all clattered to the ground, including Novitskiy, but one of the men was quick to scramble up again. He kicked Sean in the ribs, winding him. The other man got up and reached into his jacket. Sean flinched just as Grigory's colossal fist piled into the side of the man's head, knocking him out cold. The man still standing turned to

Grigory, deflecting a blow and landing one of his own. Wheezing, Sean crawled over to Novitskiy, who was trying to get up. There was a loud crack, and Sean turned to see the second man dropping to the floor with a bloodied nose.

'Are you okay?' Grigory asked, shaking his hand and wincing.

'I'm fine,' Sean said, breathing fast. 'What about you, Captain?'

Novitskiy had backed himself up against the wall.

'Who the hell are you?' he said, looking terrified.

Chapter 21

There was so much to be learned, and Sally was learning it fast. She had successfully completed her black hole analysis, gathering data that to her knowledge had never been seen before, and as each day passed, her time on board was proving to be more and more lucrative. She had only hit one dead end: with UV One, she had discovered nothing.

There was a battery of equipment with which she could analyse the vessel. She had performed tests, repeated them and varied them, all to no effect. She was running out of ideas, and so for the time being, she stopped experimenting on it altogether. Whatever its secrets were, whatever it wanted to do, she felt it would be done in its own good time. A little disappointed at this anti-climactic conclusion, she focussed her attention on the puzzles for which she at least had a few of the pieces, and relished her time doing so. The annoyance at her failure to understand UV One disappeared fast, as the runner-up prize turned out to be even better than she'd hoped. She was in space, doing research she never thought she'd get to do, so she was the happiest she'd ever been.

With the station operating in a low energy mode for the three crew before her — compared to the station's usual compliment of six to ten — she had little by way of daily chores to do, but still there were some. As it happened, she didn't resent the time away from her studies: it gave her a valuable opportunity to distract her mind and let her subconscious figure out whatever her conscious was stuck on.

Today, she had already cleared the air vent filters in each module — that had taken an hour and a half — and she had bundled the week's laundry and food waste into containers and put them in the FGB, where they were stored for collection. Now she was checking the water reclamation tanks to make sure they were working as they should. Novitskiy had shown her how to do it, and it was fairly simple: most of the work only required her to check on self-regulating automated systems.

There was a clipboard fastened to the wall next to the water reclamation tanks, and she ran through each step, pushing the corresponding button indicated and checking that the LED flashed green. The system confirmed that all was well. With no one else on board there was less humidity and urine to reclaim, but because she was drinking less it seemed to even out and the storage tank remained within the safe limits.

'Done and done,' she said, affixing the clipboard back to the wall.

Just one more thing to do today: air mix test. The main tanks and readouts were located in the front portion of the FGB, and she paddled her way from the American half, through the tight, conical PMA One, and into the FGB. It was a different environment in here compared to the quiet, computerised water reclamation tanks. It was noisy, industrial and complicated. Pipes wound in from every direction, valves and gauges sprouting from them like wild mushrooms, hissing and vibrating to the touch. Another checklist was fastened to the wall, and she followed through it. Most things were fine, but the odd valve needed a tweak here and there to bring the gauges back to their centres. One smaller valve was particularly tight, and as she gripped and twisted with all her strength it snapped open, exhaling a jet of gas that made her jump. She tightened it up again, watching as the gauge needle crept back into the safe zone, and breathed a sigh of relief.

The clipboard had been flung out of her hand by the jet of gas and was still spinning off towards the service module. She pushed off to get it. As easy as weightlessness made some activities, for others it was a pain, the casual ability for small items to wander off being one of them. As the clipboard tumbled, it collided with the walls, and soon it came to a stop against a laptop. She breezed over the storage crates in the FGB and entered the service module, and as she reached out for the clipboard, something caught her eye. With a small flutter of apprehension, she looked downwards into the MLM, but saw nothing. Dismissing it as a trick of the light, she grabbed the clipboard, but then she saw the movement again. She hesitated, then entered the MLM, letting her eyes adjust to the dark.

'Hello?' she called out, her own voice making her skin prickle.

A flash of shadow from the bulbous end of the MLM made her stop, her heart beating fast in her throat.

'Hello?' she called again.

There was no response, so she continued downwards, feeling the horrible closeness of fear wind her senses into overdrive. And then she saw it: completely naked and curled up into a ball, was a man.

* * *

It didn't take much persuasion to get Novitskiy into the car. Bales' stooges were coming round, and once that was pointed out to him, he did as they asked. Sean filled him in during the car journey back to Grigory's.

'That's quite a story,' Novitskiy said. 'If only half right.'

'What do you mean?' Sean said.

'You said that me, Romanenko and Williams were back. That's not right. Gardner's back — Romanenko isn't. Neither is Fisher.'

This revelation made no sense to Sean. He thought about it for a moment, but nothing came of it. There was no reason to leave Romanenko and Sally up there together.

'Why bring Gardner back? Why not Romanenko?'

Novitskiy pulled a face. 'I guess you haven't heard, then. Mikhail — he disappeared.'

The car swerved as Aleks turned to look at Novitskiy from the driver's seat. He didn't look happy. 'What? Is he hurt?' he said, snatching at the wheel to correct the wobble.

'He just upped and left, taking Soyuz, but not before destroying the comms system.'

Sean shook his head. He wasn't disagreeing with Novitskiy, just trying to understand what he was hearing. It made no sense. 'And he didn't come back?'

'Nope. Chris was mortified. He unwittingly helped Romanenko take Soyuz during what he thought was a routine check.' He faltered, and looked out the window. 'I can't say it was easy for me, either. He was a good friend.'

'Yes he was,' Aleks said from up front.

'The strangest thing,' Novitskiy said, turning back to Sean with a thought lighting his face, 'was when we recovered Soyuz.'

'I thought you said Romanenko didn't come back?' Sean said.

'That's the strange thing. Soyuz was empty. Romanenko was gone. Gardner had fallen into a coma trying to recover it, and Williams, he … he injured himself. Neither could stay.'

It was like there was a brick wall just behind Sean's eyes. What Novitskiy was saying was going in like it should but bouncing off without him being able to fully comprehend what had happened. He struggled to focus — trying to understand

Romanenko's behaviour seemed like an impossibility. But from the mist, one thought came through clear as a bell. 'So Sally's on her own?'

Novitskiy looked out the window again. 'Yes.'

'Jesus...' Aleks said.

Aleks and Novitskiy continued talking about Sally and Romanenko, but Sean wasn't really listening. He was busy untangling the world's largest ball of mental wool. What he realised was that Bales would need to send someone else up soon. His logic was simple: Gardner had gone to plant the bomb, but had failed. He deduced this from the fact that the station was still in one piece, and as a consequence, so was Sally. That made it a straightforward connection to realise that Bales would need to replace Gardner with someone else, send them up to kick start the mission and destroy UV One. *But what if he hasn't done it because he doesn't want to kill Sally?* No. That didn't fit the profile. Bales had killed Lev for standing in his way, and Sally was a much more insignificant blot than he was. Sean imagined that Bales was probably mortified at Gardner's return, coma or no coma. Maybe UV One knew what Gardner was trying to do, and stopped him? The thought made a cold shiver run down his spine.

'Did Bales say how he felt about you coming back?' Sean asked.

'Well, he wasn't to fussed about *my* return,' Novitskiy said. 'But he seemed pretty concerned about Gardner. I wanted him to let me go back, you know, to get Sally, but he said no. That was when I left. It made me so angry.'

If Sean was certain of his hypothesis before, he was convinced now. Novitskiy may not have known it, but by coming back to Earth he had bought Sean — and Sally — a bit more time. 'How long do you think it'll be before he can send someone else up?'

'I don't know ... a few weeks at best? There's a resupply mission due soon, I expect he'll commandeer that.'

Two weeks. It wasn't long, but it was better than nothing.

Back at Grigory's — and after another delicious meal while Novitskiy filled them in with all the details of UV One — Sean discovered through a twenty-year–old scanned news clipping that Ruth Shaw's last-known address was the Indian Hills Home for the Aged, Nevada, but that was the most recent thing he could find on her. There was nothing on her relatives, her current state of wellbeing—nothing at all. Pretty much every trace of her personal life was absent from public record. Sean needed to go and see her, but first he needed to make sure she was still alive at the very least, and that meant a trip to the forest.

'Hi, my name is Donald Hopfield,' Sean said in his best Texas accent, 'I'm from the *Evening Post.* I'm calling about an article I'm putting together on the well-being of elderly residents in retirement homes, and I'm told your home is one of the best. I'd like to arrange an interview with some of your patrons if I may.'

It was cold out in the Russian wilderness; evening seemed to be coming in early. Sean shivered as he waited, satellite phone pressed to his ear. The response came, finally, with a hint of attitude. 'We operate on a strict friends and family only basis, no reporters. We've had issues before with the press—you understand, I'm sure.'

'Can I at least get some basic info, a few facts, a quote maybe?'

'I'm afraid not.'

'Okay, thank you.'

'Goodbye.'

Sean hung up and redialled.

'Hello, I'm looking for some information on a Ruth Shaw, currently residing in the Indian Hills Home for the Aged, Nevada. Do you have anything on record?

'One moment, please, sir.'

Hold music blared from the speaker, crackling and screeching. A minute passed, and then another, and Sean's heart sank more with each one.

'I'm sorry sir, it looks like that record has been made private by the account holder.'

Shit.

'Thanks for your help.'

Sean made a few more phone calls, all with the same result.

'No good?' Aleks asked.

'Nope. No one's telling me anything.'

'So what do we do now?'

'There's only one thing left: I have to bite the bullet and fly out to Nevada.'

Grigory laughed. 'You won't get anywhere near airport security, not with your record.'

'I know. That's why I've got to call in a favour …'

Again the phone rang, but this time Sean knew exactly who he'd be speaking to.

'Hello?'

'Hi, Sean here.'

'Sean, how are you? How's the time off going? We've got the empty ISS story coming along nicely this end — we're looking to run it in the Sunday edition.'

'Great. Look, I've managed to get some intel that verifies everything.'

'Everything? What are you talking about?'

'UV One.'

The phone hissed a faint static for several long seconds.

'Sean, I thought I told you to drop that story.'

'I know, but —'

'Let me tell you something, Sean. I believe you. I have from the beginning. But we're poking around some seriously high-level shit that we should *not* be getting involved with. I need you off this story immediately. I mean it, Sean.'

First, confusion filled Sean, then disappointment, but as he thought through what he had just heard, that disappointment turned into a feeling of betrayal, which became a hardened anger. 'Oh, I see how this works,' he said through gritted teeth. 'What did they do? Pay off your mortgage? Get you that holiday home you always wanted? Buy you a new car? Come on — *what?*' Sean was yelling by the time he'd finished his sentence, and his voice echoed around the trees.

'Sean, it's not like that. Look — they threatened to close the paper. They said that if I didn't cooperate, they'd … they'd ruin my career, everything I've worked for. I can't let that happen.'

'So you sold out?'

'No, I didn't sell —'

'You sold your impartiality and your dignity to protect yourself. That's what you did.'

A pause.

'Okay, I did, but so did all the others. We're fighting powers beyond our reckoning here; you would've done the same thing.'

Another pause. Sean couldn't think of anything constructive or pleasant to say, so he said nothing.

'Look, Sean, just because we aren't running the story, doesn't mean we can't still work on it. We can build up a case and leak it, just like we did with the Ramirez story. Clean slate, job done.'

It was a compromise. Sean's anger reduced from a bubbling apoplexy to a gentle simmer. 'Okay. But I need you on my side.'

'Of course. What can I get you? Name it and it's yours.'

'A plane out of here. No passports.'

'Where to?'

'Nevada.'

'Jesus Christ, Sean, you don't want much.'

'You said *anything*.'

'Okay, okay. I'll arrange that for you. Call me early tomorrow for the details.'

'I will. Thank you.'

'And keep this under your hat.'

'I always do.'

Back at Grigory's house, Sean checked the computer in the vain hope that the search had dug something else up, but it hadn't. On the plus side, the group of three had become four, and they sat together enjoying the thick-cut roast venison sandwiches that Grigory had made.

'These are really good,' Novitskiy said, tucking into his with ravenous appetite. 'I've been eating hospital food for the last few days, and space food for forever before that, so this is a real treat.'

Grigory nodded his thanks for the compliment.

'So you're sure there's nothing else you can do?' Aleks asked, licking his fingers.

'I'm running out of time,' Sean said. 'I have to go to Nevada. I'll go it alone to avoid rousing suspicion. It's hard not to draw attention to yourself when you've got three Russians following you around — particularly when one is as big as a house.'

The others laughed, except for Grigory who didn't seem to follow that Sean was talking about him.

'I'll be leaving tomorrow,' Sean continued. 'It'll be a hard slog, but hopefully I won't be gone for long.'

'We'll stay here and keep searching online for anything more,' Aleks said.

'Good. Hopefully we can find out who this Ruth Shaw is and work out what the hell's going on. Lets just pray she's not dead.'

The next day before sunrise, after a call confirming the details, Sean made his way down to a small airfield east of Troitsk, boarded the plane that awaited him and set off towards the land of the free: America. He hadn't expected a private jet, but this was ridiculous. The plane was small, really small, and it bounced along through the air in a way that seemed to defy the laws of physics.

'We're going to be crossing the Pacific, *in this?'* Sean had said when he first saw the plane.

'Oh no,' the pilot, an old boy called Thomas McBride had said. 'No, no, no. We'll be crossing the *Atlantic*.'

Crossing the Pacific meant spending a few hundred miles over the Bering Strait between Russia and Alaska, but crossing the Atlantic was a journey of about *two thousand miles* over freezing-cold ocean. It was a more dangerous choice, but it was quicker. According to Thomas, the small plane was fitted with large fuel tanks, which would make the crossing with ease. A happy side-effect, he'd said, was that as the fuel started burning off, the plane would become more stable. His confidence wasn't rubbing off onto Sean, but there was no other option so they flew on in silence, the engine and wind noise — 'She's fast, but she's noisy' — too loud to talk over. They were going to stop off at a small airfield in Chantada, Spain, to brim the tanks before the trans-Atlantic trip, but even that was a good ten hours away.

From up in the sky, the sunrise was the most beautiful thing Sean had ever seen, a strip of azure blue growing from a ball of burning red. And McBride was right: as the fuel burned off and they climbed to thinner air, the plane stopped buffeting and sailed along without so much as a shimmy. Sean's nerves settled and he began to enjoy the changing scenery below, watching dark greens grow light and then turn to dust as they ventured closer to the equator. It was a long ten hours, but the lack of conversation gave him a chance to think and reflect, so it wasn't as bad as he'd thought. In fact he rather enjoyed it, feeling a small twinge of sadness as McBride pitched the nose down to land in Chantada. The coastline had just been visible through the haze, a strip of pale blue fringing the sky.

They landed in a dusty airstrip that was more a patch of dirt than an international hub, and Sean stretched himself out while McBride filled the plane with stinking fuel. The ground rippled with midday heat, and even the sweat patches growing around Sean's armpits felt warm against his skin. He wished he'd brought his sunglasses — no duty free to buy them from here. There wasn't even a toilet to piss in.

'Probably a hundred degrees today,' McBride said. 'And as clear as you like.'

He wasn't wrong: the sky was spotless. A good omen for the journey ahead, after which he would meet Ruth Shaw and all his questions would be answered. Or she would be dead. He didn't want to think about that.

Plane ready, they took off and skipped along the Atlantic at a good pace, but with nothing to look at but rolling blue ocean, the trip was long and tiring. Before, Sean had enjoyed the solitude afforded to him by the noise, but he resented it now, forcing himself not to look down at the dashboard clock every few minutes. Or seconds. His joints were beginning to set with ache and his muscles with cramp, and he wished the hours away with desperate prayers. Six hours in, his body begged him for sleep, but it wouldn't come. He felt sick, not from the motion of flying, but from the torturous position he was pinned in. Somehow, McBride seemed to soak it all up in his stride, and so Sean tried to follow his lead and keep a brave face. Day faded to evening, and then to night, and they continued to buzz along in the pitch black, with not a single light on save for the ones illuminating the instruments. Sean was impressed by McBride's piloting abilities, and that was the last thing he remembered before falling, at last, into a fitful state between waking and sleep.

When he awoke, it was still dark, except for a flash of the deepest purple behind them. The sleep wasn't the best — a long way from it — but he didn't feel as bad as he had done. He could just make out McBride from the instrument lights: he looked tired, but focussed. McBride saw he was awake, tapped his watch and held up two fingers: two hours left. It was a blessing. Sean worked out how many blocks of ten-minute segments that was, his tired mind finding it much harder than it should have done, and he chalked them off in his head one by one. By the time the coastline appeared, it twinkled like a string of jewels through the darkness of the early morning.

McBride put the plane down in a place he later told Sean was Walterboro. He refuelled, ready for the last hop to Tonopah, which was about two hundred miles from Carson City where Sean would find the Indian Hills Home for the Aged.

'I'm gonna catch a few winks before we go,' McBride said.

Sean thought he wasn't tired, but once they'd pitched a tent and climbed in, he fell right to sleep. It seemed like just a blink from his eyes falling shut to him being prodded awake again by McBride's boot.

'Time to get going,' McBride told him.

The smell of fried meat drew Sean from the tent, while the heat chased him out of it, and, bleary eyed, he accepted a plate with two of the fattest sausages he'd ever seen.

'Get those in you,' Thomas said. 'That'll give you the energy to see the day through.'

Back in the air, the plane jostled the sausages about in Sean's stomach, but he managed to hold them down. He imagined it was the sheer size and weight of the things that was stopping them making a bid for freedom, and he wished Indian Hills closer every second of the flight. It was the shortest stint of the three, but after a few hours of freedom he really had to force himself to climb back on board, where the old aches and cramps came flooding back. Although the flight was over land, the view was as uninspiring as the Atlantic. Sand in every direction, dotted with the occasional lake or town, bored Sean senseless, but every one drew him another mile or so closer to Ruth.

Thomas landed the plane at early dusk. The agreement was for Sean to call McBride when he was done, and he would meet him back here in Tonopah. McBride didn't like to hang around, and was buzzing along the strip before Sean had even reached the main road.

There was a town a few miles' walk away, where Sean caught a bus that took him along route ninety-five into Fallon. From there, he would catch another bus into Carson City along route fifty. Sean had never much liked the bus — they always made him travel sick — but he was so exhausted that he slept right through, waking just in time to make the change. The second bus wound through dusty desert marked by the occasional small town, and by midnight, Carson City appeared on the horizon as a nest of star-like pinpricks shimmering in the haze. He checked into a motel, where the cotton sheets and air conditioning were like a sedative, knocking him out cold. When morning came, he slept through it, and woke as afternoon was knocking on the door.

'Damn it!' he cursed aloud as he saw the time.

After a quick, cold shower, he found a phone in the hotel lobby. He scanned the business cards thumbtacked to the noticeboard next to it and called one of the taxicab firms.

'I need a taxi from the Best Value Inn to the Indian Hills Home for the Aged, please.'

'Right away, sir.'

The taxi pulled up outside not long after. The driver was pleasant enough, and Sean spent the half-hour journey listening to him talk about how his daughter was going to play cello with the state orchestra. He feigned happiness for the driver, whose name he had already forgotten, while trying to ignore the building tremor in his stomach as they approached Indian Hills. Before he knew it, the taxi stopped. Cash and pleasantries exchanged, Sean got out. It had taken him several days, and he had travelled halfway around the world, but he had made it. He was at the Indian Hills Home for the Aged, which was, fingers crossed, the residence of Ruth Shaw.

Section 4 — Vessel
Chapter 22

'Who are you?' Sally said, her throat so tight it strangled her voice.

The naked man unfurled, his stringy muscles tensing under his pale skin. Sally drifted over to him, cautious at first, then stopped, realisation hitting her so hard she clapped a hand over her mouth.

'You're — you're Mikhail Romanenko ...' she said through her fingers. It wasn't possible. *It couldn't be possible.*

Mikhail looked at her, his eyes wide against his gaunt face. 'Where am I?' he whispered.

Sally helped him into the service module, where she found him some clothes and gave him some food. He ate fast, as though he hadn't eaten in days, and she had to slow him down for fear he would choke. She waited until he finished before she asked him any more questions, her curiosity and concern for him overwhelming any lingering traces of trepidation. He seemed harmless enough, at least for now. The tremor in his hands worried her at first, but it seemed to pass after he'd eaten. Colour also returned to his cheeks and he no longer seemed quite so fragile.

'How did you get here?' she asked him, watching his every move with fascination.

'I don't know,' he said, looking around.

'Do you remember anything before being here?'

'No.' He narrowed his eyes, as if trying to dig up an old memory. 'No, wait, I do. I remember a feeling of — I don't really know how to describe it. Warmth, I suppose. Safety. Like I was being protected. Then I was here.'

'Nothing else?'

'No. Nothing at all.'

'Do you know where you are? Do you recognise any of it?'

Mikhail shook his head. Sally couldn't help but be intrigued by him. This man had Mikhail's looks — his hairstyle, his nose, his stubble, everything — but he remembered nothing. All this time she had been trying to communicate with UV One without success, and now — now it was communicating with *her*. There was no way Mikhail could have got on board without it. The thought made her heart leap, and she had to tell herself to calm down before she spoke again.

'We're in space,' she told him.

He looked blank.

'Space — in orbit. Not on Earth.'

'I don't know these things.'

'Earth is home.'

At the word *home*, the last of the fear and rigidity in Mikhail's body seemed to melt away. 'Home ...' he repeated.

'That's right,' Sally said, smiling. 'Home.'

Mikhail smiled back, a boyish grin that gave his middle-aged features a wash of youth. Sally felt a rush of warmth at the thought of having someone to talk to again.

'I know where you've come from,' she said, watching to see how he reacted. 'Where you've been all this time.' She had always thought that an encounter like this would make her scared, or at least nervous, but she was neither of those things. She was excited.

'Where?'

'Do you remember the vessel? UV One? You could see it through the window where I found you in the MLM.'

Mikhail looked as though he was about to speak, but he didn't. His grin faded, and he stayed silent.

'You do remember, don't you?'

He nodded. 'Home.'

Although Mikhail seemed to know and understand very little, he caught on fast, and over the next couple of days he and Sally became something of a team. He helped her with her experiments, setting up the equipment and logging the results, as well as assisting with her daily housekeeping chores, which she was now able to do in half the time. He even livened up her exercise regime, which he joined her for. Explaining to him that he needed to exercise to stay healthy and fight off muscle atrophy took some doing, but he got it after a while and they laughed about it together afterwards as they got themselves something to eat.

'It's entirely true, I swear,' Sally said through a mouthful of macaroni cheese. 'I used to be a little fat kid.'

'No way! I don't believe it.'

'All the other kids in school used to call me Fat Sally. Not a particularly original or creative nickname, granted, but it stuck with me for a long time.'

'How'd you get slim again?'

'We'll, I'd like to say I joined a gym and got really healthy,' Sally said, ignoring Mikhail's confused frown at the word *gym*, 'but I actually got so involved in my research that I just damn well forgot to eat. It's amazing how hard it is to stay fat when you eat as little as I do.'

'What do you research?'

'Long-distance communications, mainly. NASA has me working on a little project to develop faster-than-light comms, but I don't think it's possible, at least not with any technology we have today. Made a few breakthroughs along the way, though. But what I really love doing is searching for life.'

Mikhail, whose pouch was halfway to his mouth, stopped. 'Life?'

'Yeah. Extra-terrestrial life. *Aliens*,' she said, emphasising the last word with a wiggle of her fingers.

'Am I an — alien?' Mikhail asked, looking apprehensive.

The topic seemed to concern him; Sally could see his body language change almost in an instant. She felt a pang of sympathy: he was neither man nor alien. He was more like a confused and frightened boy. 'Don't let it worry you,' she said. 'You're back, you're safe, and that's all that matters.'

He smiled again, and ate the rest of his macaroni cheese. His good humour soon returned as they tucked into dessert. 'I like this,' he said, squeezing the apple puree and breadcrumb mix into his mouth. 'What is it? It's really good.'

'Apple pie. You should try the real thing. It's much better.'

'When? Now?' Mikhail said, his eyes bulging at the idea.

Sally laughed. 'No, not now. When they come and get us.'

'They? They who?'

'The RFSA and NASA, I suppose.'

Mikhail looked at his coveralls, at the logo on his chest. He pointed to it.

'That's it,' Sally said, nodding.

'What do they do?'

He was like an eager child, wanting and willing to learn about everything.

'They send people like me and you into space to do research.'

'Me?'

'Yes — you're a cosmonaut. A spaceman.'

Mikhail swelled with pride. 'I am,' he said, then squeezed some more apple pie into his mouth.

They cleared the table together. When they were finished, Sally led Mikhail through the station.

'I've got something I'd like to show you,' she said as they wormed their way through PMA One and into the American side. Ducking into Node Three, they surfaced in the Cupola, which was bathed in shadow. 'Watch this,' she said, and released the window coverings one by one. They fell away to reveal a view of blue, green and white: Earth.

'It's beautiful …' Mikhail whispered, touching the glass with his fingertips.

'That's home,' Sally said.

They looked out at it together, watching the clouds change shape and formation as they lazily navigated the globe. Sally hadn't much thought of home since she'd been left up here, and she realised she missed it. She wasn't sure what she missed about it, but whatever it was it left an aching hole in her chest.

* * *

The lobby was hot. Really hot. A wall-mounted fan arced back and fourth, but it did little to disperse the sweltering humidity. Sean approached the reception desk where a woman was sat reading a gossip magazine. 'Hello?' he said, trying to catch her attention.

She held up a finger, scanned through the rest of the page, then turned to Sean. 'Yes?'

Her voice was familiar. Sean realised it must have been her he spoke to on the phone. 'I'm here to see Ruth. Ruth Shaw.' Sweat trickled down his neck, slow and sticky. The moment of truth had arrived.

'And who might you be?' the receptionist said, raising her eyebrows.

'I'm her great-nephew,' Sean lied. 'I just flew in from Europe this morning, and I thought I'd pay her a visit.'

'Is that so?' the receptionist said, folding her arms. 'I ain't never seen you before.'

A scratch of metal on wood came from a doorway behind the reception desk, where a scrawny, sweaty man with a gleaming bald head now stood. 'I couldn't help but overhear your conversation,' he said, dabbing his brow with a grubby handkerchief. He put it in his pocket, and reached across the counter to shake Sean's hand. 'I'm Todd, I'm the manager here.'

'Hi Todd,' Sean said. 'I'm Pete.'

'Well, Pete — I'm afraid I have some bad news. Do you want to come into my office? We'll get a bit more privacy in there.'

Sean followed Todd around the reception desk and into his office, feeling the receptionist staring a hole into his back. Todd shut the door and the temperature went up even further.

'Please, have a seat,' he said, directing Sean to the only chair in the room. Sean sat, and Todd leaned against his desk, which was covered in paper, mostly bills.

'Did you have a pleasant flight over?'

Small talk before the heavy stuff, Sean thought, his stomach sinking. 'Yes, thanks. A little cramped, but fine nonetheless.'

'You're telling me. Those airlines don't mind cramming 'em in.'

The man had no idea just how crammed Sean had been. 'No, they don't.'

There was an awkward pause before Todd said, 'I'm sorry. That's not why you're here.' He sighed, folded his arms and looked at the floor, examining his shoes. 'This is against protocol, and I hate to be the one to tell people this sort of thing, I really do, but I don't think there's any harm in it now. Ruthy died a couple of weeks ago.'

Sean was already certain that she had, but hearing it out loud made him feel sick. The miles travelled was one thing, but Ruth was the only door to an answer left, and it had been slammed in his face.

Todd mistook his disappointment for him being upset. 'Oh now, there's no need to be sad,' he said. 'Ruthy lived a good life, a long, strong existence and died peacefully in her bed. She was a happy woman if ever I saw one.'

Sean nodded, not really listening. 'How did she die?' he asked.

'Doctor said it was natural causes. She just stopped breathing in her sleep one night.'

'Was there anything suspicious about her death? Anything at all? Did anything unusual happen just before she died? Did she say whether she'd met anyone new recently?'

Todd eyed him with caution. 'Who did you say you were, again?' he asked, wariness in his voice.

'Never mind — I'm being silly.' Sean said, and Todd seemed to settle back to his normal, sweating self. 'I'm a journalist; I always look for the hidden agenda, even if there is none.'

Damn. He shouldn't have said that. Hopefully it would be a detail that Todd overlooked.

'A journalist? Now that *is* interesting. What publication do you write for?'

Double damn. 'I work freelance. I mostly write for music magazines.'

'You ever get to go to those after parties? With all the girls?'

'No, not really. I'm not that rock and roll.'

Todd nodded. 'Probably for the best.'

Sean thought hard. There must be something he could find out while he was here. After all he *was* a journalist, and he *did* always look for the hidden agenda. 'Hey,' he said, 'do you mind if I have a look through her things? We were very close when I was a kid, and it would be nice to, you know — catch up with her memory.'

Todd smiled. 'Of course.'

They left the putrid humidity of Todd's office and wandered the halls.

'Ruthy really liked it here,' Todd said. 'She said it was her favourite place. She loved to sit in the lounge and tell stories. She had this one story about a scientist and an alien spacecraft that she used to tell. Boy that woman had a hell of an imagination. She could've made it as one of those science-fiction writers by my reckoning.'

This sounded interesting. 'Could you tell me that story?'

'Ah, well — I forget most of it …'

'Please try. It's very important to me.'

Todd stopped and scrunched his eyes up, thinking. Then he opened them again. 'Gah, I don't know. Tell you what — why don't I show you her room while I think about it, see if I can remember?'

They turned off the corridor into room twenty-four. It was a modest but tidy space, with a small bed in the middle and a big glass window overlooking the desert.

'Great view, huh?' Todd said, looking out with his hands on his hips.

'Sure,' Sean said, giving it a cursory glance before scanning the room. There was a desk opposite the bed, so he opened the drawers and looked through them.

'Let me see then, the story,' Todd said, scratching his neck. 'There was a scientist — a whole bunch of them in fact — and they found a box in the desert. Or was it a box the size of a house? I can't remember. Anyways, they find this box and they take it back to a top secret laboratory.'

Sean rifled though the sheets of blank paper and stationary littering the drawers, but besides that, there was nothing. He closed them, and moved on to her bedside cabinet.

'Say — are you looking for anything in particular?' Todd asked.

'No,' Sean said, rummaging through a drawer of socks. 'What happened after they found the box?'

'Ah yes, the box. They took the box back, but they couldn't do anything with it. It was solid — no way in, no way out. Come to think of it, that box must've been the size of a house or they wouldn't have tried to get in it. A house is pretty big though, don't you think —'

'It doesn't matter. What happened next?'

'Er — no, I suppose it doesn't matter,' Todd said, sounding a little flustered. 'Well, after a while, the scientists began seeing things, having visions. Like, real powerful stuff. Then one day the box takes one of them, and he was gone, just like that. But he returns, and he's not the same as before he disappeared — he's *changed*. It's like he's become one with the box. But the box makes the other scientists lose their minds, and so it's decided that the box should be destroyed. They do, and the scientist that came back from the box dies with it. And that's it.' He shrugged. 'I'm not too good at telling stories. Not like Ruthy was.'

Sean had stopped looking through the drawers and was fixed on Todd. 'So it's true …' he whispered.

* * *

'What do you think it wants?' Sally asked, gazing out the window of the MLM at the colourless cuboid.

'I don't know,' Mikhail said, watching it with her.

'It's beautiful in an odd kind of way,' Sally said, watching a star flicker as it passed behind it. 'I think it wants to communicate with us, but it just doesn't know how.'

Mikhail leaned closer to the window such that his nose touched the glass. 'Do you think it wants to communicate through me?'

Sally looked at him, at his squashed nose, and laughed. 'I don't know,' she said, still chuckling a little. 'Maybe it does, maybe it doesn't. Maybe we'll never know.'

Mikhail pulled back from the window and turned to her, the tip of his nose bright red. Sally burst out laughing again and pushed him away.

'What?' he said smiling. 'What is it?'

'You're so silly.'

Instead of doing her usual experiments, Sally spent the rest of the afternoon explaining to Mikhail about the stars. It was a strange experience; the more she talked to him, the more he seemed to be growing up, as if the youthful brain trapped in his adult body was maturing at an accelerated pace.

'There are three hundred billion stars in our galaxy, the Milky Way,' Sally explained, 'and about five hundred billion galaxies in the universe.'

'And how many universes are there?' Mikhail asked, hanging onto her every word.

It was a good question, she had to give him credit for that. 'No one knows. Most people think there's only one.'

Mikhail wrinkled his brow. 'That's not right,' he said.

Sally blinked. 'How many do you think there are?'

He leaned back, touching his head against the canvas wall. 'It's not really a thing for numbers. Other universes exist in a state that numbers can't describe.'

At first Sally thought what he was saying was nonsense, but the look in his eye changed her mind. 'Have you been there?' she asked. 'To the other universes, I mean.'

Mikhail's face went blank for a second.

'I can't remember.'

Then his grin returned. 'Do you have any more apple pie?'

Sally shook her head in humorous disbelief. They went for some more apple pie.

'Back on Earth,' Sally said, putting her finished pouch in the waste, 'we have pies in many different flavours. You'd love it.'

'Like what?' He was still licking the nozzle of his pouch, having squeezed every last morsel of the pie from it.

'Anything you can think of. Rhubarb and raspberry, blueberry, peach, pumpkin — the list is endless.'

'Wow. I *would* love to try all those.'

'Maybe one day you will.'

Sally looked through the tiny porthole on the bottom of the service module, where a glimpse of Earth shone through.

'When are they coming for us?' Mikhail said, somehow echoing Sally's own thoughts.

'I don't know,' she said, sighing. 'I don't know.'

The atmosphere became sombre. Sally and Mikhail did their chores together as usual, but they did them with a whole lot less laughing and joking. It was as though Mikhail was feeding off Sally's sadness, her longing for home, reflecting her emotion back at her. She'd been okay the whole while she was alone, able to ignore her real feelings, but now she had someone whose company she enjoyed, the beckoning call of planet Earth seemed to tug harder at her heartstrings.

'You miss Earth, don't you?' Mikhail said as Sally ran through the readings for the water reclamation tanks.

'Yes, I do.'

'What do you miss most about it?'

Sally stopped to think. There was so much she missed: silly little things, mostly. Seeing the leaves turn a beautiful burnt orange as winter rolled in. The smell of barbecued ribs coming from the neighbour's garden. Laughing at TV re-runs of Frasier that she'd seen a thousand times before. 'I guess I miss everything.'

Mikhail gave her a reassuring smile, and said nothing.

They didn't talk again properly until the next day, while Sally was running through some gamma ray readings from a nearby star, Wolf 359.

'Did you know it's possible to create faster-than-light communication?' Mikhail said, out of the blue. 'I know that's something you're interested in, isn't it?'

Sally stopped what she was doing. Had she heard him right? 'Really? How?'

'Not how,' Mikhail said, 'where.'

'Okay — where?'

'You're limited by the speed of light within this universe, you know that much. But punch through to the next and you can move in infinite directions and speeds all at once.'

Sally shook her head, confused. 'I don't — I don't know what you mean.'

Mikhail took her hands and cupped them into a ball. 'You understand your universe to be like this,' he said, 'and so it takes time to travel from one side to the other.' He indicated his meaning by tracing a line around the ball of Sally's hands. He then spread her hands open so she held them flat together, as though she were praying. 'This is how your universe really is, and it moves between the other universes like this.' He placed his hands over the top of hers and slid them across. They were warm, soft. 'You can leave this universe, enter another and return at any point in an instant.' He released her hands and grinned. 'Just like that.'

All at once, Sally felt something inside her, something she didn't understand. It was a warm uncertainty, a feeling that, even though her future was indistinct, everything would be okay. She savoured the moment, and the lingering warmth on the backs of her hands. 'How do you know all this?' she asked.

Mikhail shrugged. 'I just do. I have these thoughts and ideas that appear in my head. One minute they aren't there; the next they are.'

Sally wondered who Mikhail really was. Was he still Mikhail? Was he still human? Or was he something else? She realised she didn't care. She liked him just the way he was, whatever he was. They talked long into the night, sharing stories between them. Well, Sally told the stories while Mikhail smiled and laughed in the right places, frowned and shook his head with disbelief in the others. She poured herself out to him like she'd never done to anyone before, told him things that had been bottled up inside her for as long as she could remember. When she told him about the death of her mother, he leaned in towards her and held her for a few fleeting moments. She felt a tight knot in her shoulders that had gone unnoticed for weeks — maybe even years — unwind as if it were nothing.

'You've been through a lot to get to where you are now,' Mikhail said, holding his untouched carton of apple juice.

Sally smiled. She never saw herself as a martyr or a hero, or even a cause for sympathy, but it was nice to have her hardships recognised. She had fought with such defiance for so long to push through the barriers of gender and intelligence that contested her every move on Earth. It was a constant battle that never had any time for the weakness of emotion, so she had hardened herself without realising it, built up an armoured shell that was held in place by the twisted bindings of insecurity and stubbornness. But with Mikhail, that armour fell away, and she wasn't afraid to leave her weaknesses exposed to him.

'Do you remember anything else about where you came from?' she asked him, to which he shuffled, looking uncomfortable.

'I — I think I do. I can't be sure. When I think too hard about it, I get these headaches' — he rubbed his temples — 'but they're not that bad. It's a strain to think, but the more I do, the more I remember, and with it comes knowledge I never even knew I had.'

'Can you tell me what it's like?'

Mikhail looked confused. 'What do you mean?'

'I mean, can you tell me what it's like to be — well, to be the first human to communicate with extra-terrestrial life?'

Mikhail grinned. 'I'm not the first. And I won't be the last. They've spoken to you, but at the moment you just can't hear it. Give it time, and the words will come. Listen, and you will hear.'

Sally hoped beyond hope that he would continue talking. She was enthralled.

'It's like opening your eyes for the first time,' Mikhail said, 'when up to then you have merely been dreaming.'

'Will my eyes ever be open?'

Mikhail stroked her hair, running his fingers down her face and under her chin. 'Yes, they will. When you're ready.'

* * *

In downtown Moscow, Detective Inspector Yefim Banin flicked through a file that had been dropped on his desk that morning. It annoyed him, partly because he was already rushed off his feet, and partly because he hadn't done traffic incidents in nearly twenty years.

Reopened case, the post-it note stuck to the front said. *Chief wants you on it. Get it done quick.*

He took a sip of his watery tea and grimaced. As he read through the file, he built up the scene in his mind: Lev Ryumin, former RFSA Flight Director, got drunk and ran his car off the road and into a ditch, hitting a telegraph pole that collapsed the roof, killing him instantly. Bad luck.

But the forensics department had found traces of someone else's skin on Ryumin's body, and now the case file was on Banin's desk. Why were forensics even looking at the body at this late hour? The case had been shut ages ago. What a waste of time.

He picked up the phone and dialled the Chief's extension. It rang, and was answered by a young woman: the Chief's secretary.

'Chief Inspector Azurov's office, how can I help?'

'It's Banin.'

'Oh, hello — how are you?'

'I'm okay. Actually I'm not okay. I've been assigned to some goddamn re-opened forensic bullshit case, and I'm already up to my eyeballs in dead bodies.'

'Oh dear — I suppose you want to speak to the Chief Inspector, then?'

'That would be *wonderful.*'

'I'll put you through. You mind yourself and don't go getting into any trouble.'

The phone bleeped, then rung. What did she mean, *don't go getting into any trouble*? He was old enough to be her father, yet she was treating him like he was her son.

'Azurov.'

'It's Banin.'

'Banin. I thought you might call.'

'Then why did you do it? Why did you put me on this stupid case?'

'I need this one out the door. Gone, and quick. You can do that for me, can't you?'

'Why? It's been done already. Did you read the file? Drunk guy crashed his car. Died. End of.'

'Come on, Banin — you don't think I know that?'

'So what's going on?'

Azurov sighed. 'This one's come from central. They've reopened the case. I don't —'

'But what —'

'— I don't know why, but they have, and so I'm passing it down to you. The main suspect is a fugitive by the name of Aleks Dezhurov, a friend and work colleague of the deceased's. Central says he did it, and now I need you to go and put the pieces together. That's an order.'

'But I —'

'No more buts. I need this done yesterday.'

Banin wanted to tell him no, but he couldn't. 'Alright, I'll do it. But you owe me.'

'I'll get the drinks in for the rest of the week, how about that?'

'It's Friday already.'

'Then you'd better get your drinking hat on.'

Banin laughed and hung up. He flicked through the file once more, stopping at the picture of the car, upside down and mangled, wrapped around the telegraph pole.

'What a mess,' he said, tossing it onto his desk.

Chapter 23

The weather flying home was not as calm as it was flying out. If it weren't for the constant battle to keep his innards down, Sean would have been terrified by the way the small plane was being tossed about by the angry sky. Death wouldn't have been unwelcome, and the journey was the longest, most torturous thing Sean had ever done. There was more than one occasion where he regretted the trip, and he had to remind himself over and over — between trying not to hurl — that the information he had uncovered, however small, was valuable beyond reckoning.

The European coastline was a welcome sight, and Sean thanked every deity he could think of for his safe arrival. From there, the hop over to Moscow was a breeze, and one that he slept through without stirring.

'I hope I never meet you or your tin-pot plane ever again,' he said, shaking McBride's hand, 'but thank you for getting me there and back in one piece all the same.'

'It was my pleasure,' McBride said.

Sean had a bit of a walk to the nearest payphone — he'd decided not to use his satellite phone any more in case that too was being tracked — and his feet felt like two distant nubs by the time he reached it. Two miles, maybe four, he'd walked, on a stomach that could not be any emptier.

'Aleks?' he said when the call was answered.

'Sean — you're back! How are you?'

'Come and get me and I'll tell you everything.'

Sean wasn't true to his word. As soon as he arrived at Grigory's, he flopped onto the sofa and fell asleep, a state he managed to maintain for over fourteen hours. When he awoke, he felt better, but starving hungry.

'Oh god …' he groaned, struggling to lift his aching limbs. He could still feel the plane tossing him about even now.

'How are you this morning?' Aleks asked him from the kitchen.

'Just south of dead,' Sean said, sitting, then waiting for his head to catch up. 'Would you mind getting me a coffee, please?'

'Sure.'

'Where are Novitskiy and Grigory?'

'Out hunting.'

Aleks heated the kettle on the hob and made Sean a fresh coffee. Sean sipped at it, relishing the soothing warmth as it spread to his extremities, chasing his aches and pains away. 'This tastes awful,' he said. 'When's Grigory coming back? His is much better.'

Aleks snorted. 'I'm glad you like it.'

Then it all came back to Sean in an instant: the plane, the taxi ride, the old people's home, the story Todd had told him — everything. He burned the roof of his mouth as he took an over-large swig of coffee in his surprise. 'Ow!' he said, fanning his mouth and blowing.

'Are you okay?' Aleks asked, looking concerned as he put dry dishes away.

'Yeah, fine. Just burned my mouth.'

'Can I get you some water?'

The heat tingled and stung Sean's skin. 'No, I'll be fine.'

'So what did you find out in America?'

'She's dead.'

'Ruth?' Aleks asked, as he brought Sean a glass of water anyway.

Sean drank it, the cool liquid soothing his mouth. 'Yeah. Died in her sleep apparently.'

'Natural causes?'

'I asked, they said yes.'

'Do you believe them?'

'I think so. There was no need to lie.'

Aleks folded his arms, looking thoughtful. 'Is it true? Do you think she was there?'

'At Roswell? Yes. She saw UV One, or something like it. But they destroyed it.'

'Why?'

'It was doing things to people, turning them crazy. They must have all died because of it — Bales' father included. Well, all except Ruth.'

'Why wasn't Ruth affected?'

'I don't know.'

'How did they destroy it?'

'I don't know that either. But Bales does. He knows what happened, he knows it killed his father, and he wants revenge at whatever cost.'

Aleks flopped down next to Sean and folded his arms. 'That confirms it,' he said. 'Bales wants to destroy UV One, and the station with it.'

'It certainly looks that way. And we've only got a week left until it happens.'

'What are we going to do now?'

'I think we've done enough research,' Sean said. 'Now it's time to get this story on the front cover of every newspaper, magazine, blog and pamphlet before it's too late.'

* * *

'What a dump,' Banin said, pulling his all-weather coat tight around him. It was raining that fine kind of rain that soaked through even the most waterproof of materials. He knew it was raining when he left the office, yet somehow he'd still forgotten his umbrella. *Stupid case*, he thought. *I should be back at my desk, where it's dry*. He blew at the bulging drop hanging from his nose, only for another to take its place. 'So this is where it happened?'

He needn't have asked: the long row of neat telegraph poles was interrupted by one leaning at a drunken angle. At its base, the dull, fume-stained wood had fresh scars gouged from it, and a few red paint streaks, too. The car that did the damage was long gone.

'That's right sir,' the accompanying police officer said. 'Came straight off the road about here' — he pointed to a scuffed section of kerb — 'and down into this ditch here. Poor bastard. Such bad luck to hit this pole. If he'd stayed on the road a fraction longer or come off a fraction earlier, he'd have missed it.'

An articulated truck whooshed by, spraying them both.

'Is it okay if I go and sit in the car while you look, sir?'

Banin nodded, and the police officer darted back to the cruiser.

Bad luck indeed, Banin thought, stumbling down the roadside ditch to study the pole. The officer was right. It wasn't in the base, it was sprouting from the bank, and hitting it was the worst feat of bad luck imaginable. The road was dead straight, too, and quiet. How had he come off in a straight line?

He trudged up the bank, his boots sinking into the slimy mud, back to the road where Ryumin's bad fortune had started. The rain would have washed any skid marks away by now, but he knew from the file photos that there hadn't been any, which struck him as odd. There was, however, the section of kerb that had been chewed away, the sign of a car hitting it at speed and grinding straight over the top. Tracing an imaginary line from the pole to the damaged kerb, he waited for a car to pass before following it into the road, where something caught his eye. He bent down to pick it up, then jogged heavy and wet back to the verge before a truck ran him down. He opened his hand and turned the object over. It was a fragment of broken headlamp glass, clean, sharp and fresh.

* * *

Sean's stomach churned as he watched the passing metropolis through the taxi window. He hadn't been this nervous in a long time — scared, yes, but not nervous like this. He shifted on the cracked leather, looking but not seeing, his mind distracting his thoughts elsewhere.

He was due to meet an old friend, James Aspen, who was working as editor-in-chief at the *Moscow Times*. Not only did James have control of the *Moscow Times*, he was also well loved and respected throughout the industry, and had the potential to be a valuable tipping point in getting the story out. Aleks and the others had offered to come with him, but he was glad he'd refused them. It wasn't safe in the density of the city with nowhere to hide, but the risk he was running wasn't what made his stomach turn: it was UV One.

The more he thought about it, the more ludicrous it seemed. An old woman, dead of course, who'd had a UFO encounter, and a young woman, who no one knew or cared about, having the same experience all over again. He knew it was true in his heart, yet he couldn't douse the rising feeling of doubt in his guts that made him want to tap the driver on the shoulder and ask him to turn the taxi around. He sat back in his seat and dabbed nervous sweat from his cheeks with the back of his sleeve.

When the taxi pulled up outside the *Moscow Times* building, he checked his watch; he had an hour to kill before the meeting. He paid the driver and got out, crossed the street to a ream of blaring horns, and slipped into a coffee shop. No sooner had he ordered a coffee and sat down when his phone buzzed in his pocket. He had an email from James.

Can you meet me somewhere else? I don't think it's best we meet at head office.
James

That was fair enough. Sean tapped out his reply and sent it.

The earthiness of his coffee soothed his nerves as he waited, and when the phone buzzed again, he wasn't feeling anywhere near as bad.

Great. Meet me at The Beijing Tiger restaurant in ten minutes.
James

Sean looked at his watch; it was half eleven. Taking a last mouthful of coffee, he gathered up his phone and his bag, and left the shop. Ten minutes was enough time to walk to The Beijing Tiger, so he threaded his way through the streets and alleys on foot. He could get a bite to eat while he was there.

Nestled between a fabric shop and a Jewish deli, The Beijing Tiger was a sorry sight. The plastic golden tiger above the sign was as faded and cracked as it had ever been, and the waft of hot sweet-and-sour sauce hit him as soon as he opened the door. The restaurant may have been old, but it was a place he knew well, many a hazy memory gathered under its eaves. The maître d' bowed his head, and Sean nodded in return. 'Good afternoon.'

'Good afternoon, sir. Would you like to eat in or take away?'

'I've got a lunch with James — James Aspen Is he here?'

'Yes sir. Come right this way.'

Sean followed the waiter into the bowels of the dark, empty restaurant. It was a strange atmosphere: it wasn't exactly dingy, but this was no family eatery. In the corner, he could just about make out James sat at a table, and he gave him a nod. James looked grim.

'Hi, James, how are you doing?' Sean said, shaking his hand as he rose to greet him.

'I'm good, Sean, I'm good,' James said, although his usually friendly face was a little ashen. Perhaps it was the light, or lack thereof.

They sat, and the waiter gave Sean a menu, then left them to decide. James already had a menu, but he seemed to be looking through it rather than at it.

'How have you been?' Sean said, and James gave a small sideways jerk of his head.

'Not bad,' he said. 'I understand you've been getting involved with the US Department of Defense?'

He looked at Sean, his eyes hollow and searching. Sean struggled to read whether they expressed concern, or whether they were admonishing him.

'That's right …' he said, the uncomfortable feeling building in his stomach again. 'How do you know about that?'

James slapped his menu on the table. 'Come on, Sean, everyone knows. You've practically got a price on your head. What are you doing messing around with high level stuff like this?'

Sean couldn't believe it. This didn't seem like the James he knew. Something had spooked him. 'This is what we do, remember? We investigate, we report, we make public the affairs that concern the people and their future — is that something you've forgotten?'

'No,' he said, 'but this is too much. You've got to know when to draw the line.'

'You don't even know what's going on here,' Sean said, struggling to keep his building frustration under control.

James looked him in the eye with a stare that took him aback. There was fear in it. 'I know what's going on. The whole board does. I don't know whether to believe it or not, but frankly, if we *are* on the brink of some alien invasion, I think the public would do better to be kept in the dark.'

Sean shook his head, flabbergasted. He couldn't believe it — he'd respected James for a long, long time. The man sat in front of him could've been someone else by the way he was acting. 'You've given in too, huh?'

'Sean, don't …'

'Tell me, James,' Sean said, leaning close and jabbing the table with his finger, 'what happened to the dignity of professional journalism? Why are you, and everybody else in this damn industry folding like a wet deck of cards?'

James balled his fists, and at first Sean thought he was going to strike, but then he realised he was trying to hold back tears.

'They said they'd take my family away,' he whispered. 'They said they'd take them away if I didn't do what they told me to do …'

He took a quivering hand and covered his mouth with it as tears began to roll down his cheeks. Sean's anger washed away in an instant, a cold dread taking its place. 'What do you mean?' he said. 'What did they want you to do?'

James looked at Sean, his red eyes wide. 'I'm sorry, Sean …'

The restaurant door crashed open, letting a bright shaft of light into the room that was filled with black-suited bodies.

* * *

'Mikhail? Where are you, Mikhail?'

Sally had scoured the station, but Mikhail was nowhere to be seen. She felt an unnerving panic the longer she looked, and as she scurried from module to module it occurred to her that she hadn't checked his quarters. He was in there sleeping, but with an agony on his face that frightened her so much she jerked away. He twitched and he contorted; Sally didn't know what to do.

'Mikhail?' she said, but he didn't respond.

She grasped his shoulder and shook him.

'Wake up, Mikhail,' she said a little louder, and he stirred, his pained expression fading. As his eyes came to focus, he looked to her, and smiled.

'Hello, Sally. What's the matter?'

'You looked like you were in pain so I woke you up.'

The smile dulled a little as Mikhail thought. 'I was dreaming,' he said.

'What were you dreaming about?'

Mikhail frowned. 'I think — I think I was dreaming about —' he winced in pain, and held his face in his hands. When he resurfaced, his expression was normal again. 'No, I don't remember.'

Sally was worried for him. She knew he was having headaches, but she hadn't seen one before, and it looked far worse than he was letting on. 'Can I get you anything?' she said. 'For the pain?'

Mikhail smiled again, and shook his head. 'No, I'm fine. Really.'

Mikhail did seem fine now, and continued to for the rest of the day. He was back to his cheery self in no time, and they laughed and joked their way through their daily routine, which was sprinkled with more of Mikhail's wondrous insights.

But although Sally was happy, the expression of suffering on Mikhail's face when she'd found him that morning stuck in her mind, and no matter how much he told her that he was fine, she couldn't dismiss it. Over dinner, she brought up the topic again.

'Do you think your headaches are getting worse?' she asked, trying to sound casual while popping a piece of bread in her mouth.

'Please,' Mikhail said, patting her on the arm as if to reassure her. 'You don't need to worry.'

'But do you think they're getting worse? I want to know.'

Mikhail's face dropped a little. 'Yes.'

'Why do think that is?'

He shook his head. 'I don't really know. The only thing I do know is that when I get them, it feels like a tap has been opened in my mind. The knowledge that comes flooding in is too much for me to hold. It's like my head's going to burst.'

'What kind of knowledge?'

'I don't know — a bit of everything, really. Some parts I can actually understand, and that's what I tell you, but there are other things that hurt to think about.'

He pulled a pained expression, and Sally chewed her bread, thinking.

'Why do you think the vessel is doing this to you? Do you think it means to hurt you?'

'No, I don't think it does. I don't know what it's doing, but I don't sense any malice in its actions. Perhaps I am too fragile. Too weak.'

'Do you think you'll survive?'

Just saying that made Sally's throat go dry, and it caught Mikhail off guard, too. She watched him as he struggled to form an answer.

'I — I don't know. But if I don't survive, I'll die having experienced what very few ever have, so I think it's worth it.'

A passionate longing, like she'd experienced when she wanted to get into CalTech; like when she'd submitted her research to the NuStar team; like when she'd first looked up to the heavens and decided she wanted to visit them, sparked a flame inside Sally. 'Can I experience it too?'

This made Mikhail laugh for some reason, and without knowing why, Sally did too. She liked to laugh with him.

'Soon,' he said. 'Soon.'

After dinner, they resumed Sally's research. With Mikhail's help, Sally was making incredible progress, recording data she never thought she'd get to see, which she stored and backed up on the station's computers with religious zeal.

'You have no idea,' she said as she copied her data files across to the backup server, 'how useful this information is going to be back on Earth. This stuff could give us a ten-year technological advancement in less than a year. It's incredible.'

'I'm glad I could help,' Mikhail said as he switched off the equipment.

'This is seriously going to move the field of quantum physics forward faster than anyone's ever seen. God, I hope I can see the look on John Heisenberg's face when this information gets presented. It'll be a classic.'

'Who's John Heisenberg?'

Sally blushed — she felt a little silly for having brought John Heisenberg up at all. 'He's a guy I studied with at CalTech. He was a real jerk. I turned him down on a date, so he decided to make my life as difficult as he possibly could from then on. He even broke into a professor's car to steal a paper of mine once, can you believe that?'

'And it would be satisfying to show him this research?'

Sally played with her hands in the way she did when she felt awkward and uncomfortable. 'Yeah, I suppose. He's an accomplished physicist in his own right, and he did apologise to me a few years ago, but still — I'd like to show him what I can do.'

'Do you like him?'

Sally nearly choked she was so taken aback by the question. 'What? No! He's quite cute, but I can't get past all the horrible things he did to me. Not now, not ever.'

Mikhail smiled and nodded with a glint in his eye. They continued packing up and shutting down the equipment in silence.

'What if you could go back?' Mikhail said after a while.

Sally wasn't sure if she'd heard him right. 'Pardon?'

'What if you could go back — in time, I mean?'

It was something Sally had considered on more than one occasion. With a retrospective look back to how things *could* have been, there were many possibilities — infinite, even. She did it often, about many aspects of her life, even though she knew it was just a futile waste of imagination. Of course, she had never given any thought to *actually being able to do it*.

'I — I haven't really considered it.'

'It can be done.'

Sally wasn't sure if he was mocking her or being serious; his face, however, suggested the latter. 'How?'

'Not only can you enter this universe from any of the others at any point you like, you can also enter it at any time.'

'But how do you get from one universe to another?'

'Through a doorway.'

'What doorway?'

'It is created. The vessel is a doorway.'

Somehow, that made sense to Sally. She thought about the times she had stared at UV One, and how it had shown her things she didn't understand. Now she realised she had been staring through into another universe. 'You've been there, haven't you?'

Mikhail nodded.

'What's it like on the other side?'

Mikhail opened his mouth and then shut it. 'I — I can't really describe it,' he said eventually. 'Not with these words.'

'Can you take me there and show me?'

The question made Mikhail look frightened. 'No! I can't take you, it's much too dangerous. I wouldn't know where I was going — we'd get lost for certain.'

Sally took Mikhail's wide-eyed expression as a signal to move on. She finished packing up and went to the Cupola to take pictures, a hobby that she'd discovered during her research a week ago and found to be quite therapeutic. She had never been interested in photography on Earth, but on Earth she didn't have a view like the one she had now. She tracked a cloud formation before snapping it as it passed over India.

'Do you think humans are supposed to be in space?' she asked as she framed another shot.

'What do you mean?' Mikhail said, looking out the window. 'Ooh, there's an interesting cloud just about to reach Oman — look.'

Sally aimed her camera at Oman and clicked. 'You're right. It looks a bit like a dog, doesn't it? What I mean is, should humans be in space at all or are we taking things too far? For example, we can't breathe out here and we'd die pretty quick in a vacuum, so should we be floating around up here at all?'

'I think the question is, *why not*?' Mikhail said. 'Exploration is the path to discovery — surely you agree with that?'

Sally lowered her camera. She was exploring a thought that had been bugging her for a long time, from way before she had come to the station. It seemed insignificant, but she needed to air it and get it out of her system. 'Everything we humans touch, we break. Put it this way — we don't play well with others. Surely venturing into space is just going to give us more opportunity to ruin things on an inter-planetary scale.'

Mikhail chuckled, which annoyed Sally.

'What's so funny?'

'I'm sorry,' Mikhail said, 'but you sound like you're talking about an adolescent.'

At first Sally was going to tell Mikhail what a ridiculous notion that was, but when she thought about it, it made surprising sense. 'I suppose I pretty much am. An adolescent species that doesn't care if what it does affects others, destroys eco-systems and pollutes on a global scale.'

'But how does an adolescent learn? By being locked in at home, away from everything? Or out in the big, wide world?'

Sally knew the answer, but was too stubborn to say it.

'Mankind needs room to grow, to learn,' Mikhail continued, 'to become wiser. Sure, it might break a few things on the way, but soon enough, it will understand. And when it does, it will become greater than you can ever imagine.'

'How do you know this?'

'I've seen it.'

'So why can't whoever has opened this doorway just tell us how to grow up?'

Mikhail laughed again, but this time Sally didn't get annoyed. She could see there was no ridicule in his humour.

'Have you ever tried to tell an adolescent what to do?'

Sally tittered. 'I suppose you're right.'

'But you can always give them a push in the right direction.'

'Is that why you're helping me?'

'I suppose so.'

'How much more will you help me?'

'Enough. Just enough.'

Chapter 24

'Like I said in the notes, detective, we found traces of skin on the knuckles of the deceased's right hand.'

Banin sighed. He hated dealing with these white-coated nerds. 'Why have you only found it now?'

'Look, we only get a short amount of time to look over a body. We didn't find anything, he goes to the morgue. But then we get a phone call from head office telling us to have another look, so we do.'

And Banin had to somehow pin it to this Aleks Dezhurov person, whoever he was. Fingers crossed it would be *his* skin on the corpse's fist. 'Have you got a match yet?'

'I wish it were that simple, detective. We're running a sample through the database now. We could get an answer in a week or we could get one today. Or not at all. It's pot luck.'

'Fine, whatever. Just let me know when you get a match.'

'I will.'

Banin mumbled his thanks and left the room. As he climbed the stairs out of the basement — which smelled like hospitals — back up to his office, his mind whirled with questions, mainly: *why me?*

'Abram,' he said as he passed his junior's desk, 'go door-to-door to all the bars within five miles of the Ryumin crash and check if there was a brawl on the night of his death.'

'Yessir,' Abram said.

'And Abram?'

'Yes sir?'

'Do it quickly.'

Abram grabbed his coat from the back of his chair and left immediately. It made Banin smile to know that at least it wouldn't be him getting a soaking this time. He flumped into his chair, and as soon as he did, his phone rang.

'Banin.'

'The results have just come through for the DNA search.'

'Really?'

'I said it was pot luck, and you got lucky.'

'Okay, shoot.' *Please be Aleks, please be Aleks.*

'Well, that's the sticking point. I can't tell you.'

'I thought you said you'd got a match?'

'I did. But it's classified.'

'Classified?'

'Yes. US Department of Defense level one. That's their top clearance level.'

'Holy shit … alright, thanks,' Banin said, and hung up. He lifted the receiver again and dialled the Chief's extension. His secretary answered.

'Hello, Chief Inspector Azurov's office, how may I help you?'

'It's Banin. Can you put me through, please?'

'Sure thing. But I don't know why you don't just come in person. We're only the floor up from you.'

'I have a hernia,' Banin lied.

'For fifteen years?'

'Just put me through.'

'No need to be a grumpy so-and-so. I'll put you through now.'

Thank goodness, Banin thought.

'Azurov.'

'It's Banin.'

'Banin — why don't you just come up here instead of calling me?'

'I get that a lot. I have a hernia.'

'No you don't. What can I do for you?'

'Forensics matched the DNA.'

'To who?'

'Don't know. Classified. US Department of Defense.'

'Shit, really?'

'Really.'

'Shit.'

'I know.'

Azurov sighed. 'Okay, let's get this mess sorted,' he said. 'Give the US embassy a call and get this one out the door before it blows up in our faces.'

'I'd be glad to.'

'See that you are.'

Banin put the phone down, then picked it up again and dialled another number. The phone rang for a while, then the dial tone changed and it rang a while longer.

'US embassy, good morning,' a cheery voice said.

'Hello,' Banin said in his best English. 'I'm calling from the Moscow City Police. We have a case that I think you might be interested in.'

The conversation didn't go as well as he'd hoped. After a lot of waiting, transfers and more waiting, the embassy decided that the US government would neither take ownership of the case, nor reveal state secrets and identify the classified DNA, which meant he was stuck. With any luck, Abram would call with some good news. Four hours later, following a fruitless desk search for Aleks Dezhurov's latest whereabouts, Abram *did* call.

'Banin.'

'Hi, sir, it's Abram — I've got something here you should probably take a look at.'

'On my way.'

* * *

Sally couldn't sleep. Her mind whirled with thought, about Mikhail, about John Heisenberg — god, the last time she'd seen him seemed a lifetime ago, even if it was just a few months back. She felt as though her brain couldn't shut off until she'd made sense of everything, but for some reason, she couldn't. She shifted in her floating sleeping bag, trying to find a spot that would let her release her conscious and drift off, but no matter which way she turned, her brain would not shut up.

Wriggling from the cotton cocoon, she pulled on a vest and shorts and climbed out of her quarters. The lights were dim, and she paddled herself in the direction of something to eat. A hot chocolate, too. As she passed Mikhail's quarters, she heard a sound that made her skin prickle. It was a low gurgle, a glottal noise that seemed almost inhuman. It was coming from inside, and she waited, listening. The noises didn't stop so, hesitantly at first, she unzipped the door. Inside, Mikhail had knitted himself into a tight ball of limbs, and his face was contorted with agony. He writhed without warning, and Sally jumped, backing away from him as he thrashed in his sleep. She could hear his teeth grinding together, and that noise, that horrible, throaty noise continued to seep from his mouth. Summoning all her nerve, she grabbed him and shook him hard.

'Mikhail,' she said. 'Wake up, Mikhail.'

He struggled against her grip, eyes still shut, but she clung on and shook harder.

'Wake up, Mikhail!' she yelled, and with a sudden convulsion, he did. He looked around in sudden jerks, his eyes wide with fright. When their eyes met he blinked, and normality fell upon him once more.

'Sally …' he whispered. 'I thought I heard you calling. Are you okay?'

He was shiny with sweat and his veins pulsed under his skin. Sally's heart calmed to see him acting normal again, and to no longer hear that blood-curdling noise.

'You were in pain,' she said. 'I had to wake you. Was it another dream?'

Mikhail nodded. He wiped his forehead, slicking his fingers back through his hair. 'I'm so hot,' he said, and Sally reached out to cup his brow.

'God, you're burning up,' she said, alarmed. 'Let me get you a damp towel to get your temperature down.'

When she returned Mikhail was looking a little better. She dabbed his head and cheeks, and he shut his eyes.

'What did you dream about?' she asked as she leaned forward to run the towel around the back of his neck.

'I don't know,' Mikhail said, eyes still shut. He screwed his face up and shook his head, looking on the brink of tears. 'I can't keep doing this …'

'Is there anything I can do?' Sally asked, and Mikhail opened his eyes. Their faces were inches apart, so close that she could feel his warm breath on her lips.

'You're already doing everything,' he said, and before Sally even knew what was happening, she was kissing him.

* * *

This is going to kill me if it doesn't make me insane, the Director of the Baikonur Cosmodrome thought as he surveyed the Kazakhstani desert, the skies above it as topaz as he'd ever seen them. Another launch re-scheduled, another change of mission and another ridiculous deadline. He had a right mind to make a complaint, for the sake of the safety of his team, but the American — Bales — had been as clear this time as he had been the last. Despite his sleep deprivation, the Director remembered the phone call word for word, as clear as if he were having it face-to-face right there and then.

'You want *what*?' he'd said, feeling his knees weaken as Bales' words sank in.

'I know it's last minute and I apologise, but the situation has changed and the mission needs to change with it. A specialist has been forced to return, and we need to get someone else up there as soon as we can. I have the people — I need you to build me the rocket. Can you do that for me?'

'Well,' the Director had said, his mind torn in two, 'we're not far off a scheduled resupply, so I suppose it *is* possible —'

'That's exactly what I wanted to hear, thank you. Don't think this effort will go ignored, because it won't. The fate of a lot of people rests on this.'

And then he was gone.

The Director watched the gantry preparations as he recalled the conversation over and over in his head. He knew it wasn't his business to question the goings on of his superiors, and he knew that NASA had the best interests of the station and its crew at heart, but he couldn't help but feel that something was off. Nevertheless, the preparations for Soyuz TMA Eleven M pushed on, drawing closer and closer to completion. He squashed the nagging feeling back down again as a cool wind blew in across the expansive launch site, bringing with it the fine sand of the desert. Shielding his eyes, he retreated from the observation balcony and back into the protection of the Cosmodrome. Only one more day of this and it would be done.

* * *

Banin pulled up alongside a rough-looking bar just outside of the Moscow city limits, a place only two miles from the crash site. The neon sign — which buzzed in what Banin thought was a painfully stereotypical way — said: *The West House*. He'd heard of The West House before, and the stories didn't exactly fill him with glee. This was the place to come if you wanted to hide from someone — or just plain hide someone. Someone usually dead. There was a cruiser already parked outside, and leaning on it, waiting for him, was Abram.

'Thanks for coming, sir,' Abram said, walking with Banin to the bar's entrance. 'I think I found just what you're looking for.'

They went in, and Abram led Banin to the bar, behind which a stout, ugly man wearing a dirty shirt and overalls was standing.

'This is Ruslan, Ruslan Vasnetsov. He's the owner.'

'Hello, Mr. Vasnetsov,' said Banin, offering his hand, which Vasnetsov didn't take. Banin retracted it again. 'Right. So, what do you know?'

'I know lots of things, officer.'

This was going to be difficult. Banin gritted his teeth and told himself to stay calm. 'I'm not an officer. I'm a detective. What do you know about the night that my friend here' — he gestured to Abram, — 'has been asking you about?'

'I know there was a fight.'

'Good. Tell me more.'

'There's always fights here, and you boys don't show up most times.'

'I'm sorry about that, Mr. Vasnetsov, but we're very overworked and understaffed —'

'I get robbed nearly every month and you boys don't do anything.'

Banin took a breath and mentally counted to ten. 'Well, we're here now. So what can you tell me about this fight?'

'Well, it wasn't much of a fight. Just a punch. This old boy shows up for a drink like he does every night, and then about a hour or so after, a whole bunch of Americans came in and rounded on him.'

Vasnetsov now had Banin's full attention. 'Americans?'

'That's right. They were in smart suits — about four of them I think — and they were questioning him for a while. They didn't even sit down, let alone buy a drink.'

'So when did the punch happen?'

'Be easier if I show you.'

'You have CCTV?'

Vasnetsov snorted. 'Of course I do. How else am I going to get you police to do anything when you finally start paying attention to me?'

He had a point, Banin thought, but he didn't fancy arguing the toss with him right now, so he bit his tongue and followed him around to the back, to a small, dirty room with an old TV and VHS player, and a stack of tapes.

'I've got all my tapes labelled and I store them in the cupboard there,' Vasnetsov said, pointing to a bulging piece of flat-pack furniture. 'I've got the one you want all lined up and ready.'

He turned the TV on, and once the static had settled, there was a picture. It was the bar, as seen from above, in soft black and white. In the top right hand corner of the frame there was a man on his own having a drink. Lev Ryumin.

'Watch,' Vasnetsov said.

Sure enough, four men entered the bar and walked straight over to Ryumin. They all looked distinctly American, crew cuts and wide jaws, and the one taking the lead seemed familiar to Banin.

'Abram,' he said, 'you recognise that guy? The one with the white hair?'

Abram squinted at the fuzzy picture, then nodded. 'Yeah — I saw him on the news. He's the RFSA Flight Director.'

'Doesn't look Russian to me,' Banin muttered.

'He's not,' Vasnetsov said, tapping the screen, 'he's American to the bone. I'd recognise that accent anywhere.'

Vasnetsov pressed the fast-forward button, and the picture sped up, taking on a strange, leaning distortion. The Americans had stayed with Ryumin for over fifteen minutes by the time Vasnetsov pressed play again. On the screen, Ryumin leaped up from his chair and squared up against the white-haired American, who backed up a step and held up his hands, as if turning down the confrontation. Ryumin staggered, then took a clumsy swing that the white-haired man easily deflected with his hand.

'There's our DNA,' Banin mumbled to himself.

Caught off balance, Ryumin tumbled to the ground. Using a bar stool, he hoisted himself up, then after making a rude gesture at the Americans, he left. The Americans talked to each other for a minute, then followed.

'That's all I've got,' Vasnetsov said, stopping the tape.

'You don't have any cameras outside?' Banin asked.

'Outside? There's enough crap happening inside for me to worry about what happens outside.'

Fair enough, Banin thought. 'Okay, Mr. Vasnetsov, you've been very helpful. Thank you for your time.'

Banin made a move to leave, but Vasnetsov grabbed his arm.

'Wait! What about my tapes? What about the other crimes?'

Banin yanked his arm from Vasnetsov's grip. 'I'll send an officer down to collect the evidence — tell *him* about it.' Then he walked out the room with Abram following, leaving Vasnetsov grumbling to himself.

'Look's like we've got ourselves a motive,' Abram said, struggling to keep up with Banin's quick strides.

'It looks that way,' Banin said, but he wasn't convinced. Why would these people, these Americans, come and visit Ryumin in a grotty bar in the middle of nowhere? And why would they try to kill him? And who was the white-haired man? The TV said he was RFSA, but his DNA said he was US government. And where the hell did Aleks Dezhurov fit into all this? It made no sense, none of it did. Whatever was going on had got under Banin's skin, and he needed to work it back out again. There was no backing out now.

'Shit,' he muttered to himself.

* * *

When Sean came to, it was pitch black. It was also hot, close, and there was a musty smell in the air. He struggled, but he was bound with his hands behind him to a post with what felt like rope. A thin crack of sunlight beamed in ahead of him. Everything was quiet.

* * *

'Did Sean say when he was going to be back?'

Aleks peered through the blinds, watching cars trailing by at the end of the road, hoping one of them had Sean in it.

'No, he didn't,' Novitskiy said as he read the morning paper.

Aleks left the blinds and returned to pacing the room. 'He can't have meant to be gone for this long. It doesn't feel right.'

'It's only been a day,' Grigory said from the kitchen. He was cracking eggs into a frying pan, which filled the room with a loud sizzling. 'He was gone longer than that last time.'

That much was true, but he *had* gone to America, not half an hour down the road. Aleks wandered back to the blinds to look through them again. 'I think something's wrong,' he said.

Novitskiy threw his paper on the table. 'Well what do you suggest we do? He didn't say where he was going, what he was doing, and probably for good reason.'

'But, he's just a kid …'

'He's not just a kid,' Novitskiy said. 'He may look like one, but he's not. He can look after himself.' He retrieved his newspaper and shook it back open.

In a flash decision, Aleks grabbed his jacket and walked to the door. 'I'm going out.'

'You won't find him,' Novitskiy said from behind his paper.

'What about your eggs?' Aleks heard Grigory shout as he shut the door behind him.

Something didn't feel right, not at all. Something felt very wrong, in fact. Novitskiy was correct about one thing: Sean wasn't just a kid, and so far he'd managed to keep himself out of trouble. Whatever it was he was doing, he'd missed something, been caught out. Aleks needed to find him before he landed in real trouble, if he hadn't already.

He started Grigory's truck and turned it around. He waited, engine running and road open ahead of him, frozen in his seat. Novitskiy was right about another thing: what *could* he do? He slapped the steering wheel out of frustration, and the horn gave a pathetic honk. He knew *exactly* what he needed to do, even if he didn't want to admit it to himself. It was simple: he had to go to the police. It was going to be suicide. He was a wanted man, but a lifetime in prison without the blood of the innocent on his hands was far more preferable than freedom and the weight of a guilty conscience. At least, that's how he felt right at that moment; before he had a chance to change his mind, he put the truck into gear and set off for Moscow.

Chapter 25

The Director of the Baikonur Cosmodrome gave himself a mental pat on the back. They'd done it again, and he watched the last few wisps of trailing smoke dissipate with a sense of pride and satisfaction. It had been touch and go, but the deadline had been met and TMA Eleven M had left the ground without fault. The whole thing did, however, leave him feeling twenty years his senior.

'I'm getting too old for this,' he muttered to himself.

* * *

Sally dreamed that she was on a boat, lost at sea. There was a storm, and the waves crashed higher and higher around her, rocking the boat, tossing her from side to side. The waves rose over the edge of the hull, falling as foam around her, on her, soaking her to the bone. But the water was warm, and it caressed her, folding around her in soothing blankets that gave her a feeling deep inside that was wonderfully comforting. She felt safe.

She awoke in Mikhail's arms, and she savoured the warmth of his breath on the back of her neck until she could no longer ignore the complaints of her bladder. She slid free of Mikhail's gentle grasp, unzipped his quarters enough to slip through, zipped it shut again and took herself to the toilet, giggling as she enjoyed the feeling of weightlessness for the first time since she'd arrived — she really was walking on air.

Finished, she floated on down to the galley to fix herself some breakfast. She was hungry, and her stomach gurgled as she heated up some honeyed porridge. She wasn't normally a porridge fan, but today she fancied it. It wasn't long before the pouch of steaming paste was emptied, consumed with a gusto usually reserved for quiet nights in with ice cream and a good movie. Pouch deposited in the waste disposal, she decided that she would go down into the MLM and have another look at UV One. It had been a while since she had last been down there, and her intrigue piqued at the thought of seeing it again.

Swooping down the tunnel and into the ball at the end, she spun and cushioned her deceleration with her bare feet, bringing herself to a stop with graceful agility. She smiled: her control in a weightless environment was improving day on day, and it was very satisfying to pull off a complicated manoeuvre like that one. When she got back to Earth, walking would be boring by comparison. At the reminder of Earth, which was glowing bright through the window, her thoughts turned to Novitskiy, Gardner and Chris. She hoped they had got home safe, and that Gardner and Chris were recovering well. The pathetic state of those three as they had left saddened her, and she looked beyond Earth to the lifeless craft floating on the black sea.

'What is it you're looking for?' she whispered to herself.

She almost expected a response and felt a little disappointed to receive none. UV One, its colourless surface catching the light of the occasional star, shimmered dully, a distant reflection in an interstellar puddle. Perhaps it was a dead relic, floating without aim through the cosmos, searching for life and trying to communicate its pre-recorded message. The beings that created it could be — and probably were — long dead; perhaps even the whole species was gone. This singular vessel could be all that was left of an extinct race, a drifting artefact of a once-great civilisation. She reached out to touch it, pressing her finger on the glass, covering it. When she lifted her finger away, it was still there, still following. She sighed.

At once, a bloodcurdling scream filled the station, and then it was gone.

'Mikhail …'

Sally pushed off the floor and shot up the tunnel, crashing into the wall at the other end. She scrambled forwards, building momentum to get back to the crew quarters as fast as she could, snatching for handholds to pull herself along with. As she entered the Destiny lab, she could see that that Mikhail's quarters were still shut, and as she reached it she hurried to pull the zipper open. As the door flapped down, a small globule of blood floated out, and she clapped her hand over her mouth as the sight filled her with terror and revulsion. Mikhail was contorted into a scarcely believable position, his eyes rolled back into their sockets, his ears and nose leaking globular blood into the cramped quarters; there was little white surface left uncovered with red.

'Mikhail!' Sally screamed, and began unfastening him from his sleeping bag. He writhed, blood spraying from his nose. Sally pushed him back against the wall to keep him still, wrestling with the sleeping bag as her heart threatened to leap out of her chest. Once he was free, she towed him to the medical bay at the end of the module. He thrashed some more, but in the short time it took her to reach the vertical stretcher and to start strapping him to it, he had gone limp, his eyes shut.

'Come on, Mikhail, hold on …' she whispered, pulling the last few Velcro tabs tight. She struggled to find his pulse, which she then realised was because he almost didn't have one. The blood flow seemed to have stopped and his skin was turning grey. Sally felt for his pulse again; now it had gone completely. Without wasting a moment, she ripped into the first aid container and retrieved the compact defibrillator. Peeling the backing off the electrode pads, she stuck them down, thinking back to the first aid part of her brief training. She thought she was doing it right. God, she hoped it was right. Taking a deep breath, she thumbed the button, and Mikhail jolted against the stretcher's straps. She felt for his pulse — still nothing. Pressing the button again, Mikhail jolted, but this time with less energy. Again she felt for his pulse, but still there was nothing.

'Come on!' she yelled, tears filling her eyes.

She thumped the button, and a tremor shot through Mikhail's body. He thrashed against the stretcher violently enough to start peeling the Velcro apart. He spluttered, thrashed some more, and went limp. Sally watched him, her breath held. She didn't want to watch, but she couldn't turn away.

'Eaurghhh …' Mikhail moaned, opening his eyes. 'What — what's happening?'

Sally could feel herself quivering. She spoke, but the words came out distant, like they weren't hers. 'It's fine. You're fine. There's nothing to worry about.'

Mikhail looked at the blood down his front, and his eyes widened. 'Oh my god,' he whispered, wiping it with a finger and watching it glisten on the tip.

'I'm so glad you're okay,' Sally said, clasping her hands around his. She tried to smile in a reassuring way to comfort him, to help her believe what she was saying, but she couldn't hold back the hot pressure pushing against her eyes. She never, ever cried, but seeing Mikhail like this brought tears quicker than she had ever thought possible. She wiped them away, still trying to smile, but they just kept coming. Mikhail looked frail, weak; almost as though he'd aged a decade overnight. Now her tears were in full flow, and she buried her face in his chest and sobbed.

* * *

Everything about Aleks was numb as he pushed open the door to the Moscow Police Department headquarters. He washed through the entrance lobby in a haze of immediacy, his thundering heart sapping his senses of clarity. People were looking at him, stopping their conversations and watching him pass, he was sure of it. He could feel it. Or perhaps he was being paranoid. He stopped at the reception desk, where the receptionist smiled at him.

'Can I help you?' she said, either unaware of who he was or uncaring.

'Yes,' Aleks croaked. He coughed, dislodging the uncomfortable sweat that had formed on the back on his throat. 'Yes. I need to speak to an officer about the International Space Station.'

The receptionist's smile wavered, her eyes narrowing a fraction. 'Okay ... one moment please,' she said, reaching for her desk phone.

'Say it's about Ryumin. Lev Ryumin. I have information about him.'

This seemed to strike some sort of chord with the receptionist, because her eyes lit up and her hand retracted from the phone. 'Oh, of course. You need to speak to Detective Inspector Banin. He's out at the moment, but he'll be back soon. If you go to the second floor, his desk is the third on the right. You can wait for him there.'

Aleks nodded his appreciation and quickly made his way upstairs, feeling like he'd somehow broken a serious law by doing so. He was a wanted man, and here he was, making his way to the desk of the person who was trying to apprehend him. He sat down in front of it, feeling awkward, and focused on the things scattered about on top, avoiding the questioning looks he assumed people were directing his way. Aside from the usual stationary and equipment, there was a picture of a young dark-haired boy he presumed was Banin's son. It seemed that even the boy in the photo was glaring at him with accusing eyes. He scanned the room, and the people working continued uninterrupted, unaware of his presence.

'You must be Aleks,' a hardened voice said, snapping him from his thoughts. Aleks looked to see a short, stocky man holding out his hand.

'Yes, that's right,' he said, standing and shaking the offered hand. He was acutely aware that he hadn't shared his name with the receptionist, even though this man had just used it.

'I'm Banin,' Banin said, shedding his coat and throwing it over the desk. 'I understand you have some information for me.'

'Uh, yes — I do.' Aleks was quite taken aback by Banin's distinct disinterest in him. 'How do you know my name?'

'I've been looking for you.'

'So you know what they say about me?'

'I do.'

'It's not true, you know.'

'I know.'

Aleks couldn't quite believe what he was hearing. 'I'm sorry ... what did you say?'

Banin gave a casual shrug of his shoulders, dismissing Aleks' crime as though it were a mere practical joke. 'I know it wasn't you. As soon as I got the call I had a gut feeling it wasn't you, but I've been thinking about it more, and now I'm certain. You've been set up. I've seen it happen before. You must have really pissed someone off.'

Aleks felt a distant glimmer of hope. 'How do you know that?'

'I've been in this business a long time,' Banin said, 'and I know better than anybody that sometimes the obviously guilty are innocent, and the obviously innocent are guilty. I took the liberty of making a few calls; I found out the person who put the price on your head works in the same department as someone whose DNA I'm trying to trace.'

'Okay,' Aleks said, not really following, but still grateful not to be cuffed and dragged away to the cells.

Banin sat down, then fished a notepad out of his pocket and unthreaded a pencil from its binder. He gestured for Aleks to sit with him. 'Please,' he said. 'So — what do you know?'

Aleks sat. 'I know that John Bales killed Lev Ryumin.'

Banin frowned. 'Bales … why do I know that name?'

He snapped his fingers. 'He's the one that called head office about you. *He's* the one that put the price on your head. I wonder … what does he look like?'

'White hair, broad shoulders —'

'The guy in the CCTV video.'

Aleks didn't follow. 'What video?'

'Doesn't matter. Let's just say that Ryumin was mixed up with some seriously top-level American government shit.'

'The US Department of Defense, you mean?'

Banin stopped writing notes and raised an eyebrow at Aleks. 'You know about that?'

'Yeah. Bales is a Major General.'

'Shiiiiit,' Banin muttered, throwing his pencil on the table. 'This gets better and better.'

'They're running a covert cover-up operation, and Ryumin got in the way. Knew too much. That's why they killed him.'

Banin was shaking his head. 'What kind of cover-up?'

It was at this point that Aleks was overcome by embarrassment at the ridiculousness of it all. He cleared his throat, readying his mouth to say the words his brain begged him not to.

'Aliens.'

* * *

Sally had been in love once before, or at least she thought she had. She had lied to Mikhail: it was *she* who had asked John Heisenberg on a date, and it was *he* who had turned her down. She had loved him from afar, and when she revealed her weakness for him he had brushed her aside as if she were nothing. The days and weeks afterwards were what she remembered the most. If she tried, she could just about remember what it had been like to love him before, when he was pure and untainted, but the feeling of having her soul torn in two stung her heart with vivid tenacity even now. It was a feeling she never wanted to replicate, a feeling even stronger than the one she'd felt at the passing of her parents. She could understand her grief when they died, and accepted it as part of a natural process. But she hadn't wanted to fall in love with John Heisenberg, and that made the heartache afterwards a confusing and agonising experience. Since then, men and women were merely colleagues, acquaintances. The door to her heart remained tight shut, her emotions sealed away from the weathering intensity of human contact. It had never been so much as ajar — until now.

She watched Mikhail through the open door of his quarters as he slept, as he twitched and frowned. He wasn't a handsome man, but he had a charm that warmed her, made her smile, and she couldn't help but bathe herself in it at every opportunity. Unwittingly, he had thrown the door to her heart wide open, leaving the inner workings bare and exposed, and with the tentative caution of a new-born foal, she relished it. Mikhail stirred, blinking himself awake, and when he saw Sally watching him, he grinned.

'You don't need to keep watch,' he said, levering himself from his quarters. 'I'll be fine.'

'I don't want you getting hurt,' Sally said. And she meant it. She still felt guilty for leaving him to suffer for as long as she did the first time.

'That's very kind of you.'

Sally drifted over to him. His dark eyes followed her.

'Can I get you any breakfast?' she asked. 'I can bring it to you here if you like — breakfast in bed.'

Mikhail laughed. 'Okay — that would be nice, thank you.'

Sally was close to him, daring herself to get closer, feeling every digit of each hand and foot tingling with his proximity. It was a new sensation, and it made her feel more alive than she'd ever felt before. He watched her as she watched him, and she ducked in quick, kissing him on the cheek. She had pulled away before he had time to react, her heart beating like a drum, skin fizzing with anticipation.

'See you in a minute,' she said, feeling her face flush with heat.

They shared breakfast together, eating and talking and laughing between mouthfuls of sticky porridge, and she told him the story of how she had come to be interested in science.

'After my mother died,' she began, sinking her thoughts back to her cloudy and muddled youth, 'I began to question life. What *was* life? What was the point of it? Why did we have to endure it, generation after generation?'

'Deep thoughts for a six-year-old.'

'Tell me about it. Anyway, I had come to the conclusion that a deity was just too far-fetched, left too many holes. I couldn't understand why a god would allow us to live just so that we might suffer for our entire existence before snuffing it.'

Mikhail nodded, watching her as she spoke.

'But I could see that we weren't the only ones suffering. I saw a documentary about the plains of Africa, and I remember struggling with the idea that the antelope seemed to exist solely for the lions to eat. I couldn't fathom why all the animals didn't just eat vegetables. Of course, back then I didn't realise that plants were just as much a living cellular structure as the things that ate them, but you can see my train of thought.

'And then it struck me — for every living thing, there's another, bigger, smarter and stronger than it. From the smallest plant to the biggest mammal, there was a distinct hierarchy that culminated with us humans.'

She nodded to herself, feeling that her pre-adolescent thoughts were as valid now as when they were free of the corruption of adulthood.

'I began to understand why people chose to believe in god,' she continued. 'With so much that we don't know, there must be something above us in the hierarchy — something we couldn't understand, just as the antelope doesn't understand why the lion eats it. That's when I decided that I wanted to find that being, trace the hierarchy to the next level, and it's what I've been searching for ever since.'

She looked at Mikhail sitting in front of her, hanging on her every word.

'And I think that's what I've found.'

Mikhail didn't say anything, looking down at his half-eaten porridge.

'You haven't finished?' Sally said. 'Are you okay?'

'I'm not really hungry.'

'How are you feeling?'

Mikhail looked at her, his face hollow, his eyes sad. 'I'm fine,' he said, but she knew he was lying.

Sally took his food pouch, set it aside and burrowed in under his arm, and there they floated, not sharing so much as a word with each other for several long, blissful minutes.

'You're right, you know,' Mikhail said out of the blue.

Sally looked up at him from underneath his arm. 'About what?'

'About everything. Life, the universe — me.'

'I wish you could tell me all about it.'

'I wish I could too, but even if I think of it, it …' he trailed off, his last words sounding pained.

Sally wrapped her arm around his back and squeezed him. 'Don't think about it,' she said. 'Don't.'

'There will be someone one day who can, someone who can share the secrets of the universe with you.'

Sally smiled. 'I hope I get to meet them,' she said.

'I expect you will.'

Chapter 26

'Hello?' Sean yelled, his voice hoarse, but still no one came. He had seen shadows flit past the crack of light, but he wasn't sure if they were people or just plants moving in the wind. He was thirsty — very thirsty — and the stench of urine continued to shamefully remind him that he hadn't been able to hold on long enough. His wrists were raw from pulling against his bindings, but the pain was almost numb to him now. He was sure they were loosening; he would try again soon. He'd also discovered he could slide up the post into a standing-up position, but for the moment he sat as he yelled for help and tried to wriggle free. No matter what happened, he couldn't give up. He *wouldn't* give up.

'Hello?' he yelled again.

* * *

Banin drummed the desk with his fingers, shaking his head. 'Aliens?'

'I know it seems far-fetched,' Aleks said, sensing the tangible incredulity in Banin's tone, 'but it's true, I swear it.'

'Aliens?' Banin repeated.

'Okay, forget the aliens —'

'Forget the aliens?'

'Forget the aliens. There's something in space that Bales is trying to destroy, and he won't stop at anything to do it.'

'Uh huh. And what's that got to do with me?'

'He's wiping out anyone that stands in his way.'

Aleks searched Banin's face for any sign that he was getting through to him, but he wasn't sure. 'And that includes Lev Ryumin. But worse, I think Bales is going to do it again.'

'To who?'

'A journalist called Sean Jacob.'

Banin sighed a long, drawn out sigh, and held his hands up in defeat. 'It sounds like I've barely scratched the surface of this crazy picture,' he said, 'but I've got a case to solve and you're the only clue left.'

A little prickle of flame leaped in Aleks' chest. 'So what now?' he asked.

'We find Bales.'

Before Aleks could ask, *But how do we do that?,* Banin was on the phone.

'Hi, can you get a twenty-four hour ANPR scan of all government vehicles — foreign included — and let me know the results, please? Thanks.'

He hung up.

'We have a list of all the diplomatic vehicles and their registrations,' he explained to Aleks. 'Run that through our number plate recognition cameras around the city and we can get a rough idea of where those vehicles are and where they're going. It's not fool-proof, but it's a start.'

The phone rang.

'Banin. Uh huh. Okay. Yep. Thanks.'

'That was quick,' Alex said after Banin hung up.

'It's all digital now,' Banin replied, waking his computer with a wiggle of the mouse. 'I'll print it off.'

He went to fetch the printouts, holding a thick wad of paper on his return. Each page had a map with circles on it, some numbered and some greyed out, and underneath each map was a list of information.

'Here,' said Banin, handing Aleks half the wad and a pen. 'Each page is a different vehicle, and each circle is a camera. The numbered circles correspond with an ANPR trigger, and the time of the trigger is listed below. The greyed out circles are cameras that haven't been triggered. Trace the route on each map and make a note of any extended stops, plus the time the vehicle passed its last camera. This is a week's worth of data, so look out for suspicious vehicle behaviour — frequent journeys out of town, spending a long time in a single location, that sort of thing.'

Aleks did as he was told. Most of the vehicles didn't seem to have moved at all in the last week. Some had been out into central Moscow and back a few times. All fairly normal. Others had left Moscow completely, and a few of those had not yet returned. That last set of vehicles was the one Aleks piled up separately. By the time they were finished, that pile contained seven vehicles.

'Right then,' said Banin, leafing through the sheets. 'This one is a prison van, so I doubt it's going to be that … this is the Mayor's car — I doubt he has anything to do with this …'

He continued to read through the sheets, stopping at the last. 'Hmm …' he said, brow wrinkled in thought.

'What?' said Aleks, leaning over the desk to see.

'This is an imported US vehicle, and it seems to have passed one ANPR camera along the highway south out of Moscow, but not the next one a mile later. It must have pulled off at these warehouses and stopped. That was half-an-hour ago.'

'That could be him.'

Banin nodded, still looking over the print out. 'I think you might be right.'

'Shall we go check it out?'

'Whoa there—since when did you become the partner I never wanted?'

'It's either that or you arrest me, because if you leave me here I'm straight out the door. You'll never see me again.'

Folding the paper and putting it in his pocket, Banin grumbled to himself as he eyeballed Aleks.

'Fine,' he said at last. He stood, grabbed his jacket, and beckoned Aleks to follow. As they walked back down the stairs, Banin adjusted his pistol holster, stopping at a landing halfway down a floor.

'Let me tell you something before we step outside into the free world,' he said. 'You're under my supervision and, like you so eloquently put, you should be in bracelets, so if you even think of making a run for it I'll shoot you deader than dead.'

Banin may have been shorter than Aleks, but that didn't make him any less frightening.

'Understood,' Aleks said, holding his hands up in submission. 'After all, I came here to you in the first place, didn't I?'

'Yes. I suppose you did. But that doesn't change anything.'

Banin started down the stairs again, then stopped, turning back to Aleks, finger pointing. 'And if I find out this story is a bunch of bull, I'll shoot you dead for that, too.'

Aleks swallowed and nodded. 'Sure …'

'Good. Let's go.'

They climbed into Banin's rusted car and set off at breakneck pace. It seemed that Banin knew his way around a steering wheel like he did the backstreets of

Moscow. The back tyres squealed as Banin hurled the car around another tight corner, dodging a lorry coming the other way that honked at him. Banin gave his hidden lights and siren a short blast and the lorry stopped its honking.

'Idiot …' Banin muttered.

Aleks stayed quiet, thinking it best not to correct Banin on his understanding of right of way. They peeled away from the city and onto the freeway, which shot bullet-straight due south and into the countryside. Bridges whipped overhead, Banin pushing the old car far beyond any kind of comfortable — or legal — limit, blasting his siren at any car dawdling in front. Aside from the roar of the wind and engine, the journey was a silent one, Aleks quite happy not to distract Banin from his frightening speed. As late morning became early afternoon and the clouds rolled in, Banin took an exit off the highway that turned into a overgrown, bumpy track.

'This seems pretty secluded,' he said, and Aleks silently agreed with his observation.

Ahead, a pack of dilapidated warehouses came into view, the corrugated sheet walls flaking with rust. A large sign hung over the road, peeling to the point of near-indecipherability. It seemed to indicate the warehouses were once home to a car assembly plant.

'I'll park up here and we'll walk in,' Banin said, pulling up behind a small shed. He turned the car so it was facing the exit and killed the engine. When they got out, Aleks noticed how quiet the place was — eerie even. The rush of the motorway they had left not a few minutes ago was made silent by the crest of the hill between them and it. Rusted shells, stacked up on top of one another, were dotted about the open space, memorials of a dead industry. Grass sprouted from between bricks and through concrete, the consuming power of nature swallowing this abandoned place up whole.

Following Banin, Aleks crept towards the first warehouse. As they approached it, they saw a black SUV parked up around the corner of what looked to be an old paint shed. Banin nodded at the SUV, drew his pistol, and they moved on. The warehouse door was ajar and, indicating to Aleks to stay outside, Banin slipped into the shadow. Aleks waited several long moments before he returned, shaking his head.

'No one's here.'

They continued their sombre tour of the car graveyard, Banin checking every warehouse, each time coming back empty-handed, until they reached a chain-link fence at the far perimeter. Banin holstered his pistol, looking out at the hilly fields beyond.

'This place is deserted,' he said. 'They must have been here at some point, but they sure as shit aren't here now.'

'Why did they leave the car here?'

Banin shrugged. 'Probably to throw us off the trail.' He turned his back to the fields. 'We should go. We don't have a warrant to be here.'

Aleks wanted to stay, to look some more, but deep down he knew there was no point. There really was no one here. Dejected, he turned to follow Banin, who had already begun his retreat, when something caught his eye. 'Banin, wait — what's this?'

Banin turned to look at what Aleks was pointing at: a part of the chain-link fence was missing. The shrouding shadow of the trees either side made it hard to see, but as they approached, it was obvious it had been cut. Banin, frowning, stooped down and ran his fingers through the dirt.

'That's about a big enough space to fit a quad-bike,' he said, and Aleks looked down to see a pair of faint tyre tracks. He followed them with his eyes; they headed towards a barn poking up between the cleft of two hills about a half-mile away. As he watched, the wind picked up, and the faint buzz of an engine blew in with it.

* * *

Even through the pain, Sean continued to cry out, his throat dry and his lungs burning. If he stopped, he knew he would miss that one fleeting chance to get someone's attention, someone who would continue on their way without ever knowing he was there, tied up, alone. He was sure that his bindings were indeed loosening: his right hand moved further into the loop of rope now than it had done when he had first awoken. But he'd passed the numb phase, and now the raw agony doubled with every attempt to pull his hand through.

'Hello …?' he yelled with weak indignation, coughing the last syllable into the fuggy air. So expectant was he not to hear a response that he braced his throat for another yell, almost missing the sound of a small engine buzzing towards him. He held his breath, concentrating hard to hear if the noise was getting louder — it was. A jolt of excitement fired him up, and he slid his way up the post to stand upright, his joints and wrists screaming in unison. Hopefully it was a farmer coming to get something from his shed, who would then discover him and free him, but even as he thought it, he knew it wasn't true.

The engine got louder — a bike engine perhaps — and it pulled up outside. It cut out, and footsteps headed his way. The small crack of light went dark, and the sound of a chain being unthreaded from between two metal handles clattered in his ears. Sean had wanted to be found, had been calling out to be found, but now he held his breath as he waited in terror, knowing that whoever had the key to the chain's lock would surely be the same person that locked him up in the first place.

The door opened, flooding a blinding white sunlight in, and he turned his head away until his eyes adjusted. Cautiously, he looked back, and the doorway dimmed as the silhouette of a figure filled it, walking towards him with slow, easy strides.

'I wondered when we'd finally meet,' the voice said.

'I know who you are,' Sean said with as much ferocity as he could muster, despite his stinging throat.

'I don't doubt that, not for a second. In fact I'm glad you know who I am. That means you know I'm serious.'

Sean looked at the man, catching a flash of grey hair atop a tanned face, set with narrow, piercing eyes. 'Bales …' he whispered.

Bales, hands clasped behind his back, did not stop in front of Sean. He continued walking, wandering around Sean, circling him. 'You've become quite a nuisance to me,' he said from behind. 'And so has Aleks.'

Sean tried to twist round to see him, but his bindings held him fast. 'Where is he? What have you done with him?'

Bales completed his loop, coming around into Sean's view again. He stopped in front of him, hands still behind his back, a wicked smile on his face. 'He's safe — don't worry. Safe and secure.' His eyes flashed. 'For now. He'll have you to thank when he's not.'

Despite his thirst, his hunger and his exhaustion, a prickling anger riled Sean's senses into overdrive, chasing away any hint of exhaustion. 'What are you talking about?'

'You should've listened to your friend James Aspen. Nice man. Knew his place in the world. If you'd listened to him, you wouldn't be in this mess, so you've only got yourself to blame.'

'What have you done with Aleks? Tell me!'

Bales' smile dropped, and he approached Sean. 'You had the chance to leave this alone, to walk away and not get hurt. I gave you that chance. I risked everything to let you keep your nose out, and you chose not to. Why not? Everyone else did.'

Sean didn't say anything, but behind the post he was pulling at the ropes as hard as he could, his anger stronger than the agony.

'So you've brought this on yourself. Aleks, too. You dragged him into this, Sean, this is *your fault*.'

'It's a trap …' Sean whispered. 'You're using me to get to Aleks …'

Bales grinned. 'You're smart, Sean, yes you are, and that's what got you into this mess in the first place. You know too much, and now you're going to have to pay the price, and so is Aleks. I believe he's on his way here now. At least you did that much right for me and got that nuisance of a man out of hiding.'

'This is insane,' Sean said. 'You have no right to silence anyone. Not me, not Aleks — not Sally.'

Bales dropped his grin and his eyes narrowed. 'You have *no idea* what you're talking about,' he said. 'And I don't think you're in any position to be arguing about it, either. I get what I want whether you like it or not. You had your chance to stay out of my way and you missed it.'

'I have every idea what you're talking about. I know about UV One, I know about Gardner — I know everything.'

Sean's right hand was screaming bloody murder, but it was almost free. He did everything he could to stop his eyes tearing up from the pain.

'You don't know *anything*!' Bales yelled, stabbing his finger at Sean, spittle flying from his mouth. Sean saw a madness in Bales that, for the first time, scared him to his core. All of sudden he realised how real Bales' threats were. He gave up on trying to pull his wrist free subtly, and yanked hard at the rope. Bales saw what he was doing, and took a step back, reaching into his jacket. Sean's hand tore free, fresh fire burning his skin, and he threw it round in a flash to connect with Bales' jaw. Bales staggered back, the gun he was extracting clattering to the floor. They both looked at it, then at each other, and as Bales dropped to pick it up, Sean took another swing. It landed on Bales' ear, knocking him sideways, but before Sean had a chance to recoil, Bales was on him. Blow after blow landed on Sean's ribs, head and arms, knocking the wind from him, turning his vision fuzzy. He did his best to block, but he couldn't stop the impacts raining down on him. As the world spun, he thought to himself how stupid he had been, how Bales was much bigger than he was, and how badly he had failed. He didn't remember falling to the floor, but he was down, and a high-pitched ringing filled his head. Bales, who was swimming from side to side, picked up his gun and pointed it at Sean.

'I was hoping to wait for Aleks so he could see what you've done, but I suppose he'll have to miss out,' he said.

Chapter 27

Sally didn't talk to Mikhail about his brush with death. She tried not to think about it herself either, but the best she could do was push it back into a corner of her mind that only spoke in whispers. While she was asleep, however, she could not control her mind, and flashes of Mikhail's face — eyes rolled back, lips contorted in agony, blood rushing from his ears and nose — haunted her dreams. It would happen to him again, she knew it, she could *feel* it, and it would be worse next time. He had aged considerably since they'd first met, but that didn't stop her enjoying the company of Mikhail as he was: a wonderful and enchanting human being.

'No I don't,' she chuckled, pushing him away.

'You do,' he said, laughing himself.

'I don't have a freckly nose …'

'You *do*!'

Sally ripped a small mirror from its Velcro home and had a look. Sure enough, she had a smattering of freckles across her otherwise pale nose.

Mikhail raised an eyebrow and grinned. 'See?'

Sally made a grumbling noise and returned the mirror to its pad. She must have got those working outside under the hot Californian sun a few months back. She'd been testing a deep space comms array she'd developed; the lab she was allocated was too small. That seemed a lifetime ago, and not usually having the time for vanity, she hadn't even noticed the appearance of the freckles. She stuck her tongue out at Mikhail and laughed, despite trying to keep a straight face. He winked back in a, *I told you so,* kind of way.

'You have freckles too,' Sally said. 'Dark ones.'

'I know I do.'

'I like them.'

'And I like yours. They suit you.'

'They don't,' Sally said, covering her nose. 'They look silly. I'm too pale.'

Mikhail took her wrist in a light grip and pulled her hand from her nose. She let him, the micro gravity pulling them closer together.

'They look beautiful,' he whispered.

His voice washed through Sally, a torrent of healing emotional warmth that cleansed her soul, filtering out all the hurt and pain she'd stored up over the years with its purity. For such a long time she'd avoided proper human contact, burying herself deep in her work, and it made her sad, regretful of the time she'd lost out in feeling such an unadulterated joy as the one she felt with Mikhail. In a strange way it also made her think of her parents, and for the first time in a long while, she missed them. She longed to be with Mikhail forever, to go to a place beyond the Earth that had left her cold and empty, to find a new level of emotional peace she was sure he knew of. If he left her behind, she would have to face the worst kind of pain all over again.

'I want you to take me with you,' she said, looking deep into his dark eyes.

He looked down, searching. 'I can't.'

Sally moved her head to lock their eyes together again, pulling his gaze back to her. 'But why? Why can't we both go there and be happy together? There's nothing for us here.'

'I wish I could, I really do. But the time isn't right. Maybe it will be one day, but there's something you have to do first.'

The laughter was gone. Mikhail's words were sombre. Sally took his hands and held them to her chest.

'What is it? What do I have to do to be with you? I'll do anything it takes — *anything.*'

Sally knew as the words came out of her mouth that she meant it. Her mind was constantly evolving, hunting for knowledge, and she'd learned to keep her eyes forward and focussed on the next stepping-stone, because her past had no home for her. And now, looking into Mikhail's eyes, into the reflection of her future, she could not bear the thought of returning to a life she'd outgrown. But as much as she knew what she wanted, she also knew what Mikhail was going to tell her.

'When the time is right, you'll know,' he said.

'Tell me now!' Sally shouted, gripping Mikhail's hands harder. She was shocked to hear the panic in her own voice, and realised that her chest was light with breathlessness. Mikhail pulled away, massaging the backs of his hands. Deep nail marks were visible in his skin, and Sally gasped when she saw them.

'Oh my god, I'm sorry,' she said, reaching out to help him, but he retracted from her.

'It's okay,' he said. 'I understand your frustration. But I'm not what you need; I can't be. You need another. A more perfect being, someone you can love from here to eternity.'

What Sally was hearing numbed her mind, and everything felt distant. 'I want that to be you,' she whispered.

Mikhail shook his head. 'It can't be. I'm just a very small part in a very big world. You are a big part. *He* is a big part. Together you will change the world.'

Sally had nothing left to say. She could see that Mikhail was pushing her away, not just physically, but emotionally, detaching himself from her and leaving her alone once again. Where her voice fell silent, her tears cried out, and they flowed from her and clouded her vision. Through the blurry haze, Mikhail had just two more words for her: 'I'm sorry.'

With that, he bucked, clutching his head and screamed an ear-splitting scream that cut through Sally like a blade. Wiping her eyes, she pushed forwards to help him, but he thrashed so violently that he threw her back against the wall, knocking her head against something hard. Dazed, she swam on the boundary of consciousness, her fading sight catching the dying convulsions of the man she loved.

* * *

'Soyuz TMA Eleven M, TsUP. First stage of docking underway, please confirm range of three zero zero zero metres,' came the voice of CAPCOM over the radio.

'Three zero zero zero metres confirmed, TsUP, first stage of docking underway,' Major Sam Taylor responded.

'Switching to docking camera,' Captain Tim Wilson — sat to Taylor's right — added. Using a small, metal rod, he stretched from his harnessed position to prod the relevant button.

'Copy, Soyuz. Approach looks good.'

* * *

"I'll get the car,' Banin said, setting off at a sprint.

'No! Wait!' Aleks yelled after him. 'You'll never fit it through that gap!'

Banin slowed to a stop, looking back at the fence. 'I was going to ram it,' he said, panting.

'Those posts look concreted in pretty deep.'

'Are you sure?'

'Positive.'

Aleks didn't understand how Banin couldn't see it, but to him it was obvious that the posts would have made mincemeat of Banin's old relic, even with Banin and his intense driving style at the wheel.

'Shit,' Banin groaned, wandering back, chest still rising and falling. 'Then we've got some running to do.'

Each stride over the field took Aleks another step closer to what felt like a certain heart attack, his aging organs pushing and pulling and squeezing inside him as he did his best to keep up his momentum. As he climbed the first hill of two between them and the barn, occasionally looking down to check they were still following the tyre tracks, he could do nothing but fight the urge to stop, to catch his breath, to lay down on the floor, go to sleep and never wake again.

At the top of the hill, they both slowed, Banin's fitness as malnourished as Aleks' own. Hands on hips, cold air scorching his throat, Aleks looked down over the next hill at the barn; it seemed closer, but not as much as he'd hoped. From this vantage point, however, he could see further into the crack where the barn was nestled, revealing the source of the tracks and the engine noise: a quad bike. Breathless, he pointed, and Banin nodded.

'I see it,' he wheezed.

For a moment, the sight spurred Aleks on, and he waved Banin to follow, who did so with obvious reluctance. The regret was immediate: his chest tightened and his lungs burned as he dragged air into them in long, ragged gasps, but he pushed on — they both did. Through sweat and tears he stomped down the other side of the hill and began the ascent of the next, digging his heels into the muddy-green scrub underfoot.

This time they didn't stop until they reached the low fence that surrounded the barn. After pushing so hard, stopping was a whole new agony. As Aleks had run, the cool breeze had kept him from cooking in his own heat, but now, stationary, his body temperature rose, his sticky shirt preventing it from escaping. He retched, blood rushing to his dizzy head, and he grasped the fence for balance so he could recompose himself.

'You okay?' Banin said in a strained voice that inferred his own hellish pain.

Aleks nodded. 'I'll be fine, just give me a minute.'

'Just a minute?' Banin said, laughing hoarsely. 'I think I need ten.'

As Aleks cooled off, he surveyed the barn. It faced away from them, and around it were a couple of smaller sheds. The quad bike was parked to one side of the barn, engine off.

'I reckon he's in there,' Aleks said, pointing at the barn. 'The door's probably on the other side.'

'Yeah, I think so.' Banin pulled out his phone, dialled and held it to his ear. 'Hi, can you send a patrol car up to the old factory near Pavlovskoye. Ok, thanks.'

He hung up and put the phone back in his pocket. 'Just in case.'

'So, what do we do now?'

By way of response Banin vaulted the low fence, landing heavily on the other side.

'We go in,' he said, dusting off his hands. He reached into his jacket and drew his pistol. 'While we've still got the element of surprise on our side.'

* * *

'Soyuz TMA Eleven M, TsUP. Two thousand, two zero zero zero metres. Please confirm.'

'Two zero zero zero metres confirmed,' Taylor replied.

'Soyuz, please disengage automatic docking sequence and engage manual override for control and visual.'

'Copy, TsUP.' Taylor did as he was asked, prodding the control with his rod to set Soyuz up for a manual dock, craning his neck to see through the optical view screen from the outboard periscope. 'I've been looking forward to this,' he said, grinning to himself beneath his helmet. 'I didn't think I'd ever get a chance to actually pilot something in space now everything's gone automated.'

'As long as you don't pile us into the side of the station like you did on the simulator,' Wilson said, chuckling.

'Hey, that was one time. I hadn't been on that simulator since I was on the TMA Eight M back up crew, so I'll thank you for bringing it up.'

'Okay, okay, jeez … I was only joking, no need to get so uptight.'

Taylor tutted, turning his attention to the view of the station growing larger on the screen. 'It's a shame it's the last we're ever going to see of this place,' he said.

'You got that right.'

They reflected in silence for a moment, then Taylor said, 'TsUP, Soyuz. One zero zero zero metres, entering stage two docking procedure, manual.'

'Soyuz, copy, one zero zero zero.'

'I mean, why are we even doing this? It doesn't make sense,' Wilson said.

'Shut up — you know all this stuff's recorded.'

'I'm just saying.'

'Well, don't.'

Wilson looked like he'd dropped the thought, and then he didn't. 'I just don't see what the point is. Seems like a waste to me. Surely there's another way?'

'Yeah, well, what do we know. I'm just glad we got a final chance to visit the station. You should be grateful for that.'

'I suppose,' Wilson said, sighing.

'Exactly. TsUP, Soyuz. Five zero zero metres and closing. Entering stage three docking procedure.'

'Copy, Soyuz.'

* * *

It wasn't the first time Sean had felt close to death's door, but this was by far the closest. All he could do was ask himself whether it was worth it, and a small voice from deep down inside told him that yes, it was. He'd stood by his morals, and although he'd lost against Bales, it was a victory for himself. He shut his eyes to slow the spinning of the room, and with the darkness came a peace, pure and cleansing.

'It'll be over soon,' Bales said from a million miles away. He seemed to say it over and over again, and there were hands clapping him, applauding his words, cheering him on. But *was* it hands making that clapping sound? Or was it something else? The clapping grew louder, but it couldn't have been for Bales, because he heard him turn on his heel to face the sound. That's when Sean realised that it wasn't clapping at all. It was the sound of running. He opened his eyes.

'Sean!'

Two men sprang from the white outdoor light, one brandishing a pistol in a two-handed grip. Bales had levelled his own gun right back at them

'Sean, are you okay?' one of the men said. Sean recognised the voice, and as the men edged further into the barn, he realised it was Aleks.

'I'm okay,' Sean croaked. 'You shouldn't have come for me.'

'Has he hurt you?'

'I'm fine.'

'Who are you?' Bales said, moving his gun from Aleks to the other man and back again. 'This is US Department of Defense business.'

'Detective Banin, Moscow City Police,' the man with the gun replied, his aim staying fixed on Bales.

'Aleks,' Bales said, 'what have you done? What did you tell him?'

'You went too far, Bales.' Aleks said, folding his arms.

'I need you to come with me,' Banin said. 'We need to have a talk.'

'Talk? Talk about what? We've got nothing to talk about.'

'Do as he says, Bales,' Sean said, lifting himself to his feet. At first he was a little unsteady, but his injuries weren't as bad he thought. 'Aleks, Bales means to kill us both. Probably you as well, detective, now you're here.'

'Can I ask what the problem is?' Bales said, his composure absolute.

'You're a suspect in the murder of Lev Ryumin. Like I said, you need to come with me.'

'He kidnapped me as well,' Sean said.

Keeping his eyes on Bales, Banin said, 'I'm afraid that's nothing to do with me. What US Government does to US citizens is outside of my jurisdiction. I'm no fed.'

Bales was chuckling.

'Something funny?' Banin asked him.

Bales lowered his pistol. 'As it so happens, yes there is. You see, I had nothing do with the death of Lev Ryumin. I can understand how it might look that way, and his death benefitted me greatly, but I assure you, nothing could be further from the truth.'

'Liar! You set me up!' Aleks yelled, and Banin had to stick an arm out to hold him back.

'Yes, Aleks, I did set you up,' Bales said. 'But I didn't kill Lev. That's god's honest truth.' He seemed to be enjoying Aleks' anguish.

'Can you prove it?' Banin said, his weapon still trained on Bales' head.

'As a matter of fact, I can. Give the US Embassy a call and check my roster with them. You'll see I'd left the country after my little chat with Ryumin. I tried to reason with him, make him see sense, but he wasn't interested; what he did after that is his own damn fault.'

Banin, his toneless expression showing some surprise, looked at Aleks. 'Do you know about this?'

'I —' Aleks began, but Bales interrupted him.

'Of course he doesn't know. He's too busy putting his nose where it doesn't belong to take the time to come up with the facts.'

Banin considered Bales for a moment, narrow unblinking eyes weighing up the validity of the man's statement. 'Okay,' he said, 'I'll call them. But if you're lying to me —'

'I assure you, I'm not.'

'We'll see.'

Banin dialled, then held the phone to his ear, other hand still aiming his pistol. Time stood still for a long while before he said anything. Sean looked at Bales, who didn't seem at all nervous. Sean expected him to have the jitter a man has when he knows his game is up, but Bales was steady as a rock. Steadier. It was unnerving.

'Hello, is that the US embassy? Hi. Detective Banin here, from the Moscow City Police Department. I need some information on a Mr John Bales.'

The conversation rolled on, and the more Banin spoke, the bigger the lead weight in Sean's stomach became.

'Uh huh,' Banin said. 'Okay. Thank you for your help. Yes, thank you. Goodbye.' He hung up, then cautiously holstered his pistol. 'You were right.'

Bales smiled, bowing his head a little. 'Thank you.'

'But what about kidnapping me?' Sean blurted. The whole scenario was slipping away before his eyes; he could see Banin walking away and leaving him and Aleks for Bales to do with as he pleased before it even happened.

'Sorry, kid,' Banin said. 'Nothing I can do.'

Sean's frustration was turning into anger. 'And Sally? I suppose there's nothing you can do for her, either?'

'Look,' Banin said. 'I don't know who Sally is, but I'm here to investigate the death of Lev Ryumin. I'm sorry about all this, I really am, but I'm as much use here as you are. I'm leaving.'

Banin held up his hands, and turned to leave. Bales raised his pistol, cocked it and Banin stopped.

'Where do you think you're going?'

Banin turned back in slow steps to face Bales. 'What are you doing?' he said, sounding almost peeved. It didn't seem like the first time he'd had a gun pointed at him.

'I told you,' Sean said. 'He means to kill all of us.'

Bales whipped the gun round at Sean, the cracks of madness shining through his polished exterior once again. 'Don't play innocent,' he said. 'This is all — your — fault.'

An itch in the back of Sean's mind urged him not to give in. Looking between the pistol's barrel and Bales' face, he chose the words he wanted to say, picking each one with care as if they had a direct connection with the trigger. 'You were right,' he said, saying it slow and clear. 'And I was wrong. There's something else going on here that I *don't* know about.'

'Okay, Bales,' Banin said, reaching for his holster, but Bales' sights were on him with vicious precision and speed. *Not yet, Banin, not yet*, Sean thought. He needed to get Bales back on him.

'I don't think you want to do that,' Bales said. 'Why don't you put that on the ground and kick it over here.'

Banin hesitated, then did as he was told. *And then there were three*, Sean thought.

'You're damn right there's something else going on here,' Bales said, pistol pointing back at Sean. 'And you nearly wrecked all of it. Decades of hard work and preparation, and I wasn't going to let what happened last time happen again.'

'And that's why you want to destroy UV One, isn't it?' Sean said.

Bales' pistol wavered, then steadied. 'I don't know what you're talking about.'

At that, the mental picture Sean had built up over the past few weeks of investigation shattered, falling to the ground in a thousand pieces. He stared at Bales, and Bales at him, his grey eyes revealing the truth: he really did have no idea what Sean was talking about.

Chapter 28

'Pitch twelve degrees, alignment with target confirmed,' said Taylor, concentrating hard. 'MRM Two is in visual range.'

'Copy, Soyuz,' replied CAPCOM. 'Looking good our end. Ten metres, one zero.'

'Pitch two degrees, yaw one degree. Forward thrusters fire, one second burst.'

'Forward thrusters fire, one second,' Wilson confirmed, executing the command. The deceleration made both their helmets bob forwards.

CAPCOM: 'Eight metres.'

'Eight metres, copy. Roll one degree. Pitch one degree.'

'Target aligned,' Wilson confirmed.

'Seven metres. Holding course.'

'Soyuz, looking good.'

'Copy, TsUP. Wilson, fire forward thrusters, one second, on my mark,'

'Copy, forward thrusters, one second on your mark.'

'Five metres, Soyuz.'

'Five metres, copy. Mark.'

'Firing forward thrusters, one second.'

The last few metres went by without issue, the elongated probe of Soyuz sliding straight into the docking port. The two met, and the self-locking clamps hit home without so much as a jolt.

'TsUP, we're on dry land, thank you,' Taylor said, relaxing. His brow prickled with sweat.

'No problem, Soyuz. Good docking. Much better than the simulator.'

'What? Not this crap again!'

CAPCOM laughed. 'Radio in when you're ready for departure.'

'Copy, TsUP. Oh, and bite me.'

'Copy, Soyuz, bite you.'

Taylor snorted. 'That was easy. I don't know why they have these automated systems. More to go wrong than a good old-fashioned human being.'

'It was a nice approach, I have to say,' Wilson said.

'Thanks. Now, let's get to work.'

* * *

'But —' Sean said, 'what are the explosives for?'

Realisation flooded into Bales' face, and he chuckled it back, as though Sean had told him an amusing pun. 'Oh, that,' he said. 'A small explosive, to disable Progress and keep Fisher up there with UV One. Nothing more. I know what you think of me, Sean, but you're wrong. You're all wrong. But it doesn't matter, because soon you'll all be dead, so you wont be able to damage my life's work any further.'

'Wait,' Sean said as Bales took a step towards him. Bales waited, but Sean hadn't really thought anything beyond telling Bales to wait. He looked at Aleks, whose wide eyes held no salvation, then at Banin, who jerked his shoulders in a tiny shrug.

'I'm waiting,' Bales said, 'and I'm running out of patience.'

Think, Sean, think.

'There are three of us and one of you,' Sean said finally.

'I have a gun, Sean.'

'Yes, but you can't shoot all three of us. Two, maybe — but three? Chances are one of us will escape.'

'Exactly,' Banin said, and Bales re-aimed at him. 'All it takes is one of us to escape and you're done.'

'I'd shoot you as you ran,' Bales said. 'There are open fields in every direction for at least a mile.'

'You might miss,' Banin said.

'I'm a good shot.'

'That's what, a nine millimetre? Good accuracy close up, but with some distance? Even good shooting won't make up for that.'

Banin was stalling well, but Sean couldn't see it working for long. They needed to do something else to last more than a few minutes.

'And if one of us is going to get away,' Sean said, and Bales swung back to him, 'your little secret will be out. Everyone will know about UV One and Sally Fisher, every last little detail. And you won't have the chance to do anything about it, because when more police come for you, I expect they'll be shooting to kill.'

Bales shifted his stance, looking anxious. 'Get on the ground, all of you.'

Aleks started to bend down, but Banin held up his hand to stop him. 'Stay where you are,' he said. 'Bales—you've lost. Aleks is right there in the doorway. If you shoot me or Sean, he'll get out and you won't be able to catch him. If you shoot Aleks, I'll be on top of you before you know it. One of us is leaving whether you like it or not, so you might as well let us all go and call it a day. I promise you'll never hear from us again, and we won't ever speak of this to anyone.'

Sean watched as Bales considered the idea for a moment, then lowered his gun. 'Okay,' he said. 'Then you leave me no other choice.'

As quick as the crack of a whip, he levelled the gun and filled the room with almighty thunder. The thunder came again, and then silence. Sean had dropped to the floor. The smell of gunpowder was acrid in his nose, overpowering the damp wood smell of the barn.

'Is everyone alright?' Sean heard Aleks say. The sheer volume of the gunshots seemed to have jarred his vision and he blinked to try and bring it round again.

'Oh, god,' he heard Aleks say, closer this time. 'Oh my god …'

And then he felt it, a blooming ache with a bright centre of excruciating fire. 'Have I — have I been shot?'

Aleks ran over, and Banin too. Banin was tucking a mini-pistol into a chest holster. *So that's what the second burst of thunder was*, Sean thought.

'It's in his shoulder,' Banin said, pulling off his jacket and ripping a strip from the sleeve. 'He's losing blood. We need to get him to a hospital.'

'What about Bales?' Sean said. His voice sounded distant, pushed away by the growing flower of his suffering.

'He's dead.'

'Dead,' Sean whispered. Despite the pain, he was the happiest he'd felt in days.

* * *

'I think she's over there — yeah, there she is.'

The voices sounded muffled, a blanket of semi-consciousness shrouding Sally's head.

'I think she's hurt.'

Black faded to colour, and the shadows of the voices fell on her.

'Are you okay?'

Sally felt a groan escape her lips, a groan that magnified the thumping behind her eyes. 'What's happening …?' she mumbled, the words an effort to speak.

'God, she's out of it,' one voice said to the other. 'We've been sent to get you. I think you've had an accident.'

'There's a lot of blood,' the other voice said in a concerned tone.

Sally felt the back of her head, and sure enough her hand returned with a glossy red sheen. 'I'm fine,' she mumbled, colours twinkling in front of her eyes as she tried to right herself.

'Woah there, I don't think you want to be doing that.'

A shadow loomed and a man appeared, crouching down in front of her. He pressed against her shoulders to stop her moving.

'Come on, Wilson, give me a hand here,' the man said, looking over his shoulder.

Sally felt herself being scooped up, steered through the micro gravity by guiding hands. 'Where are we going?' she asked.

'We're taking you home.'

'Home?'

'To Earth.'

A thought flashed in Sally's mind, freezing her ridged. 'Is Mikhail okay? Don't forget Mikhail.'

The guiding force stopped, and two faces appeared in front of her. They looked confused.

'Is there someone else up here with you?' one said to her.

'Yes.'

'There isn't supposed to be,' the other man — the man called Wilson — said to the first.

'Go and check,' the first replied.

Wilson darted away.

'He's here,' Sally called after him, 'and he's not well. You need to help him.'

After a while, Wilson came back. 'I looked everywhere, Taylor. This place is deserted. It's a ghost ship up here.'

'No,' Sally said. 'Look again. He's here. Mikhail's here. He needs your help.'

'Is she talking about Romanenko?'

'Sounds like it. I thought he was dead?'

'He is. Wow, she must have hit her head really hard.'

They were taking her away. Away from the station. Away from Mikhail. They were leaving him behind. 'No!' she shrieked, thrashing from their grip. They redoubled, trying to hold her still.

'Calm down!' Taylor yelled as he tried to grab her flailing hands. 'You're going to hurt yourself!'

Tears pooled in Sally's eyes as she thrashed, turning her vision to mud. She kicked and she screamed, the agony in her heart a thousand times that in her head as she was forced away from the only thing that made her happy. 'Get off me!' she wailed, trying to rip her arms and legs from the strong grip of Taylor and Wilson. 'You can't do this to me!'

'Hold her still will you —'

Sally ripped free, and took advantage of her freedom by swinging out hard. Her fist collided with a bony structure that collapsed under the weight of her swing. Wilson, blurred through her tears, recoiled.

'Shit!' he yelped.

'Are you okay?' Taylor asked, forgetting to grab hold of Sally. She kicked herself away, extracting an *oof* as her foot sunk into soft flesh, and she tumbled backwards. *He's here,* she thought, *Mikhail's here and I have to find him.* She paddled through the air, not bothering to wipe her tears away, searching blind.

'Mikhail!' she cried out, fire splitting her head in two. 'Where are you, Mikhail? We have to go now!'

Taylor and Wilson scrabbled after her, and she could hear their palms slapping hard on handholds as they dragged themselves along. She couldn't see them, but she knew they were coming.

'Have you got the first aid kit?' Taylor said.

'Yeah — here it is.'

'Good.'

A hand clasped Sally's ankle, and she kicked about to wriggle free in time to see a needle thump down into her leg. She struggled, but the more she did, the more she seemed to push herself away from the room, away from the International Space Station, until it was all just a pin-prick of light in the darkness of space.

Chapter 29

Sean was fortunate. The bullet had gone right through his shoulder, missing anything important. It still hurt like hell, though, but not so much that he couldn't manage a visit from Banin, who had come to see him at the hospital.

'How are you feeling?' Banin said, looking around the white room with distaste.

'Fine, thank you. I should be out in the next day or so, as long as I don't get an infection. How about you? You don't look like you're a hospital person.'

Banin grunted. 'I'm usually here to look at a dead body.' He didn't need to say anything more.

'I suppose that's a good reason. So, what can I do for you?'

'Do you mind?' Banin said, pointing to the edge of the bed.

'Not at all.'

Banin sat. Sean felt like years had passed since this man had saved his life.

'I need to get a statement from you explaining the whole shoot-out situation. It's a pain I know, and probably the last thing you want to talk about right now, but I've got to do it. We secured some footage from a lorry driver's dash cam that shows Ryumin veering his own way off the road, but still, I have this formality to take care of.'

'I understand. It's not a problem.'

Banin smiled. It didn't suit him. 'I appreciate it.'

They talked at length about the incident, and about the hours Sean spent in the barn leading up to it. All Banin needed was the specifics relating to the shooting itself, and nothing of the station or of Sally was mentioned.

'Once again, I appreciate your help,' Banin said, putting his notepad away.

'Not at all. I appreciate you saving my life.'

'Just doing my job.'

Banin stood to leave, then hesitated.

'Sean,' he said. 'I don't suppose you ever did get to the bottom of the whole aliens thing, did you? It's been bugging me something fierce.'

'It's been bugging me too.'

Banin sat back down again. He leaned in close, eyes alive with curiosity.

'Did you hear? They sent someone up to get Sally. She's here in this hospital, in fact. They brought her in this morning from Kazakhstan.'

'So Bales *was* telling the truth …' Sean muttered. He shifted up into more of a sitting position, which drew fresh pain from his shoulder. Banin leaned in to help him. 'Thanks. But you know what's been bugging me most?'

'What?'

'Ruth Shaw.'

Banin wrinkled his brow. 'How do you know about Ruth Shaw?'

'She was the only survivor of the group at Roswell that discovered the first vessel. Why?'

'I did some digging on Bales' — Banin reached into his pocket and passed Sean a folded piece of paper — 'and look what I found.'

Sean unfolded it.

'That's a photo of Ruth,' Banin said.

'God — she looks just like Sally.'

'I know.'

Sean stared at it for a while, thinking. 'Here's an idea: you don't suppose that Bales' father, Rupert, was the scientist in Ruth's story, do you?'

'I don't know the story.'

Sean told him.

* * *

It was the crushing weight that woke Sally, a heavy force that sat on her chest, making it difficult to breathe. She was lying in a bed — a hospital bed — and beside her was a trolley carrying a selection of machines wired to her arms and chest. It was dark, the only light the soft glow of dawn peeking through the drawn curtains. She tried to move under the uncomfortable and unfamiliar force of gravity, and the sting of the IV drip in the back of her hand made her wince. She lay there for minutes, hours, listening to the sound of talking through the door. Occasionally a head would flash past the window, too quick for her to see if she recognised the person it belonged to. As the light behind the curtains built, so did her hunger. She could feel it rumbling beneath the bed sheets, and she willed food to come to her. Eventually, it did, riding on the back of a silver trolley, wheeled in by a young, kind-faced nurse.

'Good morning, Sally,' the nurse said, smiling. 'It's good to see you awake. How are you feeling?'

'Hungry,' Sally said, wincing as she heaved herself up.

'Here,' the nurse said, 'let me.' She pressed a button on the side of the bed and the top half folded upwards, bringing Sally into a sitting position.

'If you need to adjust it yourself, it's just here,' the nurse said, showing her.

'Thanks.'

The nurse wheeled a tray over to Sally, sliding it over the bed just above her lap, then transferred the food and drink from the trolley. There was a bowl of cereal, a jug of milk and a glass of orange juice. It all looked very appealing to Sally, and she eyed it with gusto.

'I hope you enjoy it, and I'm so glad you made it back okay,' she said, beaming. 'I hear you're quite the heroine.'

The nurse continued talking, but Sally didn't really hear it. Her mouth went dry and her appetite vanished as she remembered everything.

'Mikhail …' she whispered.

* * *

'That makes sense,' Banin said.

'What does?'

'Well, here's the thing: Ruth Shaw is Bales' mother.'

'Bales' mother?'

'Yeah. That's how I came across her. She was moved to a psychiatric facility shortly after he was born. Made it a real pain to track her down. I eventually found her file in an old folder of declassified NACA material from the fifties.'

What was a smear of a thought at first grew to a clear and definite idea in Sean's mind. Bales didn't want the vessel destroyed: he wanted to *protect it*. 'So it's happened before, and now it's happening again …' he said, thinking aloud.

'What has?'

'The first vessel, the one at Roswell in Ruth's story — maybe it didn't have the chance to do what it needed to do before it got destroyed. Maybe Bales has been trying to make sure that whatever went wrong then didn't happen again this time around. The first vessel chose his father and his mother to make *him*, but when it was destroyed, the result — Bales — was tainted somehow. So now the vessel is back, and Bales has chosen Sally to … to try again.'

Banin was shaking his head in disbelief. 'That's a big stretch of the imagination …'

'But think about it: Bales said we were wrong about what we thought of him and it seems he was right, so perhaps we've been wrong about everything else, too?'

'You think that Bales is working with an alien spaceship to produce … well, I don't even know what.'

'I — I think so …'

They both laughed, Banin's a hearty rumble. 'It sounds like madness when you say it out loud,' he said, 'and maybe it is.' His laughter faded and his eyes shone. 'But maybe — just maybe — it isn't.'

Epilogue

'Doctor!' the nurse called out through the open door, before turning her attention back to Sally. 'Don't worry, everything's going to be okay.'

Sally found it hard to believe. Mikhail's memory had hit her like a train, the full force of it knocking her clean off her heels. He was gone, forever, and she was never going to see him again. A man in a white jacket skipped in through the door.

'Is everything okay?'

The nurse looked anxious. 'I think it'd be best if you update her,' she said, taking a step back.

The doctor nodded, pulled up a chair and sat next to Sally's bed. She watched him, not caring what he had to say — it wouldn't bring Mikhail back, whatever it was.

'You had some serious head trauma,' the doctor said in a kind but serious way. He brushed the greying flecks of hair that fell in front of his eyes back again. It was strange, Sally thought, being back here, back on Earth, talking with normal people about unimportant things. As she looked into the doctor's eyes, she imagined the journey she might have had, the worlds she might have visited, if only she could have stayed. She thought about everything Mikhail had told her, that she would be an important part of mankind's future, and she smiled sadly. The doctor mistook this as a positive reaction to whatever it was he was saying, and returned the smile.

'I'm glad that you're coming along well. You'll be fighting fit in no time, and despite the problems, your baby will be too.'

The doctor's words brought her thoughts back to the present in an instant. 'What?' she whispered.

'Sally,' the doctor said, his smile gone. 'I thought you knew? You're pregnant.'

All she could do was cry.

She spent the rest of the day in something of a daze, stuck in a subconscious netherworld that wouldn't let her go. Even though her body was on Earth in a hospital bed, her mind was two hundred and fifty miles up, still on board the ISS. She replayed her final moments with Mikhail over and over, watching him writhe and thrash in his last few minutes of life. She didn't watch by choice: she was trapped there, forced to relive the horrible scenario for what seemed like forever. Time had lost its power over her, until at last wake gave way to sleep and she slipped into unconsciousness. But she was not afforded rest in her sleeping state; she was still trapped aboard the station.

But this time, the station was empty. It was quiet. There was no Mikhail, no Novitskiy, no Chris, no Gardner — just her. Only the latent hum of the life support systems were there to keep her company. Perhaps she would go and look at it one last time. Perhaps that's what her mind needed to let go and move on. She could never be free of her love for Mikhail, but there was a chance she could be free of this place.

The weightlessness of low Earth orbit was a welcoming relief on her joints and muscles, which had been tender under the unfamiliar press of gravity. She floated with ease through the lab, up into the narrowing cone of PMA One, over the cargo bags filling the bottom half of the FGB. The yawning chasm of the downward chute into the MLM no longer held fear over her; she hovered above it for a time with butterflies of anticipation dancing in her chest. She took a breath and dropped down into it, the spinning orientation no more confusing to her now as her womb would be to the baby inside her. The window looking back glowed with the eminence of

Earth, the singular world that homed the billions of people who tore at each other's throats through greed and desperation.

But when she looked up to fill her vision one last time with the familiar shape of UV One — it was gone. Nothing but empty, black space was left behind. Somehow, she felt she'd known this would be the case. A part of her even wondered if it had been there at all. She stroked her abdomen, and even though it felt as it always had, the touch of flesh on flesh was enough to convince her that the part of her that wondered was wrong. An overwhelming sadness stung her eyes, but she smiled anyway. Her love was fleeting, but it had changed her life. 'Goodbye, Mikhail,' she said to the empty space.

'Goodbye, Sally.'

A jolt of surprise and excitement shot through her like electricity, and she spun round as fast as she could to face the voice. It was Mikhail, and he looked younger than he had when he'd died. More like he did when he'd appeared in this very module, naked and confused. His boyish grin and tanned skin made him glow, but there was something else ... something Sally couldn't place. He seemed *more* than alive, he seemed — heavenly.

'Mikhail!' Sally squealed, and threw her arms around him. She savoured his reciprocal hug, his gentle touch filling her with a comfort that felt like home. They parted, even though Sally never wanted the embrace to end, because she wanted to see him again to make sure he was real.

'Sally,' Mikhail said. 'I miss you.'

'I miss you, too.'

'And I'm so proud of you.'

Sally giggled. She couldn't help herself. 'Why?'

Mikhail's grin became a radiant smile, loving and true. 'Because I am. Because you're the mother of change, the seed of hope for the future of the human race. If that isn't enough reason to be proud, I don't know what is.'

They embraced again, and this time Sally really didn't want to let go. 'I can't do this by myself,' she said into the folds of Mikhail's neck. 'I need you with me.'

'I'll always be with you,' he said. His voice was so quiet, yet so close. It sounded almost like it was coming from inside her. 'You'll have my memory for as long as you live.'

Sally's grip became firmer, more desperate. She was no longer holding him to greet him, she was clinging to him to stop him leaving. 'But that's not enough ...' she whispered.

'You won't be alone,' Mikhail said. 'You won't ever have to be alone.'

They held each other in silence. Time still had no meaning, but for now, Sally didn't mind. She wanted the moment to last forever. As they floated there, together, she dozed, comfortable and at peace. 'I don't know what to do,' she mumbled, half asleep.

'Don't worry,' Mikhail said. He stroked her hair. 'You'll do just fine.'

When Sally woke up, it was as though she had awakened from hibernation, a long, deep sleep that had cleansed her body and her soul. As she blinked in the morning light, she was pleased to find that the nagging in her mind had gone. It had left a lucidity behind that was pin sharp and focussed, and for some reason, it made her happy. The radiance of the early morning sun warmed her body, pressing against her like the last lingering moments of Mikhail's caress. *You'll do just fine,* he'd said. She believed she would.

Although she felt much better, the doctor insisted she stay for a while to make sure everything was okay. It was the first documented example of conception in space, and they wanted to be certain that there had been no adverse affects. So far, so good, it seemed. The staff were understanding and compassionate, and she even had a visit from Aleks, who brought her a bunch of flowers and a card. He told her about Bales, who had set him up. He told her about Ruth Shaw and the first vessel, and she listened intently, feeling as though, somehow, she had heard the story before. But she couldn't have, so she listened anyway. Then he told her about Gardner and Chris, which saddened her. They hadn't made it.

The next day, she had another visitor, but this one she didn't know.

'Someone to see you, Sally,' the nurse said, leaning around the door. 'Says his name's Sean.'

Sean? Aleks had mentioned a Sean. The same one perhaps? 'Send him in.'

A young, scrawny guy with tatty clothes and a sling around his arm appeared in the doorway. He looked anxious, and he hovered there until Sally told him he could come in. Pulling up a chair, he sat down beside her, slicking his hair back in a most nervous way.

'Hello, Sean,' Sally said. She was curious about this man. There was a sense that she had met him before, even though she knew she hadn't, because at once she felt safe with him there. 'What can I do for you?'

Sean grinned the nervous grin of a job interviewee. 'Thanks for seeing me,' he said, 'and congratulations by the way.'

Sally stroked her abdomen. It was almost becoming habit. 'Thank you.'

'I suppose you're wondering why I'm here …'

'Aleks told me about you. He said you saved my life.'

Sean looked down. 'I don't know about that,' he said. 'I didn't do much.'

'You're being modest.'

'Yeah, well … maybe. Maybe not. I don't know. Anyway, I'm here because —' he faltered, stuck on a word, '— because I want to ask you something. I suppose you know that I'm a journalist, but I'm here on personal business. Not a press badge in sight.'

Sally gave him a polite smile, encouraging him to continue.

'What I want to say is that, I — I want to help you. With the baby. That sounds weird, I know, but I've been following your story for what feels like a lifetime, and although we've never met, I feel like I know you. I know what you're going through, and I want to be there to help you through it.'

If Sean had looked nervous before, he looked terrified now. Whether he knew it or not, he was gripping his chair tight. Sally could see from his face that his intentions were pure. Mikhail's voice echoed in her head: *You won't ever have to be alone.*

'That's very sweet,' she said. 'I'd like that.'

Sean grinned, looking relieved. 'Thanks,' he said. 'I promise I won't be any bother. It's just — you'll think this sounds silly — I had a dream the other night where I met this guy …'

He flushed red. 'Well, the details aren't important, but what I'm trying to say is that I feel this is the right thing to do. And I *want* to do it, too.'

Sally knew at once who he'd dreamed about. She and Sean talked for the rest of the day, their conversation wandering aimlessly, but staying strong. She was glad she had visitor privileges, because she found Sean fascinating, and he seemed to think the same about her, too. There were a lot of qualities in him that she had liked about Mikhail, and although the reminder of him made her sad, it cheered her to relive the joking and the laughter she'd shared with him. *I'll always be with you,* Mikhail had said.

Sean left late in the night, when he had insisted Sally get some sleep. He was right — she needed the rest, even if she didn't want it. Sean promised he'd be back first thing the next morning, and he was true to his word.

'What do you think he's going to be like?' he said, picking at the bowl of grapes by Sally's bed.

'Who?' Sally said.

'The baby. Who else?'

'Who said it's going to be a he?'

Sean shrugged, and popped another grape into his mouth. 'I dunno. It just seems … right.'

Sally didn't argue, because she agreed with him. She couldn't quite remember, but she was sure Mikhail had referred to the baby as *he*, too. 'I don't know,' she said. 'As long as he's healthy, I guess I'm happy.'

'But you must wonder what all this means? What he's going to be capable of? What he's going to do?'

'I suppose. But there's no point guessing for now. I'll just take it as it comes, with an open mind. Best to wait and see rather than fill my head so full of thoughts I miss it when it happens.'

Sean gave her a look that made her blush, something like admiration. 'You're a wise women, Sally Fisher,' he said.

Two days later, and the doctor deemed Sally well enough to leave. The thought of entering the wide world again filled her with trepidation, but not because she was scared of it, not quite — she was scared of normality, of sinking back into the routine that had left her cold and alone for so much of her life. The hospital had been something of a sanctuary, a purgatory that blurred the line between life up there and life down here. She stroked her abdomen, which made her smile. She had nothing to be afraid of, not anymore.

'Are you okay?' Sean asked, holding the door open for her.

'Yes, I am,' she said. 'I'm more than okay. I'm the best I've ever been in my entire life.'

If you enjoyed reading Vessel *and would like to read Andrew J. Morgan's* Noah's Ark *for free, please review this book and subscribe at www.andrewjamesmorgan.com, where you'll be able to keep up-to-date with all the latest from Andrew J. Morgan. Thank you, and I hope you enjoyed* Vessel.

Made in the USA
Middletown, DE
30 September 2016